Juliana Gray began writing as a chi[ld] being sentenced to her room, and later [to escape] the tedium of unsatisfactory suitors. [Despite her] residence in the most exclusive areas of London, she never met a single duke, though she once shared a taxi with a future baron.

Juliana's debut romance trilogy, including *A Lady Never Lies*, *A Gentleman Never Tells*, and *A Duke Never Yields*, was largely written when she should have been sleeping. She enjoys dark chocolate, champagne, and dinner parties, and despises all forms of exercise except one.

Praise for Juliana Gray:

'Exquisite characterizations, clever dialogue, and addictive prose' *Library Journal* (starred review)

'Charming, passionate, and thrilling . . . sets a new mark for historical romance' Elizabeth Hoyt, *New York Times* bestselling author

'A dazzling debut . . . the best new book of the year!' bestselling author Lauren Willig

'A delightful confection of prose and desire that leaps off the page' Julia London, *New York Times* bestselling author

'Fresh, delicious, witty, and devastatingly romantic' Meredith Duran, *New York Times* bestselling author

'Clever and supremely witty. A true delight' Suzanne Enoch, *New York Times* bestselling author

'Charming, original characters, a large dose of humor, and a plot that's f[. . .] [bestse]lling author

By Juliana Gray

A Lady Never Lies
A Gentleman Never Tells
A Duke Never Yields

How to Tame Your Duke

JULIANA GRAY

ETERNAL
ROMANCE

Published by arrangement with Berkley,
a division of the Penguin Group (USA) Inc.

First published in Great Britain in 2013
by ETERNAL ROMANCE
an imprint of HEADLINE PUBLISHING GROUP

1

Cataloguing in Publication Data is available from the British Library

ISBN 978 1 4722 0487 5

Offset in Times by Avon DataSet Ltd, Bidford-on-Avon, Warwickshire

Printed and bound by CPI Group (UK) Ltd, Croydon, CR0 4YY

Headline's policy is to use papers that are natural, renewable and recyclable
products and made from wood grown in sustainable forests.
The logging and manufacturing processes are expected to conform to the
environmental regulations of the country of origin.

HEADLINE PUBLISHING GROUP
An Hachette UK Company
338 Euston Road
London NW1 3BH

www.eternalromancebooks.co.uk
www.headline.co.uk
www.hachette.co.uk

To the ladies of the Romance Book Club,
and especially our sweet Emily, who gets a duke of her own.

And to all the men and women who have returned from battle
no longer whole, and those who love them.

ACKNOWLEDGMENTS

I started the month of May 2012 as an impatient writer-in-waiting. Now, with the release of *How to Tame Your Duke* in 2013, I find myself the exhausted author of six books in print: four historical romances as Juliana Gray, and two general romantic fiction titles as Beatriz Williams. Such excess could not occur without the heroic support of a great many wonderful people. Among them:

My agent and personal superhero, Alexandra Machinist, and the entire team of professionals at Janklow & Nesbit who execute so flawlessly on every front: thank you, thank you for allowing me to focus on writing alone.

My Berkley editor, Kate Seaver, whose sound advice and excellent taste improve every book; her assistant, Katherine Pelz, a miracle of organization; my meticulous copy editor, who keeps my timelines straight and my hyphens invisible; Erin Galloway, publicist of boundless energy; and all the talented and enthusiastic teams in art, production, marketing, and sales.

My husband, children, and in-laws, whose patience and love are essential and unending.

The best readers in the world, whose emails and Facebook comments inspire me daily.

And the greatest gift of all this past year: those countless instances of breathtaking generosity from the writing and romance communities. You enrich my life. There are no words big enough to thank you.

PROLOGUE

London, England
October 1889

At two o'clock in the morning, as a cold autumn rain drummed against the damask-shrouded windowpanes of his Park Lane town house, the Duke of Olympia was awoken by his valet and told that three ladies awaited him downstairs in his private study.

"Three *ladies*, did you say?" asked Olympia, as he might say *three copulating hippopotamuses*.

"Yes, sir. And two attendants."

"In my *study*?"

"I thought it best, sir," said the valet. "The study is situated at the back of the house."

Olympia stared at the ducal canopy above his head. "Isn't it Ormsby's job to take care of such matters? Turn the women away, or else toss them into the upstairs bedchambers until morning."

The valet adjusted the sleeve of his dressing gown. "Mr. Ormsby elected to refer the matter to me, Your Grace, as an affair of a personal nature, requiring Your Grace's immediate attention." His voice flexed minutely on the word *immediate*. "The attendants, of course, are in the kitchen."

Olympia's ears gave a twinge. His sleep-darkened mind began to awaken and spark, like a banked fire brought back to life by a surly housemaid. "I see," he said. He continued to stare into the canopy. The pillow beneath his head was of finest down encased in finest linen, cradling his skull in weightless lavender-scented comfort. Beneath the heavy bedcovers, his body made a warm cocoon into the softness of the mattress. He removed one hand from this haven and plucked the nightcap from his head. "Three ladies, did you say?"

"Yes, sir. And a dog." The valet made his disapproval of the dog apparent without the smallest change of voice.

"A corgi, I believe. And the ladies: two auburn and one fair?"

"Yes, sir."

Olympia sat up and heaved a sigh. "I've been expecting them."

Eight minutes later, in a yellow dressing gown rioting with British lions, with his silvering hair neatly brushed and his chin miraculously shaved, the Duke of Olympia opened the door to his private study in a soundless whoosh.

"Good morning, my dears," he said cordially.

The three ladies jumped in their three chairs. The corgi launched himself into the air and landed, legs splayed, atop the priceless Axminster rug, on which he promptly disgraced himself.

"I beg your pardon," Olympia said. "Don't rise, I implore you."

The three ladies dropped back into the chairs, except the auburn-haired youngest, who scooped up the dog with a reproving whisper.

"Your Grace," said the eldest, "I apologize most abjectly for the irregularity of our arrival. I hope we have not put out your household. We meant not to disturb you until morning . . ."

"Except that wretched new butler of yours, Ormsby or whatever the devil his name was . . ." burst out the youngest.

"Stefanie, my dear!" exclaimed the eldest.

Olympia smiled and shut the door behind him with a soft click. He stepped toward the center of the room and stopped before the first chair. "Luisa, dear child. How well you look, in spite of everything." He took her hand and squeezed it. "A very great pleasure to see you again, Your Highness, after so many years."

"Oh, Uncle." A blush spread across Luisa's pale cheeks, and her hollow blue-eyed gaze seemed to fill a trifle. "You're terribly kind."

"And Stefanie, my dear scamp. Do you know, I recently met another young lady who reminded me very much of you. It made my old heart ache, I assure you." Olympia reached for Stefanie's hand, but she instead released the dog, sprang from her chair, and threw her arms around him.

"Uncle Duke, how perfectly sporting of you to take us in! I knew you would. You always were such a trump."

Stefanie's arms were young and strong about his waist, and he patted her back with gentle hands and laughed. "You always were the most reckless girl in that damned cow pasture of a principality you call home."

"Holstein-Schweinwald-Huhnhof is not a cow pasture, Uncle Duke!" Stefanie pulled back and slapped his arm. "It's the most charming principality in Germany. Herr von Bismarck himself pronounced it magnificent. And dear Vicky . . ."

"Yes, of course, my dear. I was only teasing. Quite charming, I'm sure." Olympia suppressed a shudder. Bucolic landscapes made his belly twitch. He turned to the final princess of charming Holstein-Schweinwald-Huhnhof, the middle child, quietly soothing the corgi, who was yapping and whining by turns. "And Emilie," he said.

Emilie looked up and smiled at him behind her spectacles. "Uncle." She placed the corgi on the rug and rose.

How old was the girl now? Twenty-three? Twenty-four? But her eyes looked older, round and owlish, improbably ancient amid the clear skin and delicate bones of her face. Her hair gleamed golden in the light from the single electric lamp on Olympia's desk. The other two were handsome girls, constructed on regal lines that showed well in photographs, but Emilie's beauty was more subtle. It ducked and hid behind her spectacles and her retiring nature. A scholar, Emilie: She could parse her Latin and Greek better than Olympia himself. A strain of genius ran through the family blood, and Emilie had caught it in full.

"My dear girl." Olympia caught her hands and kissed her cheek. "How are you?"

"I am well, Uncle." She spoke quietly, but there were tears in her voice.

"Sit down, all of you. I have ordered tea. You must be exhausted." He motioned to the chairs and propped himself on the corner of his desk. "Did you make the crossing last night?"

"Yes, after sunset," said Stefanie. "I was sick twice."

"Really, Stefanie." Luisa was sharp.

"It was the licorice," said Stefanie, sitting back in her chair and looking at the gilded ceiling. "I never could resist licorice, and that little boy at the quayside . . ."

"Yes, quite," said Olympia. "And your attendants?"

"Oh, they were quite all right. Sturdy stomachs, you know."

Olympia coughed. "I mean, who are they? Can they be trusted?"

"Yes, of course." Luisa shot a reproving look—not the first—at Stefanie. "Our governess, who as you know has been with us a thousand years, and Papa's"—her voice quivered slightly—"Papa's valet, Hans."

"Yes, I remember Hans," said Olympia. He focused his mind on the memory: a burly fellow, not the most delicate hand with a neckcloth, but his eyes burned with loyalty to his master, whom he had served since before the prince's marriage to Olympia's youngest sister. "I remember Miss Dingleby, as well. It was I who sent her to your mother, when Luisa was ready for schooling. I am relieved to hear she has escaped safely with you."

"So you have heard the tale." Luisa looked down at her hands, tangled tightly in her lap.

"Yes, my dear," Olympia said, in his kindest voice. "I am very sorry."

"Of course he's heard," said Emilie, in an expectedly brisk voice. Her eyes, fixed on Olympia's face, gleamed sharply behind her spectacles. "Our uncle knows about all these things, often before the rest of the world. Isn't that so, Uncle?"

Olympia spread his broad hands before them. "I am a private man. I simply hear things, from time to time . . ."

"Nonsense," said Emilie. "You were expecting us. Tell us what you know, Uncle. I should like, for once, to hear the entire story. When one's trapped in the middle of things, you see, it's all rather muddled." She looked at him steadily, with those wise eyes, and Olympia, whose innards were not easily unsettled except by bucolic landscapes, knew a distinct flip-flop in the region of his liver.

"Emilie, such impertinence," Luisa said.

Olympia straightened. "No, my dear. In this case, Emilie is quite right. I have taken it upon myself to make an inquiry or two, in hemi-demi-semi-official channels, about your case. After all, you are family."

The last word echoed heavily in the room, calling up the image of the girls' mother, Olympia's sister, who had died a decade ago as she labored to bring the long-awaited male heir of Holstein-Schweinwald-Huhnhof into the world. The baby, two months early, had died a day later, and though Prince Rudolf had married thrice more, applying himself with nightly perseverance to his duty, no coveted boys had materialized. Only the three young ladies remained: Princess Stefanie, Princess Emilie, and—bowing at last to the inevitable four months ago—Crown Princess Luisa, the acknowledged heir to the throne of Holstein-Schweinwald-Huhnhof.

But their mother still hovered, like a ghost in the room. Olympia's favorite sister, though he would never have admitted it. His own dear Louisa, clever and handsome and full of charm, who had fallen in love with Prince Rudolf at court in the unending summer of 1864, during the height of fashion for German royalty.

Emilie, he thought, as he gazed upon the young princesses, had Louisa's eyes.

"And?" she asked now, narrowing those familiar eyes.

The electric lamp gave a little flicker, as if the current had been disturbed. Outside, a dog barked faintly at some passing drunkard or night dustman, and the corgi rose to the tips of his paws, ears trembling. Olympia crossed his long legs and placed his right hand at the edge of the desk, fingers curling around the polished old wood. "I have no inkling, I'm afraid, who caused the death of your father and"—he turned a sorrowful gaze to Luisa, who sat with her eyes cast down—"your own husband, my dearest Luisa." This was not entirely a lie, though it was not precisely the truth; but Olympia had long since lost all traces of squeamish delicacy in such matters. "One suspects, naturally, that the murder must have occurred by the hand of some party outraged by Luisa's official recognition as heir to the throne last summer, and her subsequent marriage to . . . I beg your pardon, my dear. What was the poor fellow's name, God bless his soul?"

"Peter," Luisa whispered.

"Peter, of course. My deepest apologies that I was unable to attend the ceremony. I felt I would not be missed."

"By the by, that was a jolly nice epergne you sent," said Stefanie. "We absolutely marveled on it."

"You are quite welcome," said Olympia. "I daresay it has all been packed safely away?"

"Miss Dingleby saw to it herself."

"Clever Miss Dingleby. Excellent. Yes, the murders. I thought to send for you myself, but before I could make the necessary arrangements, word had reached me . . ."

"So quickly?" asked Emilie, with her clever eyes.

"There *are* telegraphs, my dear. Even in the heart of Holstein-Schweinwald-Huhnhof, I'm told, although in this case the necessary communication came from a friend of mine in Munich."

"What sort of friend?" Emilie leaned forward.

Olympia waved his hand. "Oh, an old acquaintance. In any case, he told me the facts of this latest crisis, the . . . the . . ."

Luisa looked up and said fiercely: "My attempted abduction, do you mean?"

"Yes, my dear. That. I was gratified to learn that you had defended yourself like a true daughter of your blood, and evaded capture. When the papers reported the three of you missing with your governess, I knew there was nothing more to fear. Miss Dingleby would know what to do."

"She has been a heroine," said Luisa.

Olympia smiled. "I had no doubt."

"Well then," said Stefanie. "When do we begin? Tomorrow morning? For I should like to have at least a night's sleep first, after all that rumpus. I declare I shall never look at a piece of licorice in quite the same light."

"Begin?" Olympia blinked. "Begin what?"

Stefanie rose from her chair and began to pace about the room. "Why, investigating the matter, of course! Finding out who's responsible! I should be more than happy to act as bait, though I rather think it's poor Luisa they're after, God help them."

"My dear, do sit down. You're making me dizzy." Olympia lifted one hand to shield his eyes. "Investigate? Act as *bait*? Quite out of the question. I shouldn't dream of risking my dear nieces in such a manner."

"But something must be done!" exclaimed Emilie, rising, too.

"Of course, and something *shall* be done. The Foreign Office is most concerned about the matter. Instability in the region and all that. They shall be conducting the most rigorous inquiries, I assure you. But in the meantime, you must hide."

"Hide?" said Emilie.

"*Hide!*" Stefanie stopped in mid-pace and turned to him, face alight with outrage. "A princess of Holstein-Schweinwald-Huhnhof does not *hide!*"

Olympia lifted himself away from the desk and gathered his hands behind his back. "Of course, there's no point hiding in the ordinary manner. These continental agents, I'm told, are unnaturally cunning in seeking out their targets. Simply sending you to rusticate in some remote village won't do. Your photographs are already in the papers."

Stefanie's hands came together. "Disguise! Of course! You mean to disguise us! I shall be a dairymaid. I milked a cow once, at the Schweinwald summer festival. They were all quite impressed. The dairyman told me I had a natural affinity for udders."

"Nonsense. A dairymaid! The very idea. No, my dears. I have something in mind more subtle, more devious. More, if you'll pardon the word . . ."—he paused, for effect—". . . *adventurous.*"

Luisa drew in a long and deep breath. "Oh, *Uncle*. What have you done?"

"I admit, I had the idea from you yourselves. Do you remember, a great many years ago, when I came to visit your . . . er, your charming homeland? You were just fifteen, Luisa."

"I remember." Her voice was dark with foreboding.

"You put on a play for me, did you not? *Hamlet*, I believe, which was just the sort of melancholy rubbish a fifteen-year-old girl *would* find appealing." Olympia came to a bookshelf, propped his elbow next to a first folio, and regarded the girls with his most benignly affectionate expression.

"Yes, *Hamlet*," said Luisa warily.

"I remember!" said Stefanie. "I was both Claudius and the Prince of Norway, which proved rather awkward at the end, and Emilie of course played Polonius . . ."

Olympia widened his beneficent smile. "And Luisa was Hamlet. Were you not, my dear?"

The timepiece above the mantel chimed three o'clock in dainty little dings. The corgi went around in a circle once, twice, and settled himself in an anxious bundle at Stefanie's feet. His ears swiveled attentively in Olympia's direction.

"Oh no," said Luisa. "It's out of the question. Impossible, to say nothing of improper."

Stefanie clasped her hands. "Oh, Uncle! What a marvelous idea! I've always wanted to gad about in trousers like that. Such perfect freedom. Imagine! You're an absolute genius!"

"We will not," said Luisa. "Imagine the *scandal*! The . . . the *indignity*! No, Uncle. You must think of something else."

"Oh, hush, Luisa! You're a disgrace to your barbarian ancestors . . ."

"I should hope I am! *I*, at least, have some notion . . ."

"Now, ladies . . ."

". . . who overran the steppes of Russia and the monuments of Rome . . ."

". . . of what is due to my poor husband's memory, and it does not require *trousers* . . ."

"My dear girls . . ."

". . . to create the very wealth and power that makes us targets of assassins to *begin* with . . ."

"*HUSH!*" said Olympia.

Luisa paused, finger brandished in mid-stab. Stefanie bent over with a mutinous expression and picked up the quivering corgi.

Olympia rolled his eyes to the ceiling, seeking sympathy from the gilded plasterwork. His head, unaccustomed to such late hours, felt as if it might roll off his body at any moment and into the corgi-soiled Axminster below.

Indeed, he would welcome the peace.

"Very well," he said at last. "Luisa rejects the notion; Stefanie embraces it. Emilie, my dear? I believe it falls to you to cast the deciding vote."

Stefanie rolled her own eyes and sat with a pouf into her chair, corgi against her breast. "Well, that's that, then. Emilie will never agree."

"I am shocked, Uncle, that a man of your stature would even consider such a disgraceful notion." Luisa smoothed her skirts with satisfaction.

Olympia held up his hand and regarded Emilie. She sat with her back straight and her fingers knit, thumbs twiddling each other. Her head cocked slightly to one side, considering some distant object with her mother's own eyes.

"Well, my dear?" Olympia said softly.

Emilie reached up and tapped her chin with one long finger. "We shall have to cut our hair, of course," she said. "Luisa and Stefanie will have an easier time effecting the disguise, with their strong bones, but I shall have to wear a full beard of whiskers at least. And thank Heaven we are not, taken as a group, women of large bosom."

"Emilie!" said Luisa, in shocked tones.

"Emilie, *darling*!" cried Stefanie. "I knew you had it in you!"

Olympia clapped his hands in profound relief. "There we are! The matter is settled. We shall discuss the details in the morning. Wherever has the tea gone? I shall have it sent to your rooms instead." He turned around and pressed a button on his desk, a state-of-the-art electrical bell he'd had installed just a month ago. "Ormsby will show you the way. Tally-ho, then!"

"Uncle! You're not going to *bed*?"

Olympia yawned, tightened the belt on his dressing robe, and made for the door. "Oh, but I am. Quite exhausted." He waved his hand. "Ormsby will be along shortly!"

"Uncle!" Luisa called desperately. "You can't be serious, Uncle!"

Olympia paused with his fingertips on the door handle. He looked back over his shoulder. "Come, my girls," he said. "You shall be well instructed, well placed in respectable homes. You are actresses of exceptional talent, as I have myself witnessed. You possess the dignity and resourcefulness of a most noble family. You have, above all, my unqualified support."

He opened the door, stretched his arm wide, and smiled.

"What could possibly go wrong?"

The Duke of Olympia did not, however, make straight for his room. He walked in the opposite direction, down the hall toward the service staircase at the extreme back of the house. As he descended, the expressions of feminine outrage and excitement from the study died slowly into the walls, until the air went still.

Miss Dingleby was waiting for him in the alcove near the silver pantry. She made a little noise as he drew near, and stepped into the light.

"Ah! There you are, my dear," Olympia said. He looked down at her from his great height and placed his hand tenderly against her cheek. "Won't you come to bed and tell me all about it?"

ONE

*A ramshackle inn in Yorkshire
(of course)
Late November 1889*

The brawl began just before midnight, as taproom brawls usually did.

Not that Emilie had any previous experience of taproom brawls. She had caught glimpses of the odd mill or two in a Schweinwald village square (Schweinwald being by far the most tempestuous of the three provinces of Holstein-Schweinwald-Huhnhof, perhaps because it was the closest to Italy), but her governess or some other responsible adult had always hustled her away at the first spray of blood.

She watched with interest, therefore, as this brawl developed. It had begun as the natural consequence of an ale-soaked game of cards. Emilie had noticed the card players the moment she sat down in an exaggerated swing, braced her elbows, fingered her itching whiskers, and called for a bottle of claret and a boiled chicken with her deepest voice. They played at a table in the center of the room, huddling with bowed heads about the end as if they feared the spavined yellow ceiling might give way at any moment: three or four broad-shouldered men in work shirts, homespun coats slung over their chairs, and one stripling lad.

The stakes must have been high, for they played with intensity. A fine current of tension buzzed through the humid, smoke-laden air. One man, his mustache merging seamlessly with the thicket of whiskers along his jaw, adjusted his seat and emitted a fart so long, so luxuriously slow, so like a mechanical engine in its noxious resonance, the very air trembled. A pack of men at a neighboring table looked up, eyebrows high in admiration.

And yet his companions were so intent on the game, they couldn't be bothered to congratulate him.

At that point, Emilie had taken out a volume of Augustine in the original Latin and made an impressive show of absorption. Travelers, she had discovered early in today's journey from London, tended to avoid striking up conversations with solitary readers, especially when the book's title encompassed multiple clauses in a foreign language, and the last thing Emilie needed was an inquisitive traveling companion: the kind who asked one impertinent questions and observed one's every move. St. Augustine was her shield, and she was grateful to him. But tonight, at the bitter end of her journey into deepest Yorkshire, that godforsaken wilderness of howling wind and frozen moor, she could not focus her attention. Her gaze kept creeping over the edge of the volume to the table beyond.

It was the boy, she decided. Like her, he seemed out of place in this stained and battered inn, as if—like her—he had sought it out over higher-class establishments in order to avoid his usual crowd. He sat at a diagonal angle from her, his left side exposed to her gaze, illuminated by the roaring fire nearby. He was not much more than sixteen; possibly not even that. His pale face was rimmed with spots of all sizes, and his shoulders were almost painfully thin beneath a long thatch of straw-colored hair. He alone had not taken off his coat; it hung from his bones as if from an ill-stuffed scarecrow, dark blue and woven from a fine grade of wool. He regarded his cards with intense concentration behind a pair of owlish spectacles.

Emilie liked his concentration; she liked his spots and his long fingers. He reminded her of herself at that age, all awkward limbs and single-minded focus. Without thinking, she pushed her own spectacles farther up the bridge of her nose and smiled.

The boy was clearly winning.

Even if the stacks of coins at his side were not steadily growing into mountains, Emilie could not have mistaken the scowls of his companions, the shifting in seats, the sharp smacks with which they delivered their stakes to the center of the table. Another round had just begun, and the dealer passed the cards around with blinding swiftness, not to waste a single instant of play. Each face settled into implacability; not a single mustache twitched. One man glanced up and met Emilie's eyes with cold malevolence.

She dropped her gaze back to her book. Her wine and chicken arrived in a clatter of ancient pewter, delivered by a careless barmaid with clean, apple red cheeks and burly fingers. Emilie set down the book and poured the wine with a hand that shook only a little. The coldness of the man's gaze settled like a fist in her chest.

Emilie concentrated on the ribbon of wine undulating into her glass, on the chilly smoothness of the bottle beneath her fingers. Her wineglass was smudged, as if it had seen many other fingers and very little soap. Emilie lifted it to her lips anyway, keeping all her fingertips firmly pressed against the diamond pattern cut into the bowl, and took a hearty masculine swallow.

And nearly spat it back.

The wine was awful, rough and thin all at once, with a faint undertone of turpentine. Emilie had never tasted anything so wretched—not even the cold boar's heart pie she'd been forced to eat in Huhnhof Baden two years ago, as the guest of honor at the autumn cornucopia festival. Only duty had seen her through that experience. Chew and swallow, Miss Dingleby had always instructed her. A princess does not gag. A princess chews and swallows. A princess does not complain.

The wine felt as if it were actually boiling in Emilie's mouth. Was that even possible? She held her breath, gathered her strength, and swallowed.

It burned down her throat, making her eyes prickle, making her nostrils flare. The atmosphere in the room, with its roaring fire and twenty perspiring men, pressed against her forehead with enough force to make her brow pearl out with perspiration. Except that princesses did not perspire; even princesses in exile, disguised as young men. She stared up at the ceiling, studied the wooden beam threatening her head, and let gravity do its work.

Her stomach cramped, recoiled, heaved, and settled at last with a warning grumble. A buzz sounded from somewhere inside her spinning ears.

Emilie picked up her knife and fork with numbed fingers and sawed off a leg from her chicken.

Gradually her ears began to pick up sound again, her nose to acquire smells. To her right, a rumble of discontent ricocheted among the card players.

"Unless my eyesight is capable of penetrating the backs of your cards," the boy was saying, his voice skidding perilously between one octave and the next, "your accusation is impossible, sir. I must beg that you retract it."

One of the men shot upward, overturning his chair. "Nor bloody likely, ye fuggling wee bugger!"

"You are wrong on both counts. I am neither dishonest nor a practicing sodomite," said the boy, with unnatural calm.

The man flung out his arm and overturned the pile of coins next to the boy's right arm. "And I say ye are!" he yelled.

Or so Emilie presumed. The words themselves were lost in the crash of humanity that followed the overturning of the coins onto the floor.

Emilie, who had just lifted the chicken leg to her mouth with a certain amount of relish—she had never, ever been allowed to touch a morsel of food without the intercession of one utensil or another—nearly toppled in the whoosh of air as a long-shanked figure dove from his seat near the fireplace and into the tangle of flailing limbs.

"Oh, fuck me arse!" yelled the barmaid, three feet away. "Ned! Fetch t'bucket!"

"Wh-what?" said Emilie. She rose from her chair and stared in horror. A coin went flying from the writhing mass before her and smacked against her forehead in a dull thud.

"I'll take that." The barmaid swooped down and snatched the coin from among the shavings.

"Madam, I . . . Oh good God!" Emilie ducked just in time to avoid a flying bottle. It crashed into the fire behind her in

a shattering explosion of glass and steam, laced with turpentine.

Emilie looked at her wine and chicken. She looked down
at her battered leather valise, filled with its alien cargo of masculine clothing and false whiskers. Her heart rattled nervously
in her chest.

"Excuse me, madam," she said to the barmaid, ducking
again as a pewter tankard soared through the air, "do you
think . . ."

"Ned! Bring t'bleeding bucket!" bellowed the barmaid.
The words had hardly left her lips when a thick-shouldered
man ran up from behind, bucket in each hand, skin greasy
with sweat. "About time," the barmaid said, and she snatched
a bucket and launched its contents into the scrum.

For an instant, the scene hung suspended, a still-life drawing of dripping fists halted in mid-swing and lips curled over
menacing teeth. Then a single explicit curse burst fluently
from some masculine throat, and the fists connected with solid
flesh. Someone roared like a wounded lion, a feral sound cut
off short by a smash of breaking glass.

"Ye'd best fly, young sir," said the barmaid, over her shoulder, as she tossed the second bucket into the fray.

"Right," said Emilie. She picked up her valise and stumbled backward. She had already engaged a room upstairs,
though she wasn't quite sure where to find it; but at least she
knew there *was* an upstairs, a refuge from the brawl, which
seemed to be growing rather than ebbing. Two men ran in
from the other room, eyes wild, spittle flying from their lips,
and leapt with enthusiasm onto the pile.

Emilie took another step backward, a final longing gaze at
her chicken. She'd only had a single rubbery bite, her first
meal since a hurried lunch of cheese sandwich and weak tea
at the station cafe in Derby, as she waited for the next train in
her deliberately haphazard route. She hadn't thought to bring
along something to eat. What princess did? Food simply
arrived at the appropriate intervals, even during the flight
from the Continent, procured by one loyal retainer or another.
(Hans did have a knack for procuring food.) This chicken,
tough and wretched, pale and dull with congealed grease, was

her only chance of nourishment until morning. The dismembered leg lay propped on the edge of the plate, unbearably tantalizing.

At the back of Emilie's mind, Miss Dingleby was saying something strict, something about dignity and decorum, but the words were drowned out by the incessant beat of hunger further forward in the gray matter. Emilie ducked under a flying fork, reached out with one slender white hand, snatched the chicken leg, and put it in her pocket.

She spun around and hesitated, for just the smallest fraction of an instant.

"I've got ye, ye scraumy-legged bu—" The shout rang out from the melee, cut short by an oomph and a splatter.

Emilie turned back, set down her valise, and wrenched the other leg from the chicken. The bone and skin slipped against her fingers; she grabbed the knife and sawed through until the drumstick came loose.

A half-crown coin landed with a thud on the platter, at the bisection of leg from trunk, in a pool of thickened grease. "Oy!" someone yelled.

Emilie looked up. A man rushed toward her, his nose flinging blood, his arms outstretched. Emilie took the chicken leg, left the coin, and scrambled past the chair.

"What has ye got there? Oy!"

A heavy hand landed on her shoulder, turning her around with a jerk. Emilie held back a gasp at the stench of rotting breath, the wild glare of the bulbous eyes. The chicken leg still lay clenched in her left hand, the knife in her right.

"Stand back!" she barked.

The man threw back his head and laughed. "A live one! Ye manky wee gimmer. I'll . . ."

Emilie shoved the chicken leg in her pocket and brought up the knife. "I said stand back!"

"Oh, it's got a knife, has it?" He laughed again. "What's that there in yer pocket, lad?"

"Nothing."

He raised one hamlike fist and knocked the knife from her fingers. "I did say, what's that there in yer pocket, lad?"

Emilie's fingers went numb. She looked over the man's shoulder. "Watch out!"

The man spun. Emilie leaned down, retrieved the knife, and pushed him full force in his wide and sagging buttocks. He lurched forward with a hard grunt and grabbed wildly for the chair, which shattered into sticks under his hand. Like an uprooted windmill he fell, arms rotating in drunken circles, to crash atop the dirty shavings on the floor. He flopped once and lay still.

"Oh, well done!"

The boy popped out of nowhere, brushing his sleeves, grinning. He pushed his spectacles up the bridge of his nose and examined the platter of limbless chicken. "I do believe that's mine," he said, taking the half crown and flipping it in the air.

"Wh-what?" asked Emilie helplessly.

"Freddie, ye feckless gawby!" It was the barmaid. Her hands were fisted on her hips, and her hair flew in wet strands from her cap.

"I'm sorry, Rose," said the boy. He turned to her with a smile.

Rose? thought Emilie, blinking at the broad-shouldered barmaid.

"Ye has to watch yer mouth, Freddie," Rose was saying, shaking her head. Another shout came from the mass of men, piled like writhing snakes atop one another on the floor nearby. Someone leapt toward them, shirt flapping. Rose picked up Emilie's half-empty wine bottle and swung it casually into the man's head. He groaned once and fell where he stood. "I've told ye and told ye."

"I know, Rose, and I'm sorry." Young Freddie looked contritely at his shoes.

"Ye'd best fly, Freddie, afore yer father come a-looking. And take t'poor young sod with ye. He never is fit for wrestling."

Freddie turned to Emilie and smiled. "I think you've misjudged him, Rose. He's got a proper spirit."

"I have nothing of the sort," Emilie squeaked. She took a deep breath and schooled her voice lower. "That is, I should be happy to retire. The sooner"—she ducked just in time to avoid a spinning plate, which smashed violently into the wall an instant later—"the better, really."

"All right, then. Don't forget your valise." Freddie picked it up and handed it to her, still smiling. He was a handsome lad, really, beneath his spots. He had a loose-limbed lankiness to him, like a puppy still growing into his bones. And his eyes were pure blue, wide and friendly behind the clear glass of his spectacles.

"Thank you," Emilie whispered. She took the valise in her greasy fingers.

"Have you a room?" Freddie asked, dodging a flying fist.

"Yes, upstairs. I . . . Oh, look out!"

Freddie spun, but not in time to avoid a heavy shoulder slamming into his.

"Jack, ye drunken taistril!" screeched Rose.

Freddie staggered backward, right into Emilie's chest. She flailed wildly and crashed to the ground. Freddie landed atop her an instant later, forcing the breath from her lungs. The knife flew from her fingers and skidded across the floor.

"Right, ye wankley whoreson," said the attacker. He was the first one, Emilie thought blearily; the one who had knocked the coins from the table to begin with. He was large and drunk, his eyes red. He leaned down, grabbed Freddie by the collar, and hauled back his fist.

"No!" Emilie said. Freddie's weight disappeared from her chest. She tried to wriggle free of the rest of him, but Freddie was flailing to loosen himself from the man's grasp. Emilie landed her fist in the crook of one enormous elbow and levered herself up, just a little, just enough that she could bend her neck forward and sink her teeth into the broad pad of the man's thumb.

"OY!" he yelled. He snatched his hand back, letting Freddie crash to the ground and roll away, and grabbed Emilie's collar instead.

Emilie clutched at his wrist, writhing, but he was as solid as a horse and far less sensible. His fist lifted up to his ear, and his eyes narrowed at her. Emilie tried to bring up her knee, her foot, anything. She squeezed her eyes shut, expecting the shattering blow, the flash of pain, the blackness and stars and whatever it was.

How the devil had this happened to her? Brawls only happened in newspapers. Only men found themselves locked in meaty fists, expecting a killing punch to the jaw. Only men . . .

But then . . . she *was* a man, wasn't she?

With one last mighty effort, she flung out her hand and scrabbled for the knife. Something brushed her fingertips, something hard and round and slippery. She grasped it, raised it high, and . . .

"OOGMPH!" the man grunted.

The weight lifted away. Her collar fell free.

Emilie slumped back, blinking. She stared up at the air before her. At her hand, grasping the tip of a chicken leg.

She sat up dizzily. Two men swam before her, her attacker and someone else, someone even broader and taller, who held the fellow with one impossibly large hand. Emilie expected to see his other fist fly past, crashing into the man's jaw, but it did not. Instead, the newcomer raised his right arm and slammed his elbow on the juncture of his opponent's neck and shoulder.

"Oy?" the man squeaked uncertainly, and he sagged to the ground.

"Oh, for God's sake," said Freddie. He stood up next to Emilie and offered her his hand. "Was that necessary?"

Emilie took Freddie's hand and staggered to her feet. She looked up at the newcomer, her rescuer, to say some word of abject thanks.

But her breath simply stopped in her chest.

The man filled her vision. If Emilie leaned forward, her brow might perhaps reach the massive ball of his shoulder. He stood quite still, staring down at the man slumped on the ground with no particular expression. His profile danced before her, lit by the still-roaring fire, a profile so inhumanly perfect that actual tears stung the corners of Emilie's eyes. He was clean-shaven, like a Roman god, his jaw cut from stone and his cheekbone forming a deep, shadowed angle on the side of his face. His lips were full, his forehead high and smooth. His close-cropped pale hair curled about his ear. "Yes," he said, the single word rumbling from his broad chest. "Yes, my dear boy. I believe it *was* necessary."

Dear boy?

Emilie blinked and brushed her sleeves. She noticed the chicken leg and shoved it hastily in her pocket.

"I was about to take him, you know," said Freddie, in a petulant voice.

The man turned at last. "I would rather not have taken that chance, you see."

But Emilie didn't hear his words. She stood in horrified shock, staring at the face before her.

The face before her: *His* face, her hero's face, so perfect in profile, collapsed on the right side into a mass of scars, of mottled skin, of a hollow along his jaw, of an eye closed forever shut.

From somewhere behind him came Rose's voice, raised high in supplication. "Yer Grace, I'm that sorry. I did tell him, sir . . ."

"*Your Grace?*" Emilie said. The words slipped out in a gasp. Understanding began to dawn, mingled with horror.

Freddie handed Emilie her valise and said ruefully, "His Grace. His Grace, the Duke of Ashland, I'm afraid." A sigh, long and resigned. "My father."

TWO

The carriage rattled over the darkened road. Each jolt echoed through the silent interior before absorbing into the old velvet hangings, into the cushions with their crests embroidered in gold thread.

Emilie took in shallow breaths, hardly daring to disturb the heavy air. How many years had this carriage sat inside the duke's stables, taken out for polishing every month or so and rolled back in again? She tried to think of something to say. She had been educated to speak into silence, to keep conversation flowing during interminable state dinners and family visits, but on this occasion she could not produce a single word.

Young Freddie sat next to her, or rather slumped, dozing against the musty velvet. Freddie, by courtesy the Marquess of Silverton, as it turned out. Across from them sat the duke, still and massive, his head bent slightly to avoid the roof of the carriage. He stared without moving through the crack in the curtains to the wind-whipped moors beyond. Emilie could scarcely see him at all in the darkness, but she knew that he was facing to his right, that he was shadowing his flawed side from her view. She sensed, rather than saw, the rise and fall of his chest as he breathed. The rhythm mesmerized her. What was he thinking, as he sat there with his steady breath and his steady heartbeat, while the wind pounded the carriage walls?

The Duke of Olympia had told her little about him. He lived in deepest Yorkshire, at the Ashland family seat, from which he rarely ventured. He had been a soldier before assuming the title—he was a younger son of some sort, and not expected to inherit—and had fought in India or thereabouts. (Emilie, her skin prickling at the memory of the duke's elbow landing expertly on the drunkard's neck, could readily believe this.) His only child, Frederick, was nearly sixteen, extremely clever, and already preparing for the entrance examinations at Oxford; his old tutor had left a few months ago, which was why they needed another scholar without delay.

There had been no mention of a wife.

She opened her mouth to say something, anything, but the duke's voice checked her.

"Well, Mr. Grimsby," he said, without turning his head, just loud enough to penetrate the rising howl of the wind with his extraordinary deep voice, "this is a fortuitous coincidence indeed. Another instant, and I should have been forced to find Frederick a different tutor."

Emilie cleared her throat and concentrated on keeping her words steady. "And I thank you again, Your Grace. I assure you, I am not in the habit of engaging in tavern brawls. I . . ."

The air stirred as Ashland waved his hand. "No doubt, of course. Your references are impeccable. Indeed, I rather believe I trust Olympia's judgment in such matters above my own."

"Still, I should like to explain myself."

He turned at last, or at least Emilie thought he did. Her eye caught a flash of movement, the sliver of moonlight striking his pale hair, and she turned away with a blush.

"No need at all to explain yourself, Mr. Grimsby," he said. "You rescued my young scapegrace of a boy, after all. I daresay it was simply a case of being in the wrong place at the wrong time."

"Exactly that, sir. As for the inn itself . . ."

Another stir of the air. "I ought to have had a carriage sent to the railway station, of course. I can't imagine why no one thought of it. My butler is rather old, I suppose, and unused to visitors. As am I."

The wind screamed, the carriage jolted violently. Emilie reached for the strap, but not before she and Freddie shot forward in tandem against the opposite seat.

For an instant she was flying, suspended in the air, and then she landed with a crash into Ashland's right shoulder, just as Freddie's head connected into the small of her back.

Ashland shuddered at the impact. His iron arms closed around them both, steadying.

"Oh! I'm so sorry!" Emilie felt for her spectacles, her whiskers. Freddie was disentangling himself slowly, muttering, fumbling for his own spectacles, which seemed to have flown from his face and onto the seat.

"Not at all." The duke's tone was even, but to Emilie's ears it vibrated with some sort of emotion, distaste or impatience, and as she struggled to right herself, she sensed that his flesh was shrinking from hers. That his very bones, from the instant of impact, had convulsed with agony at her touch.

Had she hit him with such force? She hadn't felt any pain; just the ordinary sort of thud, not even worthy of a bruise.

"You're all right?" he asked. He didn't wait for an answer. His arms opened wide, releasing them both, almost pushing them away.

"Yes, yes. Quite all right." Emilie nudged Freddie away and settled back in her place. Her face burned against the cold air. *Embarrassment.* Yes, that was it. Of course the duke had been embarrassed. That was natural; she had felt it, too. They were strangers. It was simply the awkwardness of it all.

"Speak for yourself, Grimsby," said Freddie. "Where the devil have my specs gone?"

"Here," said Ashland, from the darkness.

"Oh, right-ho." Freddie leaned backward and sank into the seat, just as it rose up in another jolt to meet him. "I take it we're near the drive?"

"Almost there." A pause settled in. Ashland shifted his big body. "We will save our interview for tomorrow morning, Mr. Grimsby, if it's convenient for you. I daresay you'd just as soon head straight for your room."

"Yes, Your Grace." The carriage slowed and lurched around a corner. Emilie found the strap just in time.

"I believe they've already prepared it for your arrival. You shall instruct my butler, of course, if anything is amiss."

"Yes, of course. Thank you, sir."

Freddie coughed. "You're going to have to show a great deal more spirit than that, Grimsby, if you're hoping to survive a winter up here. Once the wind starts to kick up, things turn dashed melancholy."

A gust rattled the windows, shrieking along the seams.

"Hasn't it rather kicked up already?" Emilie ventured.

"This?" Freddie laughed without mirth. He rapped his knuckles against the glass. "Nothing more than a gentle breeze, this. A zephyr."

"Oh. I see."

Freddie laughed again. "You're in Yorkshire now, Grimsby. Abandon hope and all that. If I were you, I'd be counting the days until my first weekend off and booking the early express up to London. We *are* giving him a weekend off now and again, aren't we, Pater?"

Ashland did not stir. "If your progress is satisfactory, of course."

"Then I shall do my best for you, Grimsby. It's the least I can offer you. And I'm dashed clever, you know. Never fear."

"Quite clever, I'm sure." Emilie said this with conviction. No doubt at all, young Lord Silverton was altogether too precocious.

The carriage slowed, lurched, stopped. Almost before the wheels had fixed, the door was swinging open and the duke leapt out as if from a spring.

"That's Pater for you," Freddie said resignedly. "Not at all fond of closed spaces. You first, Grimsby. Hero of the hour and all that."

The moon shone round and full behind a raft of skidding clouds. It illuminated the Duke of Ashland's hair to whiteness as he turned and stared down at Emilie. She met his gaze squarely beneath the brim of his hat, afraid of letting her eyes trail downward to his ruined jaw. The single eye enveloped her whole. In the moonlight, it might have been any shade from pale gray to vivid blue. "Simpson, this is Mr. Grimsby, Silverton's new tutor. Have your staff see to his comfort tonight."

Emilie was aware of an enormous dark mass to her right, immense with gravity, obscuring the night sky. A single figure resolved itself from the pitch, white collar gleaming with its own luminescence from the corner of Emilie's vision. "Yes, Your Grace," said a low voice, crackling with age. "You may come with me, Mr. Grimsby."

"I shall send for you in the morning, directly after breakfast, to discuss the terms of your employment here." A sudden gust of wind nearly tore his words away, but Ashland didn't move, didn't raise his voice by so much as a single decibel. "In the meantime, I urge you to make yourself comfortable in my home."

"Thank you, sir." Despite the numbing shock of the wind, Emilie's cheeks glowed with warmth.

"In other words," Freddie put in, "you've been dismissed for the night, Grimsby. I'd dash while I could, if I were you. In fact, being a hospitable sort of chap, I believe I'll take you up myself." His hand closed around Emilie's upper arm.

"*Frederick.*" The single word snapped out of the duke's throat.

The boy paused, one shoe poised above the gravel. "Yes, Pater?"

"In my study, if you please. We have a certain matter to discuss."

Freddie's hand dropped away from Emilie's arm. "What matter, sir?"

"Frederick, my dear boy. We have all been to a great deal of trouble tonight. I believe some sort of reckoning is in order. Don't you?" Ashland's silky voice nudged upward at the very tip of the last word, implying a question where one didn't really exist. Emilie heard a little slap, as of gloves hitting an impatient palm.

Emilie didn't dare look at Freddie. She couldn't have seen him well anyway, as the moon had just retired behind one of the thicker clouds. But she heard him gulp, even above the thrum of the wind about the chimneys. Her heart sank in sympathy.

"Yes, sir," Freddie said humbly.

"That will be all, Mr. Grimsby," said the Duke of Ashland.

The butler stepped aside in a meaningful crunch of gravel, and Emilie turned and walked up the steps, guided by the dim golden light from the entrance hall, and into Ashland Abbey.

The Duke of Ashland waited until his son's footsteps had receded entirely up the stairs before he allowed the smile to break out at the corner of his mouth.

Well, it *had* been an entertaining evening, after all, and he couldn't deny he stood in need of a little excitement from time to time. A chuckle rumbled in his throat at the image of poor Mr. Grimsby, eyes wide, whiskers a-flutter, one slender, scholarly fist closed at his side and the other brandishing a chicken drumstick. But he had shown spirit, after all. The young chap had put himself in imminent danger to rescue Freddie. That was all Ashland needed to know.

He rose from his desk. On the cabinet near the window, a tray beckoned alluringly with a single empty glass and three crystal decanters: one of sherry, one of brandy, and one of port. Ashland's right hand—the one that no longer existed—throbbed with eagerness at the sight.

He walked with steady steps to the cabinet, picked up the sherry with his left hand, and filled the empty glass nearly to the brim. A single glass of spirits each night: That was all he allowed himself. Any more, and he might never stop.

The first sip slid down his throat in a satisfying burn. His nose and mouth glowed with the familiar taste, the taste of relief. Ashland closed his eyes and dug his fingers into the diamond pattern of the bowl, giving it time, letting the sherry spread through his body to fill all his parched and aching cracks. The stiffness on the right side of his face began to ease, the throb of his phantom hand to fade.

How Grimsby had stared at first. Ashland had almost forgotten the effect of his ruined face on the untrained eye. How long had it been since he had encountered, unmasked, a genuine stranger, one who hadn't been prepared in advance for this abomination? But Grimsby had recovered in a flash and composed himself politely. Well-bred, that fellow. Outside the carriage, he hadn't shifted his eyes away, hadn't looked at the ground or his hands or Ashland's hat. Another point in the young man's column. He might very likely do. Only a few months, after all. Only a few more months until Freddie's Oxford examinations, and then Ashland need no longer bother with this business of bringing tutors into the house, into his well-ordered routine, only to have them pack their valises and leave after a week or two. Freddie would be off, would likely only return to the howling moors for the odd dutiful week or two, and that would be that.

The Duke of Ashland would be alone at last. No tutors; no Freddie spreading about his profligate charm, so like his mother's; no lingering reminders of the days before he had shipped off to India, plain old Lieutenant the Honorable Anthony Russell, leaving behind a beautiful wife and infant son, and two perfectly healthy cousins between himself and the dukedom.

Ashland took another drink, longer this time, and lifted aside the heavy velvet curtain. The window faced north; in full daylight, the view was bleak beyond description. Tonight, however, all was black. The clouds had moved in completely, propelled by the incessant wind, and there was no further moonlight to illuminate the spinning grasses, the rocks, the few scrubby bushes that had once formed a sort of garden along this side of the house. In her last year, Isabelle had worked obsessively on that garden, employing a raft of men from the village to eke out some sort of civilized order to the landscape. She had ordered plantings and statuary, tried for shade and windbreaks, and all for nothing. Only the statues remained, like the ruins of some lost Roman town, limbs cut off abruptly where the wind had toppled the poor fellows off their pedestals.

Rather fitting, that.

Another drink. Nearly finished now. How had that happened? Must ration out the rest, one tiny sip at a time.

What would Isabelle have thought of young Grimsby? She would have liked him, Ashland thought. She liked young people, clever people, and there was no doubt that Grimsby was clever. It radiated from those large eyes of his, covered by his spectacles. What had Olympia written? That he knew no scholar more perfectly grounded in the subtleties of Latin and Greek than Mr. Tobias Grimsby, and that his mathematics were without flaw. Isabelle, who had been well-educated by an exacting governess, would have had Mr. Grimsby to the drawing room for tea every afternoon. She would have taken pleasure in teasing him out, in discovering his opinions and tastes and family history.

Isabelle. If Isabelle were here, Ashland would even now be climbing the stairs to his bedroom. He would even now be changing into his nightshirt and dressing robe, dismissing his valet, knocking politely on the door between their bedchambers.

Ashland tilted his glass and let the last golden drops slide down his throat. A very slight vibration now caressed his brain, the edge of intoxication just perceptible at the rim of his senses. It was all he allowed himself, to head off the lust that assaulted him every evening at this hour, as he prepared to climb the stairs and fill his lonely bed.

Isabelle's body, white and rounded in the candlelight. Isabelle's flesh, yielding to his. Her little sighs in his ear, her fingers on his back, her quickening movements. The drive to climax, the shudder of release, the slow pulse of its aftermath. Isabelle's kisses on his unmarred skin, her body tucking itself in the shadow of his.

Ashland let the curtain fall back.

With exaggerated precision, he placed his empty sherry glass back on the tray and straightened his empty right cuff.

The hall was deserted. The servants had all gone off to bed, knowing the duke's preferences. He climbed the stairs alone, and alone he readied himself for bed, because the challenge of handling his own buttons and sleeves kept his mind fully occupied.

THREE

Emilie awoke from a profound sleep to a familiar sound: the rough, metallic rattle of the coal scuttle as a maid lit the fire in her bedroom.

She opened her eyes, expecting to see worn velvet hangings and rioting unicorns on a medieval tapestry, to see sunlight pouring past the cracks of her sapphire blue curtains and her escritoire covered with books and notes and pencil stubs. She put her hand out, expecting to feel the warmth of her sleeping sister.

But her hand found only the coolness of empty bedsheets, and her eyes found only a thick gray darkness smudged with the shadows of unknown furniture.

She flung herself upright.

"Sir!" A crash sounded from the fireplace, and then the clatter of metal on stone.

Sir.

Emilie covered her cheeks. She had taken off her whiskers last night, because they itched so abominably, but her head was encased in a long woolen nightcap and her body bundled in a purely masculine nightshirt. "I'm sorry," she gasped out, hoping the maid couldn't see her clearly. She brought the bed-clothes up to her nose.

"I thought ye was sleeping still, sir," said the maid, turning back to the grate. She was nothing but a pale outline in the darkness; her basket of kindling seemed larger than her body. The grate itself was smaller still, which was of course natural, Emilie reminded herself, since Tobias Grimsby slept upstairs with the servants and not in the grander bedrooms below.

The grander bedrooms, the bedrooms for the duke and his family and their honored guests: paneled and papered and gilded, hung with silk and oil paintings, spacious and well furnished.

Emilie remembered few details from the night before, as she'd readied herself for bed, but she had a general impression of a clean space, plain and pleasant, with a few sticks of necessary furniture and a single window, curtained in striped cotton. The bedclothes beneath her fingers were smooth and woolen and unadorned. Comfort, not luxury.

"Have you the time?" she asked the maid.

"Why, I do suppose it's near enough six," said the maid, straightening. "There, then. Nice and hot afore ye knows it."

"Thank you."

The young woman turned and grasped the handle of her basket. "Ye'd best be up soon for breakfast, sir."

Breakfast? Emilie's mind was still aching with fatigue. Five hours' sleep had not been nearly enough to recover from the drama of the previous day. Breakfast? Her belly echoed with hunger, but she couldn't imagine pushing her heavy limbs out of bed and into her shirt and trousers and plain woolen jacket.

The maid left, banging her basket behind her. Emilie lay back down to contemplate the gray ceiling. Dawn was no more than a rumor beyond the glass. The wind, at least, had stilled for the moment, lulled by the approach of sunrise.

Breakfast. The duke was an early riser, then. And since early risers tended to look with scorn on those who weren't up at the first searing crow of the nearest cock, Emilie had better take the maid's advice and stir herself.

Half an hour later, her trousers buttoned and her whiskers neatly in place, Emilie arrived in the center of the great hall- way. Dawn had finally begun to leak through the windows, a dawn of surprising strength and brightness, suggesting actual sunshine. Emilie took absent note of the classical dimensions, the polished marble, the depth and intricacy of the plaster-work. Ashland Abbey had likely been rebuilt a century or so ago, she judged, and at considerable expense. When Emilie was a child, she had been to stay with the Devonshires at Chatsworth (her mother had been a great friend of Lady Frederick Cavendish in her girlhood), and she felt echoes of its formal grandeur here, that sense of scale and proportion. Each gilt-framed painting was mounted in its place, edges exactly squared; each fold of drapery hung downward without a mote of dust to mar its color.

The breakfast room, Emilie knew, would be positioned to make the most of the meager Yorkshire sunrise. She rotated, took note of the angle of the light, and set off to the right: the eastern wing, she supposed.

She passed through one doorway and the next, a succession of impossibly perfect salons, ending in a grand corridor hung with portraits. She paused. A clink of china met her ears, followed by a low and resonant voice.

Emilie straightened her collar and stepped in the direction of the sounds.

"May I help you, sir?"

Emilie stopped and turned. The butler stood before her—what was his name? Simpson?—looking arch, his voice much sterner than his words, his bearing almost painfully correct. His white shirtfront might have been made of plaster instead of linen.

Emilie's back stiffened. She lifted her chin. "On my way to breakfast, thank you. If you'll excuse me."

"Mr. Grimsby," said the butler, laden with ice, "I believe you'll find that the staff breakfasts below stairs, in the service dining room."

The staff.

The blood drained from Emilie's face, and then returned an instant later in a hot flush that made her skin itch beneath her whiskers. She stared into Simpson's impassive dark eyes and willed herself not to flinch, not to betray herself by a single flicker of her eyelids. "Of course," she said, when her throat was calm. "Perhaps you could direct me, Mr. Simpson, at your earliest convenience."

He didn't turn. "Back down the corridor, Mr. Grimsby, and to the right. You'll find the service stairs at the end of the hall."

"Thank you, Mr. Simpson. Good morning to you."

Emilie turned and forced her legs to carry her along the echoing hallway. The service dining room, of course. This grand architecture, this clink of priceless china, was no longer meant for her.

I have dined at Chatsworth! she wanted to shout, over her shoulder. *I have sat to table with sovereigns! I am a cousin to the damned Tsarina!*

All right, a distant cousin. But nonetheless.

It was better this way, of course. She could conceal herself better below stairs. What if Ashland had noble guests, guests she might have met in some previous stay in Great Britain? At the duke's table, she might be seen and noticed. Questions might be asked. Among staff, she was invisible. Nobody noticed the servants.

And that was the point, wasn't it? To hide.

Emilie's shoes clacked hollowly on the marble tiles. She turned right and found the stairs at the end of the hall, descending into the unknown world below.

T wenty heads swiveled as Emilie passed through the doorway into the servants' dining hall. She was used to that sort of thing, of course: When a princess of Holstein-Schweinwald-Huhnhof entered the room, people generally noticed.

But this was different. Emilie was dressed not in pearls and silk, but in padded black broadcloth and curling whiskers. The eyes turned in her direction brimmed not with awe, but with an impertinent and even hostile curiosity. She recognized one face: the maid from this morning, thin-cheeked and wide-eyed. She was the only one smiling.

"Why, good morning, sir! Ye nearly missed yer breakfast, nobbut like I warned ye."

"I beg your pardon," Emilie said. "I am unfamiliar with the plan of the house."

Somebody tittered. An older woman, to the right of the empty seat at the head of the table, set down her spoon and dabbed at the corner of her mouth. "Good morning, Mr.

Grimsby. I am Mrs. Needle, the housekeeper. Ye're welcome here, of course, though I'm sure Lucy will be happy to bring you a tray in t'morning, if that's yer preference. Ye may take Lionel's place at t'left. He's serving upstairs at t'moment."

Lionel, who sat to the left of the butler's seat: No doubt he was the head footman, and now busy anticipating Ashland's wishes in the breakfast room. Emilie ran her gaze once more around the table, more carefully this time, taking note. After all, servants were just as conscious of rank and precedence as their masters, and the appearance of a tutor had likely disturbed everything. Tutors and governesses occupied that liminal space between stairs, neither servant nor lord, of the educated class and yet a household employee. Hence the offer of a breakfast tray, which would make things easier for all concerned. Lionel, whose place she'd usurped, would be delighted.

But here she was. She couldn't turn tail and run.

Emilie walked around the table, head high, and pulled out Lionel's chair. His place was already set with bowl, plate, fork, knife, and spoon. She sat down and nodded at Lucy, who sat on the opposite side, several places down. "May I trouble you for the toast, Miss Lucy?" she asked.

Lucy smiled. Her eyelashes swept down. "Why, of course, Mr. Grimsby."

Emilie ate quietly, head bowed slightly to her plate, doing her best to be invisible in the heavy silence. The clatter of cutlery began to resume. Someone asked a low question; someone answered a bit more loudly. Emilie drank her tea.

"Ooh, Lucy," said one of the maids, "they've another story in t'paper today about them lost princesses in Germany. Pictures and owt."

The tea made an immediate detour down Emilie's windpipe.

"Ooh, have they?" exclaimed Lucy. "What do they look like? Are they beautiful? Have they got them tiaras on?"

"Yes, great big ones, and t'great blue sashes across their chests. I thought t'oldest one were t' prettiest. She's got lovely curling hair, just like yers. They do say . . ."

"I say, are ye all right, Mr. Grimsby?" asked Lucy.

"Quite all right," Emilie gasped, between spasms.

"Have ye heard about t'princesses, Mr. Grimsby? It's t'most terrifying story."

"No, I haven't. Mrs. Needle, may I trouble you"—cough, cough—"for the teapot?"

Mrs. Needle poured Emilie a solicitous cup. "Small sips, Mr. Grimsby. That's it."

"It's nobbut some little kingdom in Germany, Mr. Grimsby, and t'king . . ."

"T'prince, Lucy," said the other maid knowingly. "It ain't never a kingdom, it's a prin-ci-pality. Ruled by a prince. That's what t'paper said."

Lucy sighed. "Them Germans. Anyroad, t'prince died a pair of month ago, out hunting, shot dead with his poor son-in-law, t'one what was just married to his oldest daughter. And a week after, when they was supposed to crown t'oldest daughter as ruler—the prince never having no sons what might take over—they had all gone missing. Every one. Even t'Royal Governess." She leaned forward and said it with capital letters.

Emilie cleared her throat at last. "How shocking."

"And do you know what t'morning post do say today?" The other maid bounced in her chair. "They think t'princesses came to England!"

"England! Oh, Jane!" said Lucy.

"Whatever for?" whispered Emilie.

"Why, because their mother were English, seems like. She were t'sister of t'Duke of Olympia," said Jane.

A single sigh drew forth around the table. Emilie spotted a pot of marmalade near her teacup and snaked her hand around the china to snare it.

"His Grace knows t'Duke of Olympia. Great friends, they are," said one of the lesser footmen, down the table. "Thieves ain't in it."

"Imagine," said Lucy dreamily, fingering her teacup. "Imagine if them princesses was to be hiding right here in t'village. Imagine if we was to be standing next to them at t'shops."

"Nonsense," said Mrs. Needle. "I doubt a gaggle of fine princesses could find their way to Yorkshire on a map. Anyroad, they'd be in disguise, in course."

Emilie's marmalade spilled onto the tablecloth.

Lucy snapped her fingers. "*I* could spot a princess in disguise, just like that."

"You couldn't," said Jane.

"I could. It's sommat in t'way she looks and talks," said Lucy. "She couldn't never fool me."

Emilie dabbed furiously at the marmalade.

"Twaddle. Ye've never met a princess in yer life, Lucy Mudge."

"I saw that Princess Alexandra in London once't, didn't I?"

Jane laughed. "From how many street away?"

"Don't matter. I could tell."

"Ye couldn't."

"I could!"

"Lucy," said Mrs. Needle, "have ye tidied up the schoolroom yet? I'm sure t'gentlemen are being to need it this morning. Isn't that right, Mr. Grimsby?"

Emilie folded her marmalade-smeared napkin next to her plate. Her face was still warm. "Yes, madam, if it's convenient."

A suppressed laugh from the female side of the table.

"That'll be enough, Lucy," said Mrs. Needle.

"Well, it ain't as though t'young master is being to be up for hours yet . . ."

"That be enowt, Lucy," Mrs. Needle said again. "You will lay a fire in t'schoolroom directly after breakfast and give t'room a thorough cleaning."

"Oh, as to that, Mrs. Needle," said Lucy, "I'm *happy* to make owt ready for Mr. Grimsby."

Emilie looked up in surprise. Were Lucy's eyelashes actually *fluttering*? At *her*?

"I'm sure she is," said Jane petulantly.

"Lucy's duties are never yer concern, Jane." Mrs. Needle drank her tea.

"I never do mind serving Mr. Grimsby mysen," Lucy said. "Even though I were up while all hour last night, waiting for His Grace and his lordship, and I'm being to be up again tonight . . ."

"That will be all, Lucy." Mrs. Needle's voice was sharp.

". . . and t'Lord knows how late His Grace will be out *this* time . . ."

"*Lucy.*"

A footman coughed next to Emilie's left shoulder. Someone's chair scraped lightly against the wooden floor. Emilie glanced up through her eyelashes and watched Lucy finger the handle of her knife, her lips pursed in a dainty pout. She mumbled something deep in her throat.

"What was that, Lucy?" snapped Mrs. Needle.

Lucy looked up. "I said, nobbut what I blame t'poor man."

"His Grace is not a *man*, Lucy. He is a duke." Mrs. Needle reached for the teapot and refreshed her cup. "Ye may be excused."

"Aye, ma'am." Lucy rose, gathered her empty plate and teacup, and left the room.

Mrs. Needle picked up the sugar tongs and selected a lump. Her fingers were clean and round tipped, the nails trimmed nearly to the quick. "Ye will pardon us, Mr. Grimsby. We've all served together since His Grace first came to live here, and many afore. It makes us all a little overfamiliar."

"Not at all, madam. I quite understand."

Footsteps thumped down the nearby stairs, and a moment later the black-and-white figure of Simpson the butler filled the doorway with correctness. "His Grace has finished breakfast," he announced, and the maids picked up their teacups in unison and drained them.

Mrs. Needle wiped her mouth and stood. "Girls, clear t'breakfast room. Jane, ye may set another place for Lionel. Mr. Simpson, how is His Grace this morning?" There was something oddly warm and solicitous in her voice.

Emilie had finished her tea. Her breakfast sat in lumps in her belly. From the corner of her eye, she watched Simpson approach, saw his gaze rest for an instant on the spot of marmalade on the tablecloth next to her plate.

"His Grace is well enough," said Simpson, sitting down at the head of the table with a flip of his tails. He reached for his teacup and said, without preamble, in his crackling voice, "Mr. Grimsby, when it's convenient, you may attend His Grace in the study. One of the footmen will show you the way."

The Duke of Ashland stood by a tall window, cup and saucer in hand. He turned when Emilie entered, and the unexpected sunshine gilded the left side of his face, the perfect side, casting the rest in shadow.

"Good morning, Mr. Grimsby," he said. "Yorkshire appears to be welcoming your arrival in a most unseasonable fashion."

That voice of his! Emilie had thought she'd only imagined it, or that its richness derived from the close quarters of the taproom and the carriage. But this room was large, its ceilings high, and still Ashland's voice made the air dance.

"I'm grateful for the warm welcome I've received throughout your house, Your Grace."

Ashland stepped away from the blinding sunlight at the window. Emilie held back her breath. He was wearing a black half-mask over his useless eye and scarred cheek, giving him a distinctly piratical air, and the close-cropped hair that she had assumed last night to be a very pale blond was actually silver white.

She had never seen anyone so extraordinary.

"I hope my staff has been courteous. You had breakfast?"

"Yes, sir."

He set down the cup on the corner of his desk and reached with his left hand into his watch pocket, and only then did Emilie notice that the cuff of his right sleeve was empty.

Her eyes widened and flew to his face. Emilie had been trained since girlhood to remain polite and impassive, no matter how jarring or extraordinary the sight in front of her, but this man, all of him—his size, his physical beauty, his voice, his white hair, his scars, his empty cuff—was too much. Her wits had scattered about the room.

Ashland consulted his watch. "My son is at that time of life when a young man sleeps late and rises late. I have had a breakfast tray sent to his room, however, and at nine o'clock I shall expect you to begin his studies in the schoolroom." He looked up and smiled, and the hint of warmth made the backs of Emilie's knees turn to India rubber. "With or without the boy himself."

"Yes, sir," she whispered. She pushed her spectacles up her nose. Why couldn't she find her voice?

Ashland had been to war, Olympia had told her. He'd seen action in some remote part of India, before returning to

England to assume his title. Undoubtedly he had been injured there; thus the scars and the empty cuff and possibly even the white hair. Physical shock could do such things. It was all perfectly natural.

"Yes, sir," she repeated, putting more muscle into it.

"Very good. Would it disturb you at all if I were to come in and observe, at some point in the afternoon? Solely to judge my son's progress, I assure you, and not your own ability." His voice resonated with command, the way it had with Freddie last night, and Emilie knew once more that he was not asking a question.

"Of course not. You have every right."

Ashland replaced his watch in his pocket and picked up his cup. "Do you drink coffee, Mr. Grimsby?"

"I do not," she said. "I am accustomed to tea."

"I picked up the habit abroad, and I'm afraid I can't seem to shift it. I hope you don't mind. In any case, if you have a moment, I should like to sit down and review your planned course of study." Ashland gestured to the chair before the desk and walked around to find his own. Despite his great frame, he moved like an African cat. Like one of the leopards in the Berlin zoo, noiseless and swift, pacing with restless grace along the perimeter of his cage. "The Duke of Olympia, by the way, recommends you highly. Do you come from him recently?"

Emilie settled herself in the chair and resisted the urge to touch her whiskers, which were itching fiercely. Ashland watched her with his beautiful ruined face, his impassive face, and her nerves vibrated to a keen pitch. Keep as close as possible to the truth, Olympia had instructed her. "Yes, sir. I have the honor of informing Your Grace that he was in excellent health, not two days ago."

"I am delighted to hear it. You're a fortunate young man, to have such a patron."

"Yes, sir. We are related, on my mother's side."

"His Grace does take care of his own," said Ashland. His hands—his *hand*—was in his lap. At the edge of her senses, Emilie sensed a faint frisson of tension under his calm.

"He is all that is kind." Emilie knit her hands together.

"Kind. Yes." Below the duke's black leather half-mask, a

muscle twitched, as if he were holding back a smile. "I bear no blood relation to him at all, and yet he watches over my interests in London with an almost paternal care. I believe he likes the role. In ancient times, I daresay he would have acquired a kingdom."

Emilie smiled at the image of Olympia on his throne, dispensing favors and plotting campaigns. "You know him well, I see. How did you two become acquainted?"

Ashland studied her without answering, and Emilie realized belatedly that the question was impossibly personal, not at all the sort of question a tutor would ask his employer. She had forgotten herself already. The blood prickled in her cheeks.

"Oh, the usual channels," Ashland said at last. He lifted his left hand and waved it negligently. "He took an interest in me, early in my career, when I was a mere lieutenant in the Guards. But we stray from the matter at hand. The examinations, if you'll recall, take place in only five months, and while I admit his lordship is far too clever for his own good, I doubt that cleverness alone will convince the dons to accept him at such an early age."

Emilie gathered herself. Voice low, voice calm. Inhabit Grimsby. *Become* Grimsby. "If I may ask, Your Grace, why exactly is he trying for a place so soon? Might he not benefit from another year or two of private study before university?"

Ashland squared the single sheet of paper against his leather blotter. "It was my son's own idea, Mr. Grimsby. I expect he wishes to escape."

"Escape, sir?"

Ashland looked up, and his single perfect eye was ice blue as he regarded her. "Yes, Mr. Grimsby. Escape Yorkshire, escape this rather large and chilling house, escape the uninteresting company of his father."

"I doubt that, sir. You don't strike me as uninteresting at all."

A small movement disturbed the corner of Ashland's mouth. "How kind, Mr. Grimsby. Nevertheless, my son wishes to try for a place at Oxford, and I have agreed to assist him with his preparation."

Emilie parted her lips to say something appropriate, something obliging. He was, after all, her employer, and she was required to please him. But just then a draft brushed her cheek, frigid and untouched by the determined fire at the other end of the room, and Emilie heard herself say, "Do you *want* him to pass his examinations, sir?"

Ashland's white head startled back an inch or two. "I beg your pardon?"

Another blunder. Emilie flushed. She had performed her role so well yesterday, so grave and reserved, keeping every word and action under the strictest control. Why did she keep forgetting herself with *this* man, the one whom she must above all others keep without suspicion? But the words could not be called back. She went on bravely: "That is, do you wish him to leave your house and attend university next year?"

"What an extraordinary question, Mr. Grimsby."

"I didn't mean to pry, of course . . ." Emilie began.

"Yes, you did."

". . . but of course it is a tutor's business to understand his pupil's motivations, in order to better design the course of study."

Ashland's eyebrow arched. Emilie resisted the urge to fidget, to push her spectacles up the bridge of her nose; to tug at her whiskers, which grew steadily itchier under the duke's gaze.

At last Ashland reached for the fountain pen in its holder at the top of the blotter. He shook it with a single brisk stroke, set the nib to the paper before him, and began to write, with his left hand curled awkwardly around the pen and his empty right cuff braced at the side. He spoke without looking up. "Your *business*, Mr. Grimsby, is to prepare my son for his entrance examinations in five months' time. You shall conduct this *business* as you see fit. The staff and conveniences of this house are entirely at your disposal. Do you ride?"

"Yes, sir."

"A horse shall be provided for your use. I encourage you to enlist a groom in your explorations, however, as the surrounding terrain is notably treacherous. Is there anything else you require?"

"No, sir."

He looked up. His gaze was hard. "Then you may go, Mr. Grimsby. I shall be upstairs later today to observe your progress."

Emilie's back straightened. She was perfectly prepared to make allowances for the duke's misfortunes, which might make anyone hard and abrupt, and for the subservient relationship she bore to him. *Remember*, Miss Dingleby had said, schooling the three sisters in Olympia's attic last week, *that you are not princesses anymore. You are commoners. You are employed to perform tasks to your superior's satisfaction. You will be subject to his demands and his unvarnished opinions, and you must submit to them.* Emilie had repeated those words to herself last night and again this morning, as she attached her whiskers to the sides of her face with the special glue Miss Dingleby had given her.

You must submit to him.

Still, she didn't have to enjoy it.

"There is one thing, sir," Emilie said stiffly.

"Yes?"

"Apart from my duties, may I consider my time my own?"

Ashland fingered his pen. "I suppose so."

"I may, for example, venture into the village from time to time?"

"As you wish. I regret there is not more to entertain you." Ashland's voice grew a touch silkier, a touch more pointed.

The blood began to simmer in Emilie's ears. "As for entertainment, I require very little, sir, other than a book. But I do have affairs of my own, which require my attention from time to time." She stood and stared down at Ashland's white head. "If you will excuse me, I believe I shall begin work at once."

"Admirable, Mr. Grimsby. Good morning." Ashland returned his attention to the desk before him.

The scratch of pen against paper dismissed her.

FOUR

Frederick Russell, Lord Silverton, sauntered into the schoolroom at half past ten o'clock, dressed for riding. "What ho," he said, flinging his scarlet jacket on a nearby chair. "You're up early, Grimsby."

Emilie removed her spectacles, wiped them, replaced them on her nose. She took out her pocket watch and tilted it toward the window. "It is half past ten o'clock, your lordship. Your lessons began at nine. I regret you have missed them all."

Freddie's eyes popped wide behind his own spectacles. His hair was askew, clearly unbrushed, and the bones of his thin shoulders propped up his white shirt like tent poles. "I beg your pardon?"

Emilie slid her watch back into place. "Have you broken fast, sir? Before we begin each morning, I require you to have eaten. One cannot properly concentrate on an empty stomach."

"I say, Grimsby . . ."

"*Have* you, sir? Eaten?"

"Why, yes, but . . ."

"Then sit down and we will discuss your plan of study. I understand you drink coffee. I have instructed Mrs. Needle to have a tray sent up at eleven. And Lord Silverton?"

Freddie slumped into the chair. "Yes, Grimsby?"

"It is *Mr.* Grimsby. Please put on your coat and fasten your necktie properly."

"Dash it, Grimsby . . ."

"Dash it, *Mr.* Grimsby."

"Dash it *all*, Mr. Grimsby," Freddie said, but he reached for his coat.

By the time the coffee arrived at exactly eleven o'clock, borne on a silver tray by a simpering Lucy, Emilie had confirmed what she already suspected. Lord Silverton was clever, brilliant really, quick to grasp ideas and connect them with one another. He was also undisciplined, studying what he enjoyed with obsessive fervor and avoiding what he did not. He did his reading at night—into the morning, if absorbed—and took no notes. If a concept proved particularly difficult or unruly, he moved on to the next.

In short, his examiners would shred him to pieces.

"Your examiners will shred you to pieces, your lordship," Emilie said. "Thank you, Lucy. You may go."

Freddie leaned back in his chair and pushed a hand through his hair. His eyes wandered to Lucy's departing derriere. "Rubbish. I daresay they'll all be sleeping in their chairs."

He was probably quite right, but Emilie knew better than to agree. "Your Greek is not unworthy, but your Latin is execrable."

"My mathematics, however, are excellent." He reached for the coffeepot and filled his cup to the brim. "Coffee?"

Emilie eyed the black liquid with suspicion. "Perhaps a little."

He filled the other cup and picked up the cream pot. "That's how I win at cards, you know. Mathematics." He tapped his temple with a teaspoon. "I keep track of what's played, calculate probabilities. Easy enough, once you have the knack."

"But not without risk. You must have known they'd think you were cheating." Emilie added a careful splash of cream and a lump of sugar. She sniffed the results hesitantly. It did smell rather nice. Earthy, rich.

"Go on. It doesn't bite. Unless you take it black, of course, as Pater does. Ah, that's the stuff. Particularly handsome when one's been up late."

Emilie sipped and shuddered. "He drinks this *black*? With nothing at all?"

"He's the do-or-die sort, you know. He probably thinks it's dishonorable to add cream. Muddying the purity of the coffee or some such. Is that lemon cake?" Freddie stretched one gangly arm over the tray and snatched the cake.

"Plate and napkin to your left, Lord Silverton."

"Oh, right. He's not a bad sort, Pater," Freddie said, somewhat muffled by cake, "but he's rather implacable. Take his face, for example."

Emilie dabbed her mouth, remembered herself, and wiped with gusto. "What about his face?"

"Ha-ha. What splendid manners you've got, Grimsby. *Mr.* Grimsby, that is." He winked. "I mean, of course, that hideous mug of Pater's, the one that makes children scream in terror and angels faint away. For twelve years now, since he returned home from whatever godforsaken adventure blew his face apart and took his hand for good measure, he hasn't left Yorkshire, hasn't received visitors, hasn't attended a single event of a social nature. And do you know why?"

"It's no business of mine, your lordship," said Emilie, ears straining for more.

"Of course it's not, but I'll bet you're desperate to know, aren't you? You might think it's pride—that's what I used to think, and I daresay that's something to do with it. But as time dragged on, and I began to acquire a bit of wisdom"—here Freddie gave a worldly sixteen-year-old shrug—"I began to realize it was nothing more than sheer bullheaded stubbornness. He'd begun by not going out, and by God he wasn't going to change his mind midstream. And then my mother bolted . . ."

"Lord Silverton, *really*. These are hardly confidences for a stranger." Emilie ventured another sip of coffee. How strange; she was feeling rather dizzy.

"Rot. Someone's got to tell you, so you don't go about making awkward remarks. Nobody likes an awkward remark, Mr. Grimsby." Freddie grinned. "I was only four years old at the time, so I hardly remember anything, only that she was quite remarkably beautiful. Or perhaps I don't even remember that; it's just what people have said. *Oh, the duchess, she was beautiful, she was legendary.* Well, they put it about that she'd gone

abroad for her health, but the fact is she bolted, pure and simple. And if there *were* any possibility of changing Pater's mind
about entering society again, it died right there. Cake?"

"No, thank you." Emilie set her cup aside. The clouds had
blown in, deadening the sunlight that had spilled so cheerfully
through the window at nine o'clock, and the room was turning
chilly. She rose and went to the coal scuttle. Clearly the schoolroom was not in much use. The lemony scent of a recent scrub-
bing could not quite disguise the mustiness, the old-wood smell
of a space unaccustomed to human habitation. "She *is* still
alive, however?" Emilie heard herself ask, as she tossed a few
pieces of black coal atop the sizzling pile in the grate.

"Oh, I don't know about that. You'd have to ask Pater."
Freddie's voice was thick with additional cake.

"Of course I shan't ask your father. It's not my concern."

"I don't personally care one way or the other, really. I daresay she's not losing sleep over me and Pater, wherever she is."

Emilie sat back down and straightened her lapels. "Then
she is a fool."

"I do wonder what she was like, though." Freddie leaned
back and drained the last of his coffee. "They were most spectacularly in love at first, I'm told. Honeymoon in Italy, though
as I was born nine months after the wedding I don't suppose
they saw much of the sights, if you see what I mean. Then
Pater's regiment was called up, and that was that."

Beneath her whiskers, Emilie's cheeks burned. "That will
be quite enough, your lordship."

"*Indeed.*"

The single word boomed through the air like a cannon
shot. Emilie jumped, spilled her coffee, and whipped around.

The Duke of Ashland filled the open doorway, his hand on
the latch, his white hair glowing above his masked face.

T he taut room snapped into panic at Ashland's appearance,
like a platoon caught malingering by a sergeant. A useful
skill, this ability to move and observe without being perceived. He owed Olympia that, at least.

Freddie leapt to his feet; his chair toppled to the floor
behind him. "Sir!"

On the other side of the table, Mr. Grimsby set down his coffee cup and rose. His fingers curled around the edge of the table: shaking, probably. Poor fellow. "Good morning, Your Grace," he said, in his gruff little voice.

Ashland stalked into the room, closing the door behind him with a decisive click of the latch. The sound helped to quell the sick feeling in his chest.

They were most spectacularly in love at first.

"I see your studies are proceeding apace, Frederick," he said.

Freddie picked up his chair, righted it, and sat down. "Oh, don't be cross and sack poor Mr. Grimsby, Pater. Was only making conversation over coffee. I assure you, he was putting me through my paces at a smart clip a few minutes ago."

"No doubt." Ashland angled his body over the table and ran over the papers and books clustered about the coffee tray. He picked up a sheet. "Are these your Latin conjugations, Frederick?"

She bolted, pure and simple.

Ashland locked his fingers to keep them from crushing the paper.

"Hideous, I know. I've already been broken to bits by Mr. Grimsby. On the other hand, he's quite impressed by my maths."

"He should be." Ashland laid the paper back on the table. "Well, Mr. Grimsby? What's your assessment?"

Grimsby's face still glowed pink beneath that startling bush of wheat-colored whiskers. He cleared his throat. "Lord Silverton is immensely clever, Your Grace, as I suspected, but he will need to study with a great deal more discipline over the coming months. He's not yet sixteen, and his education has been haphazard at best; meanwhile, he will be competing for places against older public schoolboys who have been drilled in Latin every day for the past eight or ten years. I suppose his name will help him slide through . . ."

"I say," Freddie muttered.

". . . but I doubt his lordship wishes the lucky accident of his birth to nudge out some better-qualified young man from the chance for advancement." Grimsby's eyes gleamed as he said this, as if he actually cared about the fate of that deserving schoolboy shunted aside for the son of a duke.

Ashland raised his eyebrows. "Well phrased, Mr. Grimsby. Frederick? Do you agree?"

"When you put it that way," Freddie said sulkily. "I'm not a complete rotter, after all."

"I believe Mr. Grimsby is quite right. Britain's great strength is her ability to discover and encourage boys of exceptional ability and allow them to better their condition in life through hard work and application to duty. Nowhere else in Europe can a talented boy of little or no social connection advance himself to prominence, and the result on the Continent is stagnation, decadence, and tyranny." Ashland tapped his finger against the topmost book in Grimsby's stack, a neatly bound edition of Newton's *Principia*.

"I say, Pater," Freddie grumbled. "That's coming it rather thick."

Grimsby's face had flushed to an even more furious shade of red. "That is not altogether the case, your lordship. I would not go so far as to say tyranny."

"Tyranny and disorder," Ashland said. "Take the recent case of this principality in Germany, this Holstein-Schweinwald. A trifling, backward state, to be sure; quite second-rate and of very little interest to the world at large . . ."

"Backward!"

"Yet even there, an absolute ruler, a despot, attempts to rearrange the succession to suit his own interests, to prevent the natural growth of a democratic form of law . . ."

"Was it fair, Your Grace, that the succession must die out because the prince's children happened to be girls instead of boys? Britain herself, and by extension half the world, is ruled by a woman." Grimsby's voice shook with passion.

"Your views are admirable, Mr. Grimsby, but I beg leave to remind you that Great Britain is ruled by her people, as you well know. Queen Victoria, God bless and keep her, has only a ceremonial role in governing our country. But we are not here to discuss political theory, after all. We are here to discuss Lord Silverton's application to his studies, and his duty to earn his place at university by merit alone." Ashland picked up the book and gave it a little slap.

Grimsby dropped his eyes to the papers in front of him. He squared them neatly. "We are quite in agreement on that point,

Your Grace. I shall do my best to ensure that his lordship is prepared."

"Very good." Ashland took a chair, the sturdiest available, and drew it out from the table so that his right side would be shadowed from the window. The adjustment was so instinctive, he hardly noticed he made it. "Carry on, then," he said, with a wave. "Simply pretend I'm not here."

Grimsby's large blue eyes blinked slowly behind his spectacles. "Your Grace?"

"I have arranged my schedule to allow an hour or two of quiet observation." Ashland smiled benignly at them both.

"Pater, it's not possible. You're about as easy to ignore as a bull elephant."

Ashland fingered the edge of his empty cuff. His stump was aching more than usual this morning; perhaps the weather was changing, winter was coming on. "Nevertheless," he said.

"Don't be ridiculous, Pater . . ."

"Your lordship's father is perfectly welcome to stay and observe," said Mr. Grimsby. "He is, after all, paying for your instruction."

Ashland folded his arms and studied Grimsby. He had always considered himself a decent judge of character, with a few glaring exceptions, but he could not quite make out the young man. He had a certain freshness about him, a dewy innocence. His fair hair gleamed beneath a layer of sleek pomade; his skin still radiated surprise at Ashland's unexpected entrance. Were it not for those whiskers, curling luxuriously about the young man's jaw, he might have seemed like a youth, hardly older than Freddie himself.

And his eyes. Ashland angled his head, watching the two of them. Grimsby was explaining some point of Latin conjugation to Freddie's bored and sloping body, and his blue eyes narrowed with seriousness, causing a few lines to invade the skin between his eyebrows. An old soul, Ashland's mother would have said, nodding her head. Old and wise.

Again, Ashland thought of Grimsby in the taproom last night, brandishing his chicken leg, face ablaze with determination.

Grimsby, straightening his lapels a moment ago, as Ashland observed them noiselessly from the doorway. Speaking in his sturdy voice: *Then she is a fool.*

An older fellow, Freddie's last tutor. Seventy at least, with thinning hair and a querulous tone, complaining about Frederick's lack of attention here and Frederick's lack of discipline there. *I cannot be expected* and *these conditions* and that sort of thing.

Ashland adjusted his arms at his chest, keeping his empty cuff hidden, relieving the slight pressure on the stump from his opposite forearm. Grimsby's voice was low, a bit gruff, almost intentionally so, as if he were making up for his lack of years with a manufactured resonance. Determination, patience, intelligence. This young man was nothing like the other tutors, who had left after two days, a week, three weeks, fed up with Freddie's quicksilver brilliance and the incessant howling bleakness of the landscape.

Which begged the question: Why had Olympia sent Grimsby to Ashland Abbey, instead of putting the young fellow to use himself?

Olympia, after all, did nothing without reason.

Ashland rose abruptly. "Thank you, Mr. Grimsby," he said. "I shall leave the two of you in peace."

He walked from the room and back down the stairs to his private study. He had a great deal of estate business to work through before venturing out tonight.

FIVE

By afternoon, Freddie's restless body was nearly bursting through the walls of the schoolroom, and Emilie, sensing opportunity, prescribed a spell of outdoor exercise. A message was sent down to the stables, and in short order they were trotting from the stable courtyard, wrapped up against the weather in coats and woolen caps.

"You ride well," said Freddie, sounding rather shocked.

"Of course I ride well. I've ridden nearly every day of my life." Emilie kept her head rigid as she said this, but the remark warmed her innards. True, she had begun riding horses nearly as early as she could walk, but she'd only ridden astride for those two preparatory months at the Duke of Olympia's remote Devon estate. Even now, the leather felt odd and rather chafing along her inner thighs, though she liked the intimate feel of the horse's body moving between them. She felt closer, more connected to the animal's mind and motion.

"Well, it's a good thing," Freddie said. He motioned with his riding crop at the swilling grass around them. "Riding's about the only thing doing around here, without going into town."

"Where's town?"

Freddie pointed. "About four miles in that direction. You

come to a track, after a bit. Then there's the Anvil, which of course you know from last night's doings, and then the railway station, which you know as well, and then there's the town proper." He sighed. "Not much to that, either. Dull factory, turning out crockery, and not even any discontented workers to liven things up since Pater took it over a decade ago. Everybody's so happy, you'd think they were piping in opiates to the factory floor."

"And that's all? The factory?"

"No, no. Surely you've heard of the Ashland Spa Hotel? No? Dashed fine hot springs, which Pater's turned into a proper health resort, a mile or so out of town. Then there's shops, smiths, that sort of thing. Burghers strolling about like sheep." Freddie stifled a yawn into his sleeve. The chestnut gelding beneath him jigged with surprise. "Hardly a decent-looking girl among them, of course. I daresay it's the wind that does it."

Ashland Spa. A proper hotel, a mile or so out of town.

Clouds were scudding by, each one darker than the next. Emilie glanced up at the sky and back down to the beaten grass before her. "Do you mind if we ride in? I confess I've rather a curiosity."

"Ah! Surveying the territory for your weekly half day, eh?"

"Something like that." Emilie kept her voice even.

"Tally-ho, then." Freddie nudged his chestnut to the left.

Freddie was right; the town was unremarkable, an English village turned factory burg, the jumble of old half-timbered buildings at its heart surrounded by orderly rows of identical two-over-two workers' houses with well-kept gardens the approximate size of pocket handkerchiefs. A packet of rain hit Emilie's cheek just as they trotted through the outskirts. Freddie slowed his horse to a walk and peered at the sky. "Blast," he said. "We can turn back, if you like. Stop at the Anvil and wait it out."

"Surely you're made of sturdier stuff than that, your lordship." Emilie tucked the brim of her cap downward.

"Hell. You're *that* sort, are you?" Freddie hunched his bony shoulders and heaved a melancholy sigh.

Well, she was, after all. Emilie never had gone in much for the pomp and circumstance of her earlier life, which Stefanie found such fun and which Luisa performed with such stately grace. Emilie had always preferred curling up in an alcove with a book, or else riding across the soggy fields of Holstein-Schweinwald-Huhnhof on her horse. The worse the weather, the better: On a fine day the villagers would be out, bowing and scraping at her approach, and she'd have to straighten her back and nod regally, and her thoughts would fall back into conventional lines. No more adventure and scandal running riot in her head.

Emilie peered out into the gathering drizzle, at the townspeople pulling out umbrellas or else dashing for cover, and without warning, the Duke of Ashland's words echoed back in her head. *An absolute ruler, a despot, attempts to rearrange the succession to suit his own interests, to prevent the natural growth of a democratic form of law . . .*

Easy for an Englishman to say, of course. Nobody in Holstein-Schweinwald-Huhnhof had ever thought of democratic rule. What would the villagers do with the vote, if they had it? Papa had ruled so benignly, so benevolently. The poor had been taken care of. The wealthy had paid their taxes. The middling classes had prospered and sent their sons to school. The winds of change blowing over much of Europe had left the little principality untouched.

The assassin's bullet had come out of the blue, a shock to Emilie's own heart.

Her fingers went cold under her gloves. She pushed the thought away, as she usually did, but she could not push away its physical effects. The horse sensed her agitation, the clenching of her hands about the reins, and tossed his head.

They hadn't let her see Papa's body, when they brought it back. Luisa had gone in, white-faced, and confirmed the death of their father. And Peter, of course. Poor dear Peter, childhood friend, heir to the neighboring province of Baden-Cherrypit. Stefanie had snuck in later, before they had prepared the bodies, and said that Peter had been struck in the neck, and that his dead flesh was as white as a sheet. Had bled out, probably, into the fallen October leaves of the Schweinwald.

The horse jigged; Emilie cursed and put him right. "I say, Grimsby," called Freddie, forgetting the *Mr.* in his damp distress, "what are you about? Can't we turn back and have a pint at the Anvil instead?"

"I've a great curiosity to see this spa of yours," Emilie said, over her shoulder.

"Bother the bloody spa!"

Emilie kept riding, down the high street, taking careful note of the post office at the corner of Baker's Lane. A hostelry stood nearby; that might be of use.

But the spa, the hotel, with a variety of visitors coming and going! A place where strangers were expected and welcome, where private rooms might be had; a place easily found and yet outside of the main part of town.

It seemed ideal.

The rain began to pound her hat in earnest.

"Look here, Grimsby!" Freddie was growing petulant. "You can't mean to go on in this! It's three o'clock in the afternoon, we'll be missing our tea, and in a moment my coat will have bloody well soaked through!"

"You must learn fortitude, Lord Silverton."

"I have plenty of damned fortitude, Grimsby!"

"*Mr.* Grimsby," said Emilie, "and your language is reprehensible in a boy of your years. I must ask you to exercise a little more ingenuity."

"How's this for ingenuity, *Mr.* Grimsby: We're missing our lessons."

Emilie looked back in surprise. If Freddie was choosing schoolwork over shirking, he must be in sorry straits indeed.

Poor Freddie. He *was* rather bedraggled. His cap dripped with rain, and his shoulders were soaked. Moreover, he had inexplicably gone out without his gloves, and his hands had taken on a rather alarming blue cast. With his bony frame and his brown tweeds, he looked like an exceptionally wet insect.

Emilie let out a long breath, cast her eyes longingly up the road toward the beckoning promise of Ashland Spa Hotel, and turned her horse around. "Very well," she said. "But I must call in at the post office."

The dainty clock above the mantel—Isabelle's favorite, a wedding gift—was chiming four o'clock by the time Ashland laid down his pen, squared his papers, and rose from the chair in his study to join his waiting valet upstairs.

"It's come on to rain, sir," his valet said quietly, helping him into a coat of silken superfine wool.

"Then I shall require a mackintosh, of course," Ashland said. He turned to the mirror above the washstand and surveyed himself. The mask had come a little askew during his shaving; he straightened it, adjusted his necktie. His short white hair was smoothed neatly with a touch of pomade.

Not that it mattered, really, but he felt he owed the woman that much.

Wilkins came up behind him with the mackintosh. He shrugged himself into it and allowed Wilkins to handle the buttons. His own fingers were shaking slightly. Hat, settled snugly into his brow; glove, fitted to his left hand like a . . . well, like a glove. That was better. Secure, well covered. The breath eased from his lungs.

"Thank you, Wilkins," Ashland said. "No need to wait up."

"Of course, sir."

Ashland descended the stairs and ducked through the door, opened at the last well-timed instant by an impassive footman. Outside in the drizzle, a groom stood holding his horse. The gray November horizon was already darkening. "There's a lad," Ashland said tenderly, rubbing Wellington's muzzle, taking the reins. "Sorry about the rain, old man. We'll have to bear on like troupers."

He nodded to the groom, swung into the saddle, and made off along the four soggy miles to town.

The letter burned through the inner pocket of Emilie's jacket, right against her heart. She couldn't read it here, of course, with the rain filling the air in front of a curious Freddie. She would have to wait for the security of her room.

"Couldn't you have posted your note from the house?" said Freddie. "I'm sure Pater would have franked it for you."

"Of course. I shall remember that next time."

The rain couldn't decide how it wanted to settle: one moment mist, the next drizzle, and back to mist again. Emilie kept her shoulders straight, her back straight. She peered under the brim of her hat at the track ahead and recognized the Anvil, hunched by the side of the road, looking even more ramshackle than it had by night. A few lanterns had already been lit on the eaves, and a pair of men were sliding drunkenly off their horses in the courtyard.

"Only a pint, Mr. Grimsby. You can't say no," said Freddie, casting a longing glance.

"I can and I do. There will be nice hot tea waiting for us in the schoolroom when we return."

"The schoolroom," Freddie said, as he might say *the army latrine*, and then, "What ho! It's Pater, by God."

"Language, your lordship," said Emilie, but her blood was already singing, her eyes already peering through the gloaming ahead. The swift physical reaction shocked her.

Freddie was not mistaken. There *was* no mistaking the figure ahead, tall and resolute atop a magnificent dark horse, his left hand on the reins and his other arm resting on his thigh.

How does he manage? Emilie wanted to ask, but she bit the words back and concentrated instead on calming the skip of her heart, the flush in her cheeks. This was ridiculous. She was the daughter of a prince. She had met the Kaiser more than once. She was accustomed to powerful men. She could not possibly be nervous at meeting a mere English duke on a rain-dashed Yorkshire road. She of all people knew that princes and dukes were simply men, made of clay, requiring food and drink and rest, subject to wind after ingesting an excess of cabbage.

Perhaps because he was her employer. That would account for this shortening of breath. He held an absolute power over her fate at the moment, more than any human being had before. No wonder her senses were so wary, so filled with every detail of him.

"Pater!" Freddie hailed cheerfully, as the horses drew near.

The Duke of Ashland pulled up. "What the devil are you two doing here, on such a night?"

"Language, Pater! Mr. Grimsby's frightfully strict about it. It's hardly night, though, is it? Not even teatime."

"It grows dark early in November, as you very well know, and Mr. Grimsby is unfamiliar with the area." Ashland took in Emilie with a single enveloping glance, and then returned to his son.

"But *I'm* familiar with the area. I know every blade of

grass between here and Ashland Spa. Daresay I could find the house blindfolded on a windy night. In fact, I believe I *have*, once or twice." Freddie laughed. "I take it you're bound for your own amusement this evening? Fourth Tuesday of the month, isn't it?" He laughed again. "You're like clockwork, Pater."

Ashland was frowning. His cheeks were damp with rain and slightly pink from cold and exercise. The color rather became him. "See that you bring Mr. Grimsby straight home. None of your tricks, do you hear me? I shall expect a report from Simpson."

The dark horse danced underneath him, either from eagerness to move on or from some agitation communicating itself through his master. His ears had swiveled backward, trained on Ashland.

"That would be a great deal more convincing, Pater, if you weren't off on your own lark. But never fear! I shall escort Mr. Grimsby home without incident, I promise. Virtue quite intact. Shall we leave the lights on for you, or do you plan to stop the night this time?"

"Don't be impertinent," said Ashland. He urged his horse forward. "I shall expect you to attend Mr. Grimsby in the schoolroom at nine tomorrow."

"Have a smashing evening, Pater!" Freddie called back, laughing.

The horses' hooves rattled against the wet stones on the track. Emilie waited until the sound of the duke's horse faded into the fog behind them, and said quietly, "You should not speak to your father with such disrespect."

"Pater? Oh, he doesn't mind it a bit. He likes to make out that he's a dreadful brute, but really he's nothing but a pussycat on the inside."

"That's because he loves you. You're all he has."

"Oh, rubbish." Freddie shifted the reins to one hand and flicked the rain off his cap. "I didn't mean that he's the tender sort, only that his bark is worse than his bite."

"You're mixing metaphors. We were discussing cats."

"Oh, you know what I mean. I'm a bother to him, really. A reminder of my mother, I suppose. He lets me get away with that sort of impertinence because I'm not worth the trouble of scolding." Another flick of the cap. "Hence the plot to head off early to university."

"*Your* plot."

"He didn't object, did he?"

The horses walked on, *thump-thump* against the low patter of the drizzle, the creak of leather. Emilie burned to ask Freddie where Ashland was going, what on earth could bring him out on horseback on such a night. A lark, Freddie had said. Fourth Tuesday of the month.

Perhaps she didn't want to know.

But Freddie broke the silence with sudden force. "Anyway, he hasn't a leg to stand on, does he? Off on his own immoral philanderings, isn't he?"

"Really, your lordship."

"Well, it's true. He's off to meet some woman, his mistress I suppose, right there at his own hotel. Goes every month, rain or shine. Not that I blame him, of course, but he needn't come off so high and holy."

Emilie saw, for an instant, a naked Ashland heaving in some strumpet's bed. His back was arched and gleaming; her breasts were bare. "Perhaps you're mistaken."

"No, I'm not. I asked one of the maids. The woman's escorted up the back stairs, to the suite at the rear. Keeps things respectable, you see. He joins her there. Stays a couple of hours and goes home." Freddie laughed. "Good old Pater. Doesn't waste time, even in sport."

"There might . . ." Her horse was tossing its head. Emilie swallowed and looked down, to where her hands were clenched on the reins. She loosened her grip, finger by finger. "Your father seems to me a man of principle. There might be another explanation."

Freddie laughed again. "You're a funny old fellow, Mr. Grimsby. Another explanation! Ha-ha. Look here, I'm dashed hungry. Let's see if these animals can stretch their legs, shall we? Or else it will be dark before we get back, and Mrs. Needle, for one, is more than happy to scold the living daylights out of me." He urged his horse into a trot.

Emilie's brain said *yes, of course* and sent the necessary communication down her spine. But her body did not want to obey. Her legs, the muscles of her calves, remained heavy and immobile. Almost as if her body did not wish to tighten about the horse's girth; as if it had no desire to quicken the pace at which they pulled away from the town of Ashland Spa, from Ashland Spa Hotel, from the Duke of Ashland himself.

As if her body wanted, instead, to weigh itself into a pivot and turn the horse around. To intercept Ashland before he reached his destination.

She forced her heels into the horse's side. He sprang forward into a trot, and the motion caused a little tear to open up inside Emilie's rib cage, right underneath her inside jacket pocket and the letter from the post office. It stung her all the way back to Ashland Abbey.

SIX

Lucy was appalled.

"Oh, Mr. Grimsby! Ye're fair soaked!" She clutched her hands together. "Ye must go straight up and doff yer things, and I'll draw ye a hot bath afore ye catch yer death."

"What about me, Lucy?" said Freddie. "I'm just as wet."

She bobbed an obedient curtsy, but her look was murderous. "I'm being to tell Jane to draw your bath and all, your lordship, though I *knows* whose fault it all is."

"I protest! Grimsby was the one who wanted to ride through town! I was all for a virtuous pint of ale at the dry old Anvil."

"T'Anvil!" Lucy drew in a shocked breath. "Taking dear Mr. Grimsby to t'Anvil! Oh, yer lordship! T'very idea." She turned to Emilie with limpid eyes. "Do ye let me have yer wet things directly, Mr. Grimsby. I'm being to dry and brush them mysen."

Emilie blinked. Lucy's eyelashes trembled.

"Yes, of course. Thank you, Lucy," she said.

"She fancies you," Freddie said, sotto voce, as they climbed the stairs.

"Nonsense."

"You'd be a splendid catch for her. Get her out of Yorkshire, for one thing." Freddie's elbow poked Emilie's ribs.

"I *assure* you I have no such intention."

They had reached the landing. Down the hall would lie the family bedrooms; upstairs, two more flights, Emilie's room awaited her. Lucy had already scampered up to run the hot water. Freddie glanced at the staircase and shook his head. "Doesn't matter, Mr. Grimsby. *Lucy* has the intention. And once the girls have designs, why, it's all over for the poor old chaps, mate. Might as well have your neck measured for the iron collar."

"And where did you obtain this worldly wisdom, your lordship?" Emilie asked, hand on the rail.

He winked. "Why, from Pater, of course! How do you think my mother shackled him at twenty-two years, and still a Guardsman?" He took off his dripping cap and shook it, sending a heedless spray across the marble floor. "Best of luck to you up there, Mr. Grimsby."

It was easy to find the bathroom upstairs. Steam billowed past the door in wanton clouds, and Lucy's voice carried cheerfully above it all. "Ye can come straight in, Mr. Grimsby! His Grace had t'hot water pipes put in straight after he came to t'abbey. It's just like one of them fancy hotels."

The water shut off, and Lucy emerged from the bathroom, hair frizzing from under her cap. "There we are! I've putten out yer towel and a bit of soap. Ye can hand me yer wet things through t'door." She beamed at Emilie hopefully.

"Yes, of course." Emilie's mouth was dry. She went into the bathroom and closed the door. The sky outside the little square window was black, and rain gleamed in tiny drops against the glass. Lucy had lit two candles—wax, not tallow—and laid out a white Turkish towel. Ashland evidently took good care of his staff.

The water lapped against the enamel sides of the tub, curling with steam. Emilie removed the letter from her jacket pocket and read the short lines swiftly.

> *Both birds have landed safely. Visit next month as scheduled. D.*

Emilie let out a breath she hadn't realized she was holding. Her sisters were safe, at least for now.

She took off her cap and gloves and coat, unwound her scarf, and unbuttoned her trousers. She set her shoes neatly next to the chair and opened the door a crack. "Here you are," she said, handing Lucy her wet clothes.

"Thank ye, sir. Oh! Don't forget yer linens, sir! I'm being to put them in t'laundry directly."

Emilie closed the door again and unbuttoned her long, damp shirt. The fibers stuck to her skin stubbornly; she had to peel it off. Drawers next, and then she slung the entire lot over her hand and opened the door a bare two inches.

"Sir, I can't quite . . ."

Emilie opened the door a trifle more and shoved the linens out by force.

"There we are, sir. What lovely hands ye've got, sir, if ye don't mind my saying."

"Thank you, Lucy."

"So many young men never do bother with their hands, but yers are clean and nice nor a lady's, Mr. Grimsby. I daresay they're fair sensitive, aren't they, Mr. Grimsby?"

"They are as any other hands, Lucy. Thank you."

Lucy shifted her feet. Emilie sank farther behind the door. "If t'water cools overmuch, ye can open t'tap for more hot water," Lucy said. "Ye knows how to open t'tap, in course, Mr. Grimsby?"

Emilie thought of her bathroom at home, in which the latest plumbing had been installed a few years ago as a wedding gift to the Prince's newest bride. She had been dainty and violet-eyed and rather silly, and about the same age as Emilie. Hopes for an heir had run very high. "Yes, of course," Emilie said.

"Because I can show ye, if ye're not certain."

"I'm quite certain. Thank you, Lucy."

"Do ye see where I did laiden t'towel, Mr. Grimsby? Because I . . ."

"Yes, Lucy. I see the towel, and the soap, and the candles. You're very clever. Thank you. That will be all."

"Ye can ring t'bell when ye're done, Mr. Grimsby. It's right there on t'wall. I'll bring yer supper straight up to yer room, nice and hot."

"Thank you, Lucy."

Lucy's footsteps sounded at last down the hall. Emilie closed the door and sagged against it.

But only for an instant. The steam beckoned her, warm and alluring. She turned the lock on the door and unwrapped her breasts from their binding. They sprang free with a relief Emilie felt to her bones.

A clock ticked calmly on the wall, just above the gentle rattle of the rain. Emilie stepped naked into the bath and slid her body under the water.

The warmth made her chilled skin tingle. She lay unmoving for a moment, eyes closed, knees bent, arms floating. The bath was not large, but it was deep enough to cover her to the neck, like a cocoon. Her whiskers tickled her cheek. She longed to take them off, but then she must put them on again before she left the bathroom, and that would be impossible without the glue.

Lord, the bath felt good. As if she were being caressed with warmth in every aching corner of her body. She opened her eyes and looked down at herself, her hidden female form. Her breasts bobbed at the surface, the tips hard against the cool air. They were not especially large, but they were round and firm and well shaped, and she was happy to see them freed of the long linen bandage that flattened them under her shirt. With one hand she touched her right breast, cupped it, lifted it like a plump little island from the water.

What would Ashland think of them, if he could see her now?

She gasped and put her hand down. Where had *that* thought come from?

From seeing him on the road, of course. Off to his mistress, to his monthly night of copulation. He was probably touching the woman's naked breasts now, holding them, caressing them.

That was why Emilie had thought of it.

Emilie shut her eyes again. She knew a great deal about the act of carnal union, far more than her family could have imagined. Well, possibly Miss Dingleby could have imagined. Miss Dingleby had seen the books stacked on Emilie's bedside table, and knew what they contained behind their scholarly Latin titles. Miss Dingleby had even discreetly added to the stack. Emilie was curious, and she was studious, and of course she had wandered through her father's ancient library and founds things of tremendous interest to a curious and studious girl who had never once even been kissed.

Whose virgin body belonged not to herself, but to the state of Holstein-Schweinwald-Huhnhof, to be preserved and used and given away according to its interests.

Who, beneath her quiet and dutiful exterior, craved adventure.

Well, she had adventure now, hadn't she? She had her daring life, her disguise, even her books and her studying. No stiff ceremony now. No father with his disapproving glances, the tightening of his lips when she had not quite measured up to the rigid standards of a princess of Holstein-Schweinwald-Huhnhof. Her father was dead now, lying entombed in Holstein Cathedral, and she was free.

Emilie opened her eyes and looked down at her body, innocent and untouched, curving and feminine, wavering beneath the candlelit water. She wondered what Ashland's mistress looked like. Did the duke prefer tall goddesses or dainty china dolls? Slender women or buxom? Clever or silly? Did he take the trouble to talk to the lady in his rumbling voice, to touch her with his massive fingers, to kiss her with his dented lip? Or was it simply a transaction to him, a frictional meeting of the necessary parts?

The water was cooling. Emilie thought about opening the hot water tap, but she was afraid her whiskers might suffer. Instead, she rose to a sitting position and reached for the soap.

Not that it mattered what sort of woman Ashland preferred, or how he made love to her. The subject had nothing to do with Emilie. She had only thought of it because they had encountered him on the road, on his way to his mistress, and hers was a curious nature.

That was all.

The Duke of Ashland, having returned home and finished his nightly sherry in a single long draft, was walking down the hall to the main staircase when he noticed a faint light creeping from the open door of the library.

Surely it couldn't be Freddie. Freddie might stay up to all hours on one scholarly mania or another, but he liked to do so in the comfort and privacy of his own room.

Grimsby, then.

Ashland prepared to continue down the hall. Awkward things, midnight conversations with staff, and he was in no mood to talk at the moment, with his clothes still damp from the penetrating drizzle on the way home from Ashland Spa Hotel. Why did he persist in these monthly adventures? As always, he had left the room restless and dissatisfied with himself, full of disgust and yearning, vowing it would be the last time and knowing it would not.

The last thing he wanted now was contact with another human being.

But his right foot did not strike down on the marble floor as expected, propelling his body forward down the hall. Instead, his left arm moved of its own accord and pushed open the library door.

Mr. Grimsby shot from his chair with a start. "Your Grace!"

"I beg your pardon." Ashland gestured with his arm. "Pray be seated. I had no wish to disturb you."

Grimsby's hand dropped to the open volume on the table before him. "I hope I haven't presumed, sir. I was unable to sleep, and thought a little reading might settle my mind."

"My library is at your disposal. Books are meant to be read, after all." Ashland found himself walking into the half-lit gloom, and the two candles on the table wavered in surprise. "*Do* sit, Mr. Grimsby. I don't stand on ceremony after midnight."

Grimsby dropped into his chair and watched Ashland warily as he strolled to the other side of the room. "Did you have a satisfactory evening, sir?"

Ashland ran his index finger along a row of leather bindings. The titles slid unseen past his eyes. Was that a trace of irony in the tutor's voice? "Not particularly. And you, Mr. Grimsby? You said you were unable to sleep. I hope you're not uncomfortable. You are quite free to change rooms, to order anything you like. We are earnest for you to stay."

"I have hardly yet proved my worth."

Ashland turned and leaned against the shelf behind him.

Grimsby sat up straight, shoulders square, chin brave against the candlelight. "At this point, we have little choice. You have us at your mercy, Mr. Grimsby."

"You might wait another year before his lordship sits for his examinations." The brave chin jutted a trifle.

Ashland stifled an admiring smile. He remembered a young trooper once, scarcely eighteen and newly joined, with just such a jutting chin. What had happened to that young man? Ashland didn't want to know. He drew in a long breath, and the scent of the library laid upon his soul, familiar and comforting: leather and lemon oil, dust and wood. "We might. What are you reading, if I may be so vulgar as to ask?" He nodded at the book and crossed his arms.

"A novel, in fact. Miss Brontë."

"Well, well! Making yourself familiar with your surroundings, are you? Though I assure you, life at Ashland isn't nearly so romantic."

"The mood is captured well, however. The bleakness, the grand scale of it."

"My wife read them all constantly, over and over. That's her copy, I expect."

Grimsby made a startled movement, flipping the cover over. His eyes widened at the inscription on the frontispiece. "Oh! I beg your pardon."

"There's no need. It's only a book, after all. Leather and paper." Ashland pushed himself away from the shelf and walked toward the table where Grimsby sat, whiskers twitching with dismay. "I hope my son hasn't impressed you with gothic tales of the family. The duchess's name is not forbidden here." He laid himself into the opposite chair and stretched his legs across the darkened rug.

"It is an awkward subject, however."

"It is simply a fact. The duchess left this house over a decade ago, and we have since reconciled ourselves to the loss." He watched for Grimsby's reaction, but the young man only stared down at the cover of the book, at the small gilt lettering imprinted on the leather. "Are your parents still alive, Mr. Grimsby?" he heard himself ask.

Grimsby looked up at last, his blue eyes solemn behind the sheen of his spectacles. "They are not, Your Grace."

"But you speak of them still, do you not? Time, you see, heals all wounds. Well, not all," he said, lifting his right arm briefly and letting it fall into his lap. "But there's no point in ignoring our misfortunes."

"No, I suppose not."

Ashland leaned forward. The sherry, perhaps, was making him bold. "You're a circumspect fellow, Mr. Grimsby. I own myself curious. Have you nothing to relate about yourself?"

"Nothing to interest Your Grace, I'm certain."

Grimsby's face did not change; his gaze did not waver by so much as a lowered eyelash. But Ashland's finely honed senses came awake. Olympia's words echoed back from a dusty Kashmir road: *Beware the man who has nothing at all to say for himself.*

The Duke of Olympia, who had dispatched this young man to Ashland Abbey.

Ashland reached into his waistcoat pocket and produced his watch. Only a few minutes past midnight, after all. He replaced the watch, stretched his arms, and rose to his feet. "I believe I shall have a glass of sherry, Mr. Grimsby. Will you join me?"

"No, thank you, sir."

Ashland felt Grimsby's wary eyes follow him once more across the room to the tray of decanters on a little round table near the window. "Come, Mr. Grimsby. I insist. I find a glass sets me up perfectly before bed." He uncorked the crystal decanter with a clink and poured out two glasses.

Grimsby's eyes widened behind his spectacles as Ashland returned, the two glasses held between the fingers of his left hand. "Sir, I . . ."

Ashland set the glasses on the table. The candlelight flashed across the neat snowflake facets on the bowls. "I insist."

Grimsby reached out one delicate hand and picked up a glass.

"A toast, Mr. Grimsby," said Ashland, lifting his own glass and tilting it forward. He ignored the singing of anticipation in his veins. "To a prosperous relationship."

"Indeed, sir." Grimsby clinked Ashland's glass and took a cautious sip.

"Drink up, my good man. It's excellent sherry. I have it brought in directly from Portugal every year."

Grimsby drank again, more deeply. "Yes, very fine."

"You are wrong, you know, Mr. Grimsby. I am, in fact, genuinely interested in you. A young man of obvious intelligence and breeding, to say nothing of self-possession. Why, I find myself asking, would such a promising fellow accept a position of very small importance and remuneration, in such a lonely outpost of the world?" He drank his sherry and stretched out his legs, still encased in their polished leather riding boots, dark with use.

"You are too modest, Your Grace. The salary is more than generous."

"You haven't answered my question."

"Possibly you do not comprehend the limited opportunities available to a man my age, of no practical experience."

"You have the patronage of the Duke of Olympia." Ashland snapped out the words with a trifle more force than he intended. He was woefully out of practice at this. *Keep your emotions in check, my boy*, came the voice in his head. *You are a man of great animal passion; it is both your strength and your weakness.*

"Many others enjoy the patronage of the powerful. And after all, I am not particularly ambitious." Grimsby took another sip of sherry, as if to cover a hesitation. "I don't wish to be a man of business, in charge of important affairs. I only want my books, and enough money to keep myself."

"And a wife? Family? You have no desire for these comforts?"

"I . . . I suppose so." A flush rose from beneath Grimsby's whiskers. "One day."

"No inclination at all for female companionship?"

"Not so much as you, it seems."

Ashland had been drinking steadily, and his glass was now empty as he twiddled it between his fingers. "You disapprove of my errand tonight?"

"It is not my place." Grimsby looked down to the book before him and ran his finger along the edge of the binding. "I suppose it's no more than natural for you to . . . for the physical urge . . ."

"I understand you perfectly, Mr. Grimsby. I can only hope word of my appalling licentiousness does not find its way to my friend Olympia's ear. I am afraid he might disapprove."

Grimsby's head shot up. "Of course not, Your Grace! I shouldn't dream of such a thing!"

His tone was so shocked, so full of genuine dismay, so entirely innocent of the irony in Ashland's words, that Ashland found himself poised in the air, vacillating between suspicion and admiration. He said softly, "Then my friend Olympia has merely done me a favor, out of the generosity of his heart, in sending you to me?"

"I . . . I don't believe I understand you, sir."

Ashland stood. His head swam briefly, and righted itself. He placed his empty sherry glass on the table and observed how the candlelight radiated about Grimsby's golden hair like a halo. "Nothing at all, Mr. Grimsby. My intellect is a little disordered tonight, I fear."

Grimsby was rising from his chair. "Are you all right? May I help you at all?"

"I am entirely well. Thank you for the conversation, Mr. Grimsby. I hope we may repeat the pleasure often, of an evening, as the winter howls outside." He waved his hand at the window.

"You are retiring, Your Grace?"

"Yes." Ashland studied Grimsby's face, his narrowed eyes behind his spectacles, the tiny crease of concern between his eyebrows. He was so earnest, so wise and naive all at once. "You are rather an intriguing young fellow, you know," he said absently.

Grimsby's hand fell upon his book. "I am nothing of the sort."

"I can't help wondering if there's a great deal more to you than you let on."

"I beg your pardon. What do you mean?"

Ashland straightened himself. He should not have drunk that extra glass of sherry; his body wasn't used to it. But it was rather nice, after all, to have his brain pleasantly encased in numbness, to feel that hum in his blood again, to sense nothing in his missing hand but a comfortable bluntness. "I don't quite know what I mean, Mr. Grimsby," he said. He smiled, reached out his hand, and chucked the poor fellow's astonished jaw.

"But I look forward to finding out."

The door closed behind the Duke of Ashland's imposing body, and Emilie crumpled into her chair. She closed her eyes, but she could still see his face in front of her, the black leather mask against the smooth skin, the single bright blue eye examining her with minute care.

You are rather an intriguing young fellow, you know.

Emilie took a deep breath. Was it her imagination, or could she smell him in the air? The sting of sherry, the wild moorland wind, the warm wool, the scent of spicy soap—sandalwood, perhaps. Or maybe it was only her. She lifted her arm and sniffed her sleeve.

No, she smelled nothing like that.

Her heart still beat quickly in her breast; her fingertips still tingled. What the devil was happening to her? That tall, broad man with his piercing eye and maimed face and empty cuff—good God, surely she was not infatuated with him? With the Duke of Ashland, not two hours out of some strumpet's bed, his powerful legs stretched out before her and his hair gleaming white against the shadows of the library?

Emilie lifted her hand again and touched her jaw with her fingertips. She could feel him now, feel the instant thrill in her veins as his hand came toward her, as her skin anticipated his touch. She, Emilie, cool-blooded and studious, a princess of Germany!

A distant thump reached her ears: Ashland, climbing the stairs to his room.

But I look forward to finding out.

Emilie reached for her glass of sherry and drained it.

This was going to be a very long winter.

SEVEN

Two days before Christmas

The common room at the Anvil was as crowded as usual, a fact on which Emilie had been counting. She clutched her knapsack and breathed the stale and humid air as shallowly as possible. Around her, the men laughed and swore and ate and drank. The fire burned smokily along the wall. Rose the bar-maid bustled about, her hands never free of tankards, her mouth giving as good as she got, which was plenty.

Emilie observed her closely. When she ducked into the tap-room to fill her next round, Emilie followed her.

"I need a room," she said quietly, and held out her palm, on which a gold sovereign caught the light from the swinging old-fashioned lantern overhead. "A private room, close to the back stairs."

Rose stared at the sovereign, then stared at Emilie. "With a girl, or without?"

Emilie blushed. "Without."

There was no furniture in the tiny chamber to which Rose led her, except for the bed that overwhelmed the space, but Emilie did not need furniture. She set down her knapsack, opened the flap, and stripped to her drawers in the cold air.

Chemise first, then stays. The fastenings gave her trouble, but she had selected a new corset with efficiency in mind, knowing she would have no lady's maid to help her. Petticoats and sturdy little half boots: Her chilled fingers fumbled with the buckles until she had them all.

Her dress had rumpled in the knapsack, despite her best efforts at folding. It buttoned up the front, because she would never have been able to manage otherwise. For a moment she savored the fall of fine wool down her body, the swell of material at her hips, the lovely, heavy feminine swish of skirts around her legs.

At last she reached inside the knapsack for the final two items: a small hat, and a large false chignon, made from the thick golden pile of hair that had fallen from Miss Dingleby's scissors a month ago. She did not pause for melancholy. She pinned her short hair back, pinned the chignon at the nape of her neck, and placed the hat over all.

She stuck her head out the door. There was no one in the hall. She stole quietly to the back stairs and slipped noiselessly down.

The wind had calmed today, and the late December air lay heavy and frozen against Emilie's exposed cheeks. A steady trickle of townspeople were out, finishing Christmas errands, and instead of taking the high street down the center of town, Emilie stole around the back lanes, taking note of details and street names, as Miss Dingleby had instructed. A train pulled away from the station, the hourly service southward to York, as she passed by.

The buildings thinned; the noise of commerce died away. Ahead, the clean white shape of Ashland Spa Hotel came into view, its marble facade fronting the road like an ancient Roman bath transported to modern Yorkshire.

Emilie took off her spectacles, slid them into her pocket, and went around back to the garden entrance.

"My dear." A slight figure rose from his chair in the restaurant, straightened his lapels, and grasped Emilie's outstretched hand.

"Good afternoon, sir," said Emilie, smiling, as the man bent over and kissed the air above her gloved knuckles.

"Good afternoon, Miss Bismarck." The gentleman looked up, and Miss Dingleby's eyes danced in place before her beneath the curved brim of a neat black hat.

"How very good it is to see you, Mr. Dingleby," said Emilie.

"Sit, my dear. You must be exhausted." Miss Dingleby gestured to the other chair.

Emilie settled herself into her chair, remembering at the last instant to complete the action with a graceful swoop of her skirts. "It's only four miles. Hardly half an hour's brisk riding."

"But your delicate constitution." Miss Dingleby winked and picked up the menu. "Rather elevated fare, isn't it, for such a godforsaken outpost of civilization?"

Emilie cast her gaze about the room. She had taken tea here with Freddie a week or so ago, and had looked with the same surprise as Miss Dingleby on the spacious, high-ceilinged grandeur of the lobby, the fluted pillars and the shining marble floor, the intricate plasterwork and the oval domed skylight aglow with tinted glass. The soaring space had swarmed with people. Where had they all come from? Ladies, mostly, dressed in trailing veils and enormous bustles, attended by maids with white caps and neatly buttoned collars. They had gone back and forth between the lobby and the bathing pools in the enclosed courtyard at the center of the hotel, and as teatime advanced they had trooped into the blue and white interior of the restaurant and sat at the elegant marble tables and drunk their tea with fingers extended into the lily-scented air.

"It isn't so remote," Emilie said. "I believe they see a great many fashionable guests. The duke has transformed the spa into an establishment of repute."

"Has he, now? The clever fellow." Miss Dingleby's voice lowered a trifle. She was wearing dark whiskers along her jaw but no mustache, and her cheeks twitched. Emilie's own skin itched in sympathy.

"He's spent the last ten or twelve years diligently improving the town and the estate," Emilie said, leaning forward. "And he's got even more plans in contemplation. You ought to see the schemes, really. It's remarkable."

"No doubt."

"Of course, it all depended on the railway link. He petitioned for it himself; did you know that? And helped to fund its construction. Olympia assisted him in getting the necessary approvals and so on. You know how well connected my uncle is."

"Indeed, I do. Good afternoon," said Miss Dingleby, addressing a waiter who hovered nearby. "Tea, if you please. Do you have a decent Lapsang souchong?"

"Indeed we do, sir. An excellent blend."

"The Lapsang, then. And the usual complement of sandwiches and biscuits." Miss Dingleby smiled at the waiter and tented her fingers together on the tablecloth. "I find myself famished after such an arduous journey."

"Yes, sir." The waiter bowed and left.

Emilie folded her hands in her lap. The unbroken stretch of her skirt felt foreign beneath her fingers. Her chignon rested heavily on her neck, and she resisted the urge to touch beneath the brim and assure herself that some stray lock hadn't fallen away from its pins to betray her. "Are you certain this is wise? Meeting like this."

"Well, you can't simply meet me as Mr. Grimsby, when someone about town might recognize you and ask questions," said Miss Dingleby. "And nobody here would recognize you as Emilie, particularly without your spectacles, and particularly in tête-à-tête with a young man."

"But it's so public. So exposed. Anyone might see us."

"My dear, if we were to meet furtively behind the inn, or steal upstairs to a bedroom, we would most certainly be suspected. The best place to hide a clandestine meeting"—Miss Dingleby waved her hand, and her signet ring flashed in the bright electric light—"is in plain sight."

Emilie glanced idly at a nearby table. "Is it necessary, though?"

"Your uncle wishes to assure himself of your well-being."

"But surely my letters . . ."

"Could easily be forged by some clever agent." Miss Dingleby picked up her napkin and laid it upon her lap with a practiced and decidedly masculine movement, quite unlike the Miss Dingleby Emilie had known for so many years. "He was not willing to take such a chance."

Emilie studied the curve of Miss Dingleby's hair, which had been combed back with pomade and clubbed at the back, in a rather bohemian manner. Clever, she thought, remembering rather wistfully the heavy golden piles of her own hair on the bedroom floor, as Miss Dingleby had shorn her for her disguise. "He trusts you a great deal, my uncle."

"Yes." Miss Dingleby exposed her neat white teeth in a smile. "He does."

The tea arrived; Emilie poured out. "And you seem to know a great deal about clandestine meetings."

"I read a great many detective stories. Far more than is good for me, I daresay. Ah, that's lovely," she said, working her whiskers as she swallowed the tea. "The swill in York station was all but undrinkable. But to work. I regret to say I have very little to relate . . ."

"How are my sisters?"

"They are very well indeed. Settling in nicely, I believe." Miss Dingleby patted her waistcoat pocket. "I have letters from them for you."

"But they're not allowed to tell me where they are."

"We could not commit such details to paper, of course. The risk would be dreadful. Still, I think you'll find they're both as well as could be expected, under the circumstances."

"And we have discovered nothing more about my father's murderers?"

"Inquiries are being made, of course."

Emilie curled her left hand into a fist on her lap. With her right, she gripped the teacup hard and brought it to her mouth. "I wish," she said, when the tea was safely down the appropriate pipe, "you'd tell me more. I have a brain, you know. I might be able to help."

Miss Dingleby shook her head. "If you were to help, you'd expose yourself, and I doubt you have any idea how ruthless, how cunning these men can be."

"But why should anybody want to kill my father and Peter?"

"Any number of reasons. No doubt you're aware of the political situation in Europe." Miss Dingleby selected a piece of cake and applied herself with enthusiasm.

"Anarchists, you mean?"

"Perhaps."

Emilie's cup fell into its saucer with a clatter that echoed against the genteel marble shell of the Ashland Spa restaurant like a gunshot. "How I do wish you would tell me something."

"My dear! What a fuss. Look," Miss Dingleby went on, a little more kindly, "if you must know, we have heard a few vague clues. A group of men dissatisfied with the pace of political liberation in Europe. We are investigating."

"*We.* You and Olympia, do you mean?"

"No, no. I'm merely a messenger, you understand." Miss Dingleby slipped the last of her cake into her mouth. "As a trusted retainer of the family. But I did not come here to speak of His Grace's investigations, of which there's little to tell. I came to assure myself that you're well, and to offer my ear and shoulder. I imagine you must find it difficult, playing a part at all times. And Ashland's household, so I understand, is not the most convivial. You must be dreadfully lonely." Miss Dingleby's eyes regarded Emilie steadily.

"Not so much as I feared," she said. "Lord Silverton is lively and intelligent. Amusing company, really, when he's not sulking. And the servants are quite nice. Far more familiar than I've been accustomed to, though perhaps that's only because I'm one of them."

"Not quite, my dear." Miss Dingleby smiled. "And His Grace, the Duke of Ashland? A difficult man, they say."

Emilie had just begun on a rather large piece of cake, which gave her time to consider her reply. "I don't think so, really. He's only lonely."

"Lonely?"

"He's had no one to talk to, until now."

"He talks to you?"

Emilie's cheeks began to warm. "We meet in the library sometimes, in the evening. Chess and that sort of thing. We don't speak much. He's not talkative. The current news, the weather, a bit of politics. How Freddie's getting on." Even saying those meager words, Emilie drew the scent of sherry and leather into her head, saw the glow of the flickering candles. He did not come every night, of course. She would sit in her leather chair, reading and waiting, pretending that her heart didn't quicken at the sound of his heavy tread in the hallway, or that her limbs didn't lighten as the footsteps grew louder and approached the library door. She always left it cracked

open invitingly, always laid a few extra coals in the fireplace
and lighted another candle or two as the usual hour drew near.

Hoping, and hoping not.

Most nights, the footsteps went right by the door. Occasionally, Emilie felt a pause, a gentle hesitation in his pace, as
if he were considering whether to go in. She would shift her
seat, turn an unread page, grip the leather binding to stop the
quivering of her fingers.

Usually, the footsteps resumed, and the Duke of Ashland
climbed the stairs to his bedroom. But every so often, perhaps
once a week, the heavy door would creak open and he would
fill the empty space, his giant form outlined against the darkened hallway, his face lit into splendor by the golden glow of
the candles, his bleached hair cropped against his head, a tiny
smile lurking at the corner of his mouth. "Good evening, Mr.
Grimsby," he would say, in that sonorous voice. "Studying late
again, I see."

Somehow she would remain calm. She would close her
book around her index finger and say something like, *Yes,
Your Grace. I find the reading steadies my mind before bed*,
and of course the word *bed* would ricochet like a rifle about
the room and she would hope that the candles weren't bright
enough to reveal her blushing cheeks beneath her whiskers.

Ashland would saunter in, all economical grace, and select
a book from the shelves, or drop down on a chair and make a
few lines of conversation, or offer her a glass of sherry. "Do
you play chess, Mr. Grimsby?" he'd asked, just the night
before, and she'd said, *Why, yes, I do, though I'm sadly out of
practice*, and he'd brought out a chessboard and played with
her for nearly an hour, mostly in silence, but occasionally
offering observations and even once an anecdote about a chess
match during a wretched storm on the steamer out to India.

He had won the game last night; Emilie had been too nervous to play her pieces well. But she had put up a good defense,
she thought proudly. She had not disgraced herself. And when
at last Ashland had risen and stretched, had put away the
chessboard and bid her good night, she had sat there and
remembered all the moves she should have made, and thought
that perhaps she could have taken him, if she'd really tried.

"And how is Freddie getting on?" Miss Dingleby asked, smiling.

Emilie blinked. "I beg your pardon?"

"Freddie. Your charge, my dear. How is he getting on?"

"Oh, yes. Very well, in fact. He's terribly undisciplined, but having watched you with Stefanie all these years, I am quite prepared to deal with that sort of thing."

"Grateful to be of service." The teacups were empty, the cake in crumbs on their plates. A faint whistle threaded through the air: the late afternoon train from York, arriving at the station. Miss Dingleby took out her watch and a few sealed envelopes from her waistcoat pocket. "I fear I must go. I believe it turns around in twenty minutes. Here are your letters." She replaced the watch and motioned for the waiter.

Emilie placed the letters next to her plate and tried to quell the desperation that surged through her movements. Miss Dingleby was settling the bill, preparing to leave, and nothing had been said. She'd been looking forward to this meeting for over a fortnight, this scrap of familiarity from her old life, and yet it hadn't felt familiar at all. Miss Dingleby had changed; she wasn't the quietly firm governess of Holstein-Schweinwald-Huhnhof anymore. She was someone else, someone in confident disguise, someone who clearly harbored secrets she wasn't about to relate. "Must you go?" Emilie asked, rather ridiculously, since they both knew this was the last train to make the connection to London until the next morning.

"I must, I'm afraid," Miss Dingleby said kindly. "But I'll return next month, of course, unless something happens in the meantime."

Something happens.

"You'll keep me apprised of anything you learn, of course. Anything at all."

"Anything at all," Miss Dingleby said, and her voice was empty of even the pretense of sincerity.

Something went cold inside of Emilie's chest. She reached inside the pocket of her dress and pulled out her own envelopes. "For Stefanie and Luisa," she said, pushing them across the table.

"No identifying details, of course."

"None. As you instructed." Emilie's voice sounded flat and cold, even to her own ears.

"Very good." Miss Dingleby rose. "I am so glad to find you well, Emilie, my dear. You look flourishing."

"I am not flourishing," Emilie said. "I want my sisters back. I want my life back."

"Believe me," Miss Dingleby said, and this time her expression was full of sincerity, "that is my constant aim, waking and sleeping."

Emilie sat a few minutes at the table. There was still a little cooling tea left in the pot; she poured it out and read her letters.

Her sisters seemed well, but then a princess of Holstein-Schweinwald-Huhnhof never complained, at least on something so permanent as paper. There was evidently some overbearing daughter of the house in Stefanie's case, and Emilie smiled at the image of her heedless sister forced into the necessity for meekness. Luisa was more vague; she seemed to be a personal secretary of some kind, and the household was not a happy one. But she closed with an eager wish to hear of Emilie's safety and happiness, and to be reunited soon in better circumstances.

Somehow, Emilie had been hoping for more. She and her sisters were so close. She had shared a bed with Stefanie almost from infancy; this person who had penned the few lines before her seemed almost a stranger.

She folded the letters back in their envelopes, tucked them into her pocket, and rose from the table, just as a familiar voice carried across the air from the lobby.

A deep voice, patient and commanding.

The Duke of Ashland.

For an instant, she could not move. Her feet seemed to have frozen to the marble floor; her brain locked into place.

He was speaking to some member of staff, it seemed. His voice was low and discreet; she couldn't pick out the words, but she would recognize that vibrating tone anywhere. She cast her eyes desperately to the archway leading to the lobby. Miss Dingleby must have swept right past him on her way out.

The back entrance.

Emilie's brain fastened on the thought, and came gratefully unstuck.

She turned, and with great calm and dignity—the dignity for which a princess of Holstein-Schweinwald-Huhnhof was famous—walked toward the rear of the restaurant, as if she were simply bound for the ladies' retiring room.

The floor here was covered with carpeting. Emilie moved soundlessly down the corridor, past the ladies' retiring room. Somewhere here a hallway came off, leading to the rear of the building; she had come through on her journey in, but the way had been obvious in that direction. She had been led by the abundant light in the electric chandeliers. Coming from the restaurant, any number of blurry hallways might be the one she sought, while the others only led to the service rooms.

Voices ahead. She whipped around a corner and flattened herself against the wall.

". . . know what to do," a woman was saying. "She ain't come, that's for certain. The passengers is all off, and never a sign of her."

"What's His Grace being to say?"

"He won't be fair pleased."

"Well, if ye asks me, he can ride on back to his grand estate and swive one of t'girls there, if he has to have it," said the other voice, a man's voice, quite hardened.

"T'poor fellow. He's too decent to plow his own soil, is what. Oh, t'poor fellow."

Emilie's mind flew. Good God. Could it be? Ashland's monthly night of recreation, in a discreet back bedroom of his own hotel, with a woman who came in from elsewhere. Was this the date for it? It was a Monday, not a Tuesday. Was it the third or the fourth one?

Her throat stung. She could almost taste the bile rising up. Ashland, in some other woman's bed; some other woman, knowing Ashland's body, his lips, his voice saying her name. *Not* knowing, probably, how fortunate she was. Perhaps not even caring.

Or perhaps she did care. Perhaps she came because she loved him; perhaps she wasn't a whore at all. Perhaps he loved her but was too discreet to keep a mistress in the regular way.

Except the woman hadn't come this month. Hadn't even sent word, apparently.

The shadows seemed to darken around her. Emilie brought up her arm and bit down on her sleeve. She ought to feel pity for Ashland's disappointment tonight. Lonely Ashland, with no wife for comfort. He would have to wait another month for . . . well, for whatever relief this woman gave him.

What did they do in that discreet back bedroom? What might it be like, to be in bed with the Duke of Ashland?

"She were badly, maybe," said the male voice. "Lots of women are badly."

"Then they would have sent another, wouldn't they?" The woman's voice was growing louder. In a moment they might be upon her, find her lurking in the hallway like an eavesdropper. What would she say? *Oh, I beg your pardon, I was only looking for the retiring room.* Emilie looked down the dark hallway, leading Heaven knew where. Should she try to slip away? Or would that lead to even greater risk of discovery? A lady deep in the bowels of the hotel: Even if the hotel staff didn't call the police, the incident would stick in their minds. They would remember her face, her nervousness.

"They might have mixed up t'date," said the man. Emilie heard the footsteps now, making soft and hurried thumps along the carpet. Lord, he was nearly here. In another instant she would be caught. "It's never His Grace's usual date."

"Because of Christmas Eve tomorrow," said the woman. "I don't know what I'm being to tell him. I hazard . . ."

Better to brazen it out. Emilie drew a deep breath and turned around the corner.

"Oh! I beg your pardon. I must have gotten lost," she said, with an almost panicked breeziness.

The woman nearly thumped into her, a slender, middle-aged woman with severe dark hair and a housekeeper's aspect. "Oh! Thank t'Lord, madam! There ye are!"

Emilie started back, horrified. "*What?* No, I . . ."

The woman's hand closed around her arm. "New, are ye? Well, that's all right. Ye gave us quite a turn. We thought ye weren't coming altogether. I'm Mrs. Scruton, but of course ye knows that."

"No, there's been a mistake . . ." The blood whirled in Emilie's ears.

"Go tell His Grace she's here. He can come straight up," said Mrs. Scruton, with an air of authority, and the man—leering, of course—disappeared from the corner of Emilie's vision. "What sort of mistake, dearie?" the woman asked kindly, tugging Emilie down the hall with astonishing speed and strength. "Didn't they never instruct ye where to go?"

"No, I . . . Oh, please, I . . ." Emilie's self-possession had deserted her. She could not do this, she must fly away, and yet her limbs allowed themselves to be tugged around the corner to the back staircase.

"Now, don't never be nervous. It's yer first time here, isn't it? He's a fair good man, Mr. Brown. He never would hurt a fly, I tell you."

Mr. Brown?

Mrs. Scruton led her up the stairs, and Emilie's feet lifted instinctively, while her heart pumped madly, while her brain told her she must turn around, because she could not possibly go into a bedroom with the Duke of Ashland and pretend to be a whore, because he would surely recognize her and everything would be ruined, broken to bits.

But Mrs. Scruton. If Emilie told the woman she wasn't Ashland's monthly appointment, then the woman might ask questions, mightn't she? Might wonder what Emilie had been doing, lurking in the back hallway like that; she might remember Emilie's face, and if someone were to come looking . . .

The hallway was clean and well-lit, with electric wall sconces and a soft blue carpet, smelling of paint and lilies. Emilie's eyes fastened on the doors passing by, white and rather blurred in the absence of her spectacles. Good God. This could not be happening. She could not possibly be doing this.

Damn Miss Dingleby and her public meetings.

She would explain. That was it. She would go into the room and wait for Ashland, and she would turn away so he couldn't see her face, and she would tell him it was all a dreadful mistake. That was it. Ashland was a just man; he would let her go. She could steal away, and that would be that. If she were quiet and firm and did not make a scene, the incident would be forgotten in an hour, and no one would think to connect her face with those starched official photographs in the newspaper.

"Here we are." Mrs. Scruton whirled Emilie around a corner, where a single door sat in the center of a recess. She took a key from her pocket and fitted it into the lock. "He'll be up in two minute. Do ye want to refresh yersen first?"

"I . . . No, I . . ."

Mrs. Scruton ushered her through the door, into a dim and spacious parlor. The blue and yellow curtains were drawn snugly against the fading daylight, and the room was lit by a single oil lamp atop a round table in the center. A sofa and two armchairs sat companionably by a fireplace. There was no sign of a bed, but a door stood ajar along the opposite wall, suggesting another chamber.

"There, ye see? I'll nobbut take yer coat and hat, madam," said Mrs. Scruton, and in the next instant Emilie's worn black coat was slipping down her arms. Mrs. Scruton folded it neatly, laid it across the back of the sofa, placed the hat on top, and turned back to Emilie with an expression of deep relief. "There, then. All ready. Oh! Heavens, I'd near but forgotten."

"Forgotten?" Emilie asked faintly.

Mrs. Scruton marched to a polished demilune table against the wall, between the two windows. She opened a drawer and pulled out a length of black cloth.

"Yer blindfold, madam."

EIGHT

The Duke of Ashland paused briefly in the threshold. A new girl tonight, Mrs. Scruton had said.

Not that it mattered, really. So long as she was discreet and clean and well mannered, so long as she couldn't see his face, the woman herself made no difference. His craving was animal in nature, and a warm and sentient female body was all he required.

She would be obliging. She was paid to be obliging.

She wouldn't be able to see him.

He pulled the key from his pocket and let himself in.

Mrs. Scruton had, as always, put out all the lights but one. His good eye stretched and adjusted into the dimness, searching for the woman who awaited him.

A shadow moved by the window. "Sir?"

The word had an odd ring of familiarity. Had she come to him before, in the early months, when the women changed each time? Before he had settled on Sarah?

She stepped forward from the darkness near the windows, a woman of above average height, her fair hair gleaming above the black blindfold. "Are you there?" she whispered.

"I am here." He took off his hat and gloves and laid them on the lamp table. "Please sit down."

"I'm afraid I can't." She spoke very softly, almost a whisper, but her clear accent was that of a gentlewoman.

"Of course not. Forgive me." He stepped toward her and grasped her hand. It was slender and chilled, the thin bones fragile in his palm. She made a gasp. "The chair is just here, madam," he said, and led her forward from the shadows.

"No, it's not that," she said. "I fear . . . there's been a mistake, you see, and . . ."

"A mistake?"

"I was . . . lost, you see, and . . . I didn't know how to explain to your . . . to Mrs. Scruton . . ."

"Yes, I know. It's quite all right. You were only a few minutes late, after all." He smiled kindly, before remembering she couldn't see him. Her hand was still in his, trembling, unless that telltale vibration came from his own body. He summoned himself and drew her fingers to his lips. "It's quite all right."

"But I . . ."

"Please sit." He urged her into the chair. "Would you like a glass of something? Sherry, or wine? Have you eaten?"

"Yes, I've had tea. I . . ."

He had to be doing something, something to cover his anxiety. The woman was unexpectedly lovely beneath the blindfold. She had high cheekbones and a firm chin, and her mouth curved with beautiful fullness, a cherry-ripeness that fastened his hungry gaze. She seemed young, quite young, and altogether inexperienced despite her poised shoulders and upright posture.

No, this woman had certainly not come to him before. He would have remembered her. And yet he could not quite set aside an elusive sense of familiarity, a hint of that relief one felt when returning to one's own home after a time spent abroad.

Did he know her from elsewhere?

Ashland stepped away and made for the liquor cabinet. "You must have something. It's not a journey for the timid, at this time of year."

"I'm not timid."

"Of course not. I only meant . . ." He reached for the sherry and poured two glasses. The splash of liquid in the glass soothed his jangling nerves. "I only meant that your way has been long, and the weather uncomfortable. I hope Mrs. Scruton was hospitable, Miss . . . I beg your pardon. I haven't even asked your name." He returned to her and pressed the glass into her hand.

"Thank you." She took a drink. "My name is Emily."

"Emily . . . ?"

"Just Emily." Her voice was firm.

"Emily, then." He touched her glass with his own. "I'm Anthony Brown."

"Mr. Brown." She took another drink. "Do you always take the trouble to introduce yourself?"

He paused at her sharpness. "It seems the courteous thing to do. We are both human beings, after all, deserving of respect."

"Indeed." She set her glass on the table and rose from the chair, nearly bumping into his nose. "I am afraid, however, that a great mistake has been made. I cannot . . . I cannot stay with you." A little emphasis fell on the word *stay*.

He fiddled with his glass. The light gleamed on her hair: a beautiful color, a rich gold, the color of wheat in late summer. Her chin was tilted at a regal angle. Who the devil was she? Nothing like the women who had come to this room before; even Sarah only clung by her fingernails to the brink of gentility. This Emily was a lady of quality, without a doubt. Perhaps fallen on hard times? Perhaps accepting this employment as a last resort? He felt a sudden bone-crushing desire to stroke that alluring hair, and was glad—for once—he had no right hand to reach out and pillage her while his left was already occupied. "Cannot stay long?" he asked softly. "Or cannot stay at all?"

"Cannot stay at all." She whispered the words. She stood very close; the heat of her body tingled his neck and his hand, which held the sherry glass. She seemed to be breathing in shallow little gusts, as if agitated. If not for the blindfold, she would be staring directly into his collar. Ashland gazed down at her, transfixed by the perfect curve where her earlobe met her graceful neck.

He wanted her.

The desire struck him suddenly, with the force of a firing gun.

"Very well. If you wish to leave, you will find your fee in your coat pocket."

A blush crept over her cheekbones. "I don't . . . I don't want your money."

"You are entitled to it, after coming so far today."

"I don't . . . I can't . . ." She sat back down again. "Please remove the money from my pocket, sir."

He set down his untouched glass next to hers. "Have you never done this before?"

"No."

The word sent an animal thrill through his veins. He forced it back, forced himself to civility. "You are free to go, of course, if this . . . if you cannot overcome your disgust."

"Disgust! No, sir. Not disgust." Her hands knotted together in her lap. As he watched from above, the little red tip of her tongue slipped from her mouth to wet her lips.

Ashland swept up his glass of sherry and finished it.

"I will double the fee, if that might persuade you," he said.

"*No!* Dear God. I must go. This is impossible." She rose again, so abruptly that Ashland had no time to step back, and she collided into his chest with an *Oh!*

He grasped her arm reflexively to steady her.

As always, his senses crashed at the physical contact. He braced himself for the instant rush of panic, for the excruciating memory of a million nerve endings recoiling in his body.

The panic rushed, the nerves recoiled, but something lay atop the sensation: a warmth, a lithe softness, a curving femininity.

Emily's body against his.

She lay there only an instant. Almost before Ashland understood the comfort of her, she pulled away and put her hands to her blindfold. "I beg your pardon!"

His left hand still grasped her arm. "The fault is mine."

She went still. She wore a plain but well-tailored dress of some rich midnight blue; the bodice fitted her waist and chest without a wrinkle, buttoning up the front to the middle of her neck. Underneath that bodice, her lungs heaved for air, the only perceptible motion in all her body. "Sir," she whispered, "your hand."

Ashland was seething with lust, pounding with it; his

single eye blurred with it. He forced his offending fingers to drop away from her arm. "You are free to go, of course," he said. "But I ask you . . . madam . . . *Emily* . . ."

"Sir."

"I *beg* you to stay."

He knew his voice, dark and rough-edged, did not match his words. He knew his plea sounded more like a command, but he could not speak tenderly. He was too full of need, this unexpected cataclysm of sexual desire, and in twelve long years he had forgotten what tenderness sounded like.

What was Emily thinking? The black blindfold, which kept her from seeing what a monster stood before her, also kept him from reading her expression. She hadn't moved away; surely that was promising. The curve of her well-covered bosom still rose and sank deeply under the pressure of her breathing. Her chin tilted upward, as if she were trying to peer at his face through the blackness before her eyes.

"Madam?" he said, and this time, thank God, the word came out gently.

Her hand made some movement at her side: lifting a few inches, then falling back. She wetted her lips again.

Ashland closed his eye. He was going to perish.

"I think . . ."—a long pause, during which Ashland could count the seconds snicking away on the nearby clock, could hear a faint note of laughter ascend and fall from some distant room—". . . I think I will stay."

He caught her fingers just before they reached his chest. "Remember the rules."

"The rules?"

"You are not to touch me. You are not to lift the blindfold."

Relief was running through his body in a flood, mingling with the renewed surge of lust. A stout and long-suffering dam seemed to crack apart inside him.

God, who *was* she? What was she doing to him?

Emily.

"Not touch you?" she whispered. "But how . . . how are we to . . ."

He released her hand and touched the topmost button of her bodice. "Let me."

A sigh slipped between her lips.

He could not quite steady the trembling of his fingers as he undid the first button, and then the next. He could only hope she was as unsettled as he was, that her own nervousness concealed his yearning. Her throat, uncovered, glowed like new cream in the lamplight.

Another button, another, and his knuckles were brushing against the warm cloth that covered her breasts. She stood obediently before him, her hands concealed in the folds of her skirt; a scent drifted across the air between them, a hint of soap, mixed with something else: lavender, perhaps, from the sachet in her drawer. She did not wear perfume. She smelled only of herself, of cleanliness and female skin. He wanted to bury his nose in the hollow of her throat and fill his lungs with her.

Another button, and the bodice gave way from her breasts. She made another of her sharp intakes of breath, and her hands lifted again, as if by instinct.

"Shh," he said. "It's all right."

Her hands dropped, fisting around fabric, and her lips parted. Ashland undid the last button on her bodice and worked it carefully over one shoulder and then the other, until she stood before him with her arms bare, with only her corset and chemise to shield her bosom from his gaze. He folded the bodice and placed it on the chair, and as he rose again he passed by the gleaming curves of her breasts, the fine lace trimming of her chemise, and his heart nearly stopped in his chest. She was breathing in quick little pants; he wanted to soothe and excite her all at once, to hold her in comfort and to take violent possession of her.

What was *happening* to him? He had only just met her, and it was as if a field of electricity crackled between them.

"It's all right," he said again, because that was all his dizzy brain could manage. He found the fastenings of her skirt and removed it, concentrating on his awkward one-handed task to keep his lust under control. She was not wearing one of those odd and abominable bustles, thank God. He reached for the tapes of her petticoat, and she moved at last, stumbling back against the chair.

"Oh! You don't mean to . . . Is it necessary . . ." She was

blushing furiously now, an eager pink, and she crossed her arms over her chest.

"Shh," he said. "Let me. I want to see you, Emily."

He tugged gently at one of her bare arms, until both fell back away and opened her to him once more. He removed her petticoats, and this time he didn't bother to fold them; he almost kicked them aside in their frothy whiteness.

"Turn around," he whispered, and miraculously she turned, exposing her bare neck with its golden chignon, her smooth white flesh. He examined her corset, but he could not quite figure out how it went: Where were the laces? "Your stays," he said.

"They fasten in front," she said, a faint whisper, "so I can dress without a maid."

He stepped closer, until his belly and his straining erection nearly brushed the elegant curve of her backside, and he looked over her shoulder. "Ah, I see. Very clever."

"Can you manage it?" she asked, in the same faint whisper.

"I believe so." He brought his left arm around and plucked awkwardly at the grommets, until at last the stays fell away to the floor and her breasts sprang free.

For a long moment he simply breathed into her hair, not quite touching her, studying the curves of her body through the translucent veil of her chemise. Her nipples stood erect, two alluring pink nubs beneath the muslin; her waist and hips and legs flowed in elegant lines beneath. A faint shadow nestled at the juncture of her legs, almost hidden by a trick of the cloth.

You're beautiful, you're perfect, he wanted to say. His hand ached to cup her breast. She would fit him exactly, a ripe and flawless palmful of Emily. He imagined his finger running along her skin, his thumb caressing the very tip of her nipple.

"Sir." Her voice was low, almost a growl.

He turned his lips to her golden hair and held them there, exerting not a single ounce of pressure.

The clock chimed, six delicate notes into the stillness.

He stepped away, and the agony of separation rent through the length of his body. He picked up the bodice and skirt from the chair, picked up the petticoats and the stays, and laid them all across the back of the sofa.

"Sir?" she asked, a little forlorn.

"Sit." He positioned the chair just so and urged her downward. From his pocket he drew a small volume, the copy of *Jane Eyre* that Mr. Grimsby had brought out of the library cobwebs nearly a month ago. "Here you are, my dear. I will let you know when to lift the blindfold."

"What's this?" she asked.

"Remember, you are not to look back. You know the story of Lot's wife, of course?"

Emily swallowed. Her fingers curled around the book. "She looked back and was turned into a pillar of salt."

"Exactly. You are Lot's wife, Emily." He turned and began to walk across the room, to the armchair in the corner behind her, cast in deep shadow.

"But . . ." Her voice was bewildered, bereft, the way his own body felt in the absence of her warmth. "But I don't understand."

"Did your Mrs. Plimpton not explain everything clearly?" He lifted his tails and settled into the armchair. The back of Emily's body glowed before him, prim and upright in the ladder-backed chair, unbearably seductive beneath the sheerness of her chemise. Her neck was long and sinuous, curving like a swan's into the trim line of her collar. One sleeve of her chemise had fallen to expose her round shoulder.

"No, she . . . she did not."

The Duke of Ashland took in a long breath and leaned his head back against the upholstery. Above him, the ceiling coffers sat in their orderly squares, their white paint turned to pale gold in the lamplight. Inch by inch, nerve by tortured nerve, he brought his seething body under control.

"You are to read, Emily," he said softly. "You are to read to me."

Emilie stood rigidly against a column of the back portico, staring straight ahead into the dark gardens of the hotel. They were bringing around a carriage for her, to convey her back to the station for her supposed train to . . . well, wherever it was. York, probably.

Her insides were still trembling; her fingers were cold inside her gloves.

He was still up in the room, the Duke of Ashland. If she looked upward, she might perhaps see a crack of light through one of the windows, the window of the room where they had sat together. Where he had undressed her to her chemise, with his broad, firm hand; where she had read to him, taking little sips of sherry to fortify herself, while he sat behind her and watched and listened.

Her skin still burned from the knowledge of his gaze. Shame, or desire?

Shame, surely. What had possessed her to stay and submit to him? Expose herself to him? He had told her she might go. She should have left without another thought, innocence intact.

Emilie looked down at her gloved hands, twined together against her shapeless black coat. He had said good-bye courteously. He had rung for Mrs. Scruton, and when the soft knock had sounded on the door, he had taken Emilie's hand, removed her glove, and kissed the inside of her wrist. His lips, his warm, firm lips, had actually touched her skin.

She could feel his kiss still, sizzling against her sleeve.

A rattle sounded, a crisp hoofbeat. Emilie straightened herself and stepped forward.

"Madam!"

Behind her, the door opened in a hurried crash. "Madam!" came the call again, more clearly.

She turned.

Mrs. Scruton swept from the doorway, holding out her hand. "Oh, thank goodness ye've never left. There's a note, from t'gentleman."

"Thank you." Emilie plucked the folded paper from the housekeeper's hand. "Does he . . . does he wait for a reply?"

"He didn't say, madam." Mrs. Scruton's voice was deeply respectful. A wisp of hair fell away from her cap; she looked disordered, as if she'd been put to a mad rush.

"Thank you, Mrs. Scruton. That will be all." Emilie slipped

the paper into her coat pocket. The carriage lurched to a stop before the portico, and a footboy jumped from the back to hand her in.

The carriage was unlit. Emilie waited until they reached the station; she waited until the carriage had left so she could trudge down the side streets to the Anvil and change clothes; she waited until she stood inside the dim stable while they brought her horse out from his stall for the lonely ride back to Ashland Abbey.

There, under a swinging lantern, with the wind already moaning at the windows, she reached into her pocket and drew out the contents: the folded paper and a plain white envelope.

The envelope contained five crisp Bank of England ten-pound notes, still smelling faintly of printers' ink.

Fifty pounds! That was six months' salary for Tobias Grimsby, and a generous salary at that. What the devil was she to do with it?

Emilie thrust the envelope back in her pocket and opened the note.

Madam,

    I am deeply sensible of the honor you have done me this evening. Do I ask too much, if I find insupportable the idea of waiting an entire month to have that honor renewed? You need return no reply. I shall be waiting, and hoping, Tuesday next.

    In the meantime, I wish you a happy and prosperous Christmas.

Yours,
A.B.

NINE

Lord Silverton crossed his arms, cocked his head, and studied the Christmas tree through narrow eyes. "As a work of engineering, it leaves something to be desired."

Emilie, nineteen feet high on a ladder that might have been used to defend Ashland Abbey from the agents of Henry VIII, reached across the prickling boughs to nudge the extravagant gold star into a more dignified stance. "It's not a work of engineering," she said. "It's a Christmas tree. A festive . . . symbol of . . ."

"I say, I should rather watch that ladder, if I were you . . ."

". . . the season . . . a German tradition, in fact . . ."

". . . rather a dodgy reputation, that ladder, truth be told . . ."

". . . you've perhaps heard 'O Tannenbaum,' which . . . hold on, I've almost . . . nearly . . ."

". . . nearly came to a bad end myself last . . . oh, mind the . . ."

The ladder tottered and fell to one side in a long and graceful arc, leaving Emilie clinging to the upper branches.

". . . candle," finished Freddie. "Are you all right?"

"Quite all right," said Emilie, "if you don't think the tree will overbalance."

"I daresay it might, I'm afraid. Already listing."

"Then perhaps," Emilie said, between her teeth, which were stuck with pine needles, "you might possibly set the ladder back upright for my convenience in . . . disembarking this . . . very *festive* symbol of the season."

"Can't do it, I'm afraid," Freddie called up. "It's come all apart. Poor old thing. Deserved a better fate."

Emilie's sweating palms slipped along the fragile bark. *"Try."*

"No. No, it's no good," Freddie said cheerfully. "How's this: I'll just pop around to the other side of the tree, hold on like mad, and you can descend at your leisure."

Emilie risked a peep at the white marble floor beneath her. *Far* beneath her.

The tree shifted.

"Well, then," said Freddie, "since you're determined to dig in for the long haul, as it were, could I perhaps send you up a cup of punch? Eggnog, perhaps?"

Emilie searched for the trunk with her feet. "Your lordship, I don't believe you properly perceive the urgency of the situation."

"Won't Father Christmas have a jolly laugh when he spots you tonight! Bowl full of jelly and all that. Ha-ha!"

"Frederick . . ."

"You know, you remind me rather of a cat just now. If you would only move your limbs, Mr. Grimsby, I could guide you down, branch by branch, like a member of the fire brigade."

"How kind."

"Look, there's a fine stout branch just below your left foot, and . . . Oh, steady on . . ."

The tree groaned. A splitting noise came from the branch to which Emilie's right hand clung.

It had seemed like such a sturdy tree before. It had been brought down specially from Scotland last week, a noble, well-proportioned fir, fully twenty-five feet high and positioned right under the stained glass cupola in the center of the Ashland Abbey ballroom. It dwarfed even the magnificent trees her father had had cut down from the Schweinwald every year and placed in the castle's audience chamber, aglow with candles and tinsel.

Surely such a tree would prove impervious to a single modestly proportioned female clinging to its upper reaches.

Emilie grabbed another branch, which gave way at once. She grabbed for the trunk, feeling more like a monkey than a cat. The odious golden star, the cause of all this mischief, tipped away from its perch and tumbled into the thicket of needles and tinsel below.

The tree swayed. It shifted. Emilie's world began to tilt.

"*Mr. Grimsby!*" shrieked a voice from the doorway. A metallic crash followed, then the instant smash of porcelain, all of it promptly drowned out by the sirenlike wails of Lucy going into hysterics.

"Now, now," said Freddie. "He's quite all right, the sturdy fellow. We must simply encourage him to jump."

"Jump!" wailed Lucy.

"*Jump!*" squeaked Emilie.

"Jump," Freddie said decisively. "Far better than letting the tree come down on top of you."

The tree tilted another foot or two. "But the floor's *marble*!" said Emilie.

"All the more reason to jump first, before the tree jolly well falls on top of you, crushing you mercilessly into all that marble. Come on, now. Buck up."

"Ooh! Ooh! I can't never look!" said Lucy.

Emilie glanced back down at the endless blue-veined marble below, gleaming in the light from the two magnificent ballroom chandeliers. "I'd like to see you *buck up*, if you were perched up here."

"Come along, then, Mr. Grimsby! Nothing to it. You'll land on your feet, likely as not."

Lucy's shrieks reached an entirely new register of panic. "Ooh! I shall die! Ooh, Mr. Grimsby! I'm sure I can't never look. His poor brains are being to be scrambled. Who will be cleaning it all up?"

The tree moved again. Emilie swung backward; the branches now loomed above her as she clung with arms and legs. Rather like a hammock on a summer's day, she told herself. Except that hammocks did not have stomachs.

"Ooh, t'Lord save us all! He shall be kilt!"

"Perhaps a pleasant, well-padded sofa might persuade you to take the plunge, so to speak. Lucy, would you mind giving that delightfully impressive caterwauling an instant's pause, and help me . . ."

"What the *devil's* going on in here?" thundered the Duke of Ashland, from the doorway.

Lucy's shrieks stopped dead in her throat.

If the marble floor had, at that instant, opened up to expose the flaming pits of hell, Emilie would have loosened her grip and fallen into the Devil's own hands with pleasure.

"I'm afraid Mr. Grimsby's got himself into a bit of a fix," said Freddie. "You perceive the situation is rather dire, at present. I thought I might drag over one of the sofas to break his fall."

The tree staggered. A few candles fell off, blazing into the marble.

"For God's sake," said Ashland. His boots clacked briskly across the floor. "Lucy, put out those damned candles. Mr. Grimsby, detach yourself from that tree at once."

Emilie's face was flaming, her hands slipping with sweat. A piece of tinsel tickled her nose. Every muscle strained with the effort of clinging to the thin upper trunk of the festive Ashland Christmas tree. "Sir, I . . ."

"I'm right below you, never fear."

Freddie coughed. "Do you think that's wise, Pater? I should hate to lose you both."

Another candle toppled.

"Freddie, for the love of God, hold your bloody tongue." Ashland's voice was calm and steady. "Mr. Grimsby, when you're ready."

Emilie squeezed her eyes shut. The lights of the chandelier burned through her lids.

"I shall catch you, Mr. Grimsby. Never fear."

Emilie released her feet from the trunk. She was dangling now, her damp hands sliding down the needles.

"That's it. I'm right here."

Right here.

The fall seemed to last forever. The air rushed along her burning cheeks; her body coasted endlessly downward. *Well, that was easy*, Emilie thought. *I wonder when I shall hit bottom.*

Then something hit her back and folded itself around her. For a long instant she was staggering, toppling slowly, rather like the tree.

"That's it," said Ashland, enclosing her snugly in his arms, just before falling on his arse.

W ell! This is a Christmas Eve we'll likely never forget," said Freddie cheerfully, setting down his wineglass with a satisfied clink. "Nothing like a spot of mortal terror to get the blood moving in the old veins."

"Mortal terror? I thought your approach to the situation rather casual. Lighthearted, even." Emilie drained the rest of her own wine, and in the next instant Lionel the footman was hovering behind her, refilling the glass. She had been invited to dine with the family tonight; a kind gesture, though she suspected it had something to do with imbuing the cavernous dining room with a little more Christmas spirit by the addition of a third body. She and Freddie sat across from each other, separated by a wide iceberg of ancient white linen and an uninhibited display of the ducal silver. The Duke of Ashland anchored the end of the table with massive and silent dignity.

"Oh, that! I was only trying to stop you from panicking. I was absolutely crucified with fear, actually." He made a signal for Lionel to refill his wineglass; Lionel, with a glance at Ashland's face, ignored him. "For one thing, we should have had to find another tutor, and I'll be dashed if we could locate another one half so amusing as you, Grimsby."

"*Mr.* Grimsby," rumbled Ashland, his first words in the past quarter hour.

"*Mr.* Grimsby. Of course. Ha-ha! *Dashed*, I said. When of course, *you* were the one about to be *dashed* on the floor . . ."

"Frederick, for God's sake. Have you no other topic of conversation tonight?"

"Pater, you must admit, we haven't had anything half so interesting happen at the Abbey in years. The same old placid, humdrum existence." Freddie picked up his wineglass, discovered an overlooked drop or two, and tilted the vessel nearly vertical into his mouth. "Of course, they say these sorts of disasters happen in threes. Only imagine the excitement that awaits us!"

Lionel and one of the other footmen were clearing the course from the table. Emilie sat rigidly while her plate was removed in an expert swipe. "Since there *was* no disaster, Lord Silverton, due to the swift action of your father, I believe we can sleep easily."

She didn't look at Ashland as she said this. She hadn't been able to look at him at all in the past twenty-four hours. Each time her glance had fallen on him—today in the hallways and in the schoolroom, last night when he had stopped by the library for a few minutes of polite conversation—she had remembered the brush of his knuckles against her breast, his warm breath on the nape of her neck, his lips on the tender skin of her wrist.

She had remembered how she sat in her chemise, all but naked before him, and read Miss Brontë's passionate words in her softest voice, hoping he wouldn't recognize the timbre as belonging to that of his son's bewhiskered tutor. How he had sat, silent and unseen, in the armchair behind her; how she could feel his presence nonetheless, could somehow sense every slow breath in his lungs, every caress of his gaze on her body. How her skin had tingled, how her breasts had tightened, how the juncture of her legs had grown damp and aching.

How was it possible to meet his arctic eye after that?

Last night, when she heard the pause in his footsteps outside the library door, she had cursed herself. She should never have lingered there, where Ashland might tread. When he had entered and tossed her an oddly cheerful greeting, she had mumbled a reply and risen to her feet.

"There's no need to leave on my account, Mr. Grimsby," he had said, and at once she had blushed, her blood rising up in reflex at the remembered intimacy of his words at the hotel, the alluring rumble in his voice when he pronounced her given name.

Emilie.

She had told him she was on the point of going upstairs anyway, that she was quite done in. She had left in a rush, avoiding his massive body as if he had some virulently infectious disease: typhoid or diphtheria, an influenza of the senses.

God, what if he had recognized her somehow? Her hair, or her figure, or her hands?

What had she been doing in that hotel room to begin with?

She was mad. Madly infatuated, madly obsessed with his person.

Mad.

She should not have come to dinner tonight. She should have pleaded indisposition after her fall and taken a tray in her room. But she hadn't been able to resist, had she? As much as she dreaded the proximity of the Duke of Ashland, she longed for it.

"Mr. Grimsby," the duke said, and at once she felt his arms around her again, felt Emilie and Ashland crash together to the marble floor. A metaphor, if there ever were one. "Mr. Grimsby, do you attend me?"

Emilie's head shot up. "Yes, Your Grace! I beg your pardon. Woolgathering."

"Appropriate enough, for Yorkshire," put in Freddie.

"I only wished to inquire whether you were having a happy Christmas. Mortal danger notwithstanding, of course."

Good Lord, was that a *twinkle* in the duke's blue eye?

She pushed up her spectacles. "Yes, sir. Though perhaps I might suggest the duchy invest in a sturdier ladder, next year."

"I shall, of course, take your suggestion under the most serious consideration." The duke looked as if he might actually smile, but he drank his wine instead. "I daresay it must be rather grim for you, spending Christmas without your loved ones, in such a remote and rather forbidding corner of England."

"Not at all, sir. I feel quite at home here."

Ashland was studying her, she knew. She fought to keep the blood from rising again in her cheeks. The footmen had returned with the next course: the dessert, she saw with relief. A traditional plum pudding, fairly drowning in its brandy sauce. It reminded her, with an unexpected pang, of her childhood Christmases, before her mother died. Mother had always insisted on her English rituals.

"I'm glad to hear that, Mr. Grimsby," Ashland said at last.

"Rather," said Freddie. "I feel as if you're becoming quite one of the family. Awfully splendid having you here tonight, piercing the gloom of our lonely dining room." He took an enormous mouthful of plum pudding, rolled his eyes upward to heaven, and worked his jaws thoughtfully. "I say," he said, swallowing, "I've just had the most brilliant notion."

"I do hope it has something to do with your Greek iambics," Emilie said. She resisted the urge to glance at the clock on the mantel, to count out the minutes before she might flee from the unsparing regard of the Duke of Ashland. The sooner this dinner ended, the better. Then she could return to her usual routine of trays in her room, or else the occasional appearance at the servants' table, so as not to seem haughty. She would be safe. Away from the duke's presence, she could find a way to divest this mad and dangerous infatuation. This longing so intense, it had become a physical ache in her chest.

"Ha-ha! Greek iambics on Christmas Eve. What an optimistic fellow you are, Mr. Grimsby." Freddie scraped his greedy spoon through the brandy sauce. "No, no. It's this: I think you should join us in the drawing room this evening for the traditional gift-opening and wassail and whatnot. After all, you're quite a member of the family now, what with Pater saving your brains from being splattered about the ballroom floor and all that. It creates a sort of intimacy among us all. What do you think, Pater?"

Emilie's fork, on the way to her mouth with its precious cargo of plum pudding, came to a halt in mid-flight.

She cast a panicked glance at Ashland's face.

The duke was eating his pudding. He finished, swallowed, and wiped his mouth.

He will say no. Emilie put her fork back into motion. The plum pudding turned mysteriously to ash in her mouth.

He has to say no. It's impossible. It's unseemly. It's . . .
Dangerous.

Ashland seemed unaware that he was about to deliver a verdict of world-shattering importance. His face betrayed no emotion at all. He folded his snowy white napkin next to his plate with dextrous movements of his left hand.

Emilie's insides burned, but her hands were as cold as ice. *Say no*, she pleaded silently.

Ashland gazed at his son, and a smile—a *smile!*—lifted his firm lips. The same lips that had pressed against her wrist,

Emilie thought. The same lips that had hovered above her hair in the quiet electricity of the sitting room at Ashland Spa Hotel.

The duke put his hand on the arm of his chair, as if preparing to rise.

"I think that's a fine idea, Frederick," he said. "At the very least, Mr. Grimsby will elevate the tone of the conversation, with his Greek iambics." He turned to Emilie with his pirate's face, managing to look both masterful and uncivilized with that black leather half-mask gleaming next to his silver hair.

"What do you say, Mr. Grimsby? We're a dismal pair, Freddie and I, but it's better than waiting until Boxing Day, eh?"

"I . . ." Emilie swung helplessly for an instant. She had presents for them, of course, plucked from the shops of Ashland Spa a week ago. A book for Freddie, a fountain pen for Ashland. Miss Dingleby had always offered gifts at Christmas to her charges and their parents, so Emilie had bought the tokens just in case it was expected.

"Oh, come now, Mr. Grimsby," said Freddie. "The tree's been put to rights. Besides, I daresay poor Lucy's standing outside with the mistletoe this very moment, just waiting to waylay you. You're much better off with us. Safety in numbers and so on."

Emilie glanced in horror at the imposing door of the dining room.

She picked up her wineglass and slugged down the remainder with reckless abandon.

"Yes, of course," she said. "I should be delighted."

TEN

It was only four o'clock on a crisp Tuesday afternoon when the Duke of Ashland mounted his horse and signaled the groom away, but it had seemed like the longest day of his life.

The entire week, in fact, had dragged along as if towing a load of Yorkshire boulders in its wake.

Only a week, since he had stood at the window of his room at the Ashland Spa Hotel and watched the carriage carry Emily away from the rear portico. Only a week, since he had peeled back Emily's glove and pressed his impulsive lips against her pulse. Only a week, since he had sat down in his shame and misery and scribbled that hasty note, begging her to see him again. To let him bask in her sunshine again, to feel the innocent warmth of her, her knowing serenity, glowing like a beacon of promise.

His horse moved into a willing trot, and the frigid air sliced his cheeks. He hardly noticed. Physical discomfort was simply a fact, a part of his life; he had long since learned to accommodate it. To welcome it, almost, as a hardship to be overcome.

He reached the end of the long Ashland Abbey drive and turned into the lane. The wind had stilled, as if frozen in place by the sudden influx of winter; the sky above, so unnaturally pure and blue today, was already losing its color in anticipation of sunset. The sight of the white sun lowering in the east made his blood race.

The early winter evening was arriving.

Would Emily arrive, too?

He was mad. He had only known her for a pair of hours. He knew nothing of the thoughts in her head, her family, her childhood, her passions and her disappointments. He only knew that he wanted them all. He wanted them, he wanted *her*, so fiercely that he could hardly think of anything else. He had passed through Christmas week in a dream.

What would he do if Emily did not arrive with the sunset this evening?

His heels nudged the horse into a canter. He wouldn't think about that. He would not even entertain that awful possibility.

It would be far better, of course, if she didn't come to him tonight. He acknowledged that. Whatever pleasure he took from Emily would extract the most dreadful penalty from his sense of honor and duty, from the bedrock on which he had built his life in the past twelve years since Isabelle's departure.

Ahead lay Ashland Spa, huddled into the hills. The train from York would ease into the station in forty-two minutes.

He was mad.

In another moment, Emilie was going to pick up the clock above her mantel and smash it on the floor.

That would be undignified, of course. Miss Dingleby would flatten her brow in disapproval. On the other hand, Miss Dingleby had surely never been confronted with a clock so loud and tyrannical, its ticking scratches so intrusive, its quarterly chimes so relentlessly cheerful, the whole works so worthy of the most violent annihilation.

Tick . . . tock . . . Tues . . . day . . . Tues . . . day . . . Tues . . . day . . .

"Stop it!" she said to the clock. She looked down at her right hand, which was clenching the fountain pen with enough strength to crack the enamel. A graceful pen, exactly the same color and make as the fountain pen she had given to the Duke of Ashland for Christmas. *Well, well*, he'd said, lifting the pen from its box, smiling, *what a lovely instrument, I couldn't have picked a finer one myself,* and when Emilie had opened her box from the duke, an exact replica had lain inside.

Everyone had laughed at the coincidence—even the duke, whose laugh turned out to be genuine and pleasant and golden around the edges.

Of course. Even his laugh lured her in.

The pen wrote beautifully, too. She was presently composing a note to Miss Dingleby, and struggling to make it sound as innocuous as possible: *Thank you for the lovely tea this Tuesday last; however, I feel upon reflection that the location is unsuitable for such occasions in the future . . .*

She had trailed off at that, unsure what to write. Obviously she could not say *because the hotel staff believes me to be its owner's whore,* or *because I have carried out an assignation with my employer in one of the hotel's private rooms.*

The clock scratched on. *It . . . is . . . Tues . . . day . . . what . . . will . . . you . . . do . . . it . . . is . . .Tues . . . day . . . Tues . . . day . . . Tues . . . day . . .*

Emilie threw down the pen and went to the window. The incessant howling Yorkshire dankness had been swept away today by a rush of clear and frigid air from the northeast. Every detail of the landscape lay before her in almost painful detail. In the distance, a few rooftops of Ashland Spa, tucked into the moor like a handful of pebbles. The gray slate jumble of the Anvil, if she wasn't mistaken.

Of course she wouldn't go.

She could not voluntarily return to the back entrance of the Ashland Spa Hotel and be shown up to that quiet room. She could not *choose* to continue this . . . what was it? Liaison? She could not feed this shameful infatuation of hers. Starve it, and it would die.

Emilie turned from the window, but not before a speck of movement caught her eye.

She tried to resist. She fisted her hand against her side with the effort of resisting.

You are Lot's wife, Emilie. Do not look back.

She looked back.

A man rode a horse down the Ashland Abbey drive. A large, straight-backed man in a dark coat and hat; a large, well-bred horse with an eager stride. The man looked straight ahead, but his body was pitched slightly forward, as if humming with latent energy, as if in eager anticipation of the road ahead. He guided the horse with the reins in his left hand; the end of his right arm lay upon his muscled thigh.

Dizziness swirled about Emilie's brain. She had forgotten to breathe.

She drew in a deep and conscious gust of air and watched the duke as he turned from the drive, disappearing momentarily behind the gateposts and then reappearing at a sharp trot, his lean body moving in perfect association with the animal beneath him.

Emilie turned from the window and gripped the sill behind her with both hands. She was melting inside, her body held together only by the thunderous beat of her heart.

She could not. She must not.

She was mad, even to think it.

That there's yer blindfold, ma'am," said Mrs. Scruton, with a pat to the back of her head. "I hasn't done it up too tight, has I?"

"No, not at all," Emilie whispered. The sudden descent of total blackness made her head turn light, made her blood sing.

"He'll be right inside, madam. Been waiting for you this hour, he has." The housekeeper's voice held a trace of reproach.

"I'm sorry. I had . . . I had an errand to run."

"An *errand*?" A pause, heavy with disbelief. "Well, no matter. He'll be that glad to see you at last."

Mrs. Scruton's hands wrapped around Emilie's shoulders, almost motherly, and nudged her around the remembered corner. "He's been fidgety as a schoolboy. Ringing down every few minute. Bless the Lord you've come at last."

Emilie heard a knock, a rattle of the doorknob, a scrape. A breath of wind passed her face.

"Mr. Brown! She's here."

Emilie stepped forward, urged by Mrs. Scruton, and at once a hand surrounded hers and drew her into the room.

"Thank you, Mrs. Scruton. That will be all."

"Ring if you need owt," said Mrs. Scruton, and the door clicked shut.

Emilie stood without moving. Ashland stood before her, his hand holding hers; she could feel his warm immensity holding back the air, only inches away. What was he thinking? What expression did he wear, on that half-civilized face of his?

"Emilie." He lifted her hand and touched her gloved knuckles to his lips. His voice was still low, as if under the strictest control. "Welcome. Thank you for coming this evening. I hope it was not inconvenient."

"Not at all."

"It's a cold night. I hope you weren't chilled." He drew her forward, holding her hand as if leading her into a dance. "May I take your coat? I've built up the fire."

"Yes, thank you."

His hand left hers and went to her shoulder. He slid off one sleeve, then the other. Emilie lifted her own hands to her woolen muffler, but Ashland's fingers set them aside. "Let me," he said.

Emilie stood rigidly while the duke unwound her muffle, while he removed her hatpin and then her hat, with as much delicate care as if he were a lady's maid. He adjusted the blindfold. "Comfortable?" he asked, and this time his voice seemed a little more rough, a little less strictly controlled.

"Yes."

"May I remove your gloves?"

The question sounded unbearably intimate. She held out her hands. "Yes."

He undid the little buttons slowly. She imagined how much trouble they must be for his single left hand; she pictured his deft fingers working each tiny mother-of-pearl nub through its tiny hole. A vibration passed between their entwined hands. Were her muscles trembling, or his?

The last button came undone; the kidskin slid endlessly down her fingers. He began on the other one, with the same excruciating care, while Emilie's pulse ticked madly away, rather like the clock in her room, only more rapid, more insistent. Ashland's breath filled the air between them, smelling sweet and faintly spicy, as if he'd been drinking tea. Without the dominance of her eyes, her every other sense had gained a preternatural sharpness. The wooliness of his coat, the clean brightness of his shaving soap, the pressure of his fingers on her glove, the heat of his nearby body, the slight roughness of his breathing: Each one of these perceptions struck her with clear edges, with almost visual exactness.

The glove gave way. Ashland turned her hand over and kissed her wrist, the way he had done last week; he took her other wrist and pressed his lips against the tender skin. "You don't wear scent."

"No. I have never liked it."

"Come to the fire and warm yourself. I've had tea brought in."

He led her forward, guided her into the sofa. "How do you take yours?" he asked politely, like a hostess in her drawing room.

Emilie felt as if she were in a dream. Had the Duke of Ashland actually just asked her how she took her tea? "With cream," she said, "and just a little sugar."

A slight hesitation. "Ah."

The splash of liquid, the clink of porcelain. How awkward it must be for him. He had never seemed self-conscious about his missing hand; he performed all tasks with matter-of-factness, without any allowance for his handicap. And yet how did one pour tea and mix cream? How did one negotiate buttons and horses and shaving and writing? Every simple action, every last little chore, must require the utmost concentration.

"Here we are," he said.

Emilie held out her hands, and the cup and saucer were placed gently into her palm. "Thank you."

"Careful, my dear. It's still hot."

The tea *was* hot, a strong blend, just the way she liked it. She hadn't realized just how much she needed a lovely cup of tea. She felt instantly braced, instantly equal to any challenge, even sitting in darkness on a well-cushioned sofa.

Been waiting for you this hour, he has. He's been fidgety as a schoolboy.

Was it possible? Did she have some power over the all-powerful Duke of Ashland?

He was moving away, settling himself nearby, in the armchair, probably. Not the one in which he sat last week: the one next to the sofa, arranged companionably before the hissing fire. Emilie stretched out her feet a few inches. From the duke's direction came another clink of porcelain. His own cup of tea, she supposed.

"You're drinking tea?" she asked. "Not coffee?"

"Yes." The porcelain clinked again. "How did you know I drink coffee?"

Emilie's fingers froze around her cup. "I don't know. I suppose you seem like the coffee-drinking sort."

"How perceptive. You're quite right; I do drink coffee." Another silence. "May I offer you cake? Sandwiches?"

"No, thank you. Perhaps later."

The word *later* rang softly about the room.

"May I ask you an impertinent question, madam?" he asked.

"That depends, I suppose, on the question."

"Is Emilie your real name?"

Emilie sipped her tea and set it back in the saucer. "It is."

"Will you allow me to know your family name?"

"I'm afraid not. And you, sir? Is Anthony Brown your true name?"

He shifted against his chair. "Anthony is my given name. Brown is not."

"So we are equal, then, in subterfuge."

"No, Emilie. We are not equal." The deeper clack of saucer meeting wood. "I am at your mercy."

"That's not true."

"I assure you, it is. There is nothing I would not do for you."

Emilie set her cup into her saucer. It made a telltale rattle, and she swiftly braced the china against her lap. "You would not tell me your true name. You would not let me take off this blindfold."

He hesitated. "Anything else."

"Anything else is nothing at all. *That* is what's essential: you yourself. You won't give me yourself." She could not stop the reckless words. What was she thinking? She *couldn't* remove the blindfold. He would see through her disguise in an instant. This mask was infinitely more essential to her than to Ashland.

"Emilie, I cannot." He rose from the chair and paced across

the space in front of her. "If I revealed these things, you would not stay. You would never return."

"Would that be so tragic? You could simply order another lady."

"Not any longer." He said the words under his breath; were it not for the blindfold, heightening her senses, she might not have heard them.

She spoke gently. "Why the blindfold, then? What are you hiding?"

He didn't answer at once. What was he doing? Was he leaning against the mantel, perhaps, his long legs crossed? Was he watching her as she sat there, blind and defenseless on the sofa?

"I was injured, many years ago," he said at last. "My appearance is unsettling."

"How were you injured?"

"I was abroad. I was . . . I was a soldier, in India. Well, Afghanistan, really. We had gone over the border to . . ." He let his words hang in the air.

Emilie drank her tea. "To do what? Was there a battle?"

"There was a battle," he said slowly, "but I was not in it. I was performing . . . reconnaissance, of a sort. I was captured."

Emilie's cup was empty. She reached forward to place the saucer on the perceived table before her.

"Here, let me," said Ashland, and in an instant he was there, taking the porcelain from her fingers, his skin just brushing hers.

Captured. Emilie had always assumed that he had received his wounds in some sort of fighting: a shell perhaps, a rifle shot, an explosion that had somehow both ruined his face and taken his hand.

"Your captors injured you?" she asked.

"Yes. They wanted information, and I would not give it to them. Here, you must have cake. You're quite pale."

"No, I'm not hungry. I . . ."

"And you, Emilie? What brings you here to me, of all the places in the world? What injury has been done to you?" There was more rattling of porcelain; evidently he was not taking her at her word about the cake.

"Why do you think I have been injured?"

"For what other reason would a beautiful woman, a lady, possessing such obvious dignity and virtue, be reduced to meeting one such as I in a remote hotel in darkest Yorkshire?" His tone was light. He pressed a plate into her hands. "Your cake."

"Thank you." There was no fork. She broke off an end with her fingers and put it in her mouth. "Oh, it's lovely. Orange?"

"Yes. The house specialty."

She took another bite and cleared her mouth before speaking. "To answer your question, I am here because I have been separated from my family, due to a . . . a misfortune. My father was killed, and my sisters and I"—she was revealing too much, she knew, but she had to say *something*, had to reveal some little true corner of herself to him—"my sisters and I were sent to live with friends of the family."

"I am very sorry. Under reduced circumstances, I take it?"

"Yes." Emilie thought of her room, on the third floor of Ashland Abbey. "Quite reduced."

"But you were educated as a gentlewoman."

"Yes. I was fortunate to receive an excellent education. I had plans . . ." She stopped herself.

"Plans? What sort of plans?"

"Surely that's of little interest to you."

"On the contrary. I find myself passionately interested. I suspect your plans weren't the ordinary sort, for a well-bred young lady."

"No. I . . ." She stopped again. "You'll laugh."

"I won't, on my honor. Tell me."

She shouldn't speak. And yet the temptation was irresistible: Ashland standing nearby, unseen and immense, with his coaxing and sympathetic voice. She wanted to confess everything. She wanted to open every recess of her soul to him. She heard herself say, in a rush, "You must understand, I was raised in a strict environment. I was expected . . . That is, my life was quite regimented. My future was already determined for me, my person simply an object, to be given away at will. And I hated it. On the outside, I behaved myself perfectly, and on the inside I raged. I had . . . I had brains and talent, and I wanted—I *needed*—to use them."

"Yes," he said. "Yes."

Her heart swelled at that single soft word. She leaned forward and went on. "When I was younger, I wanted to disguise myself as a boy and go to university. That was impossible, of course. Then I wanted to be like my governess—an extraordinary woman, my governess; I admired her with all my heart. I wanted to be like her, to run away to seek employment as a governess under an assumed name. I could study all I liked and be independent. I could make my own decisions. I could be free. I could be myself." Her voice fell away, heavy with longing.

"And what happened?"

"I told my governess. She laughed and told me to think twice about that."

Ashland didn't laugh, didn't ridicule her. "It's a difficult life, I'm told. And you'd have been at the mercy of your employers."

"Yes, I realize that now." She fingered the delicate edge of her plate.

"What then? Surely you didn't give up."

"I thought . . . well, I thought I'd do something even braver. I'd keep my name. I'd simply pack my trunk and move to the city and live as an independent woman, studying what I liked and seeing whom I wished. I'm quite beyond the first blush of youth, after all."

"Not so far past." His voice was very low.

"I thought I'd perhaps sponsor a salon on Wednesday evenings, or start a literary journal. If polite society shunned me, I'd simply carry on with impolite society."

"Which, after all, is decidedly more interesting," said the Duke of Ashland.

"So I saved my allowance, sold a few baubles, wrote a few discreet letters. I told my governess and no one else."

"And then?"

She stared into the blackness, the depthless space beyond her eyes. "And my father died."

"I'm very sorry."

"And now I have my freedom, at least a little of it, and I find I . . . I have no one to talk to, really, and . . . in fact, it was rather an accident, coming here last week . . ."

"For which I am grateful."

"Are you?" She looked up in the direction of his voice. He had resumed his seat, it seemed.

"I have thought of little else this past week."

Emilie gripped the edges of her plate. "Come now. After so short a meeting? So . . . so unnatural the circumstances?"

"*Emilie . . .*" He checked himself. She heard him shifting in his chair, rising again, his restlessness seething through the blackness around her. He spoke in a voice so low, it was almost a growl. "Emilie, you must know how different you are. How utterly and instantly different from any other woman."

Yes, she thought bitterly. I have known it all my life.

"Of course I'm different," she said. "What other lady would undress herself for a stranger, without hesitation, for mere money? Would sit here and let him stare at her unclothed body, in exchange for fifty pounds in crisp and unassailable Bank of England notes?"

The coals sizzled and popped into the silence. Ashland stood somewhere to her left, not moving, not making a single sound. Not even breathing, that she could hear. Emilie placed her plate on the table, cake still half eaten.

"Well, then. The hour grows late. I suppose we should get to it."

He had chosen *Pamela*, out of some perverse desire for self-torture, or perhaps out of irony: Who knew?

To her credit, she hadn't blinked when she lifted the blindfold and saw the book waiting for her on the table. "Shall I start from the beginning?"

"Certainly."

She read beautifully, as she had done last week. She had an expressive voice, and she read every line of dialogue in character, with animation, almost as if she were enjoying herself: *"Is it not strange, that love borders so much upon hate? But this wicked love is not like the true virtuous love, to be sure: that and hatred must be as far off, as light and darkness. And how must this hate have been increased, if he had met with such a base compliance, after his wicked will had been gratified."*

A blush was creeping along her face, on the side of her cheek that was visible to him. He imagined himself rising from his armchair and bending over to kiss that blushing cheek. In his mind, his lips were exploring that pinkness, that rush of blood beneath her skin. How warm it was, how soft. Her throat, her shoulder, her bosom half hidden by the volume before her: He was kissing every inch of her now, taking his time, tasting the tender creaminess that glowed under the lamp. He was drawing the pins from her hair and letting it tumble, heavy and shining, into his hand. He was taking the book from her fingers and pulling the lace-edged neck of her chemise slowly downward, until a single pink nipple popped free, and he ran his tongue over the delicate tip.

Emily's voice rose and fell in his ears. *"You shall not hurt this innocent, said she: for I will lose my life in her defence. Are there not, said she, enough wicked ones in the world, for your base purpose, but you must attempt such a lamb as this?"*

"Stop," he said.

She looked up, startled. "Sir?"

"Pull down your blindfold, please." His voice rang out brusquely.

She sat with her fingers poised on the page, looking carefully away. "Have I displeased you?"

"Your blindfold, madam."

Emily sighed quietly and set the book on the table. Her long fingers went to the blindfold and adjusted it downward to cover her eyes.

Ashland let out a long breath and rose from his chair. "You will miss your train, if you don't leave now."

"Is it that late?"

"Yes." He walked to the sofa and found her stays. She was still sitting in the chair, her unsmiling face turned toward him. The opaque blackness of the blindfold made her hair seem like spun gold. Each detail of her body beneath her chemise was made perfectly visible by the direct light of the lamp.

A man who commits adultery in his heart . . .

"Come." He took her hand and urged her upward. "Your stays."

She lifted her arms, and he fitted the corset around her

waist, using his stump to hold the garment in place while his left hand fumbled with the fastenings. She showed no sign of awareness of his handicap, no knowledge at all that a mutilated limb touched her flawless young body.

God willing, she would never know.

"You don't wear drawers," he said, as he tied the tapes of her petticoats.

"I have never liked them, except in winter."

"It's winter now."

She didn't answer. Ashland brought over her skirt and her bodice, the same she had worn last week. Was she destitute, then? But the clothes were of the best quality, only slightly worn.

"The carriage will take you to the station," he said, when the last button was fastened, and she stood there primly before him, as neat and polished as a duchess. "Is there anything I can do for you? You spoke of reduced circumstances. Have you need of anything at all?"

"No, sir," she said.

"Will you come again next Tuesday?"

"If I can."

"You speak coldly."

She laughed. "You're not terribly warm yourself, *Mr. Brown*."

"Forgive me. I find it difficult to . . . I am not . . ." He glanced at the clock. "You'll miss your train. Let me bring your coat."

He rang the bell for Mrs. Scruton and wrapped Emily in her muffler and coat. The hat he placed gently on her head, just so, and he eased the hatpin exactly where he had found it two hours ago.

"Tell me something, sir," said Emily. "Why do you do this? Why do you pay a woman the princely sum of fifty pounds simply to read to you? Have you never . . . Do you never . . ." She paused and wetted her bottom lip. "Do you never want more?"

Ashland gave Emily her gloves and watched her long fingers disappear, fraction by fraction, within the snug kidskin. "I want more, Emily," he said. "I am a man. Of course I want more."

"Then why don't you take it?"

She was having trouble with the last few buttons; her gloved fingers couldn't quite manage them on her other hand. Ashland nudged her aside and fit them in himself. The warm skin of her wrist beckoned in the gap between the kidskin edges, but he didn't dare to kiss her this time. Could not kiss her, or he would lose control entirely.

"Mr. Brown?" she pressed.

He finished the last button just as Mrs. Scruton knocked on the door. "Because I have no right to take it, Emily. I am a married man."

He walked to the door and opened it. "Here you are. If you hurry, I believe you'll still make the train, madam."

When Emily's stunned figure had been bustled through the door, when the carriage had left the rear portico and disappeared into the black night, when the train whistle had sounded in the distance, the Duke of Ashland gave in at last. He went into the bedroom, took out his handkerchief, unbuttoned his trousers, and found release in a few short strokes.

Then he gripped his hand around the tall right-hand post at the bottom of the bed, and his shoulders shook with the strength of his grief.

ELEVEN

The Anvil
Three weeks later

Emilie caught sight of the familiar face an instant too late. "Why, there's a coincidence! What ho, Mr. Grimsby!" Freddie lifted his hand and waved. "Come to join us for a round or two?"

The rucksack rested like a leaden weight against Emilie's back. She cast a quick eye around the taproom. The heads were still mostly bent; the mugs of ale rested promisingly next to their owners. A hundred yards distant, the station clock was ticking away, second after relentless second, until the four thirty-eight from York would arrive at the platform in a massive hiss of steam, and a restless duke would start pacing the carpet of his private room at the Ashland Spa Hotel. "Yes," she said. "That is, no. I was hoping for . . . that is . . ."

Freddie's eyes widened with speculation. "What's that, Mr. Grimsby? You're not here on your own initiative, are you?"

Emilie drew breath. "I have come to fetch you, your lordship. What did you think? Simply because I've dismissed you early doesn't give you license to ruin your mind and your character in such an unseemly manner."

A nearby head jerked upward, and a crack of laughter broke out.

Freddie rose hastily from his chair. "Good God, Mr. Grimsby. There's no need for that sort of thing, is there?"

"There is. I am shocked, your lordship. Shocked to the core. You will return to the Abbey this instant . . ."

"I say, Mr. Grimsby . . ." Freddie pushed back his spectacles and threw a longing glance back at the abandoned ale and cards on the table behind him.

"Look here, lads," said one of the men, in falsetto, "young Freddie's nursemaid's come all t'way to t'Anvil to drag him back to his milk and pap . . ."

A roar of laughter drowned out the rest of his words. His lordship's face went scarlet.

"Now, see what you've done, Grimsby . . ."

"*Mr.* Grimsby . . ."

"You're a tyrant, is what you are. A bloody great tyrant, and after I saved your brains from being dashed over the ballroom floor . . ."

"That was your father."

"Damn my father!"

Another roar of laughter. Emilie put her hands on her hips and returned Freddie's stare.

"Your lordship," she said, with quiet fierceness, "you will return to the Abbey this instant. I shall expect you in the schoolroom at nine o'clock sharp tomorrow morning with your Latin verse complete."

He crossed his arms. "And if I don't?"

She leaned forward. "I shall fetch your father."

Freddie tilted his head to the ceiling and let out a raw laugh. "Oh, that's rich! Will you toddle on down to the hotel and give his door a sharp knock?"

"Don't be impertinent."

"I'm not impertinent. It's the truth. He's there again tonight, as we both know." Freddie's voice had lowered to a discreet hiss, but the words were sharp.

"It's none of our business what His Grace does with his evenings," said Emilie, ignoring the sting. "You will walk to that door, Lord Silverton, and call for your horse."

Freddie's eyes narrowed. Emilie's eyes narrowed back.

"Dash it all, Grimsby," he said sulkily. He turned around,

picked up his tankard, drained it, and marched with petulant feet to the doorway. "Coming, Grimsby?" he tossed over his shoulder.

"No, I am not," said Emilie. "I have an errand to run."

"Bloody rich." Freddie threw open the door and let the cold Yorkshire wind burst through the ale-ridden fug of the Anvil. "Everybody gets to lark but poor bloody Freddie."

The footsteps had been dogging Emilie's shoulder for most of the length of Station Lane.

Of course it was nothing. Ashland Spa was no metropolis, nor even what Emilie would call a proper town, but it did have several hundred industrious inhabitants. Even though she chose the back lanes to make her way through town on the way to Ashland Spa Hotel on Tuesday evenings—changing her route slightly each week, just to be careful—one of those townsfolk was very likely to have business along Station Lane from time to time.

Your best defense is common sense, Miss Dingleby had said. Well, her common sense had clearly gone to hell already. What else did she have?

Emilie glanced up and crossed to the other side of the lane.

The footsteps followed. It couldn't be Freddie, could it? Had Freddie turned back and watched her ascend the steps to the second floor of the Anvil? Had he seen her emerge and creep down the back stair and out into the gathering twilight?

Keep your head, Miss Dingleby said. *Analyze the situation.*

The footsteps crunched lightly on the cobbles behind her. Too light for Freddie; a woman, then, and wearing shoes instead of boots. She strode with brisk rhythm, matching Emilie's pace; she was certain of her purpose. No aimless stroller. No daydreaming wanderer.

Concentrate your mind on the details. It will keep you from panicking, and no piece of information is so small that it might not hold the clue to saving yourself.

The last purple remains of the sun had nearly disappeared over the long and rugged hills to the west. In the spaces between the buildings, Emilie could just glimpse the darkened landscape, empty of all humanity. She chose these back lanes because she wasn't likely to encounter anyone, wasn't likely to be discovered, but now the deserted shadows echoed with the measured footsteps of her follower. The stillness of the twilight, which always filled her with delicious excitement, with anticipation of the hours to come, now pressed upon her with foreboding.

Clack, clack, clack, came the brisk female footsteps, perhaps fifteen feet behind her.

A gust of wind burst between the buildings and struck Emilie from the side. She clutched her hat with one hand and staggered around the corner of Shoe Lane.

The frozen wind howled in her ears all down the length of the lane. She couldn't hear the footsteps now; she couldn't hear anything except the wild voice of Yorkshire, turning the few square inches of her exposed skin to ice. She quickened her steps.

In the hotel, it would be warm. Ashland would have arrived an hour before (she had watched him leave the Abbey from the library window, with his back straight and his powerful legs steady against his horse's sides) and made certain the coals were sizzling and the tea was ready. He would lead her to the chair nearest the fire and tell her to warm herself, never knowing that her body heated instantly when she sensed him near. That his large frame looming above her, his long, hard bones and his heavy muscle, turned her skin to flame.

A cart rolled past ahead, wheels rattling loudly, making its way along the high street. Emilie forced her legs to remain at a brisk walk, though she ached to run.

What had Miss Dingleby's weekly note said? *All is well*, or something like that, and then a few noncommittal lines about Emilie's sisters, and then, at the end: *We hear that an inquiry has been made in your neighborhood, though gossip is so hard to trace. Remember that a true gentleman always speaks and acts with discretion.*

What did that mean? *An inquiry has been made.* Miss Dingleby and her wretched passive constructions, which told one nothing. What sort of inquiry? Who had made it? Was this inquiry part of Olympia's investigation, or did her unknown pursuer make it?

Emilie glanced back over her shoulder, as if looking for traffic. A dark-clad woman walked behind her, perhaps ten yards away, thickly veiled.

A widow, no doubt, making her way home after a day's employment.

Emilie walked on determinedly. She was a princess of Holstein-Schweinwald-Huhnhof, made of stern German stuff, and not to be alarmed by a mousy Yorkshire widow dogging her footsteps.

Dogging.

Dogging.

Emilie dropped her cold-numbed hand to the pocket of her gown, where a thin stiletto lay in its sheath. Miss Dingleby had shown her how to use it (*"skin is much tougher than you might think, my dear, so slice across the neck with vigor"*), and she had practiced the movement diligently. Unsheathe, lunge, slice. Unsheathe, lunge, slice. Surprise was the key, of course. Surprise was always the key, according to Miss Dingleby.

A faint white mass began to interrupt the darkness ahead. Emilie drew a relieved breath. The hotel at last. The lamps were lit along the drive and the portico, in eerie pools of blue white light. From behind came the sudden rattle of hooves and wheels, the warning shout of the driver. An instant later, a carriage bounced past at a smart trot, drowning the sound of the widow's footsteps. It swung into the drive of the hotel with an eager tilt.

Just before the drive lay the path to the back garden. Emilie turned sharply through the black wrought-iron gate and strode down the neat paving stones, her legs straining against her heavy woolen skirt.

The path was unlit, bordered by young trees. Emilie inhaled the frozen silence, the hint of impending snow. The branches shone faintly in the reflected light from the hotel, like skeletal fingers. A high and trilling laugh came from the front portico, cut off abruptly by a closing door, and then Emilie heard the decisive and unmistakable clack of a woman's half boots on the paving stones behind her.

She went on, faster now, her hand clutched around the stiletto in her pocket. If she could just reach the back entrance.

Through the garden, across the drive and stableyard: A minute or two was all she needed.

She pushed her footsteps a little faster. The paving stones were uneven, left in picturesque disorder by the hotel gardeners, and her heel caught on an unexpected edge. She staggered forward, caught herself, and went on.

A sharp voice called behind her. "Ma'am!"

Emilie strode out, nearly running, and then the world lurched and streaked around her, and she hit the ground with a bone-rattling thud.

"Ma'am! Ma'am!"

Emilie didn't wait. She scrambled up, found the stiletto in her pocket, and flashed it out in front of her.

"Why, ma'am!"

The voice was high and surprised. The woman stood a few feet away, her veil thrown back, her face shadowed. She held her hands out before her, as if to beg.

"Who are you?" Emilie demanded breathlessly.

"Why, nobody, ma'am!" The woman took a step back, and one of the hotel lights moved across her face, revealing a flash of young features and wide, astonished eyes.

"You've been following me!"

"I haven't! Not a-purpose, anyroad. I . . . I have business here, that's all." The woman nodded at the sprawling building to her right.

"Business! What sort of business?" Emilie lowered her hand a trifle. Her pulse beat rapidly in her ears.

The woman drew herself up. "Why, that's my own affair, it is. I'm a respectable woman."

"Indeed! And what sort of *respectable* affair brings a woman to a . . ." Emilie let her words trail away. Understanding began to dawn.

"No less respectable than yours, ma'am, begging your pardon." Her tone was laden with irony.

Emilie tucked Miss Dingleby's stiletto away in her pocket. "I *do* beg your pardon. You've come for Mr. Brown, haven't you? The fourth Tuesday of the month."

The woman hesitated, and then said, a little defensively, "Why, yes, I have. Though I don't see it's any of your business."

Emilie peered through the darkness, searching for details. The woman had a sort of dignity to her, carrying herself with elegance, though her speech marked her somewhere in the middle rank, neither gentlewoman nor worker. One of those many nameless women holding precariously to respectability, as the economic ground shifted and split beneath their feet: a widow, or perhaps never married, or perhaps married to a drunkard or scoundrel or worse. Ashland's fifty pounds a month would lift her from penury and into a comfortable life, with a genteel house and a few servants. It would make all the difference.

The woman's head was tilted at a proud angle. Did Ashland admire that about her? How well had he known her? Had he simply watched her read books in her chemise, or had he been moved to do more? To touch her, to kiss her?

A surge of jealousy rose up in Emilie's chest, so sudden and violent it burned the back of her throat.

"I'm afraid there's been a change," she said. "Mr. Brown and I have come to an understanding. I have been seeing him weekly since just before Christmas."

"*What's* that?"

"I mean your services are no longer required. I'm very sorry," she added, after a brief pause.

"Why, that's . . . That's when I was badly, at Christmas. When I couldn't come. I *told* them, I'm sure I did, I sent a telegram . . ." The woman shook her head and said plaintively, "And now you've crowded me out, have you?"

"It isn't that. I had no intention of . . . We simply got along so well . . ."

"Every *week*, you say?" The woman's dark-clad shoulders sagged in the faint rim of gaslight. She locked her hands together at her belly. "He must fancy you proper, then."

"I don't know about that." Emilie spoke quietly. "He's not a man easily overcome by emotion."

"No, he's not."

Emilie reached for her pocket, and the woman stumbled back warily. "No, no," she said. "It's just this. I haven't touched his money. You can have it, if you want. Two hundred pounds."

The woman gasped. "Two hundred pound? In your *pocket*, ma'am?"

"I couldn't touch it." Emilie drew the envelopes from her coat and held them out. "Please. Take it all."

"I couldn't, ma'am."

"Please take it. I'm sure you were counting on the money." Emilie thrust her arm insistently.

The woman stood quietly. Her breath came out in ghostly clouds, uneven and somewhat rapid. "Two hundred pound," she said again, quite softly. "It would set me up, it would."

"Take it." Emilie stepped forward and placed the envelopes against the woman's knotted hands, until her fingers loosened and accepted the precious cargo.

"I shall miss him," the woman said, "though he were such an odd one."

"Yes." The word stuck in her throat.

"I always thought, maybe, if we kept on . . ." She shook her head. The veil trembled around her shoulders. "Every week, you said?"

"Since Christmas."

The woman turned, paused, and looked back over her shoulder. The shadows made her face look strangely ancient. "Do he ever touch you, ma'am? Touch you proper, I mean."

Emilie gathered herself up and tightened her woolen muffler around her throat.

"Not yet." She tilted her chin. "But he will."

TWELVE

S he was late.

Ashland pretended not to notice the clock ticking away on the mantel. He walked to the round table, Emily's table, and picked up the book he'd selected for the evening. It was new; he'd just picked it up in the bookshop the other day, and the scent of new paper and fresh ink rose up to meet him as he flipped unseeing through the pages.

He put the book down and went to the window. No sign of her; no neat black-coated figure illuminated by the gas lamp on the rear portico.

The clock ticked on, unmoved. She should have been here ten minutes ago. She had promised to come straight from the station now, so he wouldn't worry. He should have sent the carriage; that was it. What was he thinking, trusting the darkened winter roads of Ashland Spa to bring his Emily safely to his side? He should have . . .

A knock sounded on the door.

He turned. "Come in."

The door opened, and there was Emily, gloved hands outstretched, blindfold in place. "Good evening, sir."

"You're late." He meant to punish her, to make her endure the same few minutes of unreasoning worry he'd felt himself, but the sight of those outstretched hands dissolved his anger. He strode across the room and seized her kidskin fingers and kissed them. "You're shaking. What's happened?"

"Nothing." She withdrew her hand and laughed, a high and artificial laugh. "It's frightfully cold outside, that's all."

He studied her mouth. "It isn't the cold. What happened, Emily?"

"Nothing. I . . . I fell, that's all. On the path in the garden. The paving stones were uneven, and it's so awfully dark . . ."

"Good God. Are you all right?" He lifted his hand and touched her cheekbone, her jaw.

"Perfectly." She turned away.

"Come to the fire and warm yourself."

He led her to the fireplace and urged her into the nearest armchair. She was trembling with something, some emotion, though her hands clenched tightly in her lap with the effort to disguise it. She sat ramrod straight, as always, as if she were still in the schoolroom with a book balanced on the crown of her head by a purse-lipped governess.

Ashland plucked away her hatpin and drew the small felt hat from her hair. The golden strands gleamed in the firelight and disappeared beneath the black blindfold. He knelt before her, took off her gloves, and rubbed each hand between his large fingers. "I'll send the carriage for you, from now on," he said. "I should have thought of it sooner."

"Oh no. It's quite unnecessary. I like the walk, really. So bracing."

"Nevertheless." He examined her face minutely. She was steadier now, whether from the warmth of the fire or from the steady massage of his fingers. It no longer pained him at all to touch her like this, hand to hand; he hardly even remembered the old sensations of dread, of recoil. "You've scraped your chin," he said.

She touched the tip and winced. "So I have."

He rose and went to the bathroom, where he found a wash-cloth and ran it under the cool water, avoiding the sight of his face in the mirror above the sink. When he returned, Emily had unwound her muffler and was rising from her seat, struggling with her coat.

"Don't be silly." He drew off her coat and set her back in

the chair. "Here," he said, and held the washcloth gently to her chin.

"Oh! Don't, really. It's nothing."

He said nothing. The coals hissed behind him; the clock ticked. Emily's breath rushed warm and fragrant against his cheek. Her lips had parted slightly as he pressed the washcloth on her skin, and her teeth peeked out in a thin white line between them. He imagined running his tongue along that alluring seam of rosy lip, opening her mouth millimeter by millimeter, until he was tasting her deeply. Until she was tasting him.

Ah, how would Emily taste?

She lifted her hand and placed it over his. "Thank you."

Her fingers were still cool from the January air. The light touch trapped him, held him utterly captive on his knees before her. The glow of the fire illuminated her skin, as if she were lit from within.

Kiss her. For God's sake, kiss her.

With inhuman effort, he lifted his hand away from her chin. "Let me pour your tea. That will warm you quickly enough."

"I am quite warm already, thank you."

He rose and poured the tea with his shaking hand.

"Mr. Brown," she said, in that voice of hers, perfectly low and perfectly dulcet, "I have another impertinent question for you."

He couldn't help smiling. "What is it, Emily?"

"Why am I here?"

He added the cream and sugar, stirred with a tiny silver spoon, and placed the cup and saucer in her waiting hands. "Since you must know your own motivation, I can only assume you're asking me why *I* wish you to visit me every week. The answer is that I enjoy the pleasure of your company."

"That's not an answer. It's a drawing-room pleasantry. You know perfectly well what I mean."

Ashland did not want tea this evening. Not that he ever wanted tea; he had drunk too much of it in India, and the taste reminded him of other things, unpleasant things. He went to the fireplace instead and rested his right elbow on the mantel, which somewhat relieved the ache in his missing hand. "But I do enjoy your company. Is that somehow inexplicable?"

"You know we cannot go on like this. You must make a decision eventually."

"What decision?"

"Whether we will lie together or not."

The porcelain clinked as she lifted the teacup to her lips, drank, and set it down again. Ashland watched her lips as they parted to accept the tea, her throat as she swallowed, her fingers as they curled around the delicate white S-curve of the handle.

She went on, into his silence. "I presume you're wrestling with the morality of it all. But surely it's just as much a betrayal of your marriage vows to sit in a room alone with another woman, to undress her, to watch her nearly naked as she sits at a table and reads to you. To pay her for the service. After such an intimate relation, what does it matter if copulation occurs or does not?"

"It matters to me." He turned to the wall and rested his chin on his forearm. "It matters to *you*, I daresay."

"We will leave my own desires aside, for the moment. The dilemma is yours."

Ashland left the fireplace and walked to the window.

She continued. "Don't think me unfeeling. I can see how it pains you. I presume your wife is no longer living with you?"

"She left me twelve years ago." He fingered the windowpane. He felt he owed her the truth, as much as he could tell her.

"I see. Have you never considered a suit of divorce for abandonment?" She said the word *divorce* crisply, without emotion, as she might refer to the glazed orange cake lying in slices on a flute-edged plate atop the tea table.

"I have not. I returned from war a different man, a beast, maimed and charmless. Her departure was not without provocation." A tiny smudge marred the corner of the glass; he wiped at it with his thumb. "And I had made a vow, of course. A vow before God."

"So did she. *For better or for worse*, and yet she left you in your trouble, and did not return." The porcelain clinked again. "Did she leave alone?"

Ashland closed his eyes to shut out the dark-haired image of the Earl of Somerton. "She did not."

Emily whispered, "Oh, my dear sir."

He turned from the window to face her. She was still sitting before the fire, but she'd placed the cup and saucer on the table and sat with her hands together in her lap and her head bowed. "I don't require your compassion," he said.

"It is not compassion," she said. "It is admiration."

He stared at her golden head, and his breastbone, his ribs, his muscles and skin, his every defense fell away from his chest and left only his madly beating heart. "I have a son," he said.

She lifted her head. "I'm sure he's a fine boy."

"He is. He's nearly sixteen. He has . . ." The words had to be pushed from his throat. "He has been everything, and he is her son. He was born from her own body. To betray her flesh is to betray his."

"She didn't share your conviction."

"We are not discussing her behavior. We are discussing mine."

Emily bent her head again and stared at her fingers. When she spoke, her voice was choked with tears. "My dear Mr. Brown. Where does that leave us?"

Ashland levered himself away from the window, picked up the book from the table, and walked toward Emily's bowed figure. The nape of her neck beckoned, pale and tender. He knelt before her and placed the book in her lap.

"My dear Emily. My very dear Emily," he said. "Read to me."

The lamplight cast over the page in a yellow pool. Emilie's eyes were beginning to ache; she thought longingly of her spectacles, tucked into the pocket of her jacket back at the Anvil.

"Is something wrong?" asked Ashland from his armchair.

"I'm sorry," she said. "My eyes are tired."

"Then you must stop, of course."

She placed her finger in the book and closed it. The leather cover was new, stamped in bright gold letters. Ashland's gaze caressed her from behind. She wanted to turn to him, to nestle in his arms in the chair and listen to his heartbeat beneath her ear.

"What is it, Emilie?" he asked softly.

"Nothing, sir."

"Don't say that to me again. If something troubles you, tell me."

Emilie ran her fingers over the title. The wind was picking up, flinging itself against the windows. She dreaded the ride home, cold and lonely, her body and heart aching.

"I have a confession for you," she said.

"Indeed?"

"That first night, the first time I visited you . . ." Emilie placed the book on the table and laid her hand flat atop it. "It was a mistake."

Beneath the low shriek of the wind at the window, she could hear the heavy cadence of Ashland's breath.

"A mistake. I see."

"No, not like that. I mean that I wasn't the woman who was supposed to come. They mistook me in the hallway; I was only taking tea at the hotel."

"What the *devil*?" He moved in the chair, as if he wanted to get up, and then stopped himself.

"I don't know why I came up. I don't know why I stayed." Her voice began to break. She paused and filled her lungs with air. "I don't suppose it matters. Anyway, outside today, on my way from the station, I met a woman. The woman who was supposed to come a month ago. She was here for the regular Tuesday visit."

"Good God."

"I told her . . . I told her that she was no longer needed. I'm sorry; I ought not to have taken the liberty . . ."

"Good God."

"But I couldn't let her come up to you. I couldn't let anyone take my place. I gave her money, all the money you'd given me, and told her not to come back."

"You gave her . . . *What* was it?"

"Two hundred pounds."

A rustling, and his footsteps sounded on the carpet. "You

shouldn't have done that. That money was for you, Emilie. For your use, to help you."

"She needed it. It was only fair."

"It was for *you*."

"I've already told you, I don't want your money. I was glad to give it to her." Emilie's hand fisted with the effort of keeping still, of holding herself from turning toward the imposing figure of the duke behind her, shimmering with edgy energy.

"Emilie."

Where was he now? Back in the chair? She studied her fisted hand, the shadow it cast on the expensive tooled leather of the book. "There it is, anyway. At least you know the truth."

The truth. The word echoed ominously in her head.

"The truth." The floorboards creaked behind her, moving across the room. A clink of crystal: He was pouring himself a drink. "What is the truth? Who *are* you, then, if you're not . . . if you weren't sent here . . ."

"I will tell you that, Mr. Brown, when you tell me who *you* are."

"You know I can't."

"Yes, I know. But you see, it doesn't matter. All that—who I am, who you are, where we come from, all that nonsense—it doesn't matter. It's only a distraction, isn't it? What exists between us is clear. It's simple and pure. It's stripped of all the useless facts and assumptions that keep men and women from really understanding each other."

Ashland's voice was dark with despair. "Emilie, it's not possible. How can I accept that you simply knocked on my door and walked into my life, like a divine miracle, without explanation?"

"I am not a miracle. I am a woman."

"My God, what have I done?" A glass thunked down on a table.

Emilie fought the urge to turn around. It was like having a conversation with a ghost. "You've done nothing wrong, sir. I have told you the truth: I'm a woman of gentle birth, living in reduced circumstances, obliged to make my own way for the moment. I act for myself. I answer to no one's conscience but my own. I have entered this room in full knowledge of the consequences."

"You should have told me. I should have suspected. I knew in my heart you weren't like the others, and I went on regardless . . ." His voice was muffled, as if he were speaking into the wall or the curtains.

"I wanted you to. I wanted *you*."

"Why, Emilie?" His footsteps shuffled once, twice. His voice came clear again. "If you're a woman of gentle birth. Why do you come here every week, if not for my fifty pounds?"

Emilie stared at the wall before her, where dozens of intricate green vines trailed upward in perfect symmetry against a base of pure cream, ending abruptly in the carved molding. To her right, a thin line of golden light shone from the crack in the door to the bedroom.

"God help me," she whispered, "because I want *you*. Because I cannot stay away."

He whispered back, "Ah, God, Emilie."

Emilie couldn't move. The wind wailed upward a note, shaking the windows, and descended again. She unfolded her hand, finger by finger, and settled it into her lap with the other.

She felt his approach as she felt her own heartbeat slamming into her ribs.

"Emilie." He was right behind her now, looking down at the top of her head. The heat of his body enveloped her. Her breath stopped in her chest.

His finger touched the top of her ear, as light as air, and lingered along the curve to the little nook behind her earlobe. "Beautiful," he said.

"Sir."

"Hush." His finger sloped around her neck, drawing a slow circle at her nape, dipping down to trace the lace-trimmed edge of her chemise. "Don't say anything, Emilie."

His hand went under her arm, urging her upward. She rose to her feet. The leg of the chair rushed softly against the carpet.

Ashland's body touched her back. Her every sense was alight; she could feel each individual button of his jacket nestle against her spine. He walked his finger down her left arm, making the tiny hairs stand up. When he reached her fingertips, his hand ran over her palm and back up the tender underside, from wrist to elbow, settling in the hollow of her arm.

"*Sir*," she breathed out.

He drew down the sleeve of her chemise and kissed her bare shoulder.

She gasped and took a step, unable to support herself. His arm caught her just in time, wrapping around her ribs. His head was bent; his hair, thick and soft, brushed her temple.

"Shall I touch you, Emilie? Would you like that?"

His voice was low and gentle, that rich timbre she loved so much. Inch by inch, she let herself relax against him. He shuddered as she leaned back, and then he held firm. His lips touched her ear, her neck, impossibly soft.

His hand, spread across her belly, drew upward. His thumb found the underside of her breast through the fine linen of her shift, and warmth radiated across her skin. In silence he explored her, with bare movements of his thumb and fingertips, measuring the seam between breast and ribs as if he had no further ambition in the world.

She wanted to speak. She wanted to tell him that her breasts were full and aching for more of him, that her every nerve was concentrated under his fingertips, that she was going to burst with heat and sensation. But how could she say these things aloud? Her dry mouth opened and closed.

Gradually the little circular movements of Ashland's thumb grew bolder, singeing her skin through the tissue-thin layer of fabric between them. He slid upward around the curve, just grazing the tip, until he found the lace at her neckline and tugged it downward and her breast burst free into the open air.

Emilie could not breathe. She cast her eyes down to the impossible sight: Ashland's large hand at her breast, dark and weathered against her pale skin, his fingers curled in a perfect echo of the curve of her flesh. How was it possible that a hand so powerful could touch her so delicately? Something hard pressed into the base of her spine, and a thrill shivered her body. It must be him. Must be that male organ she had seen in books and pictures and statues, but never in person; that part of him designed by nature to be joined with her.

"Sir," she whispered. "Mr. Brown . . ."

"Don't speak, Emilie." His voice was hoarse, almost harsh.

While she watched in wonder, his fingers traced a circle around her nipple. His hand cupped around her breast, lifting it, and his thumb found the nipple at last and grazed the extreme tip. She gasped and flung up her hand to grip his wrist.

He said, into her ear, "Tell me what to do, Emilie. One word. Tell me what you want."

His breath was hot. He took her nipple between his thumb and forefinger and idled about the hardened nub. She watched the play of bone beneath the skin of his hands, the tiny movement of muscle and sinew that created the extraordinary sensations streaking through her body. She couldn't think. Who was she, this throbbing scrap of Emilie, standing here in this dim and wind-battered room while the Duke of Ashland's all-powerful hand cradled her naked breast?

Tell me what to do, Emilie.

Anything. Everything. But she could not manage the words. She watched his hand, his beautiful hand, as it caressed her body. His lips touched her ear in a whisper of a kiss.

If she asked, he would take her to bed. He had put the decision to her; he had taken his honor and placed it in her hands. Because she would not take his money, because she came to him without condition, because she had stripped herself bare before him, he had given her the only thing he could: himself. He would take her to bed if she asked it, he would become her lover, and he would bear the guilt on his own shoulders.

Would she let him?

She should not let him. His body wanted her passionately, but he would suffer afterward. The burden of guilt—however unjust—would lie on his conscience like an anvil. And she! An even greater madness, this physical surrender. She would entangle herself irrevocably, she would endanger every plan for the future. To part with him afterward would be like cutting out her own heart.

Oh, but to lie with him. To feel his skin upon hers, to know at last the eternal mystery. To show him what she felt and couldn't say. To comfort him; to bring him joy, however fleeting.

To be united with Ashland, for a precious instant.

"Sir. Mr. Brown."

He went on stroking her breast with his gentle fingers. He, too, was watching this union of their flesh, of Ashland

and Emilie; she could feel his gaze like another caress on her skin.

"Please," she said.

His hand left her breast and went to her blindfold. He tugged it down from her forehead and ran his fingers along its length, making sure it lay flat and snug across her eyes. Every movement slid against her body with tantalizing energy.

She didn't wait for him to turn her around. She rotated between his arms and tilted her face upward.

She meant to say, *We must stop. For your sake, and for mine.*

What she said was: "I want you to kiss me."

THIRTEEN

I want you to kiss me.

The words fell from her lips in the softest whisper, but they ignited like a spark in Ashland's brain. She held her face up to him, waiting, her blindfold dark against her pale skin, her mouth red and unbearably inviting.

If you kiss her, there is no going back.

It was his last logical thought.

He bent his head. He kissed her forehead and the rounded tip of her nose. Her breath was warm and damp on his chin; her body stood vibrant between his arms. It was like holding a living coal.

He lifted his hand and touched her hair, her ear, her cheek. *You are so soft*, he wanted to say. *So soft and utterly perfect, and I am a brute, a sinful and mutilated brute.*

Emily's lips beckoned, round and flushed and irresistible. He had no right to them.

He brushed the corner of her mouth with his thumb and laid his lips atop hers.

For a long second, he didn't move, and neither did she. They simply stood there, breathing each other in, lips held together in the lightest of bonds. Emily's breath was sweet from the tea, scented with orange, unsteady. Her chest moved rapidly, touching his ribs as she inhaled.

She lifted her hands, and he caught one the instant before it touched him. "No," he said, into her mouth.

"How can I not touch you?" she asked, in a pained whisper.

"You cannot." He led her hand back down to her side and released it. "Let me touch *you*, Emily. Just let me. You don't need to do anything."

He settled his mouth again on hers, and this time he nudged at her lips, he brought her body closer, and the spark in his brain fanned into flame and spread in a stunning draft through his body. He was already aroused, his prick iron stiff and heavy against the snug wool of his trousers, but this was something else. This was urgency, this was over a decade of suppressed sexual need roaring back into life; this was Emily in his arms, kissing him back with unskilled lips, meeting his every questioning movement with an ardent counter-movement.

If she could see you, she wouldn't kiss you like that.

He wrapped his arms around her, gathered her up, and kissed her in earnest. She made a surprised sound, a little mewling cry, right at the back of her throat, and he parted her lips and swallowed it up into his soul.

She *wanted* him. Her desire was a gift from God, unexpected and unlooked for.

She wasn't used to kissing, and he was thankful for that. Her lack of practice made his own less evident. He had forgotten how to be tender, how to seduce. All he knew was that he wanted to taste her.

He ran the tip of his tongue along her mouth. A tremor moved her, as if she hadn't been expecting it. He licked her again, a little more deeply, and this time her mouth opened to receive him, and her body, trapped within his, strained upward. He dipped his tongue inside to find the silken tip of Emily's tongue, waiting for him, inquisitive and uncertain. He stroked it with care, testing her reaction, tasting the sweet tea-spiciness of her mouth.

Another sound came from her throat, a demanding sound. She tried a tentative stroke of his tongue, just finding him with the tip, and the sensation crackled along every pathway of his body. He lifted his head. "Emily, I . . ."

But she went on her toes and took his mouth back. She sucked his upper lip, she thrust her tongue against his and slid it up and down, as if she were savoring him, and all at once the wooing was over. He could not restrain himself. He bent down, keeping his mouth locked on hers, mingling and tangling in desperation, and he swung her into his arms and strode across the room. He kicked open the door to the bedroom, still kissing her, and set her on the edge of the bed.

Emily started at the softness of the bed under her bottom. She broke off the kiss and braced her hands against her legs, as if to steady herself. "Sir . . . Mr. Brown . . ."

Her chemise had rucked up her thighs. He grasped the edge with his hand and tugged it upward from beneath her bottom, swiftly and forcefully, before she could protest, before she could change her mind. If she changed her mind, he would die, he would explode, leaving only a single combusted heap of ash on the carpet to mark his demise.

Emily's body unveiled before him, lit only by the dim light from the other room, full of shadows and faintly gleaming curves. Her hips swelled out from her small waist; her breasts were high and round, the nipples pointed slightly upward, puckered into hard little tips. He drew the chemise over her head and tossed it to the carpet.

She did not move to cover herself. Her hands remained at her sides, her body tilted to his gaze, as if daring him to find her wanting.

For a moment, Ashland stood perfectly still, unable to move. He had not seen a woman like this in years, had not had a woman's nakedness tilted willingly toward him since the night before he'd left for India.

He dropped to his knees. "Beautiful," he said, and with the tip of his tongue he licked her nipple.

She jolted in response. Her hands came up, reaching for him, and he snared her left wrist and pinned it to the bedspread, not relinquishing her breast for an instant. He ran his tongue over the tip and around, swirling almost in delirium, and then he drew the nub into his mouth and suckled greedily. She gasped and sighed; her body moved to the rhythm of his suckling, mimicking the act of union itself. He kissed his way to the other breast and did it all over again, the luxurious tasting of her, and then he released her wrist and rolled the abandoned nipple between his thumb and fingers, pulling gently at one while he suckled hard at the other, until her legs thrashed and sobs broke the air above his head. Her hand touched his hair and fell back again. "Sir . . . Mr. Brown . . . Oh, let me, let me *touch* you . . ."

His mouth left her nipple and kissed the underside of her breast, her ribs, the other breast, before nibbling upward to settle in the hollow of her throat. His cock was huge with need, throbbing with eager blood, but instead of reaching for the fastening of his trousers he drew his fingers down her body in lazy circles, ignoring the pain as he braced his weight on his stump. Down he went, around her breast and her ribs, finding her navel, exploring the soft skin at the side of her waist and the flawless curve of her hip. He inhaled the scent of her, her clean smell, devoid of flowers or powder or anything but Emily.

He'd be damned if he took her like a beast. If she fled afterward, he wanted no regrets. He wanted to have savored every inch of her, while he had the chance.

He wrapped his hand around her leg, just below the hip. His thumb dipped into the warmth of her inner thigh. "I'm going to touch you now, Emily," he said. "Let me in. Let me touch your sweetness."

"Great God," she whispered. Her head fell back. He swirled his tongue around the fine bones of her clavicle and let his thumb slip lower. Damp heat rose from the notch hidden within. He felt the first springing hair, and another. "Great God," she said again, and his thumb found the round promise of her mound, and he thought he might break.

So close, now. Almost there.

He lifted his head and kissed his way up the line of her throat. She was trembling, shaking visibly. "Steady. Hush. I'll be gentle. I'll be so gentle. Let me in. Ah, that's it."

His thumb slid at last through the crisp golden curls to her center, and he growled in shock. She was slick and hot, fully wet with desire for him, in the final luscious stages of arousal. For *him!* His fingers covered her mound, while he brushed his reverent thumb along the folds of delicate skin, familiarizing himself with the long-forgotten contours of a woman's body, the sleek and intricate anatomy of her. He inserted the tip of his thumb just inside her. She was murmuring incoherently into his temple, clenching and unclenching against him.

By God, she's going to spend, he thought in awe.

He covered her lips with his mouth and moved his thumb upward to find the hard little nubbin at her apex. Her body jolted again, held in place only by his steadying hand, his arm against hers, his devouring kiss. "Oh God, oh God," she moaned. He caressed her in tender and rhythmic circles, guiding her along, massaging the coil of energy beneath her skin.

"Let go. Spend for me, Emily," he said, and he drew out her tongue and sucked on it.

She spent instantly, in hard and unrelenting pulses, sinking backward on the bed as if her bones had dissolved. He followed her, still sucking at her tongue, still milking her below, while her cries vibrated in his mouth. Her arms strained upward against the prison of his body.

"That's it, darling. That's it. Off you go." He left her mouth and pressed his lips against the mad pulse at her throat. "That's it, you lovely thing. Look at you."

Gradually the quick heave of her chest began to slow. Her body sagged below him, giving itself up to the aftermath. He lifted his head and observed the flush of her skin, the tremble of her chin. The scent of climax filled the air. He brought his hand to his lips and tasted her.

"Mr. Brown." Almost too soft to be heard.

"I'm here." The smell of her, the taste of her, sent a mist through his brain. His skin was hot and covered by a film of dampness. He raised himself and shrugged off his coat, loosened his necktie.

"Sir?" Emily lifted herself on her elbows, gloriously nude, flushed and disordered. Ashland's prick throbbed in his trousers.

"Shh. Lie back, now, darling."

He dropped again to his knees and put his hand on her legs, widening her.

"What . . . ?"

"Let me." He kissed her inner lips, and was rewarded with a sweet jump of her body. God, the response of her! "Hush, now. Let me taste you."

Her breath hissed between her teeth. "You can't . . . It's not . . . My *God* . . ."

"You're going to spend for me again, Emily. I want to watch you do it again."

Emily's elbows gave way. Ashland touched her swollen nub with an experimental tongue, and she cried out. He swirled lower and dipped his tongue into her cleft, tasted her tanginess, smelled her rich musk. With his fingers he spread her farther and adored the perfect symmetry of her, the light curls and the crimson inner lips, gleaming with lubricity. He kissed her again; he drew his tongue along each precious fold, and then he began in earnest.

She was already excited, already fisting her hands into the bed. When he returned at last to her nub, she began to hum. He licked her in a delicate rhythm. "I can't bear it," she gasped. "I can't bear it!"

But he wouldn't relent. He couldn't. She felt so *good*, so eager, her passion so unguarded and real, her limbs so open and trusting. No goddamned showy modesty, no artifice. Over and over he flicked his tongue, holding her twisting hips in place, relishing her spiraling tightness under his mouth. He used his tongue to control her, varying the speed and intensity, bringing her to the brink and down again, then starting his torture anew, until she was like a live wire of electricity, humming and twitching and taut—oh God!—so rosy and perfect.

He let her loose at last. Her feral cry rent the air, her body arched in ecstasy, and Ashland inserted the tip of his finger inside her just in time to feel the wet flesh clench in a violent spasm of release.

"Go on, go on. Ah, that's good." He gazed longingly at her pulsing body: the sweet evidence of Emily's ready sensuality, her capability for abandonment. He had sensed that passionate nature, seething with promise beneath her calm skin, and now here it lay before him. No cool-blooded scholar, Emily. No perfectly bred society beauty, either, devoid of imagination and initiative. His Emily would meet him like a tigress; she would devour him as he devoured her.

Ashland rose, quivering with energy, with an unquiet and overpowering urge to mate. She had spent twice; she was slick and soft and ripe for his invasion. She murmured something; he thought for an instant that she said *Ashland*.

He watched her as he ripped off his waistcoat, as he pulled down his braces and fumbled with the fastening of his trousers. She was still panting, still flushed, drifting down from her second climax. The room was unlit, and her skin gleamed with perspiration in the faint light from the other room. His prick sprang out, huge with anticipation, nearly vertical. He'd never been so aroused, not even on his wedding night. He'd never seen such a sensual sight as Emily, sprawled invitingly before him, blindfolded and trusting, loose-limbed with sexual completion.

She was still lying at the edge of the bed, her legs spread apart. He put his hand beneath her arm, his stump beneath her bottom, and scooted her upward. Her hands scrabbled in surprise at the covers. "I . . . Sir?"

"I'm going to have you now, Emily." He sank his elbows on either side and kissed her.

She made a sound in her throat and reached for his shoulders, and this time he couldn't stop her touch. His need was too urgent. He gritted his teeth against the collision of her palms against his shirt and reached down to position himself. His cock slid against her opening, looking for purchase in the slippery abundance of her arousal.

"Mr. Brown!" She jumped beneath him.

"Steady," he muttered, gripping himself. God, it had been so long. He was fumbling like a boy, trying to lodge himself somewhere in that impossible tightness. "Almost . . . ah God . . . *there!*"

He dropped his elbow back to the mattress, braced above her, and shoved hard, all in the same instant.

Thirteen years ago, in the mountains of southeastern Afghanistan, Ashland had been captured by three tribesmen as he rode his frantic horse back toward the British lines. What he remembered most about the exact moment of his ambush was the slowness of time, the elastic way in which the seconds had stretched out, so that the near-simultaneous sequence of details—the horse throwing up his head in the air, the cloud of dust obscuring his vision, the flash of white from his attackers' turbans through that dust, the exotic high-pitched hallooing that shook his eardrums, the blue-flame slice of pain as his jaw shattered under the impact of a lead bullet at close range—each occurred in its own separate eternity.

The instant in which he invaded Emily elongated in exactly the same fashion.

He knew, in the fraction during which his hips swiveled for the thrust, that he had miscalculated her. Emily's flinch of shock, the stiffness of her body, the resistance where he pressed into her entrance rocketed across his senses; but by then he was committed. He was already in motion; the white light of animal need was already blinding his brain. There was no halting the juggernaut force of his journey up her stunned cleft. But he knew the truth, even before a slight stretching pressure wrapped around the head of his cock and then broke free. He heard the truth as Emily made a sharp cry and he surged without further impediment to bury himself to his stones in her slick body.

He arched there for a moment, his chest heaving, his belly just touching hers, his locked arms trembling with the force of his emotion. He dipped his head down and inhaled the warm scent of her neck. "Forgive me. I didn't know."

Emily said nothing. Her breath shuddered in her chest.

He lifted his head. "Are you hurt?"

Her head made a little shake. He wanted to lift the blindfold, to look in her eyes and read the truth. His balls were tightening under the waves of mind-spinning pleasure radiating from his prick, from the guilty primeval thrill that *he was the first, he had breached her, she was untouched, she was his.* God help him. "Forgive me."

Emily's fingers grazed his back. "Shh. I know." Her skin slid against his as she raised her knees. "I know."

Her breath was steadier now.

"Shall I stop?" he whispered, dreading the answer. Good God, what if she said *Stop*? Could he do it?

"No, don't stop."

Praise God. He swiveled his hips, and she flinched. "Does it hurt?"

"No."

He could tell that it did. A curse escaped his clenched mouth. Stupid, blundering beast. He kissed her lips, as gently as he could. "I'm sorry." He kissed her again. "I'm sorry."

Again, that tender brush of her fingers. She wiggled beneath him, adjusting herself to his intrusion, making his breath saw sharply. "No. I wanted this."

Emily, a *virgin*. His brain rocked with the knowledge, with the consequences. He'd known she wasn't experienced, but he'd never imagined *this*. What had a virgin been doing in these rooms? She had been so knowing, so . . . *informed*. So eager. The whole world shifted on its axis around him.

He pushed it all back. He would think about that later.

He hovered above her, not certain whether to move, desperately afraid of hurting her further. His mind cast wildly back to his wedding night, the details of which lay confused and dim in his memory. Had Isabelle enjoyed the act at all? What had he done? He didn't remember noticing. He'd been so young, so mad for it, knowing nothing about the business, thinking mostly of himself and his own need and the novelty of it all. He'd probably spent the instant he was inside her.

He was close to spending now, like the green and self-absorbed boy he'd once been. He fought back his release, fought back the sensation of clean, bright pleasure in his groin, fought back the overwhelming instinct to fill this tight little virgin quim with seed *this instant*.

Because this was Emily, *his* Emily, lying with a man for the first time in her life. She had chosen *him* to do this. She deserved everything he had to give her.

His breathing calmed; his heart calmed. He swiveled his hips again, and this time Emily didn't flinch. "Hurt?" he gasped out.

"No." She made a little urging movement of her own hips.

He pulled himself out a cautious fraction, and pushed back in.

"Oh!"

"Good?" he asked.

"Yeeeessss." She drew out the word, as if she weren't quite certain.

He pulled out a little more, and pushed back in. Emily

moaned: a moan he recognized distantly. The good sort of moan.

A gust of a sigh emptied his lungs. *Thank God.*

He pulled out halfway, and pushed. And again, a little farther now, an inch more.

Again.

Soft, slick, snug female flesh. How had he lived without this? He was going to die of it, the sweetness of shoving his rigid tool into all that lovely heat, into that greedy silken sheath.

Into Emily.

She was meeting him now, her breath coming in delicious little pants. He bent to kiss her, more confident. "Good?"

"Don't stop!"

He began to thrust in a regular rhythm, not too fast, not too hard, mindful of the damage he had already inflicted on her. His mind could hardly recall the technique, but his body remembered. His body knew what to do, knew how to fall into that ancient pattern of shove and release, shove and release, matching his movements to hers, finding his approach, finding her perfect place of friction.

She was so sweet and eager, so yielding and yet firm.

He'd thought, in the beginning, that he would be tormented by Isabelle's ghost, but all memory of his wife had long since fled his mind: There was only Emily and the little animal sounds she made, the dig of her heels into his trousers, the way her tight little slit gripped him in a wholly new way, like a handprint all her own. A surge of long-forgotten emotion began to reclaim his brain: joy and urgency and exultation, the headlong drive toward consummation.

His release was rearing up again, enormous, tightening his balls, intense to the point of pain. It refused his control. He ground into Emily with increasing speed, struggling between gentleness and desperation, his skin hot and humid beneath his shirt and his breath coming in tortured gasps.

"Emily, I'm about to spend, ah God, so *hard*, I can't . . ." He raised himself a little higher, hoping to hold it off a moment longer, but at that instant she clenched around him, she gasped his name, and the lightning burst of his own climax blinded him without warning.

He had meant to pull out of her, as a considerate gentleman

should do, but he hadn't the strength to deny himself this last selfish act in an evening of selfish acts. With a last mighty stroke he came inside Emily's flawless young body, and came and came, long, luxurious spurts of pleasure, giving her everything he had.

And then it was over. Empty, shocked, he sank into Emily and buried his head into the loosened strands of her hair.

I am damned, he thought.

FOURTEEN

She was blessed.

Ashland lay atop her, inside her, joined with her at last. *Ashland.* He had taken his pleasure with her; he had given her pleasure in return. He had made her body sting and hurt, and sing and come alive at his command.

He had been everything she had ever dreamed of in a lover, except perhaps for all that excess of clothing.

He was also every ounce as heavy as she'd feared.

Oddly enough, she didn't mind. His breathless bulk felt . . . rather lovely. A precious burden. In her black sightlessness, Ashland's enormous body was all there was in the universe.

She could not hear the clock in the other room, but she imagined that if she could, the ticks would arrive with a preternatural slowness, the way her heart beat now. As if held back by the hand of God.

Atop her, Ashland didn't move. His endless weight pressed her into the mattress, warm and delicious; his breath stirred her hair. The beat of his heart shattered through her, an even slower rhythm than her own: How was that possible?

How was it possible, that of all the manifold pleasures he had wreaked upon her unsuspecting body tonight, the greatest pleasure of all was lying with him afterward? Like this, as his breath and his heart mingled with hers, as his organ remained stiff and snug inside her? She flexed herself around him, just for the echo of sensation, and a little groan stirred in his throat.

Emilie drew a delicate line along his back with her finger. His shirt was stuck to his skin, damp with exertion. How heavenly, to touch him like this. Her thoughts meandered pleasantly through the mist in her brain. An image flashed and was gone: Ashland's nimble fingers moving a single chess piece in the candlelight. A knight. Those same nimble fingers that had just now parted her flesh, that had caressed her into ecstasy.

She could not believe her own memory.

But there was no denying the blissful lassitude in her muscles, the faint shimmer of aftermath. The stretching ache between her legs, where Ashland still laid claim.

It had happened. She had given herself to him. She had seized ownership of that invaluable and irreplaceable commodity—a princess's virginity—and awarded it according to her own choice. She had triumphed over her fate. There would be consequences, there would be endless complications, but she wouldn't think about that yet. She would only savor this simple and clear-edged moment.

Ashland stirred. She ran her hand down his arm, his right arm, and found the edge of his empty cuff. "How did you lose it?" she asked softly. "Did your enemies cut it off?"

He made as if to draw it away, but she held firm.

"No," he said. "A British army surgeon performed that service, after I returned to camp."

"How was it injured?"

He sighed and turned his head away from her. His hair prickled against her face. "The human hand contains an abundance of nerve endings, making it eminently suitable as an object of torture."

Emilie ran her fingers over the rounded end. It felt surprisingly smooth and unscarred, like an elbow. "Does it still hurt?"

"Not of any consequence."

"I don't believe you."

He sighed again, his only movement. Even the stump—oh, what an awful name for a part of him she loved, as she loved every part of him—even the stump lay like a weight in her hand. "There is a phantom effect," he said. "Well documented in medical literature. The hand feels as if it's still there."

"How extraordinary." She went on caressing him, exploring him.

He went on, in a distant voice. "In Eastern countries, the left hand is considered profane, because it's used for cleaning oneself after evacuation. That was why they maimed the right one. A rather subtle touch."

She lifted the stump to her lips and kissed it.

"Forgive me," he said. "I ought to have realized, or at least to have asked. I ought to have stopped, when I knew."

"I wouldn't have let you stop."

He raised himself suddenly, eased his organ from her body, and rolled away. "The fault was mine."

"Don't go!"

The cool air engulfed her skin in his absence. She felt the mattress dip and sway as he left. She pulled her eviscerated body up on her elbows. "Where are you going?"

"One moment," he said.

She heard his footsteps on the carpet, the creak of a door, the hiss of the faucet. A rush of wetness trickled between her legs. Panic seized her. She reached down and was shocked by the copiousness of it, by the abundant physical evidence of what had just occurred. Ashland's warm seed: She was brimming with it.

What had she done?

He returned, with a hand to her shoulder. "Lie back," he said gently, and she was too stunned to do anything but obey. Of course his semen was inside her. That was the point of everything, wasn't it? The transcendent pleasures of carnal union were no more than nature's method of ensuring that animals reproduced themselves.

Something warm and damp touched the soreness between her legs. Ashland was cleaning her silently, in tender movements, wiping her with a cloth of some kind. A wave of acute embarrassment washed over her. A moment ago, they were impossibly intimate, joined together, sharing breath; now, a kind of clinical detachment separated them as he washed away the remnants of their private act.

"Are you in pain?" he asked.

"I . . . No. Not of any consequence." She tried to smile, to reestablish the closeness. "It was rather wonderful, if you must know."

The mattress released him once more, and he went away, presumably back to the bathroom to return the cloth. Emilie sat up. The blood rushed away from her head, leaving her slightly dizzy. She put her hand to her head and found her false chignon nearly hanging from its pins. In hasty movements she repaired the damage, adjusted the blindfold to cover the untidiness. Her chemise must be on the floor somewhere. She slid off the bed onto shaky legs.

"Careful!" Ashland's hand came down on her arm.

"I was looking for my chemise."

"Right here." The hand went away, and then the material was sliding over her head and Ashland was helping her arms into the sleeves.

"Thank you," she said.

"Of course." A pause. "You're quite all right?"

"Yes."

Oh God, the awkwardness! She was flushing again. What was he thinking? Did she disgust him now? In her abandonment, had she passed the bounds of respectable behavior? Had she done it all wrong?

He had not moved away. Though he wasn't touching her, his warmth irradiated her. His voice, however, was cold and matter-of-fact. "I'm afraid you've missed your train. The room is yours, of course. I shall send Mrs. Scruton with everything you need."

"I don't require anything."

"Don't be a martyr," he said sharply.

She recoiled. "A martyr!"

"You don't have to refuse everything."

"Obviously, I haven't refused *everything*," she said bitterly.

Ashland made some movement next to her, and his warmth abruptly withdrew from the nearby air. "I see," he said. "As I said, the fault is mine. I take full responsibility for what occurred tonight. I ought to have restrained myself. I did not, however, and having . . . having committed the wrong, I assure you I . . ."

"Wrong!" She gestured to the bed. "This was *wrong* to you? I thought it was beautiful. I thought it was precious!"

"Emilie . . ."

"Go," she said. "Just go."

"I will *not* leave like this . . ."

"You *will* go. You can't have everything your own way. I meet you when you ask, I follow your rules, I discard all modesty, I give myself to you in shameless abandon without even *seeing* you. Allow me a little pride. Allow me this one dignity, at least." She was panting, her hands fisting at her sides. She couldn't even direct her rage. She was shouting into open space, unable to locate him in the darkness.

Ashland said nothing. Outside the window, the wind made a strange whistling sound, piercing the still bedroom like Miss Dingleby's finely honed stiletto.

The floorboards creaked beneath the carpet.

"Very well, then, madam." Ashland's low voice counterpointed the high pitch of the Yorkshire wind, unexpectedly close. "Remove the blindfold, if it offends your dignity. If you want to see what creature has taken your innocence tonight."

Emilie froze.

"Go ahead," he said softly. "Or do you wish me to take it off for you?"

The windows rattled sharply. A tiny draft reached Emilie's cheek, too warm to have slipped in from outside. Ashland's breath? In the darkness around her, she felt his shimmering heat, his power just out of reach, perhaps inches away.

"I . . . I cannot." She lowered her head. "I cannot."

"Ah. Well, there it is."

A wave of hopelessness washed over her. Their perfect, sacred moment had been only that, after all—a moment. Someone's voice echoed in her head, some half-drunk stepmother or another: *Don't you know, all the little beasts want is a good poke, and they're off. Give that up, and you've given everything.*

She turned away. "Go."

Ashland's hand seized her chin. "Don't turn away from me, Emilie. I've told you I'm sorry; what the devil do you want from me?"

"Nothing! Nothing at all! Only to be left in peace."

"By God, you won't have that! A moment ago you were spending beneath me. You're *mine* now, Emilie. You're under *my* protection, and I'll be damned if . . ."

"I am *not* yours!"

"You are, and by God, I take care of my own!" His mouth came down on hers, hard, possessive, and Emilie wanted to pull back. She wanted to put her hands on his chest and push him away, to sweep off with a haughty and well-delivered line.

But her principled objections stopped at the stem of her brain. Her lips, unaware of any insult, opened up and absorbed the force of his kiss. Her arm flung up around his neck and drew him closer. His clean scent, his rich taste were too good to refuse. Her body recognized his, remembered the pleasure of him, and wanted more.

At the instant of her acquiescence, Ashland's kiss softened. His tongue ran along her lips, scorching her blood; he searched her out, teased and stroked her without mercy. She pressed her hips against his massive thighs, pressed her tingling breasts against the hard buttons of his waistcoat. His hand slid downward to cover the curve of her bottom with his hot palm.

"God forgive me, I want you again." His lips crept along her jaw to her ear. "I shall take care of you, Emilie. You will let me take care of you."

"I don't need that. I only need *this*."

"*This* is not enough." He kissed her again and pulled away. "I cannot stay the night this time, Emilie, but I *will* make this right."

"I don't require . . ."

"I won't insult you by offering money," he said, "because you have done me an honor without price."

"Oh, very well put."

He said nothing. Emilie wrapped her arms under her breasts, creating a protective barrier against the chill of his absence. "I beg your pardon. That was bitterly said. I only mean that . . . that you have no obligation to me. I have come to you as an independent woman of free will. You owe me nothing for this. We are lovers, nothing more."

Still, he said nothing, did nothing. She felt him gazing at her, boiling with emotion, laying down his hard iron bands of self-control.

"I am not practiced at this, Emilie," he said at last, so quietly the words seemed to dissolve in the air as he said them. "I have no adroit phrases ready. But let me make something quite clear: I am not a man who takes lovers."

Emilie's chest constricted. "Then what do you call this? A *wrong*? An accident?"

"I don't believe in accidents." He was moving again, rustling the air. Putting on his coat, perhaps, and straightening his necktie. "Rest, Emilie. Until next week."

"Wait, sir . . ."

But his lips were brushing her forehead, just above the seam of the blindfold, and before she could say a word, she knew from the emptiness in the air that he was gone.

If the Duke of Ashland had encountered his son's tutor lurking about the servants' entrance of Ashland Abbey at one o'clock in the morning, disheveled, pale, and unsteady, he would have sacked him on the spot.

Luckily, Emilie thought, skulking across the courtyard shadows with tender care for her newly breached female parts, the Duke of Ashland was wallowing in his ducal bed of guilt at the moment. She had watched his window carefully from the stables, waiting until the last light winked out at last, before hazarding the journey into the house. Her parts had protested wildly. Her parts wanted to be wallowing in bed with the duke, getting breached anew.

You are as mad as a hatter, she told herself. *As thick as a tree*.

She crept along next to the brick wall, remaining just outside the dim yellow block of light from the lamp in an upstairs window.

You've risked everything, and for what?

What was she doing here? She'd never skulked home in the dead of night in her life. That was Stefanie's sort of lark. Mischievous, naughty, delightful Stefanie. Everybody loved Stefanie. If Stefanie were caught—which she never was—everybody would have laughed. Oh, that Stefanie. Off on a lark again. Emilie had always been the one to answer the clink of stone on their bedroom window, to go downstairs through the catacomb of service rooms and let Stefanie in through the kitchen delivery entrance, to tuck her into bed and lie next to her and listen to her stories. The village festivals, the midnight dances, the illicit sips of foam-topped hefeweizen, the sheep herded into the mayor's public audience chamber to be discovered in the morning.

Now it was Emilie's turn to sneak in the back entrance in the dead of night. She was dressed in trousers, she smelled like a stable, and she had just had her female parts thoroughly and passionately breached in a luxurious hotel bedroom. Blindfolded. With her employer. Her *married* employer. Whose child she might conceivably have . . . well, conceived.

At least there were no sheep involved.

Well, she'd wanted adventure, hadn't she? She'd wanted freedom, and choice, and independence. Perhaps it had all proved a bit more . . . *complicated*, that was the word . . . a bit more *complicated* than she had imagined, but she'd done it.

Now all she wanted was a warm bath and a warm bed. If it were warm enough, she might even forgive it for not containing one *very* warm, very virile duke.

Warm bath. Warm bed. She reached for the door latch and pushed.

The door held firm.

She rattled the latch and pushed again.

No effect.

The wind whistled around the corner of the kitchen courtyard. Above her head, the winter moon broke apart a pair of clouds to illuminate the old abbey stones.

Emilie drew in a deep breath and leaned her entire body against the door. Nothing. She slammed herself against the wood with force. She kicked. She swore. She leaned again, driving with her legs, and prayed.

Locked out. To top everything off.

She swore again, a particularly explicit vulgarism.

A low whistle came from behind her, slurred and tuneless. "What the devil did you just say, Grimsby?"

Emilie's hand froze on the latch. She straightened slowly and turned around. "*Mr.* Grimsby," she said.

Frederick, Marquess of Silverton, sordid and disheveled, hat backward, scarf missing, lifted up his gloved hand to tug at his earlobe. "Mister Grimsby. I don't b'lieve I heard you proper. That sort of thing ain't possible. Can't be done, without you . . . without . . . well, it can't be done by a vert . . . verteb . . ."

"Vertebrate animal," said Emilie. "I quite agree. My mistake. We shall consult the anatomy book in the morning for a more reasonable epithet."

"Really, Mister Grimsby," said Freddie, smiling lopsidedly, "a man of your inte . . . intel . . . brains. Surely you ain't gone out of an evening without this little beauty." His pupils worked desperately to focus. He reached one hand into his pocket and drew out a small metal object.

"The key," said Emilie. "Of course."

"Had a copy made m'self." Freddie brandished it with pride. "Most prized poss . . . possess . . . thing I own. Guard it with my life. I . . . Oh damn." He looked down at the mottled brickwork before him. "Where's it gone?"

Emilie sighed and reached down to retrieve the key. "You are inebriated, your lordship."

"I am not ineb . . . in . . . drunk."

"You are, and we will discuss this in the morning. You are far too young to be indulging in drink to such a degree. I ought to have escorted you home myself. Instead, I trusted you to follow my instructions." She fit the key into the old and half-frozen lock, praying it would turn. "I shall have to take this up with your father, I'm afraid."

"Oh, I think not," said Freddie.

"I think so." The lock gave way. Emilie's shoulders slumped in relief. She eased the door open and held her finger to her lips.

"I think not," said Freddie, in a loud stage whisper. "B'cause I think His Al . . . Almight . . . His Grace won't like your being out so late y'self. If you take my meaning." He stumbled over the doorjamb, caught himself on the wall, and stood staring at the plaster for an elongated second. "I think I might be sick."

"You *should* be sick. Violently sick. It would teach you a most edifying lesson, I believe." She looked down at the key in her palm and slipped it into her coat pocket. Freddie was right, of course. She couldn't risk the duke wondering why his son's tutor was arriving home so late on this particular night, of all nights.

"You're a cruel, cruel man," Freddie said to the wall. He swiveled his head to face Emilie, his crown still propped against its fixed and stable point, forcing back his hat. His eyes squinted shut. His voice turned quiet and serious, a little pleading. "You won't tell Pater, Mr. Grimsby, will you?"

The hallway was dim, lit only by the moonlight, which was fading quickly as the clouds resumed their rightful place in the Yorkshire sky. Emilie shut the door behind them and turned the lock. "No, I won't tell him. But you must promise me faithfully, your lordship, that this sort of affair shall not be repeated. For one thing, it's bad for your health. And for another thing, you might not be so lucky next time, arriving home in one piece."

Freddie lifted an arm in dismissal. "No one would dare. They all know Pater'd . . . He'd . . ." He swallowed, looking a trifle green. "I think I'd better go upstairs."

Emilie slung his arm over her shoulder. "Right we go, then."

Upstairs they staggered, using the back staircase, and down the long, darkened hallway to Freddie's room. Emilie kept her eyes fixed ahead as they passed the imposing door to the ducal chamber. "That's it. Just a few more steps. Remember"—she panted, because Freddie's long shanks weighed a great deal more than they appeared—"remember to drink a pitcher of water before you retire."

"How . . . how the devil do you know about that?" Freddie muttered.

"It's what my father always did. Here we are."

Emilie helped him through the door. Was it her imagination, or did the place smell different at night? The same scents of old smoke and polish and leather, but laced with something else, some tang of night air. She removed Freddie's arm from her aching shoulders. "There you are. The rest is up to you, I'm afraid."

"You're a trump, Grim . . . Gr . . . Oh damn." Freddie removed his hat and gloves and tossed them in the general direction of a blue wing chair. He looked blearily at her. "I shan't forget it."

"See that you don't." She turned to leave.

"Wait! Grimsby!"

She cocked her head back. "Yes, your lordship?"

Freddie was motioning with his fingers about his face. "There's something . . . something . . . wrong . . ."

"Are you all right, sir? Do you need a basin?" She started for the cabinet against the wall.

"No, no. I mean, yes, I b'lieve I do, godawful sick, but . . . but that . . ." He motioned about his face again, narrowed his eyes. "That ain't it."

"Are you in pain? Have you been hurt?"

"No, no. Jus' a moment. It's . . . it's coming . . . I . . . thinking . . . thinking . . ."

Emilie removed her spectacles, wiped the lenses, and replaced them on her nose. "Don't strain your faculties too hard, your lordship. You'll need them in the morning. I have in mind a most rigorous . . ."

He snapped clumsily. "I've got it!"

"Got *what*, your lordship? I really must be in bed."

Freddie pointed at Emilie's chin. "It's your whiskers, Grimsby. Your . . . damned old . . . whiskers. Where the devil have they gone?"

FIFTEEN

At half past four in the morning, Emilie gave up trying to sleep. She rose from her bed, dressed with clumsy fingers, stuck on her whiskers, and went downstairs to the library.

God knew she was tired enough. She'd slept a fitful hour immediately upon lying down, and then started back awake just as the duke's body lowered itself upon hers and began to transform from skin into fur, his growl of pleasure to sharpen into a snarl. She lay awake, breathing hard, unable to move at the vivid reality of it all.

It's your whiskers. Where the devil have they gone?

She'd told Freddie she'd shaved them. What else could she say? She could only hope that he was drunk enough to have forgotten the whole thing in the morning, or at least believe her when she denied knowledge of the episode. He was certainly drunk enough to accept the bit about the shaving without a blink of surprise. *Oh, right*, he'd said blearily, and turned around to vomit into the washbasin.

The day outside was still winter dark, as black as midnight, and the air was chilled. Emilie crept down the back stairs with every muscle aching. The sins of the night had come back with a vengeance: She felt as if she'd been wrung out, piece by piece, and laid out to stiffen in the sun. Between her legs, her flesh tingled and stung, scraping with acute sensitivity against the seam of her trousers.

Perhaps dresses weren't such a nuisance after all.

The library lay on the other side of the house. The dear and comfortable library, her favorite room: Surely there she could nestle with a book in one of the wide chairs. She could lay the fire—she knew how to do that, now—and perhaps even fall asleep for a precious hour or so, before the rest of the household awakened.

She scampered down the cavernous hallway, the spine of the house, from which all the principal rooms connected. Past glowering portraits and a pair of knights sprung from some impossibly giant race—Ashland's height was evidently not an accident of nature—and the white marble statue of Apollo, her favorite, though his essential bits had been made sacrifice at some point to delicate English sensibilities.

She was just crossing past an open doorway when a faint sound reached her ears. A rhythmic beat, sharp thumps muffled by the walls.

She turned to the door. A hint of yellow light glowed from the bottom of a long and narrow staircase.

For an instant, her dream reared up before her, more vivid than before: Ashland's snarl, his damp fur beneath her fingers.

Don't be ridiculous, she thought. *It's only the servants, beating carpets or . . . or churning butter. Some household chore or another.*

Was that grunting? Just before each beat, almost merged together.

Emilie hesitated, poised at the top of the stairs. She looked down the hall toward the library, quiet and peaceful. Empty.

Of course this was nothing. Dreams were nothing.

She would walk down those stairs right now and prove it.

Emilie gathered her breath and took one step. And another.

The sounds continued, *grunt-thump, grunt-thump, grunt-thump*. Louder now, more resolved. A scent rose up from the stones, not unpleasant, slightly damp. Like a cave at the seaside.

At the bottom of the stairs, the passage went left. A rectangle of light lay upon the plain gray stones. Emilie's last thought, as she turned the corner, was that it should have been colder down here. That the dampness held a trace of warmth.

Before her, the hall opened up into a room, lit by several oil lamps. In the center of the room danced the Duke of Ashland, barefoot, stripped to the waist, his white hair wet and blazing, both hands covered in dark leather gloves. He was thrusting his arms, punching a large oblong leather bag that hung from the ceiling and swayed mightily at every strike.

Both hands: Of course she meant his hand and his stump, but they were equal now, with those padded gloves fixed snugly at each wrist. He was facing away from her, at an angle, the massiveness of his body balanced with weightless grace on the balls of his feet. His back gleamed with sweat, each muscle etched in perfect symmetry by the light, tapering to a pair of hips covered in snug pale trousers.

He was magnificent.

She stood there openmouthed, eyes agape, not making a sound.

Without warning, Ashland whipped around. "What the . . ." He steadied the leather bag with one hand. "Oh! It's you, Grimsby. What the devil are you doing up so early?"

Emilie's limbs turned to jelly.

From behind, he had been magnificent. From the front, he was godlike. His hard face bore its black mask like a badge of honor; his shoulders were broad enough to pull a plow. His chest heaved up and down with male exertion. Not a single wrinkle of extra flesh marred the musculature of chest and abdomen, like an anatomist's model. A pair of converging grooves pointed suggestively downward under the fastening of his trousers.

"Grimsby? Is something wrong?"

She returned her eyes to his face and gulped. "Nothing, sir! I beg your pardon. I couldn't sleep. A bit befuddled, I'm afraid. I wasn't expecting you."

His eyebrow arched. "Were you wanting a swim?"

Emilie's brain was a muddled collage of blade-sharp quadriceps and flexing pectorals. Her mouth filled. "Swim?"

Ashland made a motion with his arm. "The pool."

She glanced in the direction he indicated. A flash of light came from around the corner, as if reflected from water.

"The pool," she said numbly, "of course."

Ashland angled his head to the leather bag. "Go on, if you like. I won't be finished for a while yet."

Emilie realized she was staring at his lips. A few hours ago, those lips had been *kissing* her. The tongue inside that mouth had been *eating her alive*, making her scream with pleasure. That ridged chest, those shoulders, those impossibly trim hips had been *driving into her*.

This was what lay behind those layers of clothing he wouldn't remove.

Dear. Heavenly. Father. She was going to faint.

Ashland was frowning. "Grimsby, are you certain you're all right? You look a little queer."

A mist was rising before her eyes. She really *was* going to faint.

"Grimsby, your spectacles," said Ashland.

"My spectacles?"

"They've fogged over. It's the pool, I'm afraid. We keep it heated during the colder months. Freddie's damned idea; I prefer it bracing."

"Oh!" Emilie removed her spectacles, ducking her head as she did so. She wiped away the steam and put them back on her nose. "Of course you do," she muttered.

Between her legs, she was feeling rather . . . warm. She shifted her weight.

"You're welcome to pick up a pair of gloves and spar with me, if you like," Ashland was saying. His eyes swept briefly over her. "You look as though you could use a bit of heft. Strengthen you up."

"No, no. I don't, er, *spar*, as a rule. I am a . . . a man of peace." She straightened herself. "And stronger than I look."

Ashland shrugged. "Do as you like, then. As I said, you've free use of the place, and swimming's excellent exercise. Shall stroke off myself shortly." He turned back to his punching bag, all sinuous power. His trousers fit economically around the hard curve of his buttocks.

His trousers, which he would undoubtedly remove to (dear God!) *stroke off* in the bathing pool.

Emilie swallowed. "I think . . . perhaps . . . I shall find a book in the library instead."

Why does His Grace keep a bathing pool in the lower level of the house?"

Freddie looked up from his plate of steaming morning offal. His face bore a gray green cast, like a lump of clay left to gather algae in a stagnant pond. "*Must* you do that?"

"Do what, your lordship?"

"Talk."

"The breakfast table, your lordship, is, or ought to be, the scene of civilized conversation, where members of the household come together with convivial . . ."

Freddie brought his cup to his lips, tilted back his head, and drained it.

". . . fellowship." Emilie eyed her charge. "That *is* tea, isn't it?"

"Coffee, Mr. Grimsby. Black."

"Ah yes. Just like your father. Which returns me to the point: Why does the duke maintain a bathing pool?"

The footman moved up noiselessly to refill Freddie's cup. He stared queasily at the stream of black liquid. "Oh, that. He had it installed soon after he returned from abroad. The doctors recommended sea bathing, but of course he wasn't going to a public seaside like the rest of humanity, oh no."

"It isn't *sea*water, is it?"

"It is." Freddie picked up his cup, drank, scalded himself, and set down the cup again with an oath and a clatter. "Shipped in fresh by rail every month. Haven't you noticed the delivery? Converted fire engine brings it in from the railway station. Confounded fuss."

"I had no idea. None at all."

Freddie blew carefully over the top of his cup and tried again. "Of course, I admit it's rather nice to be able to swim in the convenience of one's own home. I made them heat it, of course. It's as good as swimming in the Arctic in wintertime, otherwise."

"So your father told me."

Freddie glanced up, amused. "Caught him at it, did you?"

"No. He was at boxing practice." Emilie selected a third piece of toast from the rack at her right. She was feeling quite remarkably hungry this morning, for some reason.

"Oh yes. He does that, too. A regular John Sullivan, my Pater. Jolly reassuring, should we be waylaid by a gang of prizefighters while trotting across the moors some afternoon. Is that the newspaper?"

"It is." She pushed it toward him. Freddie's face was beginning to lose its greenish tinge, under the effects of the coffee. Her own thoughts were reeling. Did Ashland really rise before each dawn and exercise like this? Boxing and swimming and God knew what else? She had been breakfasting in the family dining room for weeks now—a single invitation that had somehow stretched into a habit—and never noticed a sign of recent rigorous exercise in Ashland's demeanor. For what reason did he do it? Why should a duke, a man who scarcely ever dined in company, let alone left his estate to face the physical dangers of the wide world, keep his body honed in such battle-ready shape? As if he were preparing for some great test. She lifted her own coffee—also black, God help her—and tried to banish the thought of Ashland striking that punching bag, his muscles bunching effortlessly under his glowing skin.

Of Ashland's body atop hers, connected with hers, heated and powerful, stroking into her with exquisite strength.

Beneath her neat jacket, her plain wool waistcoat and cotton shirt, the linen bandage binding her chest, Emilie's breasts tingled painfully. She cleared her tightened throat and finished her toast. "Speaking of which, where is His Grace at the moment? He's never been so late for breakfast."

Freddie looked up. "Oh, that. Hadn't you heard? Pater's gone off."

Emilie's knife clattered on her plate. "Gone off?"

Freddie waved his hand. "Off. Gone. Exit, pursued by a stag."

"A bear."

"Whatever it is. Absconded to London, at the crack of . . . dawn . . ." He stared at her and frowned.

"London!" Emilie's forehead stretched upward with astonishment, causing her spectacles to slide down her nose. She pushed them up hastily. "The duke in *London*! Whatever for?"

"I haven't the foggiest. I'm quite as perplexed as you."
Freddie cocked his head, still frowning, his eyes fixed on Emilie's face. "Daresay things have gone along so swimmingly with this new bird of his, he's decided to try his luck in the capital."

Emilie's fingers went cold. "I . . . I daresay."

"You know . . . the oddest thing . . ." Freddie said slowly.

Emilie stared down at her plate. The yolks of her half-eaten eggs had met a pool of grease from the kippers, and were beginning to congeal. Her enormous appetite had evaporated. "What's that?" she asked absently.

"No, no," he said hastily. "A dream. I'm sure of it. Ha-ha. A dream, of course."

She glanced up. "A dream?"

Freddie was plunging his fork into his breakfast, looking miraculously human, a living testament to the restorative powers of strong black coffee. "Ha-ha. You'll never credit it. Last night, you see, I dreamt that you'd shaved those whiskers of yours."

"Ha-ha." She picked up her cup and hid behind it.

Freddie stuffed his mouth and smiled reminiscently. "Astonishingly vivid dream. I can see your face quite plainly, shorn as a newborn lamb."

"Newborn lambs aren't shorn, as a rule."

"Well, but you *looked* like a precious little newborn baa-lamb, without your whiskers. All wide-eyed and innocent. Gone, the avenging tutor! Ha-ha." Freddie threw back another cup of coffee. "I should sketch it out before I forget. Then the next time you're scolding me, I'll bring it out to remind myself of your humiliation."

"I wasn't humiliated." Emilie glanced at the footman's impassive face. "It was only a dream, after all. *Your* dream."

"And a dashed fine dream at that. The memory has quite cheered me up." Freddie used his toast to wipe the rest of his egg, shoved the lot gracelessly in his mouth, swabbed himself with a snowy napkin, and stood up. "I shall await you in the schoolroom, Mr. Grimsby. Don't be late!" He tucked the newspaper under his arm, clicked his heels together, and swept from the room.

Emilie knew she should rise and follow him, but her limbs

wouldn't move. She stared at her toast, uncomfortably aware of Lionel the footman standing ten feet away, probably annoyed, probably impatient for the damned tutor to lift his bony arse out of his seat and leave the room to the poor sods who did the *real* work around the Abbey. She'd come to a much deeper understanding of what it meant to be a servant, these past several weeks.

The Duke of Ashland had left for London.

What did it mean? Trying his luck in the capital, as Freddie put it? Now that the ice had been broken. Now that he'd finally lain with another woman. The deed had been done. One sin might as well be a hundred.

Emilie clenched her fists in her lap.

Think logically. Of course Ashland hadn't gone to London to find more women. It wasn't in his character at all. Emilie thought of his words last night, his disciplined arms pounding the leather bag downstairs. He was not a wastrel. He was not a rake. This trip to London must be some business affair, some urgent matter.

In any case, it shouldn't bother her, even if he *were* after women. She should welcome his straying to other pastures. The sooner this tie between them was snapped off, the better. And since she didn't seem to have the strength, Ashland might as well do the snapping himself. She would spend this week of his absence constructing a very high, very thick wall between them. By the time he returned, she would be quite indifferent.

Or at least able to greet the sight of his half-naked, gloriously glowing body with perfect composure.

Emilie finished her toast, finished her coffee in a gulp. She rose and nodded to Lionel, who returned—to her surprise— an almost imperceptible nod of his own.

Outside in the hallway, she nearly crashed into Simpson as he strode toward the breakfast room. "Oh! I beg your pardon, Mr. Simpson."

"Not at all, Mr. Grimsby," said Simpson, as he might say, *Take your arse to Greenland, Grimsby, on a fucking flat-bottomed rowboat.*

Emilie was undeterred. "I understand His Grace departed for London this morning. When can his lordship and I expect his return?" She inserted Freddie's name into it, just to ensure the butler's attention.

Simpson looked as if he'd been handed a week-old pig's bladder and asked to make a sausage with it. "His Grace did me the honor of informing me that he would be absent a week."

"Seven full days?"

"So much I have always understood a week to contain."

"How perceptive you are, Mr. Simpson. I am in your debt." Emilie turned and marched down the hall to the staircase— the main staircase, used by the family—and went up three flights to the schoolroom, where the Marquess of Silverton stood in the center of the carpet, blue eyes globular, newspaper fluttering from his hand, staring at her with an expression of utmost shock.

"Good God, Grimsby!" he said. "You're a bloody *princess*, aren't you?"

SIXTEEN

A shocked silence greeted the Duke of Ashland as he paused in the doorway of the dining room at his London club.

He expected nothing less. He hadn't darkened this particular threshold in well over a decade, not since the eve of his departure with his regiment. A riotous evening, that one. He'd crawled back into his hotel room just as his old friend dawn, the rosy-fingered bitch, had broken the horizon in the east. An hour's sleep, a bracing bath, a mug of coffee, and he'd been off to Victoria Station to join his regiment massing at Southampton. God, that rattling train. His head still ached in sympathy at the memory.

The mood at the club tonight was something less than riotous, and the stunned faces turned toward him were even less familiar. He remembered the smell, though—that exact blend of roasted meat and smoke, leather and spirits, wafted out to greet him as if he'd been away only a week or two. *Eau de club*, he supposed. He kept his gaze high, scanning over the tops of their befuddled gentlemanly heads, but he could feel them take him in: his white hair, his black leather half-mask, his ruined jaw protruding beneath. Perhaps even the empty space outside the cuff of his right sleeve, which he kept defiantly at his side, in full view.

At one time—indeed, for the last twelve years—he had dreaded this moment. Tonight, for some reason, he found he didn't give a damn what everyone saw.

A chair scraped. "By God. Ashland, you old bastard. What brings you to London?"

Ashland adjusted his gaze and found his mouth breaking open in a genuine smile. "Penhallow! I'd no idea the club's standards had sunk so low in my absence." He reached out his arm, his right arm, and Lord Roland Penhallow grasped the stump in both hands without the smallest particle of self-consciousness.

"You've saved my life, old man," Penhallow said heartily, a wide grin splitting his own impossibly handsome face. He shrugged one shoulder at the mass of curious manhood assembled behind him. "This sorry lot was boring me to tears. Join us?"

Ashland shot a quick glance at the table from which Penhallow had risen. Nobody he recognized, of course. A young fellow, Penhallow, still at Eton when Ashland had left for India, but as the grandson of the Duke of Olympia he'd traipsed across Ashland's past a few times. He had even been among the few to visit at Ashland Abbey—*my grandsire asked me to pop in on you on my way to Edinburgh and try out this fantastical bathing pool of yours*—and Ashland had found himself rather enjoying the lad's company. He had a way of neither staring at nor ignoring Ashland's scars, simply carrying on as a matter of course. Rather like young Grimsby. Rather like Emily, too, and his heart cracked anew at the memory of her gentle kiss at the end of his arm.

"Tempting," Ashland said, "but in fact I was hoping to find your grandfather doddering about. They informed me on Park Lane that he might be found here this evening."

Penhallow lifted both eyebrows—he had never quite mastered the elegant art of raising just one—and said, "Why, no. Not that I've noticed." He turned back to his table of friends and called out, "Don't suppose you've seen my old grandsire dodder past this evening, Burke?"

At the table, a tall red-haired gentleman set down his wine-glass and shrugged. "Not once, I'm afraid."

"Ah well," said Penhallow. "Mind you, the chap's got a distinct habit of turning up when he's least expected. Do join us, however. You must. Burke's been trying to convince me to run off to Italy with him for a year of monastic seclusion, and I'm having the devil of a time explaining to him that it simply won't do."

Penhallow took him by the arm and led him inexorably forward between the tables. One by one, the occupants turned politely away, returning to their conversations, casting only the discreet glance or two his way. "Gentlemen," said Penhallow, "I have the honor of presenting to you the legendary Duke of Ashland, who's finally deigned to honor us rubbishy degenerates here in London with a visit, so you'd better mind your p's and all that."

At the words *Duke of Ashland*, the four men at the table shed their shared air of incurious somnolence and shot to their feet in a simultaneous volley. It was all *Your Grace! Didn't know it was you*, and *Your Grace! Most honored, sir*, and in a moment Ashland was seated with a bottle of best claret flowing freely into his glass.

Which was, he reflected, taking the first swallow, exactly how his last evening at the club had begun.

Except for all the *Your Grace*s. That had begun upon his return.

I'm afraid I don't quite understand, Your Grace." The solicitor fidgeted with his fountain pen, turning it this way and that, rolling it from finger to finger. His face was still the same mottled red it had turned when the Duke of Ashland was first announced into his chambers. "Do you wish to cut off the allowance entirely?"

Ashland stretched out one leg on the expensive Oriental rug and plucked a piece of lint from his trousers. Outside, the brown January fog had laid against his skin with a chill that went to his bones; here, the room was heated to tropical strength, coals sizzling hotly in the fireplace. It reminded him of India, of that suffocating and inescapable warmth, drenching him to the core. "Mr. Baneweather, since we made these arrangements twelve years ago, when Her Grace first left the protection of my roof, I have not seen her, nor made any effort to follow her movements. In return, I have heard nothing, either of her or from her. Having instructed you to inform me if her monthly allowance went uncollected, I have assumed her to be alive and well. At the moment, I simply wish to ascertain her whereabouts and mode of living, with a view to initiating a suit of divorce at the earliest opportunity."

"I see." Mr. Baneweather glanced down at the neat stack of papers before him. "May I ask what brought about this change of heart? I recall you were adamant, *most* adamant, that the marriage should be allowed to stand, despite my advice at the time."

"Twelve years have passed, Mr. Baneweather. My son is nearly grown. In addition, I have recently formed an attachment to a most worthy young lady." The words came out more easily than he expected. He had chosen them carefully; they sounded much more respectable than the bald truth: *I have debauched and deflowered an innocent young lady of unknown background, and it seems I cannot live without her.*

"Ah. Of course. I confess, Your Grace, I had been hoping for something of this nature. Your case has always . . ."

"To that end, Mr. Baneweather," Ashland went on, "I wish you to supply me with Her Grace's current direction. I shall wish to make such a delicate interview in person. I expect she is abroad?" As if a runaway wife could be anywhere else.

Mr. Baneweather cleared his throat. "In fact, she is not. She lives—that is to say, the address at which she collects her allowance—that particular address is in London. Putney, to be precise."

"Putney!" Ashland started forward in his chair. A sharp pulse shot through his blood: Isabelle in Putney, a mere few miles away. Doing what? Living with whom? He had always imagined her in Europe somewhere, some fashionable place by the sea, Nice or Portofino. He had allowed her a thousand pounds a year, enough to give her an independence, so she should not be obliged to find another protector when Somerton inevitably left her. A thousand pounds ought to give her a luxurious style of life abroad.

Putney. Fashionable, expensive Isabelle, living in the dreary London suburbs. What had happened?

"Yes, Putney. Five or six years, in fact."

"And you did not inform me?"

"You asked not to be informed, Your Grace. With respect." The flush was fading at last from Mr. Baneweather's face.

So Isabelle had been within reach, all this time. Within reach to . . . what? Divorce her? Take her back? The Earl of Somerton had married some beautiful young debutante about five or six years ago; the papers had been full of the news. Was that why Isabelle had returned to England? Ashland pressed his forefinger into his leg to stop the whirl of thoughts in his head. Discipline. Focus. "Very good. So I did. You will please write down this Putney address for me, Mr. Baneweather, and await my further instructions in the matter. In the meantime, I have a contract of sorts for you to draft." He reached into his coat pocket and withdrew a few folded sheets of paper. "I have written down the salient points. I shall need it drafted up properly within a week's time. I can be reached at Brown's hotel."

Ashland rose from his chair and placed the papers at the edge of Mr. Baneweather's endless and gleaming desk. The thin sheets wilted mournfully downward in the warmth.

Baneweather was scribbling furiously. "Here you are, Your Grace," he said, rising. His mustache twitched eagerly. "Is there anything else I can do for you?"

Isabelle in Putney.

Ashland looked down at the paper before him. The familiar scent of fresh ink anchored him to reality as he read the impossible lines. "Nothing else at the moment, Mr. Baneweather." He looked up. "But I expect I shall have further instructions for you shortly."

The hackney deposited him at the end of the street, as he instructed. "Wait for me," he said, tossing the driver a few shillings, and settled his hat snugly on his head.

The London fog was thick today, that grotesque and dank miasma of coal smoke and river damp. It burned his Yorkshire lungs and obscured the details of the houses as he passed: comfortable suburban villas, semi-detached, stained gray by years of fog, with neatly tended gardens and barren January window boxes.

Isabelle's house lay near the end of the street, exactly like its neighbors. The left-hand house of the pair, with a neat number 4 painted above the door. He paused for an instant at the little gate outside the steps. He hadn't the faintest idea what to say to her. An awkward interview, that was inevitable; and entirely unexpected on her part. What if a man lived there, too? What would he say? He drummed his gloved fingers on the cold wrought iron. Oddly enough, he felt not a hint of nervousness. No rattling heartbeat, no tingle of anticipation. Only curiosity, mingled with impatience: an eagerness to have this interview over, to snip off this dangling thread in his life.

He opened the gate, crunched up the gravel path, and let fall the knocker on the door.

A woman answered, dressed in a neat black uniform. She gave a start at the sight of his broad chest before her eyes, and looked up slowly to find his face. She started again. "Good morning, sir," she squeaked.

"Good morning. I am here to see Her Grace, the Duchess of Ashland."

The maid's mouth rounded into an astonished O. "The . . . the duchess?" she said, in the same helpless squeak.

"The Duchess of Ashland. Or perhaps she no longer affects that name. The lady of the house, if you please."

"I . . . I don't . . . I . . ." She swallowed, evidently torn between Ashland's intimidating appearance and her duty to protect her mistress from unwanted callers. "May I give her your name, sir?" she said at last, clutching the edge of the door.

"Certainly. I am her husband, the Duke of Ashland."

"I . . . Oh!"

"May I come in?"

"Sir, I . . ."

Ashland stepped forward through the doorway, causing the maid to fall back a step or two. "I'll wait in the parlor, if you'll show me through," he said.

"Yes, sir. Your Grace. Of course." She scuttled ahead, showing him into the front room, an overstuffed parlor thick with photographs and mantel cloths and great potted palms.

He spared not a glance for the photographs and went to the window, staring out at the foggy brown streetscape. A delivery van ambled by, pulled by a dark and elderly horse whose ears swung listlessly back and forth. Above Ashland's head, footsteps rattled about, voices muffled through the plaster. Isabelle's voice?

A light tread came down the staircase. Ashland turned to the doorway.

"Your Grace," said the maid, humbly, as she held back the door.

A woman swept in with a loud rustle of blue and yellow silk. Her hair was dark, pulled back severely from her face into a cascade of impossible dark curls; her bustle was so high and proud that Ashland feared for her balance. She stretched out her hands. "Ashland!"

For an instant, he didn't recognize her. And then, incredulous: *"Alice?"*

His sister-in-law took another tottering step. "My dear brother. You ought to have warned me."

Because it was the polite thing, he went to her. He took one of her outstretched hands and kissed the air above it, and he passed her gently into a chair.

"My dear Alice," he said, standing awkwardly by the mantelpiece. "How are you?"

"I have called for tea. Do you like tea?"

"I haven't much time, I'm afraid. I only came to ask after Isabelle. I thought she was here, or so my solicitor informed me." He knew the words sounded stiff and bloodless. He lifted his arm and laid his elbow on the mantel, in a tiny nook of emptiness amongst the bric-a-brac.

"Oh! Well, I'm sorry for the mistake." Alice looked down at her hands, which were knotted correctly in her silken lap. "She isn't here."

"Isn't here at the moment, or doesn't live here?"

"Doesn't live here." She said it in a whisper.

Ashland allowed a little silence to fall. "I don't quite understand. Her quarterly allowance arrives here, according to my solicitor. One thousand pounds a year. A rather handsome sum. I hope this is not some unfortunate *mistake*." He picked up one of the objects, a miniature golden-haired shepherdess, and turned it about his palm. "She is still *alive*, isn't she, Alice?"

"Oh yes! Oh, of course. I . . . I had a letter from her just last week. I . . ."

A knock sounded on the door, and the maid came in with a groaning tray of tea things: pot and cups and cream, cakes and buns without number. She set it down on the round table next to the sofa, made a few adjustments, and straightened. "Will that be all, ma'am?"

"Yes, Polly. Thank you."

The door closed behind the maid, and Alice leaned eagerly forward over the tea tray. "Cream and sugar, Your Grace?"

He didn't give a damn. "Yes."

She bustled about with the tea, hair gleaming in the lamplight. Ashland watched her without moving, the quick nervous flutterings of her hand, the tea spilled over the edge of the cup (*oh dear me! how clumsy*), the slice of cake laid carefully on his plate. "There you are, Your Grace. Isn't it just the thing on such a frightful January morning?"

"Yes." He laid the cup and saucer on the mantel and lifted the paper-thin porcelain to his lips. "Tell me about Isabelle. Is she well?"

"Oh yes. Very well indeed."

"I presume you forward her the money each quarter, as it arrives?" He tilted his head to indicate the well-stocked room about him. "*All* of it?"

Her mouth was buried behind her teacup. "Well . . . that is, not all of it."

"Most of it?"

"Well, that is to say . . ."

"Alice," he said, setting his cup precisely in his saucer, "suppose you tell me exactly where the money goes each month, and why."

"Oh dear." She put her own cup and saucer on the table and wrung her hands together. "I don't know if Isabelle would want . . ."

"I don't give a *damn*, Alice, if you'll pardon the expression. What I want to know is this: Where *exactly* is my wife, and what *exactly* are you doing with her allowance?"

Alice shot to her feet. "Oh, Your Grace. Please don't be

angry. I was only . . . Isabelle asked me to, you see, because she couldn't care for the girl herself, not with . . . with her present company . . ."

"Girl," Ashland said. His limbs went numb. "What girl?"

"Her daughter, Your Grace."

A furious cheeping started up from some cluttered corner of the room. Alice sprang to her feet. "Oh, the silly bird. He sees the tea things, of course. He never could resist a lemon tart." She picked up a plate and dashed to the birdcage.

Ashland watched her feed the bird, heard the chattering of female and parakeet distantly through his humming ears. A liquor tray sat at the far end of the room. He placed his cup and saucer on the tea table and strode toward it. The decanters were brimming, each with an expensive engraved label slung about the neck. He selected the brandy.

"I see." He tossed back his glass in a gulp—half full only; he had that much discipline—and set it down on the tray with a crystalline clink. The brandy burned its way comfortably to his stomach. "This daughter. Where is she now?"

"Why, upstairs with her governess, of course. I hired a French governess for her. Only the best." Alice beamed proudly. "She'll go off to Lady Margaret's next year."

"How old is she?"

"Rising thirteen, Your Grace, and a fine handsome girl she is."

Rising thirteen. "May I see her?"

"I . . ." Alice tugged at the lace on her sleeve. Her brow had compressed into a multitude of worried lines beneath her razor-parted hair. "I suppose there's no harm." She went to the tea table and rang a small bell.

Ashland could not say another word. He turned away when the maid came, and looked out the window again at the deserted street, closing his ears to the whispered conversation behind him. It was nearly noon, but the air outside hung dark and murky as twilight. A few piles of tenacious slush clung to the bases of the streetlamps. A sudden ache invaded his breast: for clean, windswept Yorkshire, for one of Freddie's jokes, for Grimsby's wry ripostes. For Emily's gentle voice, reading a book. Her quick smile, the velvet touch of her skin against his lips.

Home.

The door creaked. "Your Grace?"

Ashland turned. A dark-haired girl stood in the doorway, a tall girl, almost as tall as Alice, who stood behind her charge with ring-strewn hands upon those thin adolescent shoulders. He strained to see the girl's face, but she stood just in the shadow of the lamp burning nearby.

"Good morning," he said. "I am the Duke of Ashland. What is your name?"

She made a little curtsy. "My name is Mary Russell, Your Grace."

The breath left his body. He only just saved himself from falling on his knees. "I see. How old are you, Mary?"

"Thirteen next month, Your Grace." Her voice was reedy but firm, holding its ground before his beastly buccaneer's face.

Thirteen next month. Ashland made a swift mental calculation.

"Step forward, Mary, and ask the duke to sit down," said Alice.

Mary stepped forward, sat down correctly on the sofa, and motioned her arm to the nearby wing chair. "Won't you sit down, Your Grace?"

He eased himself into the chair. Mary's face came into focus next to the lamp.

She was not his.

Her hair was dark, and her eyes were nearly black: the exact color and shape of the Earl of Somerton's eyes, of which Ashland had seen enough to last him a lifetime.

So that was why his wife had left so abruptly. She had become pregnant by her lover. Had thought, perhaps, that a child would be enough to hold a man like Somerton.

"Have you traveled far, Your Grace?" Mary asked him.

"Yes, I have. I arrived in town yesterday, from Yorkshire."

"I hear it is very bleak in Yorkshire."

He smiled. "It is. I think it rather suits me, don't you?"

She tilted her head. "Perhaps. But I daresay such a climate might make anyone bleak, unless one had a great many friends for company. Do you have many friends there?"

"Not nearly enough, I'm afraid, though the ones I have are very dear to my heart."

Mary nodded her dark head. "That's the important thing, of course. Have you had any tea? The cake is very good."

He spoke with her for half an hour, about her studies and about Yorkshire, about the London fog and her recent visit to Hampton Court with her governess. They touched briefly on Henry VIII and all the Annes and Catherines. He rose at last when luncheon was called.

"Will you stay and have luncheon with us, Your Grace?" asked Mary, rising, too.

"I'm afraid not. I have a number of errands, and my time here in London is limited. I have an appointment in Yorkshire next week of the utmost importance."

"I see. It was a very great pleasure to meet you, sir. I believe you are my first duke." Mary offered her hand.

Ashland took her hand with his left and shook it gravely. "I am deeply sensible of the honor, Miss Russell."

When she left, he turned to Alice. "The remittance will continue, but on no account is any of the money to be forwarded to my wife. I shall expect a full report of expenses every quarter. My solicitor will arrange payment of Miss Russell's school fees. Should you have any need of an increase in income, you may apply to me at once."

"Your Grace!"

"In the meantime, I should like you to give me my wife's current direction. I presume she remains in Europe?"

"Why, yes, sir. Of course, sir. But . . . sir, I don't think . . ."

"You will give me her address, Alice, or I shall be forced to begin inquiries. Do you understand me?"

She bowed her head. "Yes, sir."

Ashland didn't open the paper she gave him until he was safely stowed inside the hackney and crossing Putney Bridge into Fulham. He unfolded it and held it up to the meager yellow light from the window, until he could just make out the rounded black letters of his sister-in-law's copperplate handwriting.

SEVENTEEN

"All I'm saying, Grimsby . . ."

"*Mr.* Grimsby."

"Look, I'll bloody well keep calling you Grimsby if you insist, but I'll be damned if I say *Mister*. It's not right." Freddie made an impatient flick of his riding crop.

"And yet, you have no difficulty employing the most offensive language in my presence," said Emilie. "Against that, a male form of address should require no effort at all." A lone snowflake landed on the tip of her nose; she resisted the urge to hold out her tongue for another. She and Stefanie used to do that, out riding in early winter, and while the gray Yorkshire moors bore no resemblance to the lush forests of the Schweinwald, the bite in the air, the unmistakable scent of coming snow, gave her exactly the same childlike thrill.

"Ha. I recall perfectly the expression that came out of your mouth last week, when you was locked out of the house. Absolute filth, Grimsby. I'm sick at the memory. And you not merely a lady, but a princess! Think of your subjects, Your Royal Highness."

"I have no subjects. My sister is the heir." She blew out a white cloud into the air.

"Right-ho. Which brings me directly to the point, now that we're finally off by ourselves. We've got to lay plans."

"Plans for what?"

"Why, for restoring you to your throne, of course!"

The horse moved comfortably beneath Emilie's seat, an easy rocking gait. The wind blew against her cheeks, the same rapacious wind as before, but she minded it less now. It was like an old friend. Even the bleak landscape felt right some-how. "I don't have a throne. And if I did, I wouldn't want to be restored to it. I hated that life. I'm grateful I escaped." As soon as she said the words, she realized they were true. She had no remaining desire to find her father's killer. She had no desire to return to her thick-walled palace existence. She missed her sisters desperately, of course, but that was all. Even dressed as a man, hiding her true identity, she felt more free, more *her-self*, than she ever had before. In her selfish heart, she didn't want justice served.

"Oh, rubbish. What girl doesn't want to be a damned prin-cess? The first thing, of course, is you've got to marry Pater."

Emilie nearly jumped from the saddle. "Marry your father? Are you mad?"

"In the first place, there's your royal honor to consider. I don't suppose he knows he's rogering the lost Princess Emilie of Holstein-whatever-it-is every Tuesday evening in Ashland Spa Hotel, does he?"

"Your *lordship*!"

Freddie tapped his temple beneath the brim of his wool hat. "I can put a few things together, Grimsby. So firstly, he's got to marry you anyway, having debauched you and all that. Sec-ondly, you're clearly in love with him, because otherwise you wouldn't be trotting off to meet him every week. And thirdly . . ."

"I am most certainly *not* in love . . ."

". . . thirdly, Pater would be the most immense use in pro-tecting you and finding those deadly assassins and all that. Imagine him going after the poor chaps with all his vengeful might, doling out justice hither and yon! They wouldn't stand a chance."

"There is a small impediment, your lordship. You forget your father is still married."

Freddie snorted. "I daresay that can be got around pretty efficiently, after twelve years of abandonment by my incomparable mother."

They walked on in silence for a moment, horses playing contentedly with their bits, saddle leather creaking in sympathy with the wind. A few more snowflakes flew by, thicker now. Emilie bent her chin into her scarf and studied the dead winter turf passing between her horse's ears.

"There's another reason." Freddie's voice cut defiantly through the air. "The last reason."

"What's that?"

"You could stay here. Not *here*, obviously, if all this glorious natural beauty ain't to your taste." He waved his crop to the monochrome horizon, the diagonal jags of building snow. "But the three of us, together, wherever it is. I'd even . . . I'd always rather fancied a . . ." He ducked his head, in an uncharacteristic display of embarrassment.

"A what, your lordship?"

"Well, a brother. Or even a sister. A bit late now to be a companion in mischief and all that, but still . . ." He shrugged, a sixteen-year-old's indifferent shrug, masking vulnerability.

Emilie looked up at the heavy sky and blinked her stinging eyes.

"The point is," said Freddie, more brusquely, "you've got to come clean to Pater. The longer you wait, the more he'll rant and rage. You can *trust* Pater, Grimsby. He'll move heaven and earth to help you, you know."

"I know." Emilie was studying the ground ahead, where a great stone formation—known to locals as the Old Lady, because it had apparently once sported a long and wart-flecked nose, before some winter frost a century ago had broken it off—loomed against the lines of snow. Was it her imagination, or did she catch a flicker of movement behind the Old Lady's right ear?

She glanced to the left, where the relative safety of the Ashland Spa road beckoned a half mile away.

"I'll help you, if you like. Warm him up a bit. *Look here, Pater, have you ever imagined old Grimsby without his whiskers? He'd look a damned prime girl.* Or else, *That old Grimsby, what a priceless fellow. Make a fine wife, if only he were a she.* That sort of thing."

"Oh, splendid."

"You could tell him tonight, couldn't you? It's Tuesday."

The noseless Old Lady loomed near. Nothing stirred about her right ear except the snow. It must have been a trick of Emilie's eyes, her overworked nerves. "So it is. But you forget your father hasn't arrived back from London."

"Oh, he'll arrive. You'll see. Pater never misses an appointment."

Emilie opened her mouth to reply, but it was Freddie's voice that shattered the air.

"Look out!"

A shape blurred along the right side of her vision. Someone grabbed her reins, turned the horse to the left, and they were galloping, galloping, the snow stinging against Emilie's face, the wind freezing her breath in her lungs.

T he Duke of Ashland sprang from the carriage almost before the wheels had come to a stop. "Have Grimsby and his lordship attend me in my study at once," he said to Lionel, tossing the footman his greatcoat and hat.

Lionel followed him down the corridor. "They have gone out, sir."

"Out?" Ashland spun about, nearly knocking the sturdy fellow to the marble floor. An odd emptiness scooped out in his chest. He realized it was disappointment. "Out, in this weather?"

"Yes, Your Grace. The weather has in fact turned for the better today, and his lordship was eager to take advantage."

"I see." Ashland turned around and resumed his journey, less urgently now. "Have them come to me the instant they arrive, then. And tell Simpson to bring in some coffee," he added, over his shoulder. "A great deal of coffee."

In the study, Ashland lit the lamps himself and settled into his chair before the desk. A neat stack of papers lay atop the blotter, waiting for his attention, but the words blurred in his empty gaze. He glanced at the clock: half past two. He'd risen before dawn to make the earliest possible train, to make certain of reaching home in time. And he'd worked furiously in the days before: going over papers and agreements with Mr. Baneweather, instructing agents with Isabelle's Italian address, concluding all his business in a burst of insomniac activity.

And that interview last night in the Duke of Olympia's private study . . .

His gaze dropped down to the papers before him, just as a distant shouting reached his ears, accompanied by thumping and clattering. He raised his head and looked out the study window.

A loud crash. Raised voices carrying through the walls. Ashland sighed and rose to his feet.

It could only be Freddie.

Sure enough, a bare thirty seconds later, the study door burst open to reveal his long and angular son, greatcoat still attached to his body, hat askew. "Pater! You're back!"

"I am."

Grimsby slid out from behind Freddie's back, and Ashland was surprised by the surge of affection he felt for the tutor's slight form, for his wheat-colored hair emerging into the light as he removed his hat.

"Good afternoon, Your Grace. How was your journey?"

Ashland looked from one to the other. They were bristling with fresh air and energy, with some strange suppressed excitement, breathing hard with it. Freddie's eyes gleamed so brightly, they nearly jumped from his head. Grimsby's hand clutched his hat a little too hard.

Ashland wanted to leap over the desk and crush them both in his arms.

Being English, and being a duke, and being Ashland, he did not. He crossed his arms and said, "Tolerable, I suppose. Did you have a pleasant ride?"

"Oh, ripping," said Freddie. "Especially that exhilarating dash at the end. Galloped along as if the Devil himself were at our heels, firing a pistol. Have you ordered coffee?"

"I have."

Freddie tossed his hat and greatcoat in one chair and threw himself in another. "Grimsby and I have had the most cracking time whilst you've been away. I've learned all his deadly secrets."

Grimsby sent Freddie a killing look and placed his hat upon a small tripod table, underneath a lamp.

"Is that true, Mr. Grimsby?" asked Ashland. "What sort of secrets?"

"His lordship is pleased to joke with us," said Grimsby, in his gruff little voice. "I have little of interest to disclose, I'm afraid."

"Oh, that depends on what one finds interesting," said Freddie. "Where the devil is that coffee?"

On cue, the door swung open in a stately fashion. The next few minutes were occupied by the usual rituals of pouring and serving. Ashland inspected the coffee, a particular strain of arabica beans he'd ordered in London and sent down to the Abbey a few days earlier with instructions to brew at double strength, piping hot. Grimsby's whiskers twitched as he sniffed his cup.

"Were your ears burning last night, Mr. Grimsby?" Ashland asked, settling back in his chair in a cloud of aromatic steam.

"Your Grace?"

"I was discussing your case with your venerable sponsor, the Duke of Olympia."

Grimsby choked on his coffee. Freddie delivered him a hearty swat to the back, causing additional coffee to spill from his cup, causing his hands to jerk, causing more coffee to be spilled. Ashland rose silently and handed the poor fellow a napkin, while Freddie guffawed spasmodically in his chair.

"Go on, Pater," he said, between gasps. "Tell us about Olympia."

"There isn't so much to tell, really. He asked after our Grimsby, and I told him he was getting along very well."

"I agree. Grimsby's getting along very well indeed. Giving *satisfaction*. That's the phrase, isn't it? A great"—Freddie coughed—"a *great deal* of satisfaction."

Grimsby ignored Freddie and looked directly at Ashland. "How kind of you, sir. Was His Grace in good health?"

Ashland laughed. "When is he otherwise? Yes, he was looking very well. We discussed your excellencies as a tutor for some minutes. He takes a great interest in you, Grimsby."

"I daresay," said Freddie.

"Very good of him, of course," said Grimsby. "Had he any personal message for me?"

"No, no." Ashland ran his mind over the rest of the discussion: the political situation in Europe, the distressing affair in Holstein-Schweinwald. Ashland had forgotten that Olympia's sister had once been married to the assassinated Prince Rudolf, that he had a personal interest in the issue. What had Olympia said? *I fear there may be a deeper game afoot.* Ashland's attention had been wandering at that point, looking forward to the next day, aching with longing. At the conclusion of the meeting, Ashland had finally worked up the nerve to say aloud what he'd been burning to say for an hour: *I have decided to initiate a suit of divorce against Isabelle. I hope I may count on your support in this matter?* Olympia had looked at him for a long moment, with that hooded gaze of his, and then he'd risen from his chair, offered his hand, and said, *With all my heart.*

It had been . . . gratifying. It had soothed that persistent twinge of guilt still buried deep in his conscience, even now.

"No message," he said to Grimsby, a little absently, and glanced again at the clock.

Freddie, setting to work on his cake, said crumbfully, "I say. Are we keeping you from an appointment, Pater?"

"Not at present."

"Because one can't help but noticing that it *is* Tuesday afternoon. Shouldn't you be upstairs, bathing and shaving and making yourself pretty?"

"Frederick." Ashland brought down his cup with a crash.

"Oh, come, sir. We quite understand. We are all *men* here, aren't we? Men of the world, I mean. Hmm, Grimsby?"

"Quite," said Grimsby, with steely masculinity. He swung his fist upward against his chest. "Men of the world, that's us."

Freddie stuffed the rest of his cake in his mouth and rose. "So we shan't keep you an instant longer. God knows it must take hours to make your frightful mug acceptable to the discriminating female eye. What do you think, Grimsby?"

Grimsby rose. The lamplight reflected against his spectacles in a flash of white. "I think His Grace is perfectly acceptable. But then, I'm hardly a judge, am I?"

Ashland felt oddly unnerved under the white light of Grimsby's gaze. He looked at Freddie instead. "Your candor is priceless, young man. Grimsby, will you do me the very great service of hauling my ungrateful cur of a son upstairs to his studies?"

Grimsby bowed, and as the light ran over his skin, Ashland thought he looked a trifle pink. All the salty talk, no doubt. Poor, innocent chap.

"With the greatest pleasure, Your Grace," said Grimsby, and he grabbed Freddie by his ungrateful collar and hauled him upstairs to his studies.

G ood God," said Emilie, as the schoolroom door closed at last behind them. "How the devil could you sit there like that, cracking jokes? We were nearly killed!"

"Oh, I've dodged the odd highwayman often enough, in my time. That leap across the hidden ditch behind North Tor unseats them every time." Freddie reclined in his chair and idled his finger in his Latin grammar.

"*That* was no highwayman." She stopped. "There really are highwaymen about?"

"Well, not really. Thieves, brigands, what have you. But not the *stand and deliver* sort of highwayman. The trains, I'm afraid, have done for the poor chaps. Still . . ."

Emilie paced across the room. "In any case, this was no common thief, that far away from the road, and a little-used road at that. No, the fellow knew what he was after. He knew where to find us, and when." She drummed her fingers on her elbows. "This is disastrous. They must know I'm here. I shall have to write to Miss Dingleby directly."

Freddie straightened. "What's that? You really think it was some foreign agent or another?"

"Without a doubt. He was waiting for us. Miss Dingleby said someone was making inquiries in the district. My God! I hope my sisters . . ."

Freddie leapt to his feet. "Well, then we've got to tell Pater straightaway! He can post guards, hunt the chap down . . ."

She spun to face him. "Absolutely not! I can't possibly embroil him in this."

"Why the devil not?"

"Because . . ." She swallowed heavily. "Because it's none of his affair."

"*You're* his affair." Freddie paused. "Literally."

"I won't, Freddie. Not . . . not yet." She closed her mind to the thought: confessing everything to Ashland, watching his blue eye grow colder and colder as he realized the magnitude of her double deception. Watching the emotion wink out of him, as surely as the wind howled over the moor.

One more evening, and she would tell him. One more meeting of Emilie and Mr. Brown. His kisses, his body linked with hers. She couldn't deny herself that.

And then it would be over. She would wire Miss Dingleby first thing tomorrow. She would warn her that the agents had found Tobias Grimsby, had connected the Duke of Ashland's tutor to the missing Princess Emilie. That her sisters were possibly in danger as well. She would slip away, she would take the train up to London and stay with her uncle, and that would be that.

No more Ashland. No more Tuesday evenings. No more excruciating, half-naked encounters in the basement of Ashland Abbey.

"In any case," Freddie was saying, peering out the window in the manner of a cornered fugitive, "I'll accompany you into town tonight and wait for you in the stables. You're not going off by yourself, not with assassins lurking around every bend."

"Oh, well played. And you'll be doing *what* in town this evening? Off to the Anvil? Cat's cradle with Rose in the corner? Sipping tea?"

Freddie turned and grinned. "I'll be as good as gold. Word of honor. Her Highness's Royal Guard does not malinger on duty." He performed a strict salute.

Emilie smiled. He looked absurdly young, all of a sudden, as he puffed his chest with assumed manhood. "I am deeply honored," she said.

"Oh, I'm not doing it for you." He went to the door, swung it open, and stood aside for her. "I'm bloody well doing it for poor old Pater."

EIGHTEEN

Emilie arrived first in the Duke of Ashland's private hotel suite. She spent a nervy seven minutes flitting about the rooms, fingering the curtains, adding coals to the fire. A week of steeling herself to him, a week of tempering her heart into hardness, and she had melted like metal in the forge the instant she had seen the duke standing behind his desk in the study, large and powerful and crackling in the exact center of that field of magnetic energy he carried effortlessly about him. His bright blue gaze had burned through her skin, and she knew she wouldn't refuse him. Couldn't refuse him.

She had already undressed to her corset and chemise. She would make no pretense that this was anything but a carnal meeting, a passionate reprise of the week before.

A knock sounded at last on the door. Emilie pulled her blindfold over her eyes and turned.

"Emilie?" His beautiful voice made the blood accelerate in her veins.

She held out her arms. "Here."

She was expecting the touch of his hand, the formal press of his lips on her fingers. Instead she heard his quick footsteps approaching, and then she was hoisted upward and crushed against his endless chest. "Ah, God, Emilie. At last."

She put her arms around his neck and breathed in the warm scent of his skin, just below his ear. "I've missed you," she whispered.

He held her without speaking, as the coals sizzled and the clock ticked discreetly. He must love her a little, she thought. He must. She listened to his heartbeat, to the steady pace of his breathing.

Remember this.

"Mine." He kissed her neck. "My Emilie."

She took his ear delicately between her teeth. "Mine."

The air sucked into his lungs. He hoisted her higher and carried her through space, set her into the cushions—the armchair, the sofa, she couldn't tell—and laid his mouth over hers, kissing her ferociously as his hand dipped below the rim of her corset to stroke her breast.

Now. He would take her *now*, before even a dozen words had been exchanged between them, and every atom of her body thrilled with wicked anticipation. She wanted to be taken right here, pinned to the cushions by his hammering body. She stroked his mouth with her tongue and arched her back to his caress.

But he pulled back. "Wait," he growled. His chest heaved beneath her hands. "Wait. Before we go on."

He rose, and Emilie struggled upward against the slippery cushions. The armchair, she thought dimly. "Where are you?"

"Here." Something dropped into her lap.

"What's this?" She laid her fingers atop the weight: a sheaf of papers.

"It is a contract, Emilie. A legal vow."

Emilie ran her finger around the edge. Her heart took on weight and sank slowly into her belly. "I don't understand."

Ashland's voice came from somewhere above her, several feet away. The mantel, perhaps. "We are past the point of subterfuge, Emilie. You were quite right last week. This cannot go on as it has, not after what passed between us."

"I don't . . . I don't need . . ."

"Emilie, I am not Anthony Brown. I am Anthony Russell, the Duke of Ashland, and I have spent the past week in London arranging my affairs. I have instructed my solicitor to begin a suit of divorce against my wife, and we will be married as soon as the final decree is issued."

Emilie sprang from her chair, clutching the papers. "*What?* No!"

"In the meantime, I cannot exist without you. You hold in your hands the freehold title of a house near Ashland Spa, a large and I believe quite comfortable house, which I have transferred to your possession in the name of Emilie Brown. I have already ordered my staff to clean and prepare the house for you. You may furnish it to your own taste at my expense. I have also arranged an initial draft of ten thousand pounds to be deposited in an account in your name, with a yearly allowance of two thousand pounds for your living expenses, to be made in perpetuity from my estate during your life. Should"—his businesslike voice wavered for an instant—"should we be so fortunate as to conceive a child, I have made provision of ten thousand pounds for each of our issue, to be paid at the earlier of marriage or majority, and a corresponding increase of one thousand pounds per annum in your own allowance. I hardly need add that I shall recognize such issue as mine, to be formally legitimized upon our marriage."

Emilie stood speechless as the sterile words whirled past her ears: *issue* and *annum* and *perpetuity*. At his pause, she gasped out, "Your *mistress*? I am to be your *kept mistress*?"

"You are to be my wife."

"Your *wife*? Are you *mad*?"

He ignored her. "But in the meantime, if we are to share a bed, with all the consequences that may arise from such association, you have the right to my protection. To my guarantee of care and comfort during your life."

"How *dare* you! How dare you enter this room and issue *orders* . . ."

"I am not issuing orders."

She held up the papers. "And what do you call these, exactly? Only the means to control me with your money and houses and children."

"Rubbish. I only want to provide for you, to make you comfortable . . ."

"This is ridiculous. I am perfectly comfortable."

The mantel rattled under his fist. "The bride of the Duke of Ashland does not live in some *hovel* with relatives who do not treat her according to her due."

"I am not your bride."

"You will be."

"Even if I were, should I instead live under your keeping before marriage? Your avowed mistress before the world? Every door would be shut against me!"

"I would exercise the utmost discretion. I don't go out in society, and the house itself is remote."

"The idea is lunatic." Emilie tossed the papers into the armchair behind her, and in the next instant she was seized in Ashland's embrace, his hand cradling her face.

"What is lunatic," he said, in a fierce whisper, "is the idea of seeing you only once during each week, less perhaps, burning for you every other endless damned night, until the wheels of the English legal system can be made to free me from that betraying, unnatural bitch I once called a wife. I want a home with you, Emilie. I want to give you all the ease and luxury you deserve. I want to sleep next to you at night. I want to reach for you when I wake up in the morning. I want to feel our child growing in your belly, and I don't want to wait—God only knows, a year, two years, more even—to claim you as mine."

She was breathless, churning. He surrounded her with his heat and his demands, his tantalizing vision of a passionate future. He crowded out her outrage. He crowded out her reason.

"You don't even know me." His lips were so close, she brushed them as she spoke. "I might be anyone."

"You are Emilie. That's all I need to know." Ashland kissed her softly. "I spoke in haste, just now. I'm too used to giving orders. I was afraid, you see, that if I asked, you'd say *No*."

"I still said *No*."

"If I ask you instead, will you answer differently?" He was nibbling her now, tiny, exquisite movements of his mouth around hers, eating her alive, bite by bite. Another moment, and she would die from it.

"Ah, you don't understand." She laid her arms lightly about his waist, and her chest glowed when he didn't flinch at her touch. "You don't understand."

"I understand everything. I understand that I can't live without you. That I can't live without *this*." His fingers went to the fastening of her corset and released her body from its cage. He pulled down her chemise and enclosed her breast with his hand, rubbed the tip with his thumb. Every nerve of her body burst into tingling life. "Can *you*, Emilie? Tell me you can live without this, and I'll stop. I'll walk away."

"No." She tugged at his coat. "No, I can't."

"Emilie, listen to me carefully. I'm going to take you right here on this chair, hard and fast, because I shall go mad if I don't have you now." His mouth replaced his hand, and he suckled her breast with sudden strength, making her cry out needfully. "And then I'm going to take you to bed and make love to you slowly. I'm going to kiss every precious inch of you, from every angle. I'm going to see how often I can make you spend, and how hard. I'm going to take hours. And then I'll let you sleep, and in the morning you'll wake up to me sliding back inside you."

His words made her blood heat to boiling strength. She was turning molten, a liquid pool of desire, her brain churning from the images he stirred there. Already her limbs were heavy and loose, preparing to receive him. "Wait." She put her hands on his chest. "Wait."

"I can't wait. I've been imagining this all week, imagining you sitting in this chair with your legs spread apart, open for me." His arm went beneath her bottom, and he was lifting her and settling her gently in the chair, drawing her chemise up to her waist, spreading her legs. "My God. Like this." He parted her with one thick finger and eased slowly inside her, all the way to the knuckle.

"Ashland!" She dissolved into the chair.

"God, look at you. Soft and wet . . ."

Emilie's hands fluttered at his shoulders, urging him on despite the throb of warning in her head. "Ashland . . . wait . . . I can't . . . I meant to speak to you first . . . I . . ."

"So beautiful." His tongue flicked her nub, just above his knuckle.

She gasped out, *"Children*, Ashland . . ."

He lifted his head. "What's that?"

"Children. I can't. We can't . . . I . . . It's impossible."

Ashland drew his finger gently from her body. "What do

you mean, Emilie?" His voice was almost too low to be heard. "What do you mean? Do you not want children?"

"I . . . It isn't that, it isn't *you* . . . but I can't. Not now."

A heavy pause rocked between them. "Emilie, I've told you already. I've laid it out in writing, legally binding. I will recognize our children as mine. I will give them my name. I will provide generously for any child with whom God chooses to bless us. You needn't worry." He said the words in a curiously emotionless tone. The tone, she knew, of his deepest feeling.

"Children need more than a banker's draft," she heard herself whisper.

He exploded at that. "Good God, Emilie. Do you think I wouldn't be a father to them? My God, I'd dote on them. I'd spend every possible minute with them and with you."

"But you have a son already."

"Whom I love with all my heart. But he's nearly grown. And I rather think he'd welcome the company."

What had Freddie said? *I'd always rather fancied a brother. Or even a sister.*

Ashland's child in her womb, in her arms. The four of them, a doting family. Laughter over dinner, chess and conversation in the library. Emilie's chest squeezed so tightly, she couldn't breathe.

"In any case," Ashland went on, more softly, "you may already be with child by me."

"But I may not. And I can't take that risk again. Not yet," she added, purely to appease him, for there could never be another time.

Not after he knew the truth.

He remained still, breathing quietly into her skin. "Very well. That is your right, of course. I can take steps to avoid conception."

"What steps?"

"I can decouple before spending. Or there are more secure means, if you prefer."

She could hardly think, with Ashland's body hovering over hers, hot with masculine power. The word *decouple* sent another surge of desire through her belly. "What means are those?"

He sighed and straightened her chemise, and then his body heaved away from hers. "Wait here a few minutes."

As if she would leave. As if she *could* leave.

The door clicked shut. Emilie sat in the chair without stirring. In her black cocoon, every sense was unnaturally sharp. She could trace each tingling nerve, each concentration of heat, each symptom of sexual arousal that Ashland had awakened in her body. There was not a single parcel of her flesh that didn't scream with the need to feel him inside her. She wanted him so badly, she hurt with it.

You are Emilie. That's all I need to know.

Emilie forced her body from the chair and felt her way to the mantel. The fire was hot and steady, glowing against her bare legs. One by one, she plucked the hairpins from her chignon and laid them on the cool marble. The false knot, her former glory, fell away into her hands. She idled it about for a moment, measuring the silky mass, before placing it next to the hairpins. With shaking fingers, she untied the blindfold, folded it into a neat square, and set it atop the golden luster of the chignon.

The hotel was oddly still this evening. Even the wind had died away, heavy with falling snow, making the air seem hollow in its absence. The room, the elegant private suite of the Duke of Ashland, lay around her, every stick of furniture dear to her, though she had scarcely ever seen it. It was the smell she knew best: lemon oil and tea leaves, the trace of smoke, the snow-clean and tea-spiced scent of the duke himself.

Emilie stared into the round bull's-eye mirror above the mantel. Her face gazed back at her, distorted by the convexity of the mirror, enlarging her blue eyes and diminishing her shorn hair and her jaw and chin. Herself, only different, deformed. She shook out her hair, combed it through with her fingers. Emilie, the disguised and ruined Emilie, the Duke of Ashland's lover. In that strange and unnatural face, not a trace remained of the studious and bespectacled princess of Holstein-Schweinwald-Huhnhof, with her outward virtue and her inward restlessness.

Who was she?

The door opened behind her. "Emilie?"

"Here," she said softly, without turning.

The door clicked shut. She listened for the sound of his footsteps on the carpet, but nothing came. He stood utterly still, his gaze burning the back of her bare neck.

"I see," he said at last.

Emilie placed her fingers on the edge of the mantel. "I was thinking, while you were gone, that . . . that we have both engaged ourselves to a great degree, in a rather short period of time . . ."

"I see."

"You are prepared to enter into . . . into a permanent arrangement with me. And it would not be fair . . . We cannot continue, without seeing each other as we truly are. As our real selves, face-to-face."

Ashland's feet shifted. "I offered to remove the blindfold last week. You refused. I assumed you were not ready to see what I am."

"And you would ask me to marry you without my having seen this face of yours? Without your seeing mine?"

His footsteps moved the floorboards at last, approaching. He came to a stop directly behind her and laid his hand softly on her shoulder. "What happened to your hair, Emilie? A fever?"

"No. Not a fever. I cut it off."

His breath tickled her neck. "Emilie, if I have understood anything during the past decade, I have understood how we poor mortals are deceived by beauty. My wife was beautiful, extraordinarily so, and when I married her, I naively presumed this physical perfection went through to her soul."

"You mistake me, sir. I am not afraid of your face. I know your character, your heart, and there is no part of you I couldn't imagine the most beautiful in the world."

"Ah, Emilie. You're afraid of my seeing you, then? That I'm not capable of the same generosity?"

Emilie gazed at the floor in wonder. This was the stiff and arctic Duke of Ashland saying these tender words to her. The reserved and formal Ashland: Where was he now?

His lips touched the nape of her neck. "In the beginning, you wore that blindfold because I chose to remain anonymous. Later, as I came to know you, I didn't have the courage to ask you to take it off. I couldn't bear the thought of you recoiling from me, your look of horror."

Emilie lifted her hand and laid it atop Ashland's.

"A moment ago, Emilie, I told you what I wanted. But what do *you* want?"

She shook her head. Her throat was tight, her eyes stinging.

"Tell me. Will it matter, Emilie? My face?"

She shook her head. "Will mine?"

In answer, Ashland's hand slipped around the ball of her left shoulder. His other arm came up to hold her right.

He turned her around.

She wanted to close her eyes, but she couldn't hurt him, she couldn't deceive him like that. Ashland's masked face shifted into view before her, jagged and familiar, his blue gaze so soft and tender with love she nearly cried out.

She stood waiting under his regard. He was blurred at the edges, a little indistinct without her spectacles. Was that recognition in his expression? How could he not recognize Tobias Grimsby in her face, in her eyes? Any second, and that all-seeing eye would widen, that skin would draw tight over his cheekbones. He would step back in horror, in disgust.

The clock ticked behind her ear. Ashland's warmth radiated through her chemise. His left hand released her shoulder to brush her cheek with his knuckles.

"Beautiful," he said, and he lowered his face to kiss her.

She kissed him back. Her shaking arms enclosed him. Dazed with relief, shamed with her own cowardice, she said nothing at all and simply gave herself up to him.

"Emilie." He hauled her off her feet and carried her to the round table at the other side of the room. He tossed the book on the floor, parted her legs, and sealed his mouth over hers in a deep and ravaging kiss, stroking her with his hot tongue, running his hand up her thighs to her belly and breasts. "Reach in my pocket, Emilie. The left pocket."

Her brain was spinning with lust. She put her hand in his pocket and pulled out a small packet.

"Open it." He took her earlobe gently between his teeth.

She opened it.

"Not the sort of thing a man uses in bed with his wife, you understand. But as my lady commands."

She stared at the gossamer-thin object in her hands. "Where did you find it?"

"The hotel keeps them—discreetly, of course—in case a guest requests one."

Emilie hid her burning face into Ashland's shoulder.

He said, "I've never used one. I can't . . . You'll have to help me put it on. You'll have to tie the strings for me."

"But I don't . . ."

He took the sheath from her hand and went to the pitcher of water on the drinks tray. "It needs to be dampened. I know that much."

"How do you know it?"

He sent her an amused look. "I *was* in the army, you remember."

He returned to her with deliberate steps. His gaze devoured her, as if she were something he might eat. Her blood thudded in her ears. She reached out as he drew near, but he didn't touch her. Instead he took off his coat and waistcoat and slid his braces from his shoulders. Her gaze dropped to his trousers.

"Take me in your hands, Emilie," he commanded her.

Something in his voice burned away the last vestige of shyness. She unbuttoned his trousers, and he sprang free, stiff and dark and . . . well, rather enormous. Far larger than she'd imagined, larger than the drawings in her books had ever led her to expect. Had he really pushed *this* inside her last Tuesday? *All* of it?

She should be frightened at the sight. She should swoon with maidenly shock.

Instead, she wet her lips. She wrapped her hands around his heavy length, ran her fingers along the velvety circle of skin at the tip. A drop of moisture welled free, and without thinking, she bent to lick it off.

Ashland shuddered.

He tasted sharp and tangy. Wild. She licked again. Her tongue found the fissure and dipped inside.

"You'll kill me," he growled. He took her hand. "Help me with this."

She struggled with the sheath, her eager fingers too clumsy for such delicate work. He strained under her touch, bumping into her belly as she bent over him and tied the strings at the base. The action was so forbidden and shameless, so charged with erotic purpose, she felt another surge of warmth between her legs.

"I can't wait, Emilie." He lifted her chemise and found her with his fingers. "God, you're drenched. Come here. Closer. That's it." He urged her to the very edge of the table, bracing her with his right arm, caressing her with his left. His fingers grasped her thigh. His tip parted her, settling just inside her lips. He said huskily, "Now, watch us. Watch me join us together, Emilie."

"*Here?*" she gasped, astonished.

"Here."

She gripped the edge of the table, breathing in shallow gasps. His damp forehead touched hers, his breath warmed her face. She looked down, and there he was, hard as steel, rope-veined, disappearing millimeter by millimeter into the V between her legs. The sight of it, of Ashland feeding his thickened member into her body with utmost control, sent wild shocks pulsing in her blood. Her delicate flesh stretched and stretched, stretched almost to the edge of pain, and she cried out at the fullness of him, of the solid weight rubbing against her sensitive tissues, too much sensation to bear.

Ashland was breathing hard. His face was hot and damp with perspiration; heat radiated from the arms that gripped her. At the base of his throat, right before her eyes, his pulse thrust aggressively against his skin. He tilted her backward slightly and worked himself even deeper, another precious inch, until his snug ballocks pressed her below and the strings of the scandalous French letter tickled her outer lips.

Emilie gripped the edge of the table with all her strength, fighting to keep herself from disintegrating under the impossible pressure. Ashland's breath pumped into her ear. He slid his hand to her bottom and braced himself. "Put your legs around me, Emilie," he whispered, and she put her legs obediently around him, digging her heels into his upper thighs. Another shock of pleasure rippled through her body. "That's it. Good girl," he told her, and with a kiss to her shoulder he began to move. He glided out slowly, in a rush of slickness, and eased himself back in. "All right?"

"Yes . . . *yes* . . ." She tilted her head back and closed her eyes. The table was hard and unyielding beneath her bottom; Ashland's rod was hard and unyielding between her legs. She was squeezed between the two. *A rock and a hard place*, she thought wildly. No escape now.

"Love, I can't hold back any longer."

"Then don't," she gasped out.

His next thrust rocked her to the core, making the table rattle. His hand tightened on her arse and he thrust again, again, faster, stopping her breath with his strength. He made little growls as he went, punctuating each ramming shove into her body, and her own cries of pleasure shot out from her throat at the force of him.

They settled into a pounding cadence, meeting each other at each thrust, never missing a single beat. Ashland struck so deep it hurt; but the hurt was a good hurt, compressing her pleasure to an unbearable extremity, so exquisitely timed that Emilie's climax began to gather in her loins after no more than a dozen strokes. It wound her tighter and tighter, this insatiable vise, each thrust more intense than the last, while Ashland's grip trapped her at the edge of the table.

Shove, shove, shove, relentless and perfect, his fierce face, his damp skin, his want, her want. His rocky voice: "I'm going to come hard, Emilie."

Her heels dug hard, beating in rhythm. *Too much, too much.* Her every nerve strained to the point of rupture, reaching, *reaching*.

"I can't, I can't," she sobbed.

He kept on pounding. "You can. You can. Let it go, love. Let yourself go. Spend for me. Spend. *Now*."

Shove, shove, shove, and climax burst like lightning. She flew outside herself, propelled by the white streaks of sensation that shot from Ashland's stiff flesh within her.

"Emilie!" He shouted her name, gave a final mighty thrust, and wrapped himself around her, taut and shuddering. A slow groan rumbled his throat, ending in a noiseless sigh.

For a long moment they remained still, breathing hard, locked together at all their various points: his arms, her legs, their faces pressed together, his staff still rigid within her. Emilie was dizzy, boneless. Without Ashland holding her in place, she might have floated to the ornate plaster ceiling.

"My God," Ashland muttered. His chest was still heaving. "My *God*, Emilie."

He lifted his head and kissed her forehead, kissed her nose and her cheeks. He braced himself on the table and withdrew as deliberately as he had first slid inside her, wincing as his tip pulled free.

Without speaking, he gathered Emilie up from the table, carried her into the other room, and laid her on the bed. "Don't move," he said, and he disappeared through the door.

NINETEEN

The Duke of Ashland stared at his face in the mirror above the sink. His skin was still flushed, still damp with perspiration; his single eye glowed back at him, pupil madly dilated. He could still feel the pulsing aftershocks of climax in his veins, the most thunderous climax of his life.

Though, to be sure, last week had come exceptionally close, even without that epic and perfectly matched rhythm he and Emily had achieved just now.

He smiled.

A well-pleasured man, that's what he was.

He looked down at his tool, which emerged from his trousers still stiffened, still covered by the damned French letter. He fumbled with the string, untying it at last, and washed it out in the basin. He dropped it carefully in a jar and removed his clothes, piece by piece, folding each one with a soldier's discipline: necktie, shirt, trousers, stockings. He placed the stack on a chair and went to the bedroom. The air rasped against his skin, recalling his nakedness at every step.

Undressed.

Defenseless.

Emily was lying on the bed as he had left her, propped by the pillows, her knees tucked up. One hand lay across her belly, and the other was up on the pillow, next to her shorn head. He hadn't lit the lamp, and the light from the room behind him left only the slightest dusky glow on her skin. He looked at her face, at her round, wise eyes, and for an instant a chord of bone-deep familiarity struck in his chest.

He knew her.

She was *his*. They belonged.

In the next instant, Emily bolted upward.

He approached with the silent steps he'd learned in Olympia's training, the steps with which he approached his prey. The Wraith, they had called him in the Afghan mountains. He tried to hold her gaze with his, but her eyes slipped inevitably downward to encompass his naked and vulnerable limbs, his maimed body, his aroused prick. The beast that he was.

"Ashland, you're beautiful," she whispered, and held out her arms.

He bent his knee into the mattress. "Wear and tear included at no additional expense."

Her face held an odd expression: wonder, and something like wistfulness. She touched his cheek. "Ashland, I . . ."

"Shh." He kissed her, eased her into the pillows. With his good hand he drew down the bedclothes and settled her inside. "We have all night. I've left instructions this time. I'm not expected back until morning."

"Ashland, I can't. I . . ."

He kissed her lips and stopped her words. "Nothing lies between us except your own pride. Just accept me. Accept *us*." Another kiss. "After last week, after what happened just now, how can you deny what exists between us? Besides"—another kiss, this time in the hollow of her throat—"having ravaged the virtue of my proper and virginal young companion, I have no honorable recourse except marriage."

She laughed at that, a melancholy laugh. "You're a *duke*, Ashland. You can do whatever you please."

"Not so." He settled her into the shelter of his body and propped himself up on his elbow. His fingers drew lazy figures along her skin. "I can't quite seem to convince you to become my duchess. I don't know why. A life of squalid luxury, a faithful husband in your bed. Granted, I shall never make a particularly decorative figure on your ballroom floor, but at least you'll *have* a ballroom floor."

Emily stared silently at his face, while the word *husband* swelled and echoed in the air between them.

She reached up and untied the black leather mask from the side of his face. He didn't flinch, didn't so much as flicker as she drew it away.

She leaned forward and kissed his empty socket, on the lid sewn shut by a long-ago surgeon. "I adore every inch of you. Whatever happens, whatever becomes of us, Ashland, remember that." She kissed his shattered jaw, his scarred cheek, his ravaged self. "Every inch of you."

He went still under her featherlight caresses. "That sounds rather like a farewell. *Best of luck, old chap, and thanks for the memories.*"

"I want you to promise me something, Ashland," she said, with her lips against his throat.

"Anything."

"When you know. When I've told you everything. Promise me you won't hate me."

"Emily." He put his finger under her chin and looked into her eyes. What beautiful eyes she had, round and blue, improbably young. Guileless. And filled with emotion, brimming with feeling, matching the love that overflowed his own heart. "I could never hate you."

She drew in her breath. "Ashland, there's so much I haven't told you. About me, about my past. Who I am."

"There's so much I haven't told *you*. The things I've done." *The men I've killed, and how I killed them.* He steeled his brain and forced the thoughts away.

Emily found his stump and covered it with her hand. Under the warmth of her touch, the ache dulled almost to nothing. "But that was long ago. This is now. Who I am *now*."

"As I told you already: You're Emily. That's all I need to know. The rest is just so much rubbish. I knew my wife's ancestry clear back to Dutch William, I knew every detail of her life, and what use was it? I never knew her at all."

"Perhaps you don't know *me* at all."

Ashland swiveled his gaze upward to scrutinize the ceiling.

He lifted his finger to tap his chin. "Let's see, then. Are you a murderess?"

She snorted. "No."

"Forger?"

"Oh, do be serious, Ashland. I'm trying to . . ."

He snapped his fingers. "I've got it. The proprietess of a house of ill repute?"

She picked up a pillow and lobbed it at his face. "And what do you know about those?"

"Well, you recall, I *was* in the . . ."

"Army. Yes, I recall." She relaxed back into the pillows. Her skin was still pink, still warm and glowing from frantic carnal intercourse. With *him*.

Ashland assembled his face into sternness. Clearly he was going to have to take the upper hand, to clear away all her feminine doubts and scruples. A rather overwhelming proposition, after all, marrying a duke. He could understand her shock. Her trepidation, even. And perhaps he hadn't handled the bit about the house and the money with the appropriate degree of tact. Ladies tended not to see such things in a practical and rational light. "It seems I haven't made myself properly clear. I don't give a damn if you were born to the meanest family in England. I don't care if you've fled some crime of the most dastardly nature. It doesn't bloody well matter to me if your past reeks of scandal, if you're living under an assumed name, if you're a modern-day Jacobite under sentence of treason. I intend to marry you, and I'll fight every court in the land, I'll damned well *bury* any scoundrel who dares to say a word against you." He captured her wrists and lowered his head to kiss her, deeply and thoroughly, until they were both gasping for air. "Is that clear enough for you, *duchess*?"

"Yes," she whispered, looking entirely subdued.

"Good, then. And now I'm going to make love to you for the rest of the night, exactly as I said I would, because I don't break my word, Emily. You're going to lose count of the number of times you spend. You're going to forget your own name, whatever the hell it is. You'll be begging me to stop. And when you wake up in the morning, I want no more talk about holding back, about waiting, about leaving things be. I don't want to waste another minute of my life without you by my side, in my bed, across my table. I shall order my carriage and take you to your new home, and I shall spend the rest of my life endeavoring to make you happy." He lowered his head to lick her breast. "Understood?"

She didn't say *yes*, but she growled, a low feminine purr of a growl, and Ashland decided it amounted to the same thing. He bent over her with fingers and lips, with tongue and teeth. He lingered over every curve and fold and angle of her body, studied and pursued her every gasp of pleasure, until she hummed like a well-tuned instrument under his caresses. Until she was shuddering and crying his name. Until her lithe body arched and her wet flesh vibrated with release. And before she had drifted back down to earth, he began all over again, doing things to her he had only dreamed of doing to a woman before, lost in the miracle of Emily.

When at last she could take no more, when she was begging him to stop, he rose and fetched the sheath from its jar and took his own pleasure at last, shoving his prick deep into Emily's luxurious wet grip. She wrapped her arms and legs around him and urged him on, and he couldn't last, she wouldn't let him last. He spent in violent spasms and sank atop her, inhaling the scent of sweat and sex and Emily. He imagined, in that instant, that he'd been released from purgatory at last and allowed through the gates of heaven.

Emilie opened her eyes to a perfect pitch blackness. For a long and panicked instant, she could not place herself in the universe. Where she was, who she was.

She breathed slowly, allowing her mind to rise up naturally from its velvet depth of sleep. A warm scent invaded her nose, rich and intimate and muscular. Such a gorgeous, familiar scent: She craved more of it. She closed her eyes again and filled her lungs, and as she did, she became aware of the heavy weight lying across her ribs, the steady breath stirring her hair, the solid mass radiating heat next to her skin.

Ashland.

Her breath tripped, and started again.

By the good Lord, he felt *heavenly*. That was *his* scent, *his* warmth surrounding her. That humming feeling of well-being in her limbs had come from his hands, his lips, his attentive and tireless lovemaking.

How often had they come together last night? She could not quite remember. On the table, that first time, hard and fast and exhilarating; and then again on the bed, after he had wreaked rapture on her body until she could scarcely move. They had fallen asleep for an hour or so, and then Ashland had risen and ordered a late cold supper and fed it to her himself, with sips of champagne here and bites of paper-thin ham there, with kisses and caresses and laughter, until at some point they were joined once more, rocking together in a lazy rhythm, whispering unspeakably dirty words back and forth. He had taught her all the names for his male organ pressed inside her, all the names for her own female parts, all the names for the act in which they were engaged, until her blood ran so hot she couldn't think. He had turned her over and finished them both off in a frenzy, her back against his front, his teeth nipping her neck, like animals. Afterward, he had curled his big body around hers and caressed her with his broad and loving hand. More sleep, and then one of them had begun again, she couldn't remember whom, or perhaps it had been mutual: a mutual waking and lovemaking followed by mutual collapse.

He was still collapsed. She listened to his breath, his heartbeat in the intimate black night. Was that the very faintest hint of a snore? She smiled and hugged the sound to herself. She rolled her memory back and recalled it all again, from start to finish, clarifying the details. Cataloging. Four times, then. He had made love to her four times. Four glorious, pounding, breathless times.

No wonder contentment seemed to roll off his unconscious body.

Four times tonight, once last week. Five times altogether. It wasn't much, really, to last her a lifetime. But she would remember each one.

The darkness in the room was not yet subsiding. It must be well before dawn.

She had to leave.

Before she could tempt herself into another minute, and another five, she lifted Ashland's arm from her middle—his right arm, with its rounded end that seemed so natural to her now, a normal and beautiful part of Ashland's body. At one point last night, during one of the slow and sleepy interludes between congress, she had asked him what it felt like, his phantom hand. He had nudged the end of his arm along the underside of her breast, lifting the soft plumpness, and said, "As if it wants to touch you, and can't."

Her heart contracted again at the memory. She sat up, laid his arm carefully in the sheets, and drew up the bedclothes, hardly daring to breathe for fear of waking him. The ever-wakeful, ever-watchful Duke of Ashland.

He didn't stir.

She slipped out of the bed and the bedroom. The sitting room was chilled, the fire nearly out. Her skin, accustomed to the cocoon of warmth she'd shared with Ashland, prickled with goose bumps. She drew on her clothes, shivering, and crept from the room, leaving her blindfold and her false chignon on the mantel behind her.

She wouldn't need them anymore.

F reddie was waiting for her in the stables, as he'd insisted. He lay curled in a pile of straw in the corner, snoring peacefully. She changed into her men's clothes, packed her dress in the knapsack, and shook his thin shoulder gently.

"Did you tell him?" Freddie scrambled for his spectacles.

"No."

He swore. "Where's your pluck, Grimsby? He's not going to take your head off. He loves you."

"He doesn't love me. He's never claimed to love me."

"Well, of course he wouldn't say the word out *loud*." Freddie snorted.

"I took off the blindfold and my hair. He didn't recognize me. I didn't have the heart to tell him outright." She led the way out of the stable and into the snow, three inches deep and building. "I just couldn't."

"Women," he said.

They trudged in silence down the deserted road, guided only by the dark lumps of buildings along the way. The snow glowed faintly on the ground, a ghostly landscape. Emilie walked with her head bent downward, and still the stinging flakes caught her cheeks, her eyelids.

At the Anvil, they collected their horses and paid off the stableboy generously. "Pardon the observation," said Freddie, swinging up in the saddle, "for I'm not well versed in these sorts of matters, but you don't seem particularly happy. All things considered."

"I don't know what you mean."

"Again, I speak without experience, but aren't women in love supposed to be beamy and delighted and that sort of thing? You look rather . . . downcast." He paused delicately as they turned into the road. "Everything all"—cough, cough— "all right?"

"Quite all right. We . . ."

He flung up his hand. "God, no. No details. This is bloody awkward enough as it is."

"I wasn't going to give you details. For heaven's sake," she added, blushing at the recollection of those details. "I only meant to say that we were quite in accord. But of course it can never happen again."

"Why not?"

"Because tomorrow morning, or rather this morning, after breakfast, I'm going to tell him the truth."

"Thank God. He'll rant and storm, of course, but at least things will be out in the open. No more of this ridiculous secrecy. Tramping through the snowy roads in the dark of night, dodging foreign agents." Freddie blew out his breath, causing a mad swirl of snowflakes around his face.

"Freddie." She looked down at the dark smudge of her hands on the reins. "Don't you see? I won't be able to stay here any longer. Disguised, disgraced. An unmarried woman . . ."

"Oh, Pater'll fix that straightaway, I'm sure."

She didn't answer. How could she? They rode along in silence, the horses keeping to the obscured road by instinct, moving briskly in eagerness to be home. The air was cold and sharp with snow; it sawed Emilie's lungs at every breath.

"Freddie," she said at last, "I can't marry your father. I simply can't."

"Why the devil not? You love him, don't you? God knows

why. Some peculiar disposition for gruff old chaps with dodgy peepers, I expect."

"That's not the point. And *do* mind your language. I am still your tutor, at least until later this morning."

Freddie's voice rose. "Then what the devil *is* the point? I thought true love conquered all, and all that rot. Why the devil not marry him?"

"Freddie."

"I beg your pardon. Why the dickens?"

"For a multitude of reasons. Because he wishes to marry me out of . . . of desire, and . . . and a sense of duty, not love. And because . . ."

"Rubbish. Just because he hasn't got the proper words for it . . ."

". . . because I am not some ordinary young lady, who can fit comfortably into your lives. I'm in mortal danger at the moment, or don't you remember? And lastly"—her voice dropped—"because I have deceived him, and what marriage can survive that?"

"Oh, *that*. He'll understand."

"I don't think he will."

"Try him. You'll see."

A dark shape was rising against the milky snow. "Here we are, anyway," Emilie said. "Do try to get some sleep. I promise I shan't insist on your nine o'clock lesson."

Freddie, for once, said nothing. They went to the stables and unsaddled their horses side by side, then put them away with oats and water. Freddie's hands moved with knowledge over the straps and buckles, the brushes and blankets. He had likely spent a great deal of his childhood in here, Emilie mused.

She let them both in the kitchen door with her key. Freddie turned to her at the bottom of the service steps. "Give him a chance, Grimsby. Please." In the light of the oil lamp, his eyes were serious and pleading. "Just trust him, will you? Let him . . . Well, just give him a chance. He needs this."

The ache in Emilie's chest was too much to bear. She placed her hand against Freddie's cheek. "I'll do my best," was all she could say.

The upstairs corridor was still and silent. A distant clock

sounded four o'clock in steady chimes as Emilie crept down the cold floorboards, guilty and churning, muscles still thrumming from Ashland's bed. She found her door, opened it without a sound, and let her knapsack slide to the floor.

A fire still simmered gently in the tiny grate. Emilie took off her greatcoat, hung it on the rail, slipped her black wool jacket from her shoulders. She sat down on the bed to remove her shoes.

The bed moved.

Emilie leapt to her feet.

"Oh, sir! Oh, sir, never be frightened! It's nobbut mysen."

A figure rose from the pillow. The firelight outlined its body, clad only in a chemise, young nipples pointed jubilantly to the ceiling.

"Lucy!" Emilie exclaimed. She clutched the ends of her unbuttoned waistcoat together. "Good God, Lucy! Your . . . your *clothes*!"

Lucy held out her arms. "Oh, sir, never go away! I nobbut . . . Why, dear me, sir. What's happened to yer whiskers?"

"I shaved them."

"Oh." Lucy blinked, took a deep breath, and plunged on. "Well, I thought . . . Oh, sir, that there wicked Freddie, taking ye out to t'Anvil and those . . . those bad women. I can't bear it anymore, sir, I can't! I pinched t'key from Mrs. Needle . . ."

"You did *what*?"

Lucy sprang from the bed and drew off her chemise in a single dramatic stroke. "Take me, sir! Take me instead!"

Emilie spun around. "For God's sake, Lucy!"

"I . . . I guess I'm as nice as those wicked women at t'Anvil, aren't I? I'll be taking good care of ye, sir. You can . . . We can be married, t'duke will let us, I'm sure, and . . ."

Emilie stared at the dark wall before her and counted to ten. "Lucy, my dear, this is *most* improper."

"It's no more wrong nor what you does!" Lucy's voice broke into sobs. "Night after night, coming home at all hour. It ain't right, sir, not for a gentleman like thassen. I'd be ever so much better to you, sir. I would. Don't I darn up yer hosen and lay them out for ye?"

"That was you?"

"Don't I bring ye t'best bits of cake and leave t'heels for His Grace? Don't I bring up yer coffee ever so hot, and keep yer nice coat brushed?"

"Lucy, I . . ."

The floorboards creaked, and Lucy's arms flung around Emilie's shoulders. "Oh, take me, sir, do!" Lucy's arms were surprisingly strong. Emilie found herself spinning around to face the maid. The girl's eyes were closed, her head flung back like a martyr facing the pyre. She was wearing her frilly white cap and nothing else.

"Have yer wicked way with me, Mr. Grimsby!"

"Lucy!"

"Sate yer unnatural lusts! Do what ye will with me!"

Emilie put her hands to her temples. "Lucy, Lucy. What sort of novels have you been reading?"

"Pluck t'precious flower of me innocence!"

"Lucy, remember yourself! Have you been drinking His Grace's sherry?"

An indignant gasp. "Why, I *never*, sir!"

Emilie's exhausted head was beginning to pound. She reached out and patted Lucy's shoulder, keeping her gaze trained resolutely upward. The faint scent of Mrs. Needle's lemon oil gathered between them. "Lucy, my dear. Put your clothes on."

"Sir?"

"I'm afraid my unnatural lusts are quite at rest at the moment. No need for any . . . any heroic floral sacrifice on your part."

Lucy crossed her arms over her breasts. Her eyes rounded plaintively, like a puppy's. "Nay?"

"Not at all, I'm afraid." Emilie smiled kindly. "You're very sweet to . . . to offer yourself up to my . . . my unruly passions in such a . . . an unexpected manner. But I assure you, I have no wicked designs on your person, Lucy. None at all."

Lucy sniffed. "Nowt at all?"

"None."

Lucy's lip trembled. Her eyes blinked.

"Now, don't cry, Lucy . . ."

Lucy lifted her arms and pounded her fists on Emilie's bound chest. "*Cruel*, that's what ye are, sir! Letting me think ye cared for me! I seen t'look in yer eye when ye thanked me for yer coffee! Burning with t'flames of desire, ye were! And then ye runs off down to t'Anvil and drains yer knackers with t'wicked ladies there!"

Emilie grasped Lucy's pummeling fists. "Lucy, do hush. I assure you . . ."

Lucy wrenched away, picked up her chemise, and threw it over her head. "Me mum were right, weren't she? Never do trust a gentleman, Lucy, she says to me. It's only t'working boys is decent."

"Now, Lucy . . ."

"Never ye *Lucy* me, Mr. Grimsby! Ye keeps yer wicked hands to yessen, from now on!" The dressing gown went on, belted at the waist with dramatic tugs. She picked up the candle on the nightstand, lit it on the coals, and swept to the door. "Satyr!" she spat, and turned in the doorway.

Emilie sank onto the bed.

"Oh, and Mr. Grimsby, sir?"

"What is it, Lucy?" Emilie whispered tiredly, not lifting her head from her hands.

"Ye looks like a lady without t'whiskers."

The door slammed, and Lucy was gone.

Emilie stared at the floor. Her head ached with fatigue, but her thoughts were jumping spasmodically, as if shocked by electricity. Ashland. Freddie. Her family. Bloody *Lucy*.

What the devil was she going to do with this mess?

She turned her face and gazed longingly at the pillow. It was dented from Lucy's head, probably still warm.

Emilie heaved herself to her feet. At least there was one place at Ashland Abbey she could be certain of peace and quiet.

A sleepy footman unbolted the door at half past five o'clock, after only a minute's brisk pounding. The Duke of Ashland swept through the portal in an urgent slap of boots on marble.

"My apologies, Lionel. Awaken my valet at once. I shall require a bath and a change. I have ordered the carriage."

Lionel made a half bow. "At once, Your Grace."

Ashland made his way around the corner of the great entrance hall and down the corridor to his study, not pausing an instant. A clatter of shoes echoed behind him as Lionel rushed to obey his instructions. He threw open the door to his study and strode to his desk.

"Pater!"

Ashland started and turned. "Freddie? What the devil?"

His son rose from a reclined position on the sofa, rubbing furiously at his eyes. A stalk of straw extended prominently from the back of his head. "Was waiting up for you, of course."

"Waiting up for me?" He let his hand fall to the desk. In all his panic at waking to an empty bed, in all his wild worry for Emily and the almost physical pain of her absence, in all the week's bustle of laying plans and settling affairs, Ashland had allowed the thought of Freddie to slip from the forefront of his mind. A stab of remorse struck his chest at the sight of his hollow-eyed son. "I beg your pardon, Frederick. I have been immensely busy of late. How are you getting along? Everything well with Mr. Grimsby?"

Freddie knit his hands together between his knees. "Well, you see, Pater, that's the thing. Grimsby . . . he . . ."

Ashland gripped the edge of the desk. "He's all right, isn't he? Has something happened?"

"Easy, Pater. Grimsby's quite all right. He's very well indeed, except . . ." Freddie raked his hand through his hair.

"Except what?"

"Well, he's not quite what I expected. What either of us expected." Freddie coughed. "Full of surprises, our Grimsby."

"What the devil do you mean by that?" The cold tension began to uncoil, replaced by impatience. Ashland felt the clock ticking away by the mantel, putting Emily farther away from him at every stroke.

Freddie jumped from the sofa. "Let's talk about this new bird of yours, Pater."

"You will not refer to her by that word," Ashland snapped reflexively.

"All right, all right. Beg your pardon and all that. This . . . this lady you've been seeing in town. Don't bother denying it."

"I haven't the least intention of denying it. In fact, I wish to speak to you about her."

"Well! Jolly coincidence, that. I was wanting to speak on the subject myself." Freddie raised his head and met Ashland's gaze squarely. "What are your intentions toward her?"

"My *intentions*?" Ashland folded his arms. "What the devil do you mean by that? My intentions are honorable. I have, in fact . . ." And, just like that, under the intensity of Freddie's expression, the words began to thicken and muddle in Ashland's throat. "Look here, Frederick. I didn't wish to spring all this on you suddenly . . ."

"Spring away, Pater, I assure you."

Ashland adjusted his throat. "I want to make things clear: I have no wish to dishonor your mother. But after the passage of so much time, and . . . and having formed an attachment . . ."

"You're going to divorce Mother at last and marry her?"

"I have that hope," Ashland said quietly.

Freddie's face broke into a grin. "Well, I say! That's splendid! Thank God! I knew you had it in you, Pater." He crossed the rug, shoved his fist into Ashland's crossed arms, and grasped his hand for a vigorous shaking. "Splendid news!"

"I . . . I . . ." Ashland watched his astonished hand being pumped. "I'm . . . glad you approve."

"Approve, by God! I'm delighted. Just the thing for you. There's just one . . . one very slight complication. Nothing of great consequence, you understand. I'm sure you'll brush it off straightaway, sensible old chap that you are, and sort everything out in an instant. Or perhaps a week or so, realistically speaking."

Ashland shook his bemused head. True, he hadn't had much sleep last night, but surely this interview ought to be making more sense. Coffee. He should have ordered coffee. "Complication?" he said numbly. "What the devil do you mean by that?"

"Well, it's rather difficult to explain." Freddie released his father's hand and stretched his arms high above his head in a gigantic yawn, like a spindly adolescent lion satisfied with his day's play. "Perhaps it's best if you see for yourself."

Emilie had learned to swim at the age of fifteen, on the orders of Miss Dingleby. "It is a skill typically overlooked by young ladies," her governess had said, "and yet it may possibly save your life, and that of others." She had been stripped of her gown, put in an awkward bathing costume, and plunged into the chilly waters of the Holsteinsee one May morning, and once she'd recovered from the shock, she discovered she liked swimming very much. She liked the freedom, the way her limbs stroked through the water, the feeling of rhythmic power. She liked the way the rest of the world disappeared, all the trappings and ceremony and restrictions of her life, to leave only herself, Emilie, immersed in the elemental forces of nature.

The Duke of Ashland's private bathing pool was nothing like the mountain-fed chill of the Holsteinsee, of course. It caressed her body with tingling warmth; it felt curiously alive against her bare skin, easing all the little aches of her passionate night in Ashland's bed, cleansing and invigorating her. She stroked back and forth for nearly half an hour, and as she turned to make her last lap, she felt as if she might conquer the world.

She would dress and go upstairs and pack. She would write a note to Ashland, to be delivered after her own departure. She would go to the station, she would send a wire to Miss Dingleby, she would take the train to London and walk into her uncle's study and demand that her father's murderers be found and brought to justice. She would end this extraordinary chapter in her life and . . . well, return to her old self. Princess Emilie of Holstein-Schweinwald-Huhnhof, only a little older and wiser.

As for Ashland himself . . .

Her fingertips touched the stone edge of the pool. She stared at them for a moment: the delicate long bones, the blunt nails, the drops of water trickling from the knuckles. Such feminine hands; how had she fooled them all with hands like this?

People see what they expect to see, Miss Dingleby had said.

She placed her palms on the smooth paving stones and hoisted herself upward. Her nipples puckered instantly at the cool air. She reached for the thick Turkish towel on the low stool nearby and froze at the sight of the booted feet before her.

The boots were well polished, enormous, planted squarely on the stone, dark leather against pale marble. She knew those boots well.

Emilie whipped about and flung the towel around her dripping body.

"Emilie," said the Duke of Ashland. His voice was the lowest she'd ever heard it, scarcely above a growl, and yet perfectly calm, perfectly controlled. "Emilie *Grimsby*, is it? Or is that a fabrication as well?"

"Not Grimsby," she said.

"What, then?"

She didn't answer.

"What a fool I am," said the Duke of Ashland. "So many clues, and I missed them all. I, of all people. My hat is off to you, my dear. Olympia has trained you well."

Emilie squeezed her eyes shut. "I never meant to hurt you."

"Tell me, Emilie. Why are you here? What information did Olympia hope to gain through you?"

"None at all, sir. I . . . He . . . That's not why I came."

"Why, then?"

"I came to hide."

"From what, Emilie?"

She filled her chest with warm, damp air. "From my father's murderers."

"Good God."

Did he believe her? She looked down at the white towel covering her body, the pool of water forming about her feet. She could almost hear the finely tuned machinery of Ashland's brain whirring about, taking in all the threads of information and weaving them into the correct pattern.

"The Holstein-Schweinwald affair," he said at last. "Of course. You're Olympia's niece."

"Yes."

"The Princess . . . Emilie, I presume?"

"I am."

The water from the bathing pool lapped quietly into the silence between them.

"You have played your part exceptionally well, madam. To have made such an extraordinary sacrifice in the name of duty."

"It was not a sacrifice."

"Ah yes. You couldn't resist me, wasn't that it? *God help me*, you said." There was a little slap, as of gloves against sleeve. "At least I had the honor of making your performance a pleasurable one. Or were you feigning that, too?"

"I feigned nothing. You must believe that."

He laughed coldly. "Believe what, madam? I confess, I don't know what to believe."

"I told you you'd hate me, when you knew the truth. I told you . . ."

"Hate you? You mistake me, madam. If I hated you, I would simply have turned and left, and given orders for you to be removed from the premises. Instead I am still here, waiting for you to turn around and continue this conversation face-to-face. Or do I remain so repulsive to your eyes?"

She turned.

He stood ablaze, his blue eye scorching with emotion, his massive body crackling with suppressed energy. His feet were planted wide apart, and his hand fisted at his side, leather glove enclosed by white knuckles. His white hair glowed silver in the shifting light from the bathing pool.

"You are not repulsive," she said. "You're . . . you're . . ."

"I'm what, Emilie?"

"Everything."

He stood staring at her, as if he were trying to burn away the outer layers of her skin and read the truth beneath. She willed it through the air between them: *I love you. I adore you. Deceiving you nearly destroyed me.*

"You are still in danger, I presume," he said. "That's why Olympia sent you to me."

"Yes."

"Hmm. I believe, my dear girl, we would all have been saved a great deal of trouble if Olympia had seen fit to send me his little package with instructions included."

"He couldn't. He couldn't have sent me as I am, as an unmarried lady to a house without a mistress . . ."

Ashland slapped his glove against his leg. "The result was the same, however. Instead of protecting you, I seduced you."

"Perhaps it was the other way around. I came to *you*, if you remember."

"Regardless." He pinned his glove to his chest with his right wrist and wriggled it onto his left hand with astonishing dexterity. "I shall leave at once for London and determine what must be done. You will stay here. You will resume your disguise. You will not leave this house, not even to the garden. I shall leave instructions with my men to lock the doors, to admit no one, to protect you at all costs."

Emilie gasped. "You can't do that!"

"I will."

"But these men, these agents, they know I'm here. Yesterday, just before you arrived, I was out with Freddie and rode straight into an ambush. A man sprang from behind the Old Lady; if Freddie hadn't known the moors so well, and lost him . . ." She let the words dangle.

Ashland's expression didn't change, but the coiled tension in his body wound, if possible, even tighter. "I see. And how long has my loyal son known of your disguise?"

"Since the morning you left for London."

Ashland swore under his breath.

"So you see, I can't stay here. It's impossible." Emilie's hands tightened on the towel, her flimsy and undignified shield from Ashland's icy rage. "Now that they know where I am, and how I'm disguised."

"And who, exactly, are *they*?"

"I don't know. That's what we—what my uncle and my sisters and I—are trying to find out."

"I see." He tapped one finger against its opposite sleeve. His face had turned hard, calculating, the way it must once have looked before battle, on his clandestine missions in the mountains of Afghanistan. "Very well. As I have no trained men here at the Abbey, you and Frederick will accompany me to London. You will change into your disguise at once and meet me in the front hall in half an hour. You will obey my every instruction to the letter, without question, or I cannot guarantee your safety. Is this understood?"

"I am not one of your army subordinates, by God!"

Ashland reached out and captured her chin in his gloved palm. "No, you are not," he said, in a dusky voice. "But Olympia, God forever damn his plotting brain, has entrusted your safety to me. You are nothing but a pawn, my dear, and you must play your role or lose the game."

The leather of Ashland's glove was cool against her skin. Though his hand was gentle, it engulfed her chin completely, humming with latent power. "And when the game is won?" she asked.

Ashland's gaze slid over her face. "When the game is won, Emilie, the victor claims the spoils." He passed his gloved thumb across her lips, turned, and walked out of the room, his boots echoing against the marble in sharp clacks.

TWENTY

The Duke of Olympia regarded the two figures seated before him with a beneficent satisfaction. "An unspeakable delight," he repeated, smiling. He steepled his fingers. "I had scarcely hoped for it."

"Nonsense," snapped the Duke of Ashland. "You had it planned all along. I daresay you were wondering what the devil took me so long."

"Not at all, not at all. My Emilie is a formidable opponent." Olympia turned his smile to the bewhiskered young person in the other chair, which still gave Ashland a start. Even knowing what lay beneath those whiskers and those spectacles, that sleek layer of pomaded golden hair, he couldn't quite believe this was Emily. *His* Emily, whose supple body had risen up so eagerly to meet his own, whose breasts he had weighed in his hand scarcely hours before. Who had whispered such tender words in his ear, who had kissed him as if she'd really meant it.

Not Emily anymore. *Emilie.*

He swallowed back the bitterness that rose in his throat. Emotion had no place here, at the present moment.

"She is indeed. But we are not here to applaud the workings of your nimble brain, Olympia, nor the skill with which your niece has played her part. We are here to determine what is to be done to resolve the crisis. You will, perhaps, be so good as to deliver me a candid assessment of the state of affairs." He allowed a slight emphasis to fall on the word *candid*.

Olympia leaned back in his chair, still smiling. "Forgive me. I have grown sentimental with age, and your case has perplexed me for so long. Yes. Holstein-Schweinwald. A damnably mysterious problem. My inquiries have turned up almost nothing."

Emilie's rigid back straightened another regal inch. "Where is Miss Dingleby?"

"Who is Miss Dingleby?" asked Ashland.

"Miss Dingleby," said Olympia, without changing expression, "has acted as my agent in Holstein-Schweinwald-Huhnhof for several years, since I first detected stirrings of an unusual nature in that state."

Emilie gasped. "All along!"

"Surely you suspected. In the past few months, if nothing else."

"I knew she . . . I thought perhaps . . ." Emilie bit her lip. "Ashland's right, isn't he? You've planned all this, from the beginning."

Olympia spread his hands before them. "It depends on what you call the beginning. I have always followed with particular intensity the political affairs of your native land, my dear, having such a close and avuncular interest there. The regular demise of your stepmothers awakened a certain suspicion in my mind."

"You believe they were *murdered*?"

Olympia shrugged. "I have no proof. And yet a rather shadowy organization exists across the states of Europe, passionate anarchists all, committed to the elimination first of the Continent's established monarchies, and then of government altogether."

Ashland's pulse skipped. "You think this is the work of Free Blood?"

"As you know, there's no more effective catalyst for political instability than a state without a legitimate heir."

Emilie had turned white. "My mother, too?"

"As I said, I have no conclusive proof."

Ashland was watching Olympia's face with keen eyes. "But you do have something."

Olympia rose from his desk and walked to a cabinet in the wall, from which he withdrew a plain silver cup. He handed it to Emilie.

She turned it over in her hands. "The Holstein crest," she whispered.

"Miss Dingleby sent it back to me. She recovered it from your third stepmother's bedside table, the night before your half brother was born dead. Upon chemical analysis, the dregs were found to contain a potent and particularly toxic abortifacient."

"Good God."

"You will note that all of your dear father's wives died in childbed, delivering stillborns." Olympia resumed his seat with a gentle flip of his superfine tails.

Emilie was still staring at the cup. Her long fingers trembled against the tarnished silver; her lips were bloodred against her white face. The sight of her distress made Ashland's chest contract, made his breath stop in his lungs.

"Why didn't you say anything before?" she asked her uncle.

Ashland laid his arms across his chest in an effort to hold himself together. "Because this sort of information is best kept to oneself until the moment arrives to strike. Isn't that right, Olympia?"

"Correct. And you were in excellent hands with Miss Dingleby, who this very moment is pursuing a channel of her own. We had your message, you see, about the ambush yesterday morning. It confirmed our fears."

"What fears?" asked Emilie.

"That someone is privy to our investigation. Someone had discovered where we had hidden you."

"Succeeded where I failed," Ashland said crisply. He looked again at Emilie. He had stolen glances at her throughout the jolting train ride into London, in the cab from the station to Park Lane, and still the mystery of her seemed hidden from him. His mind, trained to accept and act on startling new information without hesitation, could not quite encompass this. It wasn't simply that Emily was Grimsby; he'd always felt a streak of odd tenderness for the tutor, which demonstrated at least *some* sort of subconscious recognition of her true nature, thank God. It was that Grimsby was *Emilie*, the lost German princess, radiant and untouchable. He'd said scarcely a word to her all day. He didn't know whether to throttle her for her betrayal, or to make passionate love to her because she lay unmasked before him at last, or simply to gaze at her in awe and longing.

He took refuge, as he usually did, in silence.

"Don't blame yourself, young man," said Olympia. "Had I put out the least hint, you would have smoked her out at once. In any case, we are now offered an auspicious opportunity."

As always, Olympia's benign face revealed nothing of his inner thoughts. But Ashland had learned his trade at the duke's broad feet; Ashland heard the words *auspicious opportunity* and knew what they meant.

"No," he said. "You will not risk Emilie."

Olympia's well-tailored shoulders straightened an infinitesimal degree. He returned Ashland's gaze without blinking. "Emilie, my dear, would you be so good as to allow me a few minutes' private conversation with our friend the Duke of Ashland?"

"I would not."

"I thought not." His gaze continued to lock with Ashland's, dark and cool. "You will therefore forgive my candor when I inquire of the duke what, exactly, gives him the honor of acting so decisively on your behalf?"

"I will answer with equal candor, sir. Your niece is my affianced wife."

Emilie shot from her chair. "That's not true!"

"Isn't it?" Olympia looked at her at last, and this time his eyes crinkled slightly at the corners. "It hardly seems a matter to admit doubt. Either you're engaged, or you're not."

"I am bound in honor to her. I will marry her."

"Nonsense," Emilie said. "No such obligation exists between us. Especially not now, with everything changed."

"I disagree. Nothing essential has changed." He spoke to Olympia. "In the first place, I have compromised her innocence."

"Tut-tut," Olympia said.

"In the second place, there is a possibility she carries my child."

"Quite shocking. Is this true, my dear? *Is* it possible?"

"I . . ." Emilie's mouth opened and closed. Her white face was becoming rapidly overrun with a fetching pink blush. She cast a helpless look at Ashland, and back at her uncle. "It makes no difference. I will not marry him. I will not marry a man . . ."

"You will *not* walk this earth, carrying my child . . ."

". . . out of some archaic sense of duty, not to say outdated notion of . . ."

". . . without bearing the protection of my name as well . . ."

". . . will undoubtedly regret such an irrevocable step . . ."

". . . to say nothing of the protection of my body . . ."

". . . when I have resources of my own should . . ."

"QUIET!" Olympia rose from his chair and placed his hands on his desk. "Whether or not the two of you reach the altar before tearing each other apart is beside the point."

"It is?" said Emilie, finger still raised.

"It *is*?" said Ashland. He rose to meet Olympia's towering regard.

"Quite immaterial, really. You need only be engaged," said Olympia. "Publicly engaged. The Duke of Ashland and the lost Princess Emilie of Holstein-Schweinwald-Huhnhof, a terribly romantic affair. A ball would be just the thing to celebrate the announcement, don't you think?"

As the last words left his mouth, an odd buzzing sound issued from the corner of Olympia's desk. The duke's eyebrows lifted. "You'll excuse me." He leaned over to lift an object shaped rather like an elongated bell to his ear.

The buzz still seemed to echo in Ashland's ear. He folded his arms back over his chest, girding himself, while Olympia exchanged a few low words into the odd contraption in his hand. Emilie said nothing, but he could feel her vibrating nearby, her ardent young body straining with emotion. *Let me handle this*, he wanted to say. *This is my world. Be easy. Let me take care of you.*

The receiver clicked back into its box. "I beg your pardon. Miss Dingleby has been informed of developments and will be with us directly. Now. The engagement ball. Three weeks,

I believe, will be sufficient preparation. The season hasn't begun, but I daresay we can coax a few celebratory souls into the capital for the occasion. Emilie will stay here with me, of course. We will divest her of her disguise at once. Have you a house in town, Ashland?"

"Not at present."

"I believe there are a few suitable properties available for lease at the moment. You will of course call as many staff as possible down from Yorkshire; we don't want any new hires running about the house."

Ashland stepped forward and placed his left index finger in the center of Olympia's immaculate leather blotter. "As I have said before, you will not risk Emilie."

"My dear fellow, she will be in no danger at all in my house. I shall personally ensure her safety."

"In the first place, I stay where Emilie stays."

"Quite improper."

"I don't bloody care. In the second place . . ."

A knock cracked through the air.

"Come in," said Olympia.

Ashland heard the door open behind him, heard a sharp clack of heels on wood, followed by the silence of the rug. Olympia's gaze flickered to the newcomer. "Ah! Miss Dingleby."

"Am I interrupting?"

"Indeed you are," said Olympia. "Anything to report?"

Her voice was warm and businesslike, as Ashland might have expected. Olympia's female operatives always ran to type. "My errand this morning was fruitless, I fear. But Emilie's room upstairs has been secured. I shall put my own cot in there tonight. I've posted Hans on the lookout outside, meanwhile, should anyone have followed them down from Yorkshire."

"No one did," said Ashland, without turning.

"Are you quite sure?" asked the woman behind him.

He turned. "I hope you aren't questioning my competence, Miss . . ." He raked her angular form up and down. "Dingle-bat, was it?"

Miss Dingleby smiled benignly. "You did require several weeks to discover our Emilie's disguise."

"If you had done your job properly, madam, she should not have been forced into hiding in the first place."

"I beg your pardon. Have you any idea what sort of enemy we're up against, Your Grace?"

"I've infiltrated the most murderous cults in . . ."

"Stop it, the lot of you!" cried Emilie.

Ashland turned. Emilie stood akimbo, her face flushed pink, her blue eyes searing them both behind the sheen of her spectacles. Her false whiskers seemed to stand out from her jaw. "Stop talking and making plans for me, as if I'm nothing but a pawn on a chessboard, to be moved about at will! *You!*" She pointed at Olympia. "You've planned every step of this, haven't you, knowing full well I'd fall under Ashland's spell, drawing him into a . . . a possibly *mortal* danger that has nothing at all to do with him! Risking his life, just as you did in India, when you nearly killed him! I won't let you do it again!"

Ashland opened his mouth to say something, but there were no words. No words at all to riposte this extraordinary woman, this fire-fueled princess who stood there and fought for him, for *him*, with all the fury in her regal golden-haired body.

"And *you!*" Emilie turned and stabbed her avenging finger in Ashland's direction. "You will not risk yourself in a public *engagement* to me! You will not sleep in this *house* with me!"

Speech returned in an instant. He took her shoulder. "By God, I will!"

"You won't!" She stared up at his ruined face without flinching. "For one thing, you have a wife already! Or had you forgotten?"

Ashland's hand fell away.

"Because *I* haven't forgotten," she said. "And I doubt that London society has. You've no business engaging yourself to anyone, publicly or not. Lavish Park Lane ball to lure mad anarchists, or not."

He couldn't breathe. The pain in his chest was too great. He took a step back, and his foot seemed to sink forever into the weave of the carpet beneath, holding him fast. "You're correct, of course. I have no right, at present."

Her face began to soften. "Ashland . . ."

Behind him, Olympia coughed a delicate cough. "Ah yes.

Your unfortunate previous marriage. As to that, I believe I have a solution."

"There is no solution," said Ashland, without turning. The blue of Emilie's desperate eyes held him fast. "Not even you could effect a divorce so quickly. Even if you could, the haste of the engagement would be the scandal of the century."

"Ah." There was a rustle of papers, and a creak of floorboards beneath the rug. "After your recent visit, I took the liberty of making inquiries through my own channels. I received this reply within hours, just this morning."

A slip of paper appeared before Ashland's chest, just within the periphery of his vision. An odd skip moved his heart, whether dread or hope or anticipation. He grasped the note without looking and let his gaze drop slowly to the typescript message.

REGRET DUCHESS OF ASHLAND DIED RESULT
OF TYPHOID AT HOME ON VIA NATALE ROMA
ITALIA ON 19 SEPTEMBER 1887 STOP BODY
INTERRED ANGLICAN CEMETERY ON
21 SEPTEMBER 1887 .

"I'm very sorry for your loss," said the Duke of Olympia.

When Emilie found the Duke of Ashland again, he was wearing a thick wool greatcoat that made his large frame even more imposing, and a footman was handing him his hat and glove.

"Going out?" she called, from the bottom of the main staircase.

He turned, and Emilie's breath died somewhere at the base of her throat. His face was hard and pale, the mask like a black slash across his skin. At the sight of her, dressed once more in her feminine clothing, his massive body went still.

She crossed the hall. "May I have a word with you?"

He motioned with his hand to the small morning room overlooking the park. His silence unnerved her. He'd hardly said a word since Olympia presented him with that fatal telegram an hour ago; his face had taken on that same bleak expression it wore now, and he'd handed the paper back to her uncle with a low, "Thank you."

He had bowed to them both and left the room.

He said nothing now, simply allowed her to precede him into the room. A fire did its best to chase away the late January chill beneath a simple white marble mantel; Emilie crossed the room and held her hands above the glowing coals. "Did you speak to Freddie?" she asked.

"Yes. He took the news quite in stride."

"He never knew her, of course. He once told me she never really seemed alive to him at all. She was like a phantom to him."

"Yes."

Emilie turned. The duke stood near the window, staring at the skeletal row of Hyde Park trees across the street, his hat and glove dangling from his hand, the stern and beautiful lines of his perfect leftward profile turned toward her. A thin ray of winter sunshine turned his hair an almost ethereal shade of gossamer white. "Who is this man your Miss Dingleby has set to guarding the house? Hans, I believe?" he asked.

Emilie started. "My father's valet. He helped us escape."

"You're certain of his loyalty?"

"As I am of my own heart," she said.

He watched the scene outside the house with his eye narrowed in thought.

"Where are you going?" Emilie asked.

"I have a brief errand to run," he said, "and then there's much to arrange. A visit to my solicitor, wires to the Abbey. I should like the wedding to take place by March, if that does not inconvenience you."

"March!"

He turned at last. His broad shoulders nearly blocked the feeble light from the window. "If you must have something lavish, that should allow us enough time to make arrangements. In the meantime, I shall not rest until I discover and destroy this threat against you and your family. I find wholly unsatisfactory the efforts your uncle has made on your behalf thus far."

"We are not . . ."

"I shall also look about for a house in town. I daresay you

won't want to stay in Yorkshire year-round. You are welcome to accompany me in the search, as the home will be yours. The staff from Ashland will be called down to service it for the time being; do you have any objection? I shall give orders for the strictest discretion regarding your previous disguise."

Emilie drew in a long breath, which was truncated abruptly by the unexpected dig of her stays into her ribs. She could not meet him in anger, not now, when he'd just received such a shock. "I have not agreed to marry you, Ashland. I have not agreed to any of this. The engagement, the ball, all of which will occasion danger to you and your son. A marriage; a house in town, so far away from my own homeland."

He fingered the brim of his hat and tucked it under his right arm. "I am not particularly keen on your uncle's ideas myself. I see no reason to risk your life at a damned party, but Olympia always did prefer his grand schemes to a more subtle approach. Still, at least we may have the opportunity to rid ourselves of this menace at a single go, and you will be well protected. I shall not leave your side for an instant."

Emilie thought of Ashland's half-clothed and gleaming body, beating his fists with machinelike strength into the leather punching bag in the basement of Ashland Abbey.

"You're avoiding the question, Ashland. You know I wasn't speaking of the ball by itself."

He regarded her calmly with his bleak blue eye. The fire glowed warm on Emilie's back, but her front was warmer: The skin of her face and bosom and belly burned under Ashland's steady gaze, as if she were naked before him. He took two long and deliberate steps forward, reached out his hand, and traced the line of her jaw with extraordinary gentleness.

Emilie couldn't speak. Ashland's touch snaked through her body like a live electric charge.

His hand dropped. "I shall not force you to marry me, of course," he said, working his fingers into his glove. "A mere English duke, nearly forty years of age, maimed by war, widowed and with a child already, is perhaps a poor catch for a young and singularly beautiful princess of Germany. But as I have already taken the basest advantage of you, and as you find yourself in precarious and uncertain circumstances entirely without justice to your merit, I beg you to do me the

immeasurable honor of allowing me to devote my life to
ensuring your safety and happiness. Good afternoon, madam."

The Duke of Ashland bowed, put on his hat, and left the
room.

Alice's high voice carried across the room like an anxious
lapdog. "Why, Your Grace! What an extraordinary
surprise!"

Ashland turned. His sister-in-law stood in the doorway,
wringing her hands against her blue silk waist. The lamp cast
a warping shadow along one side of her face.

"Indeed," he said. "The day has been chock-full of surprises, from its earliest hour. I am not certain my constitution
can handle another, in fact, so I beg you to be as candid as
possible with me, Alice." He walked forward until he was
almost breathing on the sharp part of her dark hair. "As candid
as possible."

Alice stumbled back with a nervous trill of laughter. "Why,
Your Grace! I can't conceive what you mean. I have been perfectly candid with you."

"Ah! I suppose, then, it merely slipped your notice that my
wife has, in fact, been dead for over two years. Died in Rome
of typhoid, and buried there. Your remittances to her, perhaps,
were claimed by another?"

Alice's mouth opened, closed, and opened again. "Sir! I'm
sure I don't . . ."

Ashland took his watch from his pocket and examined the
face. "The hour grows late, Alice. I'm afraid I have no time to
waste on your denials, followed by my own threats and impre-
cations, and then by your own inevitable collapse and confession. Dreary, dull, and quite unnecessary. Pray sit down, and
I will explain matters to you in the concise and matter-of-fact
fashion to which I am accustomed. You needn't speak at all,
in fact."

Alice tottered forward and lowered her trembling backside
into a chair.

"First and most urgently: Does Miss Russell know of her
mother's death? Nod your head yes, or shake it no."

Alice's head swung slowly from side to side.

"As I thought. You are, as of this moment, relieved of your duty as her guardian. You will order her things packed at once, and you will quit this house yourself within the week. I shall allow you to keep your belongings and whatever savings you have managed to accrue during the course of your fraudulent guardianship, but you will be allowed no further allowance, nor any contact with Mary. Is that clear?"

Alice sat frozen.

"You will please nod your head, Alice, if you are quite clear on the matter."

Alice nodded her head.

"Very good. Now rise, if you will, and make the necessary orders. Mary and her governess will leave with me in half an hour."

Alice rose from her chair, white-faced and round-eyed. "But Your Grace! What do you propose to do with her?"

"To raise her as my daughter, of course."

"*Her?* But she's not yours. She's Isabelle's spawn, her and that earl, deceiving you in your own bed . . ."

Ashland spoke with slow precision. "I don't know what you mean. Lady Mary Russell was born to my wife during the course of our marriage. She is my legitimate daughter, and she has lived her life unclaimed and unwanted by those from whom she has a right to expect love and protection. This injustice will continue no longer. You will send her ladyship down to me at once, so I can deliver the news myself."

"Yes, sir." She moved to the doorway as if in a trance.

"Alice," he said softly.

She stopped.

"Did you really think I wouldn't find out? Did you really think you could carry on forever?"

Alice whipped around. "And what would it have mattered to you if I did? Isabelle finally got what she deserved. She had you all fooled, all of you, and still you followed her about like the dogs you were, sniffing under her skirts. You couldn't help yourselves around her, could you? You never saw what she really was. You couldn't believe someone so beautiful could be . . . oh, not evil, not that, but such a *child*, such a selfish child. I expect you thought the earl was her first lover, did you? I expect you thought you could traipse off to India with your regiment and Isabelle could do without the attention, she could do without everybody admiring her and flirting with her. I suppose you thought she was as faithful as you were."

Ashland looked down at her. His fist clenched and unclenched at his side. "I suppose I did."

Alice turned away, took a step forward, and paused in the doorway. She said, in a lowered voice, "It wasn't *you*, Your Grace. What she did, why she left you. Just so you know. It was *her*. And I always thought she was the greatest fool alive, walking away from you."

Ashland folded his arms against his chest.

Alice looked at her feet. Her hand touched the doorjamb. "I did Mary a favor, I did. She never knew what a whore her mother was."

"No," said Ashland. "And God help me, she never will."

The windows were already dark by the time Ashland knocked on Emilie's bedroom door. It was answered by a long, thin woman with neat hair and a pair of extraordinarily bright hazel eyes.

"Ah! Miss Dingleby. May I have a moment's privacy with my fiancée?"

Miss Dingleby's eyebrows lifted. Her rosebud mouth—far too innocent, Ashland thought, but Olympia always did have a strong sense of irony—curled upward in amusement, and she glanced over her shoulder into the lamplit interior of the room.

"It's quite all right, Dingleby," came Emilie's brusque voice. "He won't ravish me, I assure you."

Miss Dingleby turned back to Ashland. "I have talked some sense into her, thank goodness. So I'd be obliged if you didn't ruin anything with your masculine blustering and all that."

"I assure you, I have no intention of ruining anything." He paused. "Have *you*?"

Miss Dingleby raised a single challenging eyebrow and swept past, leaving the door open a respectable pair of inches.

Ashland closed it.

He walked forward to where Emilie sat in her chair before

a fine mahogany escritoire, pen in hand, lamp shining on her golden hair and brushing her delicate features. The pen trembled slightly in her fingers. Ashland's heart dropped away from his chest.

He found a nearby chair and carried it next to her and sat down, perched on the edge. The light struck her spectacles in such a way that he couldn't quite read the expression in her eyes. Expectant, perhaps. Or wary. He took her cool hand and pressed it between his fingers.

"Your Highness, I ask a boon."

TWENTY-ONE

The Marquess of Silverton blinked, removed his spectacles, wiped them with a disreputable handkerchief, and replaced them on his nose. "Good God, Grimsby. Look at you!"

Miss Dingleby adjusted the trim of Emilie's bodice by a fraction of an inch. "*Not* Grimsby. Her Royal Highness, the Princess Emilie of Holstein-Schweinwald-Huhnhof." She took a step back, passed a critical eye up and down Emilie's figure, and turned to Freddie. "And you will endeavor to recollect the fact, your lordship." The words *your lordship* dripped with scorn from her mouth.

Freddie whistled. "Regardless, that's a ripping frock you've got on, Grimsby. Has Pater seen it yet?"

"Not yet." Emilie swiveled one way and another before the mirror, hoping neither Freddie nor Miss Dingleby noticed the flush spreading rapidly over her damned telltale cheekbones.

"Then he's in for a shock tomorrow night. I do hope the poor fellow can keep his wits about him." He made a theatrical yawn, patting his mouth with one lazy palm. "I only wish I were there to see it."

"*Freddie.*" Emilie turned and planted her hands on her elegant silken hips. "You and your sister are not to move from your father's house tomorrow. *Not one step*. Is that understood? The ball is a *grown-up* affair." She cast him her sternest Grimsby glare, communicating a wealth of meaning and warning, which could be summed up pithily as: *Don't spill the beans, or else*.

"Not even a turn about the garden?"

"Don't be clever. If I see one hair of your excitement-seeking head lurking about the ball, I shall . . . I shall . . ."

"Tell tales to my father?"

Emilie looked at Mary, who sat in the corner, sketching Emilie's dress in furious strokes of her pencil. "Mary, my dear, do try to make sure your brother behaves himself."

Mary raised her dark head and smiled. "Shall I lock him in his room?"

"That's the spirit." Emilie turned back to the mirror. She hadn't meant to allow herself to become close to the girl, but how could she help it? Freddie dragged his new sister everywhere, and Emilie could hardly shut out Freddie. And then, after a week or so, Mary had begun to shed her careful reserve. She began to make her clever remarks, her flashes of humor, her startling questions, and suddenly they were all laughing and talking together, and the gaping sister-shaped holes in Emilie's heart had begun to trickle full again. Ashland would walk into the room, and his furrowed brow would smooth out, and though he wouldn't say anything—he rarely said anything now, as if conversation were taxed by the word—Emilie noticed the warmth in his eye, the softening around his mouth.

She was surrounded now, a hostage to this new family peopling itself around her, laying its claim to her. The lease for a splendid double-fronted house in Eaton Square had been signed a week ago, and Mary and Freddie had just been moved in, but they still spent most of their time in Park Lane, under the vigilant eye of the Duke of Ashland.

The Duke of Ashland, who, as the society columns breathlessly reported, was so in love with his royal fiancée, he scarcely left her side.

Even to sleep.

"Well, it's dashed dull about the old place. Hardly any furniture, and no company except the servants and that old beanpole of a French governess Mary's got. Good Lord, I'm glad

I'm not a girl. Governesses are a devil of a nuisance." He cast
a meaning glance at Miss Dingleby, which she ignored.

"Mademoiselle Duchamps is not a beanpole," Mary said.
"She has a long and elegant figure."

Emilie studied the corner of the mirror, in which half of
Mary's face caught the reflection. From the window, a pale
February sun revealed a distinct upward curl at the side of her
mouth. Emilie smiled back. "There are always your studies,
Freddie. Or had you forgotten your Oxford examinations?"

"Oxford? Who the devil cares about that anymore?"

Miss Dingleby clapped her hands. "Out, now, the both of
you! The dress is quite in order, as you can see, and I must
whisk it off Her Highness before she spills her tea and ruins
it. Off, off!"

When Mary and Freddie had been bustled away, Miss Dingleby applied herself to the infinity of fastenings at Emilie's
back.

"You're very good at that," said Emilie.

"At what? Acting as your lady's maid?"

Emilie smiled. "That, too. But I meant managing people.
When I was tutoring Freddie, I found myself using your tricks.
Your tone of voice."

The bodice loosened at last, and Miss Dingleby helped her
out of the voluminous dress, the multitude of frothing petticoats. "You are quite ready for tomorrow's ordeal?"

"I believe so. I suppose if I can't trust you, I can't trust
anybody."

"Quite true."

"Do you really think these men will strike? We've had no
sign of any danger since I arrived in London."

Miss Dingleby held out an afternoon tea dress of rose chif-
fon. "That may mean anything. But your uncle knows what
he's doing. These sorts of events tempt such organizations into
the open. They offer a prestigious target in an unguarded setting, they offer crowds in which to hide, they offer numerous
opportunities to infiltrate and strike. Most importantly, they
offer publicity. Think of the Tsar's assassination. Think of the
opera house bombing."

"Both of which were *successful* attacks."

Miss Dingleby attacked the buttons of the tea dress with

ruthless efficiency. "But we will be prepared. Your duke has the instincts of a guard dog, and we'll have our operatives posted throughout. As long as you don't turn missish, young lady. I want no last-minute airs and vapors."

"Of course not."

"You won't plead indisposition at the top of the stairs?"

"Miss Dingleby, *really*." Emilie tilted her chin.

"Very good. Because I did not whisk you and your sisters across Europe in the dead of night, agents at our heels, in order to have you disappoint me at the crisis." Miss Dingleby fastened the last button with her cool and efficient fingers and turned Emilie to face her. Her hazel eyes were all Dingleby: bright and searching, exposing Emilie's hidden corners like the uncompromising beam of a Channel lighthouse. "And now, my dear, I have an impertinent question for you."

"You, Miss Dingleby? I'm shocked."

"You must be quite honest with me, Emilie, my dear. I can't help you if you're not honest with me."

"I can't imagine what you mean."

Miss Dingleby took Emilie's hand between both of her own and pressed it. "My dear, I am trained to notice details, and having lived in such close proximity to you these last weeks— sleeping in your very bedroom—it has not escaped me that a certain visitor, ordinarily quite reliable, has not made its regular appearance. Hmm?"

Emilie tried to pull her hand away. "You're right. It's an extraordinarily impertinent question."

"Is the duke aware of this anomaly?"

"Which duke do you mean?"

Miss Dingleby arched one eyebrow. "Either one."

The room seemed to have gone quite cold, despite the warmth of Miss Dingleby's hands squeezing her own, the fiery light in the governess's eyes.

"There's no need to speak of it to anyone," Emilie said. "The visitor is not long overdue."

"How long?"

Emilie hesitated. "A week. Perhaps two."

"Two weeks. Long enough, then." Miss Dingleby pressed even more tightly. "And what are your intentions in the matter?"

"I . . . I don't know. I've hardly had time to think about it. After the ball . . ."

"After the ball may be too late. Come, sit down." Miss Dingleby drew her to the elegant leaf green settee at the end of the bed. "Now. You are to speak of this to no one, do you understand me?"

"I must tell Ashland, if . . . if the situation does not resolve itself."

"Nonsense. If you tell him, what will happen? You'll be obliged to marry him. This campaign of his, with his constant presence and his alluring ready-made family, will end in your becoming the Duchess of Ashland, if you're not careful."

Emilie forced a smile. "Not so terrible a fate, really. I'm becoming more reconciled to it by the day."

Miss Dingleby jerked back. "Good God, Emilie! I rescue you from that stifling German court of yours, from royal marriages and etiquette and the lot, and you tumble headfirst into the same chains from which I've delivered you? An English *duke*, Emilie? I thought better of you. I *taught* better of you."

"Ashland isn't like that."

"Don't be obtuse. I suppose you fancy yourself in love with him."

"If I do?"

"Then enjoy him, by all means, but don't make the mistake of marrying him."

Emilie jerked her hand free and stood. "I can't believe you're saying these things, Dingleby. You, who taught me about virtue and duty and *honor*."

"Think carefully, Emilie. Think about what I allowed you. The books I gave you. Our discussions, late at night. When did I discourage your ambitions?"

Emilie stood silently, her pulse snapping in a quick rhythm.

"You don't really want to marry him, do you? Out of the frying pan, into the fire. I'm only saying the very things you're thinking."

"I *do* love him. I want a life with him. I want . . ."

"But on your own terms, isn't that right? Without encumbrance, without obligation. As your husband, he can control your every move."

"He wouldn't do that."

"You're arguing against yourself. Come, sit down again." Miss Dingleby patted the cushion next to her.

Emilie remained standing.

"Very well. Listen to me: You have made an unfortunate error, but there are ways to correct it, without anyone the wiser."

For some reason, Miss Dingleby's words didn't sound as shocking as they should. Emilie heard them distantly, matter-of-factly, as if the two of them were back in the palace school-room, going over lessons. Luisa would be listening attentively, pencil poised, and Stefanie would be staring out the window, admiring a butterfly. Emilie's chest ached with longing.

"To rid myself of the baby, you mean," she said at last. "If indeed there is a baby."

Miss Dingleby sat on the settee with her arms folded in her black gabardine lap, forehead stretched with expectancy.

If indeed there is a baby. Emilie hadn't allowed herself to think about the possibility yet. She had pushed the suspicion away, had concentrated on other things. She had expected every day to see the signs that everything was normal, every-thing was quite all right, and every day the signs had not appeared, and still somehow she'd convinced herself that it was a mistake, that the very idea of being with child by the Duke of Ashland was absurd.

Absurd.

Her belly was quite flat. She felt quite as she usually did. Perhaps her breasts were a little sore, a little swollen, but that was surely the result of being back in corsets again, her body being shoved and squeezed into position; or perhaps because the tardy visitor was on the point of returning.

Should we be so fortunate as to conceive a child. Ash-land's child, the child he wanted. She forced herself to imag-ine it: Ashland, standing by a window, cradling a sleeping infant in his enormous arms. Her heart began to slow down, to thud in a hard and steady rhythm, returning warmth to her belly and limbs.

Ashland's child. *Their* child.

"Don't be ridiculous," she said.

"I am being perfectly reasonable. Women do it every day."

"Perhaps they do. But I couldn't do such a thing without telling him," said Emilie.

Miss Dingleby threw her hands up. "Listen to you! You're laying your neck conveniently on the scaffold, after all I did to free you."

"I see no reason to act at all just yet. Once the ball is over . . ."

Miss Dingleby rose. "Once the ball is over, and the danger is past, you'll have no escape. You'll be relieved, you'll be grateful to Ashland, you'll do whatever he asks. I am quite ashamed of you, Emilie. I'd thought you made of sterner stuff. I'd thought, if I gave you a taste of independence . . ."

Emilie's hands fisted at her sides. "Yes! Yes, I quite perceive that everybody thinks they know what's best for me. Everyone makes plans for me. Everybody moves me about at will to suit their own purposes. But I do have a will of my own, and I intend to exercise it this instant. Miss Dingleby, you will leave this room at once, and allow me *for once* to make my own decisions."

Miss Dingleby did not move. Her tender rosebud mouth tightened almost imperceptibly around the corners; her eyes regarded Emilie without blinking.

"Brava," she said at last, and left the room.

The Duke of Ashland, ascending the grand staircase of the Duke of Olympia's Park Lane town house two steps at a time, was not particularly pleased to encounter the neatly dressed figure of Miss Dingleby just as he achieved the top.

He stepped aside. "Good afternoon, Miss Dingleby."

"Good afternoon, Your Grace. You are here to see Her Highness?" she asked, as she might ask, *You are here to snatch the Grail of Our Lord from its sacred altar, you unscrupulous dog?*

"I am."

"I suppose it will not trouble you that Her Highness is resting in her bedchamber at present?"

"I shall not disturb her long."

"Certainly not. I have every faith in Your Grace's sense of honor and decency," said Miss Dingleby in precisely spaced words. "Good day."

The door to Emilie's suite stood ajar. He rapped on the thick panel nonetheless.

"Who is it?"

"Ashland."

A slight pause. "Come in."

He pushed open the door. Emilie stood at the window, her fingers pressed against the sill. The fading light cast a bluish tint over her skin.

"You're not wearing your spectacles," he said.

"My eyes were hurting."

"Are you all right?"

"Yes." She looked at him. The muscles of her face were drawn tight; her body radiated restless tension. One finger drummed against the wooden window frame. "Are you off to return Freddie and Mary to Eaton Square?"

"Yes, I am. I shall return later this evening, of course. Where is Miss Dingleby going? You shouldn't be left alone like this."

She crossed the floor toward him. "May I go with you? I've hardly been outside at all these past weeks."

"I would rather you didn't. I have an errand to run before returning."

"I see."

"Emilie." He fixed his arms behind his back to keep himself from touching her. "Are you quite all right?"

"Yes."

"If you're having second thoughts about tomorrow, I can stop everything. I'll tell Olympia . . ."

"No! No. I want this over with."

"I don't like it. You know that. There are other ways."

"It's my decision," she said.

She stood so regally, her back straight, her chin tilted. Her golden hair was parted neatly and gleamed with submission before disappearing into a snug chignon at the back of her neck. She reminded him of a citadel, all smooth stone walls and high battlements. He wanted to throw up his grappling hook and scale her, but the very thought of the act seemed profane. As if he might scar her, might mar the perfect fortress of her.

Where was Emily, behind Emilie's polished walls? Where was Grimsby?

"There are other ways," he said again. "I have a special license in my pocket this instant. You are above the age of consent; we can be married before dinner. We can go away, wherever you like."

"Nonsense. I intend to see this through. For my sisters' sake, if nothing else."

A flash of white showed between the fingers of her right hand: a balled-up handkerchief.

"Very well. Either way, I have made the necessary preparations. In the meantime, I have something for you." He withdrew an envelope from his jacket pocket and held it out to her.

"What is it?" She tucked the handkerchief into her sleeve and took the envelope. He looked at her wrist. He wanted to strip away that sleeve, to strip away the dress itself, to gorge himself on her nakedness. He wanted to tumble her backward into that bed, or possibly forward, and make love to her until she was crying with pleasure, until she was laughing out loud, until she was *herself* again.

He swallowed heavily. "It arrived in the post at Eaton Square, addressed to you."

She looked at the black scrawl on the envelope and gasped.

"Do you recognize it?" he asked.

Her gaze lifted to his, eyes wide with excitement, apprehension vanished. "It's from my sister."

TWENTY-TWO

The thin light of the gas lamps shifted across Ashland's face as the carriage rounded the corner of Cheyne Walk later that night, making his ruined face even more terrifying than usual. His thunderous expression didn't help. "I am a fool for letting you talk me into this."

"It's perfectly safe. You're with me, and nobody in London knows me as Grimsby. Well, except Freddie, and he's hardly an anarchist. A principled one, at any rate."

"This is not the time for jokes."

"Yes, it is." Laughter bubbled up in her throat. She glanced out the window at the passing shadows of the houses, the lurid pools of gaslight on the pavement. "I'm going to see my sister. My sister, Ashland! You don't know what this means to me." She reached out and wrapped her hand around his enormous knee.

"You're certain it was her handwriting? There could be no mistake?" He ignored her hand.

"As certain as I am of my own."

"This chap she's bringing. Is she a decent judge of character? You've no idea who he might be?"

"He must be the man my uncle placed her with, and you know Olympia's judgment is impeccable."

A grunting noise rumbled from his chest. He folded his arms. "I don't like it."

"You don't have to like it. Only try to be happy for me, will you?"

The carriage lurched over a rut, dislodging Emilie's hand and flinging her off balance. Like a snake, Ashland's arm flashed out to steady her. His grip encompassed her entire shoulder.

"A quarter of an hour," he said. "No more."

The carriage slowed. Albert Bridge loomed ahead, the approach shrouded with trees.

Ashland reached inside his overcoat, drew out a pistol, laid it in his lap. "You have your stiletto?"

"Put that away. Yes, I do." She craned her head against the window, trying to make out the shapes outside in the thickening river fog. The carriage jolted to a stop, and she reached for the handle just as Ashland's hand closed over hers.

"I go first," he said. He gripped the pistol with his left hand and cocked it with a nimble motion of his stump. His chin jerked, motioning her to open the carriage door for him.

The dank Thames air rushed across Emilie's cheeks. Ashland swung to the ground in a lithe and silent movement, like the enormous African cat she had imagined him, back in the library at Ashland Abbey. He tossed a single soft word back to the driver.

"Wait," he said to Emilie. "Stay back in the carriage until I've called you."

Emilie's hand fisted around the edge of the door. Ashland took a step forward, and another. "Holstein," he called out, in a low and carrying voice.

"Huhnhof," came the faint reply.

Ashland made a quick motion with his right arm. Emilie slithered down the carriage step and came up behind him, in the shelter of his broad back, looking around his shoulder to the charcoal smudges of the Embankment.

A shape emerged. "Ashland, by God."

"Hatherfield?" Ashland lowered his pistol.

"She's right in the bushes behind . . ." the man's voice began, but the rest was lost in a rush of footsteps, a flying

missile of wool and damp skin that flung itself past Ashland
and swept up Emilie in a bone-crushing embrace.

"Stefanie!" Emilie gasped out, hugging her back, crying,
shaking. She pushed the coat-clad shoulders away and grasped
her sister by the cheeks. "It's you!"

The Marquess of Hatherfield coughed discreetly. "Does
have a rather . . . a rather *odd* appearance, don't it?"

Ashland glanced at the two figures embracing on the bench
ten yards away, on whose four trousered legs only the faintest
trace of gaslight gleamed. Emilie had taken off her bowler hat,
and Stefanie was touching her hair, exclaiming at its
shortness.

He kicked his toe at the gravel. "Is she really a ginger?"

"Beyond a doubt," Hatherfield said blandly.

A squeal of delight issued from the bench, followed by an
answering squeal of equal pitch.

"What the devil are they talking about?" Ashland said.

"Us, old man. Us."

"How do you know that?"

"Four sisters. And a stepmother."

A hansom cab trotted by in a wet rattle of hooves and
wheels. Ashland watched it travel along the Embankment and
up Cheyne Walk. The fog was already growing denser, cold
and greasy against his skin. "Five minutes," he called out
gently.

The two figures on the bench paid no attention. They were
holding hands now, chattering like birds. Their words mingled
and overlapped, an astonishing tangle of verbiage. How the
devil did they make each other out?

"Women," said Hatherfield. He thrust his hands into his
coat pockets.

"Have you had any trouble?" Ashland asked.

Hatherfield sighed a weary sigh. "Nothing *but* trouble, old
man. You?"

"I mean this sort of trouble." Ashland nodded to the thick
and expectant shadows around them. "Threats, attacks. Has
anyone found you out?"

"No, no. Lying low."

"Stay low, Hatherfield. Stay low. You've heard about the ball tomorrow?"

"Invitation arrived a week ago."

"Don't go. Don't let *her* go. Do you understand me?"

Stefanie's giggle rang in the air. At least Ashland assumed it was Stefanie. He'd certainly never heard Emilie make such a sound.

"I see," said Hatherfield.

"Yes."

Another hansom rattled by, followed by a carriage. A drunken voice rolled faintly from the boats moored nearby in the river.

Ashland called out, "Two minutes."

On the last syllable, a sense of movement caught his attention: a noise, or perhaps intuition, because the movement came on his blind right side.

He turned. A dull gleam flashed from the fog-shrouded shadow of a clump of trees.

"Secure the women," he said to Hatherfield, and he launched himself toward the trees.

A loud crack split the air. Cries erupted from the bench behind him.

Another stride, and he was flying into the shadows, colliding with a solid wool-padded figure.

"Oof," it said.

The gun flew to the pavement. Ashland kicked it away with his boot and shot his left fist into the man's jaw. His head snapped backward; he toppled to the ground like a felled tree.

Ashland leaned down and gathered the man's collar in his fist. "Who are you? Who sent you?"

The man's hand moved; a flash of metal caught the gaslight. With a single motion, Ashland released the collar and thrust his right elbow downward into the man's wrist. A faint crunch, and the knife dropped to the stones with a clank. The man howled with pain.

"Who sent you?"

The man lurched up. Ashland sent another fist into his jaw, and this time he went still into the pavement.

"Damnation," Ashland muttered.

A low cry floated behind him. He whipped around.

In the blur of darkened bodies shifting through the fog, he couldn't make anything out. Four people, maybe five. The hard smack of a fist connecting with flesh. A howling cry. Emilie's voice, shouting something.

Ashland's pistol dug into his ribs, but the quarters were too close for bullets. He reached for the knife in the grass, leapt forward, and grabbed the nearest figure. Broad, bulky: not one of the women. Ashland had at least eight inches of height on the man. He brought his right elbow down hard in the juncture of neck and shoulder, and the attacker crumpled to the ground without a sound.

In the murky darkness, Emilie's pale face flashed by, her neck enclosed by a thick woolen arm.

A white glare lit behind Ashland's eyes. He let out a low growl, balanced the knife in his hand, and thrust his stump forward with exacting precision, just to the right of Emilie's ribs, directly into her attacker's gut.

The man's grip loosened. Emilie dug her elbow into his ribs. He released her with an *oof*, and even before Emilie had slumped forward, Ashland took the man about the chest and laid the knife against his throat.

"Who are you?" he growled. "Who sent you?"

The man gasped something.

"What's that?"

A shot cracked out. Something blurred before his eyes.

"Damn it to hell!" Ashland said. He threw the man heavily to the ground and grabbed Emilie's hand. "To the carriage!"

"I can't leave Stefanie!" she cried.

"Right here." Hatherfield's voice came at his ear, calm and steady. "Shot came from the river."

"Take the women to the carriage. I'll cover." Ashland drew out his pistol.

"Right-ho." Hatherfield dashed off, herding Emilie and Stefanie, and Ashland turned to the river. It was encased in fog, ghostly and impenetrable. How the devil could anyone have aimed a pistol from there?

Another shot cracked out. A bullet whistled past his ear.

Not the river. The *bridge*.

Ashland swore. At his feet, the man stirred, but there was

no time to deal with him. Ashland hurried toward the carriage, half running, keeping his pistol trained toward Albert Bridge. Hatherfield was bustling the women in, shielding the door with his body.

"Go south," Ashland said to the driver, swinging in behind Hatherfield. "Away from the bloody bridge."

The carriage lurched forward as he shut the door. Ashland found Emilie, scooped her up, and crushed her into his chest.

There will be no ball tomorrow," said Ashland. He was holding the knife in his hand, turning it about in the trace of light from the carriage window. They had just seen off Stefanie and her marquess into an anonymous black hansom cab on the Brompton Road, and the interior of the carriage had grown heavy with the shock of aftermath.

"We can't cancel it now."

He looked at her. "Are you mad? You were nearly killed just now."

"He wasn't trying to kill me. If he were, I'd be dead."

"Then what was he doing?"

"Trying to take me away. To kidnap me." She spoke quickly, her words running together. Her brain kept jumping about, as if struck by a charge of electricity, unable to settle into logic. She tried to remember the exact sequence of events, but she could only muster flashing impressions. The elation of seeing Stefanie, touching and talking to Stefanie, as if they'd only been parted for hours instead of months. The sudden attack, the arm squeezing her neck, the flight to the carriage.

Had it all really happened? To her, the quiet and unremarkable Emilie?

"Oh, a thousand times better, then." Ashland tucked the knife into the pocket of his overcoat, and a trace of a wince passed across his face.

"You're hurt!"

"It's nothing. A nick."

She grabbed his left sleeve. A rent showed through the cloth at the forearm; the edges were wet. "It's not a nick! You've been cut!"

"For God's sake, Emilie. I've seen worse."

She looked up at his scarred face. Guilt washed over her heart. "Yes, but you're not in the Afghan wilderness anymore. You're in London. You're with me."

He touched her cheek. "Yes."

A streetlamp ghosted along his face. His expression was soft with longing, the way it had looked when she had first removed her blindfold in the hotel room at Ashland Spa.

Weeks ago, a lifetime ago. How she'd missed him, the open and unguarded Ashland.

She unbuttoned her coat and jacket and waistcoat, revealing her white shirt. She pulled one tail free from her trousers. Before Ashland could protest, she took the knife from his pocket and started a tear in the fabric.

"Damn it, Emilie. We're a quarter hour from home. I'm not going to bleed to death."

But he let her ease his arm from his coat and jacket. He let her roll back the sleeve of his shirt to reveal a cut, not particularly long or deep—thank goodness for well-made winter woolens—but still leaking blood. She wiped away the excess and bound it up.

"There. That's better, isn't it?" His thick forearm lay passively in her hands, without so much as a flex of muscle.

"Much better."

His voice was husky. She looked up, and her silly eyes filled. "I'm sorry, Ashland. I'm so sorry for all this. You haven't deserved any of it."

"No, I don't. I don't deserve you at all."

She whispered, "Oh, you fool."

She released his arm and put her hands to his cheeks. They were warm and damp beneath her palms, from exertion and from the relentless London fog. The leather half-mask had molded to his skin.

"You fool. You're too good for me. You fool." She lifted herself from the seat and straddled his thighs. "You fool." She kissed his mouth.

"Emilie." The single word was hardly more than a rumble in his chest.

Ashland's lips savored hers, too slowly. She thrust her tongue between them and stroked the silken lining of his mouth.

All at once, his arms were bound across her back. He urged her into his body; his mouth returned her kiss as if to consume her. She cradled his hard and muscled lap between her legs, his unstoppable strength, and she ground herself into him. "I want you," she said. "Now."

"Emilie . . ."

"*Now*, Ashland. Please."

Ashland's fingers thrust against the waistband of her trousers and fumbled with the fastening. It fell open, and his hand slipped down to caress her, his thumb rubbing against her nub, his index finger sliding down her lips and surging inside her. She cried out.

"God, you're wet, you're so wet," he said in wonder.

She went up on her knees. He brought down her trousers in brutal tugs, forcing them past the seat cushions and down to her ankles. The air was cold on her skin, but she hardly noticed, with Ashland's hot fingers sliding up to wrap around her bottom. She tore at the fastening of his trousers, unbuttoning his flies. Her bones shook at the shape of his hardness through the fabric.

His fingers dipped into the cleft of her bottom. His cock filled her hands, too much to hold.

"Put your arms around my neck, Emilie," he said.

Ashland's breath rushed in hot gusts against her jaw. Tiny beads of sweat had broken out on his brow, as if he were fighting some unseen battle. She brought her arms up around his neck, anchoring herself, and he guided her downward, bringing her to rest on the tip of his vertical member.

"*Ashland.*" Emilie's mind went white with need.

"Easy, now." With two gentle fingers he parted her lips and nestled himself inside the outermost walls of her passage. "Make it last."

"I can't," she panted, wriggling downward on him, desperate.

He held her buttocks firmly in check. His voice was stern. "Make it last."

She eased herself down, begging softly at the infinite delight, the steady encroaching size of him.

"That's it. That's it." He groaned the words.

Deeper and deeper he went. The carriage jounced, but he

steadied her, keeping them joined, until with a last rough little tilt of his hips, he buried himself fully inside.

"Oh my God," she said. He was bone deep, lodged in place against the entrance to her womb. She shifted her hips to relieve the ache, but there was nowhere to go.

"Emilie." He kissed her neck, her jaw, her ear, frantic and tender.

She lifted herself carefully back up. Their bodies made a slick sound, wet flesh against flesh, richly carnal.

The jolting of the carriage brought her down again. A lurching turn, and Ashland swore savagely, fighting to keep her atop him. His hips tilted upward, seeking hers, and she came down hard, lifted herself, and slammed down again with an inhuman growl of satisfaction at the pleasure-pain of it, the sweet bruising heat of cramming herself full of Ashland. Over and over she drove home his eager cock, while he muttered lewd and thrilling words into her ear to the frantic beat of her movements: telling her how to use him, telling her what she did to him.

The carriage did most of the work. It jolted them together with erotic friction; it threw them apart and made them clutch and shove like a pair of lust-crazed animals. Ashland went on muttering in her ear, urging her on, his fingers prying gently at the seam of her flesh, and the dark box around them filled with the sucks and gasps of union, with the earthy scent of human desire.

It was not perfect. It was messy and disjointed, it was arrhythmic and raw. The air grew thick and humid with perspiration. Ashland's lips pressed on her skin, his arms caged her body, his cock rammed in and out, in and out, violent with need, rubbing over and over against a place of brilliant sensation. Emilie gripped his black shoulders and ground into every stroke, panting hard, straining with all her might, almost there, almost, *almost, oh God* . . .

The carriage swung right, at just the wrong instant. A keen of frustration burst from her lips.

Ashland's firm grip drew her back. "*Do* it, Emilie. Come *now*," he demanded, holding his thumb over her nub, pushing himself deep, and all at once she burst over the edge, incandescent, her body pulsing whole with the shock of release.

At the instant of climax, Ashland's arms lifted her and placed her to one side, and in a quick movement he brought out his handkerchief and spent in spasms of hot seed, as his right arm pinned her shuddering body fast against his chest.

Ashland's mind crept upward from the brink of consciousness. Emilie lay pressed against him, breathing hard, her hand splayed across the thick wool of his overcoat.

Sweet Christ. She had just swived him senseless in his carriage.

He could scarcely move. Every muscle had relaxed into a simmering torpor. With effort he shoved his handkerchief into his pocket and settled Emilie more comfortably against his side. She stirred awkwardly, raising her head, and he remembered that her trousers were still tangled around her ankles.

"Sorry," he managed. He reached down and tugged her trousers back into place; he forced his half-erect prick inside the placket of his own and fastened the buttons.

"Don't say that. Don't be sorry." Her hand curled around his neck. The simple gesture made his chest glow with warmth. *This* was the woman he knew; this was *his* woman, his Emilie.

And he would kill anyone who tried to harm her.

The carriage rounded another turn. He looked out the window just in time to catch a flashing glimpse of the Duke of Wellington on horseback.

"Hyde Park Corner," he said in her ear. "Almost there."

She lifted herself up. "You didn't need to do that. Your handkerchief."

Ashland's brain was as foggy as London itself. "What's that?"

"Ashland, I . . . I've got to tell you something . . ."

The carriage slowed and jounced over a hole in the pavement, breaking them apart. "Later," he said.

He brought her in through the area door, to which he had a key, nodding to Hans's shadowed figure as he descended the steps. Neither of them spoke as they stole through the kitchens and up the back staircase. A clock chimed one o'clock as they reached the landing on the second floor, Emilie's floor.

She turned at the door to her room. "You can't come in. Miss Dingleby sleeps with me. She's expecting me back; she'll still be awake."

"I know. I sleep in the next room."

"What?"

He kissed her lips. "Just sleep. We'll speak in the morning. Are you all right?"

"Yes."

"I wasn't too rough?"

She ducked her head. "No. *No!* You were perfect. *I* was rough. I wanted that. I needed to . . . to break free from all this . . ."

"I am at your service, madam." He kissed her again. "Take a warm bath in the morning. You'll be sore, I'm afraid. If it weren't for your damned Miss Dingleby I'd . . ."

"We've got to talk, Ashland."

"Later. Tomorrow. You need your rest."

"*You* need your rest."

"I'll be up when I've spoken to your uncle. Sleep well. I'll make sure you're safe tonight. Every night."

She tried to speak, but he pointed to the door, mouthed *Miss Dingleby*, and opened it for her.

When she was safely inside, the door closed behind her, Miss Dingleby's urgent voice asking her questions, Emilie answering in crisp, firm tones, Ashland tripped down the stairs at double time and strode to the entrance of Olympia's private study, from which a crack of light still showed.

His mind had cleared. Energy had returned to his limbs; he was vibrating with resolve. He threw open the door without knocking.

The room was empty, except for Ormsby the butler, turning down the lamps.

"Where is His Grace?" Ashland demanded.

Ormsby looked up. "I'm very sorry, Your Grace. The duke has gone out."

TWENTY-THREE

Freddie flung the newspaper onto the desk. "Look, Grimsby! I'm on the front page!"

"Your lordship," said Miss Dingleby, "you will please remove yourself from Her Highness's chamber at once. We have a ball for which to prepare her."

Emilie plucked up the newspaper. The headline shouted LOST PRINCESS FINDS LOVE IN ENGLAND; SET TO WED DUKE OF ASHLAND IN STORY-BOOK ROMANCE; ROYAL BALL TONIGHT IN PARK LANE TO CELEBRATE ENGAGEMENT; PRINCE AND PRINCESS OF WALES EXPECTED TO ATTEND in breathless capital letters. She peered at the blurred photograph on the page before her: taken, it seemed, on the steps of church last Sunday. How they had managed the picture, she couldn't imagine. Olympia had loomed at her right side; Ashland had glowered at her left. She had been practically surrounded by a Roman phalanx of oversized dukes. "Where *are* you?"

He came up next to her and pointed at the photograph. "Right there! Can't you see it?"

"That's an ear."

"*My* ear." He snatched the paper away. "And well captured. Note the noble curve, if you will."

"Your lordship, *please*." Miss Dingleby's voice rang with gubernatorial authority. "I wonder Her Highness allows you here at all. It is *most* improper."

"Improper?" Freddie looked genuinely appalled. He swung helplessly to Emilie. "What the devil's improper about it? In a matter of days, she'll be my *mother*!"

"*Hmm*," Miss Dingleby snapped. She marched to the door and held it open. "Out."

Freddie's shoulders slumped. He trudged to the door, paper dangling from his hand.

Emilie's heart gave out. She had tried all day to find a private word with Ashland, but he'd been gone from the house since daybreak, had only returned an hour ago, and had gone straight to Olympia's private study under locked door. Of the household staff, bustling with preparations for the ball, only Miss Dingleby remained to serve her. Or to guard her prison cell, more accurately. She'd spent the past hour pacing about like a caged animal, watching the inexorable progress of the clock on her mantel.

And now here was Freddie, in and out like a gust of welcome air, throwing about words like *mother*.

Stalwart Freddie.

"Freddie, wait." Emilie followed him to the door. She spoke in a low voice. "Look after your sister tonight, please. And if anything should happen, if your father or I . . . If anything should happen, you'll take care of her."

"Of course."

Emilie leaned forward and kissed his cheek. "Go. Your father's waiting to take you back to Eaton Square."

"No, he's not. He's shut up with Olympia, laying schemes. Hans is going with us."

"Hans, then. And stay put, for heaven's sake. Don't risk yourself."

Freddie rolled his eyes and turned, straight into the slight figure waiting outside the door.

"Good God," he said. "*Lucy!* What the devil are you doing here?"

* * *

The Duke of Olympia lifted the stopper from the crystal neck of the sherry decanter and motioned in Ashland's direction. "Calms the nerves," he said.

Ashland held up his hand. "My nerves are perfectly calm, thank you."

Olympia poured himself a glass. "All this hustle-bustle. I shall be very glad when it's all over and we can return to business as usual."

"I shudder to ask what constitutes business as usual for you."

"Oh, this and that." Olympia waved his hand and drank his sherry. He was already dressed for the ball in crisp whites and gleaming blacks. His graying hair shone under the electric lamp.

"If we may return to the matter at hand, however." Ashland made a minute adjustment to the starched white cuff emerging from his formal black sleeve. "I have spent the morning making inquiries regarding the matter of last night."

Olympia held up his sherry glass to the lamp and examined the play of light in its multitude of facets. "We will speak later, of course, on the wisdom of taking my niece for a midnight assignation at all, let alone without informing me first. I might have saved you a great deal of trouble, had I known."

"I was prepared to protect her, and I did. And she wanted to see her sister."

"With an imminent threat hanging over her head, Emilie's desire to see her sister is neither here nor there."

"I disagree."

"Because you are in love with her."

"Because I have seen what a few weeks of being a prisoner in this house has done to her. She is honorable, she is dutiful, she hasn't complained. But she is not happy. She is not herself."

Olympia's glass landed on his desk with a trifle more force than necessary, spilling a precious few drops of sherry onto the depthless mahogany. "How many times, Ashland, have I cautioned you not to let your *emotions* become involved in your work?" The word *emotions* dripped from his mouth, as if he'd accidentally ingested some foul concoction of earth-worm and bat's blood.

Ashland returned his gaze levelly. "The happiness of others should be the ultimate goal of any endeavor. Should it not?"

"Hmm." Olympia took out his handkerchief and dabbed at the spilled sherry.

"Do you mean simply to harangue me for my excessively emotional nature, or have you any interest in the outcome of my inquiries this morning?"

"The latter, of course."

"Very well. I met with Hatherfield . . ."

"Ah yes." Olympia sank into his chair. "Tell me about my dear friend Hatherfield."

"I daresay you know more than I do. Very clever of you, tapping us all for your project. In any case, he has not encountered any outside danger in his—ahem—association with Princess Stefanie, but he has received an odd series of notes." He drew a paper from his pocket and laid it on the desk before him. "He gave me this one for examination. Do you recognize the writing?"

Olympia took the note and smoothed it with care. "I do not."

"You will note the peculiar character of the letters themselves. It puts me in mind of the Gothic German script."

"I see your point."

"It does not awaken any particular suspicion?"

Olympia looked up and pushed the note back across the desk. "My dear Ashland, remember that this organization has members across Europe. We might attribute such writing to any number of men."

"You're not concerned that someone seems to have discovered Princess Stefanie's true identity as well? That these clever disguises of yours haven't seemed to fool our opponents at all?"

A thump sounded through the floorboards, and a faint shout. Ashland raised one eyebrow.

Olympia waved his hand. "The musicians, I believe, are setting up."

"You're quite certain of them?" Ashland folded the paper and replaced it in his pocket.

"They are all trained agents," said Olympia. "Hence the, er, difficulties in arranging themselves, er, musically."

"Any other outside staff? Has the food been examined?"

"My dear fellow, I am not an amateur. We have gone over these details countless times."

Ashland leaned forward. "One more question. This Hans. Emilie's father's valet. What do we know of him?"

"Enough."

"Can he write English?"

"He was devoted to the late Prince. Vetted by Miss Dingleby herself."

"Ah yes. The redoubtable Miss Dingleby. A finger in every pie, it seems. Vetting valets. Protecting princesses from mortal harm."

Olympia knitted his fingers together on the desk and twirled his thumbs in a kind of water mill. A faint scent of cigars and sherry drifted from the air around him, a familiar and reassuring smell. The smell of competent men, of clubs and private studies. "You do not approve of my Dingleby?"

"She has your trust. She must be beyond reproach." Ashland laid his palm flat atop his crossed leg. He was wearing knee breeches, as befitted a royal occasion, and his quadricep felt as if it might burst through the gleaming white silk. Without adjusting his own expression a millimeter, he studied the duke's face: the deepening lines about his blue eyes, the uncompromising angle of his chin. How many secrets were crammed into the skull behind that face?

Olympia sighed and leaned back in his chair. "What an observant fellow you are. Perhaps I should start from the beginning."

Ashland allowed a small smile. "Better late than never, I always say."

Miss Dingleby stepped back to admire the result of the hour's labor. "Excellent work, Lucy. Mrs. Needle was quite right; you are a wonder with hair. Perhaps that curl near her right ear might be a trifle higher?" She motioned with her finger.

"Aye, ma'am." Lucy came in again with the tongs, nearly singeing the skin of Emilie's ear.

"Excellent, excellent," Miss Dingleby said. "I hardly recognize you, my dear. Rather like your sister's engagement ball last year. What a glorious occasion! Except for the fiancé, of course. A sad sack, Peter, but that's all in the past."

"He wasn't a sad sack. He was quite pleasant."

The roll of Miss Dingleby's eyes demonstrated exactly her opinion of pleasantness in young men. "Now stand up, my dear."

Emilie rose to her feet. Lucy stepped back to a respectful distance.

Miss Dingleby busied herself about Emilie's skirts, getting each fall of fabric just so. "Excellent, excellent," she muttered, emerging at last. She stood back and cocked her head to one side. Her finger tapped her lower lip.

"What do you think, Lucy? How does Her Highness look?"

"Quite nice," said Lucy.

"Hmm. Yes. I see what you mean." Miss Dingleby reached forward and removed Emilie's spectacles. "Oh, there we are. Much better, don't you think? Our dear Duke of Ashland won't be able to take his eyes from you."

Lucy made a tiny and tortured cough, as if a small animal were strangling itself at the back of her throat.

"Yes, Lucy?" Miss Dingleby said, without looking.

"Nobbut a . . . a speck of t'dust, ma'am." Lucy laid her tongs on the dressing table.

"A glass of water, then." Miss Dingleby snapped her fingers. "In fact, that's an excellent idea. I shall return at once with drinks for us all. I have a special recipe for calming the nerves."

"My nerves are perfectly calm," said Emilie, and it was true. She felt utterly cool and collected, as if she were a doll of some kind, an automaton encased in ice, a princess of Holstein-Schweinwald-Huhnhof. Not at all the sort of hoyden who would engage in rampant carnal intercourse with dukes in midnight carriages.

The wheels of fate were turning now, and there was not a bloody thing she could do about it.

"Nonsense. I shall be back directly." Miss Dingleby strode to the door and marched out.

Emilie studied the closed door with a trace of bemusement, then went to the dressing table, picked up her spectacles, and replaced them on her nose. She stared at her reflection in the mirror.

A magnificent dress, she had to concede. Her long figure had been compacted into an hourglass of blue satin, so pale and icy it was nearly white. The sleeves were gathered up at the very balls of her shoulders in sprays of tiny blue satin rosettes, and her gleaming skirts came together in the back into a veritable river of a long ice blue train. Her bodice swooped just to the edge of propriety, and a fringe of frothing petticoats peeped out a fraction of an inch between her ice blue hem and the floor. A matching blue ribbon wound through the artfully upswept curls on her head.

To her right, Lucy was busying herself with the tongs and the hairpins, her face a study in ruddy color.

"Thank you for your help, Lucy," Emilie said.

"Aye, ma'am. I'm right fair sorry, ma'am. I mean Your Highness. What happened afoor in Yorkshire. I never did know. . . I never thought . . ."

"Lucy, my dear. Whatever are you talking about?"

Lucy looked up and met her face in the mirror. "That last night, ma'am . . ."

"I have no idea what you mean. Yorkshire, you say? The Princess Emilie of Holstein-Schweinwald-Huhnhof was never in Yorkshire." Emilie gave a delicate shudder to underscore her point.

Lucy blinked. "Ma'am?"

"As it happens, however, your arrival is most fortuitous. I am in need of a lady's maid at the moment."

Lucy's mouth dropped open. "But ma'am . . . Your Highness . . . I'm never trained at all . . ."

"That is of no consequence whatever. My interest in fashion is minimal. What I require, most of all, is discretion and loyalty." She turned from the mirror and met Lucy's astonished gaze. "Discretion, my dear, and loyalty. Offer me these, and I shall return them in spades."

"Oh, ma'am." Lucy breathed out slowly.

"Discretion and loyalty, Lucy. Do you possess these qualities?"

"Aye, ma'am."

"Good, then." Emilie turned back to the mirror. "Now if you'll help me with these shoes. I can't seem to find my feet amongst all these petticoats."

The door opened again while Lucy's head was still buried under Emilie's skirts.

"Dear me." Miss Dingleby set down a tray on the desk. "Have we lost the poor girl already?"

Lucy emerged, somewhat disheveled. "Ma'am?"

"Never mind. Emilie, my dear, I have prepared you a batch of my special elixir. Calms the nerves, refreshes the senses." Miss Dingleby picked up one of the glasses from the tray and held it out to her.

"I've told you already. My nerves are calm enough."

"Nonetheless." Miss Dingleby jiggled the glass. The light reflected in tiny wavelets across her face, making her irises appear to shift color to green and back again.

"Not just now, Dingleby. I'm not a bit thirsty."

Miss Dingleby sighed and replaced the glass. "Now, look at you. You really must remove those spectacles, my dear. It's your engagement party. Your duke awaits you below; the Prince of Wales himself is among the guests." She walked to Emilie, took off the spectacles, and folded them with care. "You see?"

"I don't, as a matter of fact. That is the point of the spectacles."

"Ashland will be by your side the entire evening. You have no need of perfect eyesight. Really, you must look your best, for his sake. You do want him to be proud of you, don't you?"

"His Grace will be proud of her, with or without t'spectacles," said Lucy. "And brains is heaps more important nor beauty, me mum always said."

"Why, thank you, Lucy," said Emilie. "How very flattering."

"Dear me. It seems the household staff in Yorkshire are encouraged to have opinions." Miss Dingleby smiled, a faint stretching of her perfect rosebud lips. She picked up the glass of elixir, her own private recipe. "Come, now. You must have a drink. You'll find yourself much refreshed."

Emilie took the glass and held it up to the light. It was pink in color and rather cloudy in its fine crystal tumbler, reminding her oddly of the thick fog drifting off the river last night. A hint of grapefruit tickled her nose. Miss Dingleby had always propounded the merits of grapefruit. She had insisted on each princess eating a half, carefully sectioned and without sugar, for breakfast every morning, regardless of season. The governess had consumed the remaining half herself; she hated waste of any kind.

The smell of the grapefruit wound through Emilie's nostrils, recalling all those mornings about the table in the breakfast room, unsweetened fruit poised expectantly on her plate, the routine and formal beginning to every routine and formal day. Each hour passing by like the drip of rain on a window, exactly like the one before. The smell, the memory itself, made her feel faintly ill.

"Come along, then," said Miss Dingleby, her hazel eyes bright in her sharp face. She put one finger to the base of the glass and nudged it to Emilie's mouth. "Bottoms up."

The nausea welled up from Emilie's belly. Saliva filled her mouth. She swallowed hard and put down the glass on the dressing table with a distinct crash.

"I think I'd rather not," she said.

TWENTY-FOUR

T he footman stood at attention outside the Duke of Olympia's private study, looking rather like a black-and-white guard dog.

"Why, Lionel," said Emilie. "I see you've been pressed into duty this evening as well."

"Your Highness." He inclined his head gravely. His face remained expressionless.

"I should be grateful, Lionel, if you'd step aside and announce me to Their Graces at once."

At this, a hint of pain touched Lionel's grave face. "I am under orders, Your Highness, not to allow anyone inside t'room."

"Pish," said Emilie. "Or posh. Whatever it is. I am the Princess of Holstein-Schweinwald-Huhnhof, a personal friend of the Kaiserin herself, niece to the Duke of Olympia, and affianced wife of the Duke of Ashland, whose persons you presently guard. I assure you, you are fully authorized to open that door to me."

"Your Highness . . ."

"Not to pull rank, of course," she added.

"Your Highness . . ."

"Oh, for heaven's sake, Lionel. For old times' sake, if nothing else."

Lionel hesitated, sighed, and reached for the door handle.

The two men inside the room bolted to their feet at her entrance, though she had eyes only for the Duke of Ashland: impossibly tall, fearfully immaculate in his white knee breeches and his tailcoat of blackest black. His white satin waistcoat gleamed against the starched pleats of his shirtfront. Her eyes drifted upward along the broad reach of his formidable shoulders and landed at last on his blurred face, his rigid jaw, his black mask, his cropped white hair, his icy blue eye open wide as he took her in.

"My dear," said the Duke of Olympia, dimly, from some other world entirely unconnected with the one in which she currently existed, "you look beautiful." He was next to her, he was kissing her hand, she was murmuring something polite, while the image of Ashland burned in perfect photographic negative in her brain.

Her dream-uncle took her hand and drew her across the room. "My dear fellow, I give you my niece," he said, and placed her hand within the broad palm of the Duke of Ashland, which swallowed it up whole.

"Your Highness." As he bowed before her she caught a glimpse of the tiny white triangle of his handkerchief poised correctly in his waistcoat pocket, and she forgot her own name.

"My dear, you're blushing," said Olympia. "Have you no loving words for your husband-to-be?"

Loving words? She pulled her eyes up from his handkerchief, from the memory of last night's handkerchief, and met Ashland's stern gaze.

Dear God. This matchless man, shimmering with controlled power, had been locked in frantic sexual congress with her. Last night. In a darkened carriage.

The sounds, the scents flooded back in her brain. The bounce of the carriage, the slick thrust of his body into hers. The filthy words he'd poured into her ear. The jerk of his hips as he lost himself into his handkerchief.

His handkerchief.

His voice, deep and muscular. "Emilie, where are your spectacles?"

She made a clearing little shake of her head. "In my room.

I was told that such things are unsuitable for balls." She managed a smile. "I am to look my best, after all."

Ashland looked down at her, unblinking. "If you'll excuse me," he said, and left the room.

"Wherever has he gone?"

Olympia spread his hands. "I haven't the faintest notion."

Ashland returned in under a minute, spectacles in hand, and fitted them to her face with infinite tenderness. "Much better."

A stinging sensation invaded Emilie's eyes. She fought it back. Princesses did not cry, certainly not in front of others. "Thank you, Your Grace. Uncle, may I have a private word with my fiancé?" The word *fiancé* seemed to swell with intimacy in the lamplit room.

"My dear, our guests will be arriving within minutes . . ."

Ashland's voice cracked above her. "Her Highness wishes a moment of my time, sir."

A weary sigh from Olympia. "Very well. I beg you not to abuse the furniture."

He left in a flash, before Emilie had time to catch his meaning and blush anew.

"Well! Why on earth would he say such a thing?"

Ashland chuckled. "Something to do with the expression on your face, I imagine."

She looked up, and his gaze came into brilliant focus: no longer glacial, but warm and amused. "I have no idea what you're talking about."

"Really? Because, if I'm not mistaken, I was thinking the same thing you were. The same thing I've been thinking about since I woke this morning." His voice slid downward into an entirely new range, somewhere between a growl and a purr. "You, straddling my lap last night, shivering as you took me inside you."

"Sir!"

He took a step closer. "The carriage bouncing us together as we shagged each other silly. You telling me to shove my big . . ."

"Sir! The footman is just outside the door!"

". . . harder and faster . . ."

"I *said* that?"

"You did." He wrapped his hand around her waist and pulled her right up against his pristine black-and-white body. "Do you know what I think, sweetheart?"

"I can't imagine."

"I think, once we're married, we should order a midnight carriage ride at least once a week."

"We would scandalize the neighbors."

"We could vary the neighborhood."

She tried to push herself away, but he held firm. "Such levity, at such a moment. I came to speak to you seriously, to discuss tonight's ordeal in detail, to discuss my suspicions and to try to dissuade you from putting yourself in certain danger like this . . ."

He swept her up, blue satin skirts and artful curls be damned, and carried her to the Duke of Olympia's brown leather Chesterfield sofa. "Oh, that. Well under control. Your uncle and I had a most productive discussion. Nothing to fear."

"What's that?" She struggled against his arms, but he simply sank down on the cushions and held her in his lap. "Ashland, there were men with pistols last night. Pistols! And Miss . . ."

"All under control. By midnight tonight, the whole damned ring of them will be smashed." He leaned down and kissed her. "And I shall be demanding the earliest possible date for our marriage, or I cannot be responsible for my actions."

"Your actions?" she said breathlessly, because his warm lips were smothering the long point-by-point discussion she had put together in her head before coming downstairs. There was something about Miss Dingleby, something important . . .

"Primarily, making love to you as often and as thoroughly as possible. Carriages, sofas. Even the occasional bed, if necessary." He slipped his index finger inside her bodice—her most conveniently low-cut bodice, trimmed with only the flimsiest excuse for a lace ruffle—and stroked her nipple.

"Ashland! It took fully an hour to assemble this dress, and I will not have you ruining . . ." Her words were swallowed in another kiss. She gave up and put her arms around his neck. What could possibly be more important than kissing Ashland, after all?

A sharp knock rattled the door.

"Ignore it," said Ashland, from the corner of his industrious mouth.

"You're certain"—he stroked her tongue; she shivered—"you're certain there's no danger? Because I think . . . Miss Dingleby . . ."

"All under control, I assure you. And I shan't leave your side for an instant. Not a thing to worry about, except this scandalously low bodice of yours." He gave her bosom a proprietary kiss.

Another knock, repeated with energy.

"Ashland, what on earth has come over you? This isn't like you at all." Her head fell back against his arm.

"Because I've just realized I'm free. Free of my wretched past, free of the imminent threat of a pack of murderers taking you away from me. Free to marry you and take you to bed . . ."

"Not necessarily in that order, I surmise."

"God forbid. I'm too old to wait for the proprieties." His hand, having abandoned her bodice, began to wind its way through the thicket of frothing petticoats at her ankles. He shifted her downward into the deep cushions of the sofa and stretched himself alongside.

"Yes, quite. Which brings to mind the final point I wished to discuss with you . . . rather important, really . . ."

The door crashed open.

"Damn it all, Ashland," said the Duke of Olympia. "I gave you strict instructions about the furniture."

The singing elation in the Duke of Ashland's blood lasted well past his third waltz with his fiancée. Everything was going along swimmingly, after all. With Emilie standing steadfast and graceful by his side, the endless receiving line hadn't proven quite the torture he'd imagined; their well-bred guests had generally taken his left hand without undue awkwardness. And Emilie looked resplendent in her pale blue satin, having been put back to rights by a hastily summoned Lucy.

Just before their sweeping entrance down the staircase— Olympia always did have a taste for grand theater—he had pulled the Ashland sapphires from his pocket and laid them about her neck, where they now glittered shamelessly in the light from the electric chandeliers.

They suited her, he thought, as he whirled her past the rapt gathering of dowagers in the northeast corner of the Duke of Olympia's ballroom. Sapphires worthy of a princess.

He told her so.

"Worthy of a princess, indeed," she said. "A banker's wife, you mean. They're quite deliciously vulgar."

He bent to her ear. "On our wedding night, I'll put them to even better use."

That earned him a swift rap of her fan, but her charming blush was well worth the punishment. He glanced downward to observe its pink progress along her bosom.

The waltz lumbered ponderously to an end. "Really, you'd think my uncle could have arranged for better musicians," Emilie said. "That was absolute rubbish."

"Tin ear, I expect." He cast a sharp eye across the room at Olympia. The duke was engaged in conversation with an attractive woman of a certain age, ablaze with diamonds, but he sensed the weight of Ashland's gaze. He turned his head slightly, made a single tug of his earlobe, and returned to his conversation.

Ashland drew Emilie along the side of the ballroom and snatched a pair of champagne flutes from a passing waiter, slipping the stems between the adroit fingers of his left hand. "You look a trifle overheated, sweetheart," he said. "Let's visit the garden."

"I'm not a bit overheated, and I do believe I see my dear cousin Penhallow over there, by the musicians . . ."

Ashland leaned down and whispered in her ear.

"Oh. Well." She patted her hair. "The garden it is, then."

Ashland's task (and it was, by far, the most agreeable mission he'd ever been assigned) was simply to keep Emilie otherwise occupied as Olympia went into action in the ballroom. He'd already begun in the library, seducing her with all the shameless exuberance of his relief, and now he had her pliant and undivided attention. As a result, she hadn't noticed any of the undercurrent of activity in the ballroom. She'd enjoyed herself, she'd sipped champagne, and she'd danced only with him. She'd looked up at him as they waltzed about the room and his heart had stopped at the miraculous glowing warmth in her eyes.

Warmth for *him*.

He was the luckiest man alive.

He sent only a single glance backward as he passed through the French doors into the cool dampness of the Duke of

Olympia's garden, his hand at Emilie's back. Olympia's silver head was crossing the room, making its way to the secret panel on the wall behind the orchestra where Miss Dingleby waited with her decoy.

Everything in place. He had only to keep Emilie away from the ballroom.

And really, the deeper they went into the garden, the more occupied her mind and body, the safer she'd be.

It was his duty, in fact.

"Oh, it's so chilly!" she said. "Let's turn back. We must. Our guests will wonder where we've gone."

Ashland set down the champagne on an empty urn, whipped off his black tailcoat, and settled it about her shoulders. "Problem solved. Drink your champagne, like a good girl." He picked up the flute and handed it to her.

"I really shouldn't . . ."

He put his hand to her back and nudged her forward. "There's an old saying, my dear. When a lady says she shouldn't, she almost certainly will."

"I beg your pardon. Where did you learn that?"

"I *was* in the army."

"I'm beginning to find that excuse wears rather thin."

But she was smiling, she was happy. She was allowing him to urge her deeper into the garden, where the light from the ballroom faded into the shadows. The beds were all barren, of course, the roses pruned ruthlessly back and the shrubs hunkered down against the February chill. A row of boxwoods lay ahead, subdued into round balls by Olympia's fleet of gardeners, and Ashland guided her deftly around them to the small glass-walled conservatory that lay beyond, filled at the moment with spring plantings.

"Oh, I remember this!" she exclaimed. "My sisters and I used to hold tea parties here, when we were visiting in the early summer. What fun it all was. I wish we could look inside, but I suppose it's all locked up for the winter."

Ashland reached his arm around her and plucked an object from the inside pocket of his tailcoat, making sure to brush her bosom as he went.

He held the object up before her.

"Oh! However did you find a key?"

"I have a knack for such things." He fitted the key into the lock.

"This is thrilling. I wonder if that old wicker chaise longue is still there. We used to take naps on it."

"It is."

"How . . . Oh!" She stopped in the doorway.

He came up against her back and put his arms about her. "Do you like it?"

"How did you . . . ? Oh, it's beautiful!"

She stepped forward into the bower of blooms, fragrant lilies and roses, gardenias cut and overflowing their vases, sensuous orchids rising up from planters.

"Some of them are your uncle's. I had a few men scour the florists for the others."

She turned in his arms. "Oh, but we can't! The ball!"

"The champagne is flowing. I daresay they won't even notice we've left." He lowered his lips to hers and tasted her gently.

Emilie's arms stole around his neck. "Ashland, you're a romantic."

"Bite your tongue. I am a gruff and taciturn Yorkshire duke." He lifted her up and carried her to the chaise longue. The Ashland sapphires glittered darkly at him.

"This is shocking. We really ought to behave more properly until the wedding." She sighed dreamily and tilted her head back, as his tongue explored the delicate skin at the hollow of her throat.

"Trust me. The wedding will take place as quickly as we can arrange it," he said.

"The sooner the better."

"I'm glad you've come around to my way of thinking." Ashland pulled down the neckline of her dress. It was a tight fit, constructed exactly to measure, but Emilie's breasts seemed extraordinarily full tonight, nearly bursting from her corset, and with diligent effort he coaxed a single dusky tip into the open air.

She made a gurgling laugh. "I had no choice, really."

He was busy suckling her tender nipple and couldn't answer. God, she was luscious. Her back arched, feeding his greed for her, and his prick swelled inside his trousers.

"Ashland, really. This is no time for that. My uncle's plans . . ."

"Bother your uncle's plans." He meant it.

"But there's something . . . I have to tell you both, about Miss Dingleby . . ."

Ashland raised his head and cupped her cheek with his hand. "We know all about Miss Dingleby. Trust me. Your uncle is managing things as we speak."

"Oh." Her eyes went round in the hint of moonlight.

He kissed the corners of her eyes, her lips. "Would I allow my guard down for an instant if you were in danger? Of course not. Olympia explained everything. You, Miss Dingleby, everything. He's taking care of it all right now. You've nothing more to worry about."

"You know *everything*?" Her voice was anxious.

"Everything."

Her body relaxed in his arms. "And you're happy about it?"

"Entirely satisfied."

Her hands went to his shoulders. "Ashland, I'm so glad. You've no idea how this relieves my mind. I've felt so trapped, these past weeks, knowing I was leading you into danger, when none of this was your choice. Not wanting to trap you, too. I didn't want to say anything until I was certain . . ."

Her soft acquiescence was sending him over the edge. "It's all over now, sweetheart, or almost. Nothing but roses ahead."

She opened her mouth again, but he laid his finger over it. "No more worries. Let me make love to you now. Let me give you pleasure."

Emilie took his finger away and smiled. "I only wanted to say, at least you won't need your handkerchief this time."

For an instant, he couldn't reply. It was as if the sun came out inside his chest.

He lowered himself back to her. "Yes."

Despite the urgent fire in his blood, he seduced her slowly, waiting until she was slick and plump before unbuttoning his flies and sinking himself into her. He thrust in a gentle rhythm. He worked her to climax with ruthless self-control, mindful of her tenderness after last night's frenzy. The passage of time relaxed around them; he was surrounded by satin and stiff petticoats, by sapphires and soft skin, by the scent of rare flowers and by Emilie's sheath clasping him snugly. The effect was so delicious, so languorous, that when she spent around him, gasping and shuddering, the instant ferocity of his own release stunned him.

He thrust his hips in a last urgent shove, everything else forgotten, Olympia and Miss Dingleby and the musicians in the ballroom. There was only Emilie and her sweet breath on his neck, her delicate body still pulsing below him as he drained himself deep inside her.

I am so glad," she whispered, moments later. He was lying alongside her, both of them breathless and rumpled on the inadequate width of the chaise; he was half atop her, half braced on his elbow, damp and flushed and heavy lidded. Whether the ancient wicker could bear them both much longer, she dared not consider.

"Very glad."

"It was so silly of me. Suspecting Miss Dingleby!" She laughed. "But when she came up with that odd drink of hers, urging me on, I had the strangest sense of dread. *Bottoms up!* she said, with that sharp look in her eyes. I suppose I've been so anxious lately that . . ."

Ashland raised his head. "Drink?" His voice held an odd note, through the huskiness of arousal and release. "What drink?"

"Oh, one of her grapefruit concoctions, I suppose. And all I could think of was that she had been there in the castle with my stepmothers, she had discovered those drinks that made them miscarry, and since I'd just admitted my suspicions about the baby . . ."

Ashland bolted upward. The crisp white bow under his starched wing tips had come shamefully undone. "The *baby*?"

"Well, she had suspected before, of course, but . . ."

"You're with *child*?"

A glacier seemed to have invaded Emilie's heart, sending off chunks of ice into her bloodstream. She opened her mouth, which had gone suddenly dry. "Why, yes. I mean, I . . . I might be. I think so. I thought you knew. When you said . . ."

Ashland's shocked gaze went to her bosom, to her belly, and back up to her face. "You're with *child*? By *me*?"

Emilie gasped and sat up, dislodging Ashland. He scrambled to his feet. "Of course, by you! What the devil do you mean by that?"

"I'm sorry . . . Of course I . . . only shocked . . . Good God! A child. Good God!" He raked his hand through his close-shorn hair. A square of moonlight caught his face through the glass, rendering it nearly white, the black mask like an abyss.

"Well, what did you *think* I meant?" Emilie realized her naked breasts were spilling over her bodice in a most undignified fashion. She stuffed them back inside. "What did *you* mean?"

"I certainly didn't mean *that*. I . . ." He shook his head. "What was that about a drink?"

Emilie stood up. "Miss Dingleby. She brought me a drink, a pink-colored drink, just before I went to see you."

"Did you taste it?"

"No! I told you, I had a strange feeling. I put it down and I went to the library to find you and Olympia, to warn you of my suspicion. And you told me it was all under control. Where are you going?"

"Back to the bloody ballroom, if it's not too late!" He staggered around the flowerpots, working frantically at the fastening of his trousers.

She followed him. "What's happened? What's the matter?"

He spun around and took her shoulders. "What's happened is that we thought Miss Dingleby was on our side. We thought she was a double agent, pretending to be in with Hans's lot . . ."

"Hans!"

"Yes, Hans! He's your inside man. He's the one behind all this; he's their operative. But Dingleby convinced him she was working with Free Blood, when in reality she'd been setting up this grand event tonight, to capture them in the act . . ."

"Good heavens!"

"Except that it appears she's been playing us instead!" He released her with an almost violent thrust and spun around.

"Wait, Ashland!"

"Stay here!" he ordered, over his shoulder. He threw open the conservatory door.

"I won't! I'm going with you! It's my country, it's my father and sisters . . ." She strained against him, trying to fit around him and through the door. The cold air of the garden hit her flushed skin in a welcome gust.

He turned and cupped her face with his massive left hand. "You're carrying our *child*, Emilie. For God's sake, stay here."

"But I . . ."

Even as she said the words, he was in motion. With lightning speed, he ducked through the conservatory door, closed it, and locked it with his key.

"Ashland!"

He had already disappeared into the shadows. She rattled the knob, she pounded the glass, she rattled the knob again. Her blood was racing through her body in a live stream, shooting with energy. She paced to one side, coming up short in front of a massive urn filled with pink orange roses. She kicked it with her toe.

Locked. He'd locked her inside.

She turned back to the door and rattled the knob again. The key was still in the lock, tantalizingly close. She pressed her ear against the glass. Was that shouting? A pistol shot? Or simply merrymaking?

Miss Dingleby. Her mind struggled to grasp it all. Had Miss Dingleby been working for them all along? Or had she turned at some point, cloistered in Holstein Castle with its stultifying life, its archaic customs, its wealth and absolute power over the peasantry around them?

Miss Dingleby. My God, how could she do it? Raise three girls to womanhood, and then murder their father. And all for a cause, a foolish and impossible cause, a violent pie in the sky.

Traitor.

Emilie pounded the glass with her fist. Her eyes wandered across the conservatory, to the chaise longue on which she and Ashland had just made love. Ashland's formal black tailcoat still lay there on the cushions, crushed by their heaving bodies.

A distant sound brushed her ears, a crash.

Emilie marched across the conservatory to the chaise. She picked up Ashland's tailcoat and wrapped it around her left hand as she strode back across the flower-strewn floor.

Without an instant's hesitation, she punched through the pane of glass next to the knob, reached through with her right hand, and unlocked the door.

I t took Ashland scarcely half a minute to run back along the garden path and up the stone steps to the French doors guarding the ballroom, and in that time his brain formed and discarded half a dozen plans.

Something was going on, that much he could tell. The sounds of music and tinkling laughter, of the buzz of conversation, had transformed into cacophony.

Shouts, screams, crashes. The wholesale smash of crystal. Ashland reached the top step and took in the scene through the glass: a melee of scrambling silk dresses and surging fists. The door flew open before him, and a man ran past, heading for the garden. Ashland grabbed him by the collar. "What's happened? What's the matter?"

The fellow jabbered. "Riot, man! Run while you can!"

"From whom?"

"Footmen! Musicians! A bloody riot!"

Ashland released the man and ran into the ballroom.

The ringing voice of the Duke of Olympia greeted him. "Quiet, everyone! The police have been called! Quiet! You're in no danger!"

But for once, no one paid attention to that glorious ducal boom. A woman flung herself at Ashland's chest. "Save me, sir! I shall be murdered!"

Ashland plucked her from his shirt and set her aside. "Calm yourself, madam. It's all quite under control."

A shrill whistle cut through the air, and then a pounding rush of feet. From the advantage of his six feet five inches of height, Ashland saw a river of blue pour into the ballroom from the hall. He cast about for the Duke of Olympia's silver head.

"What the devil's happened? It's Dingleby, isn't it?"

"She wasn't there. No decoy princess, either. Where's Emilie?"

"Locked in the conservatory. She told me . . . Oh, the devil take it. Dingleby's working for them, after all! She's planned it all out!" Ashland cast about, but all he could see were policemen.

"Complete balls-up," muttered Olympia. "The footmen, the extra ones Hans organized, got restless when the princess disappeared. Someone fired a pistol. My fellows leapt out from the orchestra and . . . Dash it all!" He wiped his brow. "Start all over again."

"But where's Dingleby?"

"God knows. I'm a blasted fool. I should have known."

Ashland dodged a flying policeman. "Look, I think she's bolted. Emilie found her out, just before she came down to the library."

"Emilie!"

"Offered her a drink of some kind, and Emilie thought it was to rid her of the baby, who I suppose would be the next blasted heir . . ."

"Baby!"

"Oh, bloody hell. We've got to find Dingleby!"

Olympia turned and let out a whistle. A man ran up in formal dress, one of the musicians. "Doing the best we can, sir. The damned chaps had the jump on us. We were waiting for your signal."

"Yes, dash it. Look, Dingleby's turned. The policemen are sorting out this mess; I want you to take your men and comb the city, do you hear me? Find Dingleby."

"Yes, sir."

Olympia turned back to him, stepped aside to allow a baton-swinging policeman to rush past, and said, "Right-ho. Go fetch Emilie and take her upstairs. You're not to leave her for an instant, do you hear me? The security of all bloody Europe may hang in the balance. If we allow her to be captured . . ."

But Ashland was already off at a run, his blood turned to cold vapor in his veins. What if Dingleby had been hiding all along, had seen him take Emilie to the garden?

What if she had arranged the riot herself, had waited for it to begin, so Ashland would leave Emilie unprotected?

The key. He'd left the bloody key in the lock, so Emilie wouldn't be trapped in case something happened to him.

He flew across the terrace and leapt down the steps. He ran down the garden path, lungs searing, and staggered to a stop in front of the conservatory door.

Broken glass glittered in the moonlight. The door stood ajar, wavering slightly in a breath of wind.

"Emilie!" he howled.

As his voice died away into the distant shouts from the ballroom, the sound of running footsteps reached his ears.

He spun around.

"Sir! Oh, sir!"

A maid was running up, clutching her cap to her head, her crisp black-and-white uniform springing from the shadows.

"Who's that?" he barked.

"Oh, sir! It's me, it's Lucy. Lucy from t'Abbey, sir!"

"Lucy!" He grabbed her shoulders. She was heaving for air. "What's the matter? What's happened?"

"It's Her Highness, sir! I come to tell you! You was flying up t'garden that fast, I couldn't keep up!"

Ashland drew a deep breath, willing himself to calm, willing his racing pulse to quiet. "It's all right, Lucy. Quite all right. What did you come to tell me?"

"It's Her Highness, sir. I'm sure it's nowt, but it seemed so odd, sir. With t'party going on, and t'feighting."

"What's odd, Lucy? Tell me." His heart was smashing violently against his ribs.

"Why, it's Mr. Simpson, sir."

"Mr. Simpson? My butler? But he's at Eaton Square, isn't he?"

Lucy shook her solemn head. "He did come over here. He did come over here, sir, just afore t'feight started in t'ballroom. And then I sees him . . . him and Her Highness . . ."

"What, Lucy?"

"They've gone off together, sir. Off in a hansom cab, as fast as you please."

TWENTY-FIVE

"Thank goodness you had the cabman wait around the mews, Mr. Simpson," said Emilie. "The carriages have entirely closed up Park Lane."

"Indeed, Your Highness," said Mr. Simpson.

She craned her neck to see around the horse's ears. The cold wind rushed against her face, heavy with fog. "Can he not go any faster? Every second counts!"

"Of course, madam."

"Lucy's gone off to find the duke. Oh God! If they've harmed Freddie and Mary in any way, I'll never forgive myself." She looked down at the crumpled paper in her hand, crushed in the panic of reading the terse message.

"If I'd had any idea of the contents of the note, madam, I should of course have stayed to defend his lordship." Mr. Simpson sounded quite calm, but then he was trained to remain calm in the face of crisis.

As was she, she reminded herself. She sat back in the cab and tried not to think of Freddie and Mary in Hans's power, Miss Dingleby's power. *As you read this Note, Lord Frederick Russell and Lady Mary Russell have been taken into the Custody of the Revolutionary Brigade of the Free Blood. You will repair at once to 28 Eaton Mews North and await further instruction.*

Await further instruction. What did *that* mean?

They were trotting smartly down the eastern side of Belgrave Square now. The traffic had thinned somewhat, and Emilie's belly tightened, as if the strain of her own muscles could somehow push them faster.

"There was no one at the house when you left?"

Mr. Simpson coughed. "No, madam. The footmen, the maids—all of them were at Park Lane tonight. Only Mrs. Needle and I were in residence when the note arrived for you. I took it upon myself to deliver it."

"I'm so terribly sorry. It's all my fault. She knew I'd found her out, and she must have raced directly over, knowing how much . . . how much I . . ." Her voice faltered. She couldn't say the words *love them*, not in front of Mr. Simpson. "How much His Grace is attached to his son," she finished, gripping the edge of the wooden door before her.

"I'm afraid I don't quite understand, madam."

"No, of course not. Damn it all, can we not go any faster?" She rapped on the trapdoor.

The driver opened. "Yes, ma'am?"

"We're in a dreadful hurry. An emergency. As fast as your horse is able, please!" She looked at Simpson. "Have you any money with you?"

"Yes, madam." An injured air.

"Thank God for that, at least."

Simpson accepted her unladylike language without a flinch. "Yes, madam."

The hansom jolted over a rut in the road and swung left onto Belgrave Place. Only a minute or two, now. Simpson was reaching into his pocket for the fare. Emilie closed her eyes and listened to the rattle of the wheels, to the clop-clop of the horse drawing her closer and closer to . . . what?

It might be a trap. She mouthed the words to herself.

Well, of course it was a trap. That was the point, wasn't it? To gain control of Emilie's person. Freddie, Mary, Ashland, Simpson, poor Mrs. Needle—they were simply innocent collateral. All this planning and danger, all this suffering: It was all because of her, because of who she was.

She'd allowed them to put themselves in harm's way.

Her fault.

The hansom turned again with a sharp jerk, forcing Emilie's eyes open. The paving stones in the mews were rough and deeply rutted, causing the entire vehicle to bounce as they trotted down the length of buildings.

"Twenty-eight, you said?" came the driver's voice through the trapdoor. "Here it is."

The hansom rolled to a stop. Simpson thrust the money through the door, and Emilie was flying off the cab the instant the driver released the doors, tangling in her blue satin ball gown with its princely train. The building stood before her, with its wide carriage door to the left and the servants' entrance to the right. A few wisps of straw lay limp and dirty on the pavement outside.

Her slippers scrabbled over the wet cobbles. She clutched Ashland's tailcoat to her shoulders and staggered to the door and pounded with her fist.

The wooden panel swung open.

She fell forward into the damp-smelling hall. "Freddie! Mary!"

The unmistakable voice of the Marquess of Silverton floated from somewhere above. "Go *back*, Grimsby! Go *now*!" The last word was cut off by a thump.

"Freddie! I'm coming!"

"No, Grimsby! Go away! Get Pater! We're all right!"

A small feminine scream, cut short.

"Mary! Oh God!"

The hall was dark, almost perfectly black. Emilie lurched into the gloom with her hands stretched out before her, trying to find the stairs. From behind her came the thump of Simpson's footsteps, then the hiss of gas, and suddenly a ghostly circle of gaslight illuminated the space.

A pair of horses thrust their surprised noses over the stall doors. The duke's fine black landau sat in the middle of the space, polished and ready for a morning turn about the park. Where were the grooms, the servants? Park Lane?

"Freddie?"

"*Go*, Grimsby!" Another hard thump, a blow on flesh, followed by a grunt of pain.

Emilie looked wildly upward in the direction of the sound. Freddie and Mary sat back-to-back in the hayloft, bound together with rope. A glowering Hans stood above them, brandishing the rope's end.

A pistol dangled from his other hand.

"Let them go, Hans! I *order* you!" shouted Emilie in German.

"By what right?" he asked.

"I am your *princess*, by God!"

"By God, you are not." He spoke calmly, with infinite conviction. "You are a tyrant, and your kind has held sway over the people of Germany long enough. Your time has passed, and you don't even know it. Look at you in your gown, your jewels, your ridiculous yards of silk. What have you done for the betterment of the world? What right do you have to rule over anyone?"

"Look here," said Freddie, "I can't understand a word you've said, but I do know you can't talk to my stepmother in such a fashion."

A voice floated out from the doorway. "Now, now, your lordship. This is no way to conduct a negotiation of such a delicate nature."

Emilie spun around. In the instant before the gaslight winked out into darkness, the image of Miss Dingleby floated before her: eyes bright, one hand reaching for the lamp and the other holding a pistol.

Ashland found Mrs. Needle in the Eaton Square scullery, bound and gagged. "Where are they?" he demanded, the instant the rag came free from her mouth.

"Oh, sir! I'm that sorry! He took them off, he did. He was in like a flash, right through t'area door." She worked her jaw, wincing.

Ashland pried with his desperate left hand at the ropes around her wrists. "Who? Who took them?"

"A great German fellow, he was. Scarce a word of English to him. Oh, sir. Has he taken Lord Freddie and her ladyship?"

"I fear he has, Mrs. Needle. You must tell me everything you know. Was there anyone with him? A tall woman with dark hair?"

"Nay, not anyone, sir. They went off through t'back, they did."

The ropes loosened at last. Ashland tugged them off and rubbed Mrs. Needle's wrists, one by one. "The back! To the mews, then?"

"Why, aye, sir!"

"By God." He rose to his feet. "Mrs. Needle, ring Scotland Yard at once. Ask for a chap named Parker, tell them it's urgent, tell them it's from me. Parker will know what to do."

"Aye, sir! Right away, sir!"

He ducked under the doorway to the hall. "And Mrs. Needle?"

"Aye, sir?"

"If Simpson and Her Highness arrive here, for God's *sake* don't let them leave."

In the absence of light, Emilie's mind cleared of anxiety. She had learned, in her long hours of blindfolded conversation with the Duke of Ashland, how to accept the loss of sight. How to compensate. How to listen and smell, to stretch out the net of her senses. Next to her, Mr. Simpson reached out to lay a protective hand on her arm; above her, Mary cried out.

But Emilie knew Miss Dingleby hadn't moved from the entrance. She still stood there, with her pistol in one hand, unable to aim and fire it in the darkness.

What was she waiting for?

"Miss Dingleby!" Emilie heard her own voice ring out, clear and confident, and the sound gave her strength. "You have what you want. I'm here. Release Freddie and Mary, and I'll go with you willingly."

A slight shuffle along the floorboards. "My dear, whatever do you mean?"

"I know you're working with Hans. I know you're in league with these anarchists, my father's murderers. I daresay you have some sort of plan for me, or else you'd have killed me outright by now. Whatever it is, I stand ready. Let them go."

Miss Dingleby laughed in the darkness. "Good gracious! What an inventive mind you have. Plans for you? My plans are only to keep you safe. I've spent the last few hours tracking down our German friend here, once I learned he'd left his post in Park Lane. Thank goodness one of us thought to bring a pistol along. Or had you hoped to bribe him with your sapphires?"

Emilie had quite forgotten about the sapphires. She put her hand to her neck. There they were, cold and heavy, worth a fortune. She wrapped her fingers around them, as if they were an anchor that might hold her spinning thoughts in place. "The drink. The drink you offered me before the party."

"To refresh you. Really, Emilie! What the devil's come over you? Stand aside, please, so I may deal with Hans without fear of injuring you."

Emilie shook her head. "No. I saw the look in your eye. And Ashland said . . . when he heard about the drink . . ."

"My dear girl, you've put yourself in such a muddle. If I meant to kidnap you, why on earth would I have sent you into Yorkshire? For months? And your sisters. Wouldn't I have kidnapped them, too? You're not making any sense at all."

Emilie forced her brain into logic. "Because of my uncle. Because you had to make him think the danger came from elsewhere, or he would have found you out. He would have stopped you in your tracks." She gasped. "Olympia! He was your real target tonight, wasn't he? He was the one you meant to kill. You could have put a bullet through him tonight, and no one would have suspected you!"

"I say!" exclaimed Freddie.

"What went wrong tonight, Miss Dingleby? Did you think I'd found you out, and switched plans? Or was Hans disobeying orders, coming to Eaton Square?" She turned in the direction of the hayloft and cast her voice upward into the blackness. "Hans!" she said in German. "What was the plan at Park Lane tonight?"

Silence.

"So he *is* working with you," said Emilie, turning back. "It was your idea, luring me here tonight while everyone else was at the party. Your secondary plan, because the first went awry when I refused the drink."

"Nonsense. Hans!" Miss Dingleby barked, in German. "You will release the two children at once."

"Fräulein?"

"At *once*, I said."

Hesitation, and then, "*Nein*, fräulein."

"Let them go, Hans," said Emilie. "I have a fortune in

jewels around my neck. They're yours. Let them go, and you'll have me, you'll have the jewels. They're innocent. They have nothing to do with this."

"Stop it, Grimsby!"

A shuffling sound came from the hayloft, a thump. Mary squealed.

"Turn on the lights, fräulein!" shouted Hans. "Now!"

At once, the gaslight illuminated the interior of the mews in a sickly glow. Emilie stumbled back, held up only by Simpson's firm hand on her arm, trying to keep both Miss Dingleby and the hayloft in sight.

The hayloft, where Freddie was half standing, struggling furiously with the ropes around him, and Hans stood with the rope end held above his head, about to strike.

Where the Duke of Ashland, poised along the rafters, dropped silently to the hayloft floor and knocked the pistol out of Hans's astonished hand.

In India, in Afghanistan, they had called him the Wraith. They had called it impossible, a miracle, that a man so large and solid could move about without disturbing a single breath of air, a tiny pebble on a path. Could creep up on a sentry in a mountain pass and kill him, without either of them making a whisper.

Impossible, the Afghans had said. He cannot be human. He must be a spirit, a ghost.

They had put a price on his head anyway, and had increased that price to a princely sum. Some among the British ranks had thought he should head home while he could, that he'd done enough, that no man could take such chances forever. But Olympia had disagreed. *We cannot do without him, not with the British army poised to make its advance over the border.*

And Ashland himself? He'd believed himself invulnerable. Everything in life had come naturally to him: his looks, his strength, his brains, his talent, his beautiful wife. He had conceived a healthy male heir on his wedding night. He was the favorite of the gods. How could he fall?

The Wraith had been caught within the week.

But the body remembered. His muscles knew how to

perform the little tricks of movement, how to slide soundlessly along the rafters of a mews until he lay inches from the head of his target.

How to lie quietly, waiting for the moment to strike, even as the woman he loved pledged her own precious life in exchange for that of his children.

The woman he loved.

As Emilie's voice floated up from below, serene and determined, he thought his own body might burst from the love he felt for her. He was suffused in it; he was made of it.

The gaslight switched on, and he dropped to the ground.

The pistol clattered to the floor with one efficient cut to Hans's elbow. He wrapped his right arm around the man's neck.

"Let him go, Ashland!" snapped Miss Dingleby.

Hans made a strangled noise. He dropped the rope end and clawed at Ashland's arm with his powerful fingers, but Ashland held firm. A preternatural strength filled his limbs: the strength of battle. The strength of a man protecting what he held most dear.

"Ashland, be careful!" Emilie cried.

"Let him go, by God! Or I'll shoot this pistol!"

"You'll miss," he said. Thirteen years ago, with a hand attached to his right wrist, he could have killed Hans in an instant. Now it was messy work, a brute test of his arm against Hans's thick neck. Hans's right hand had dropped away to scrabble at his jacket. A knife?

"Then I'll hit Hans, and we'll never know who the devil is really after the princesses!"

"*You're* the one after them!" he roared.

"I am *not*! But kill him now, and we're back to the beginning! And where does that leave Emilie? Where does that leave her sisters?"

Ashland paused. Trust her, or not? If he killed Hans, what would she do? Use her pistol on Emilie? Could he reach her in time?

"Emilie, is she speaking the truth?" he asked softly.

"I don't know! I . . ." Emilie's voice was agonized.

Ashland eyed the pistol on the ground, a few feet away.

"Very well," he said. In a single movement, he released Hans with a violent toss, dove for the pistol, rolled, and trained it on the German valet. "Now, Hans. You will kindly untie my son and daughter."

"I say, Pater! That was well done," said Freddie. "Most efficient."

Hans raised himself up on his elbows.

"Emilie," Ashland said, "kindly explain to our friend what must be done."

The German words rushed past his ears. He kept his pistol trained between Hans's baleful eyes, which narrowed with comprehension as Emilie finished. Hans looked at the pistol, at Freddie and Mary, and back at Ashland.

"Do it." Ashland's tone of voice required no translation.

Hans rose to his knees and crawled to Freddie and Mary.

"That's the spirit, old chap," said Freddie. "Mind the knots."

"Keep your hands where I can see them, Hans. Emilie?"

Emilie translated swiftly. Hans shot him a murderous look.

Mary slumped forward first. Freddie sprang free and began to rub her wrists. "That's all right, then, old girl. See? I told you Pater would ride up on his cavalry. Reliable chap, Pater."

"Nonetheless," said Mary, "I should much prefer not to repeat the experience."

Ashland's shoulders eased a trifle at the sound of Mary's composed voice. A thoroughbred, his newly adopted daughter.

"Now then, Miss Dingleby," said Ashland, without shifting his gaze an inch, "what do you propose to do to keep Hans's valuable brain to ourselves?"

"I shall take him off at once for questioning, of course," she said crisply. "You and Emilie are free to go."

"How very kind. And if I'd rather stay?"

"I hardly see the use. You have no German."

"Indeed. Perhaps we'd better wait for reinforcements, however. Just to be on the safe side." From the corner of his eye, he saw that Emilie was turning in Miss Dingleby's direction, her right hand hidden in the folds of her satin ball gown.

The stiletto. Did she have it with her?

He kept talking, kept Miss Dingleby's attention focused on the hayloft.

"What I wonder, Miss Dingleby, is why you didn't press him on these matters before. Unless you're the one pulling the strings, of course. Then it would all make sense. Then it would be *your* valuable brain we must seek to preserve."

She sighed. "How tiresome you all are. *You* of all people, Ashland, should know that a clever agent does nothing to reveal his hand. If I'd probed Hans for the names of his leaders, I'd have been suspected at once."

"A clever agent has ways of discovering these things."

Emilie was doing something with her left arm, twisting it. He couldn't see more, because Simpson was standing right next to her, immobile, his gaze trained on the small window next to the door.

"In any case," Ashland went on, "I believe I shall have Freddie do the honors of tying up our good friend Hans. It's only fitting, after all."

"With pleasure." Freddie picked up the rope.

Simpson shouted out.

Ashland felt the vibration in the wood below his feet, the electric rush he knew as well as his own heartbeat.

The door flew open.

"*Now*, boys!" someone shouted.

Hans launched himself forward. Ashland, off balance, stepped aside an instant too late. His left hand gripped the pistol; his right elbow took the force of the fall. Hans landed atop him and pressed the blade of a knife against his throat.

"Pater!" shouted Freddie.

A pistol shot shattered the air.

Hans's eyes opened wide. He mouthed something, but no sound emerged from his throat.

Ashland gave a mighty shove, overturning the body from his chest, and sprang to his feet.

The Duke of Olympia stood near the doorway, as a stream of men eddied around him. In the center of the room, right next to the wheel of the landau, stood Miss Dingleby with her pistol still raised, surrounded by a cloud of acrid smoke.

In the end, it solves nothing," said Miss Dingleby, sipping her sherry from the comfort of the Duke of Olympia's best club chair. "Emilie is safe for the moment, but there are others involved in the plot, and they will strike again. Hans was the key. I had spent years cultivating him, gaining his trust."

Emilie turned to the window and stared at the midnight blackness. Her brain ached with fatigue, but her thoughts insisted on jumping about. The image of Hans's head, at the moment of impact. The sight of Ashland with a knife to his throat. Simpson's hand on her arm, holding her still. "I'm very sorry to have overturned all the plans."

"Not at all, my dear. It was not your fault." The Duke of Olympia presided at his desk. His own glass of sherry sat next to the blotter, half full. His left hand twiddled a pen.

Ashland rose from his own chair and laid his hand on Emilie's shoulder. "I shall not make such a mistake again, I promise. Are you quite sure you're all right?"

His hand was warm and strong, enveloping her shoulder. She longed to turn to him, to let herself be swallowed up in his reassuring bulk, but her limbs were too stiff, her heart too heavy in her chest. "Yes, quite all right. A good night's sleep, that's all I need."

Miss Dingleby set down her empty sherry glass and stood. "As do I. You'll excuse me, all of you. We shall, of course, discuss all this in the morning. What's to be done. The danger to the girls is only diminished, after all. We must find another way in."

The Duke of Olympia had risen, too. "Thank you, my dear, for all your bravery tonight."

She inclined her head. "Of course."

When the door had shut softly behind her, Ashland turned to Olympia. "Well, then? What's to be done? The other girls have their disguises, which may continue to shield them for a time, as long as Hans's superiors aren't aware of their exact whereabouts. But Emilie is now known to be alive and residing in this house. She's the most obvious target."

"Indeed." Olympia's sharp eyes moved to Emilie. "Particularly if—as I understand it—she may be carrying the next heir to the principality of Holstein-Schweinwald-Huhnhof."

Emilie returned his gaze without speaking.

Ashland's hand tightened on her shoulder. "We will marry without delay, of course. She will have the protection of my name and my body. I will . . ."

"Marry you!" Emilie spun to face the duke, dislodging his

hand from her shoulder. "You forget, Your Grace. I never agreed to marry you. I agreed to a public engagement, nothing more."

He stared at her, his pale blue eye wide with astonishment. "Not marry me!"

"I am *not* a pawn to be moved about. We might have scored a total success tonight if you'd let me in on your schemes. Instead you played at making love to me, you spent the evening seducing me in order to keep my poor witless self away from your terribly sophisticated, terribly important plans . . ."

"*Played* at making love to you!"

". . . and then, without ceremony, you announce that we'll be married without delay, that having deflowered and impregnated me, you'll do your duty and—what was it?—*protect* me, particularly since I'm no longer simply a valuable political object in my own right, but a vessel for another one!"

"A *vessel!*"

"What an honor for me! What joy, to look forward to a future of being married to an overbearing iceberg, protected and moved about and used for everyone's purpose but my own! To bear a child for exactly the same fate! By God, I was better off as your son's tutor. At least then I was free to act for myself, to leave your employment if I wished!"

She was breathing hard now, her hands fisted into her skirts. She thought for an instant of Ashland's tender words, his gentle touch in the conservatory, making love to her as if she were the most precious object in the universe. And it had all been an act, simply to distract her. His charming words, his roomful of flowers, his romantic gestures were all meant to deceive her. To lull her into a lovestruck trance to keep her away from the real business of the evening.

Her blood ran so hot, she couldn't think.

Ashland's face was deeply flushed. "My *duty!* You think I wish to marry you out of *duty*? You honestly believe I was *pretending* that scene in the conservatory? I was *using* you?"

She snapped her fingers. "Oh, of course! I'd forgotten the inexplicable animal lust you feel for me. I stand corrected. Let us not to the marriage of true loins admit impediment."

The Duke of Olympia made a strangled cough into his handkerchief. "My dear Emilie, I cannot help but feel that I am somewhat *de trop* in this most . . . er . . . edifying conversation. Perhaps I should retire and allow you and your . . . er . . . *overbearing iceberg* to continue . . ."

"No." Ashland's voice whipped out to cut the duke short. His face was ablaze. His single blue eye seemed lit from within, focused with extraordinary intensity on Emilie's face. "No, sir. I want you to hear this. I want you both to witness what I have to say."

He fell to one knee.

"Here we go," Olympia muttered.

"Forgive me, Emilie. I have behaved unpardonably. I have not trusted you as you deserve. I haven't been open with you. Instead of asking, I have demanded."

"Nothing wrong with that," said Olympia. "A woman likes to know what's what, don't she, my girl?"

Ashland ignored him. "May I tell you why, Emilie?"

She looked down at the top of Ashland's head before her, bristling with close-cropped white hair, his proud face turned up to her. She couldn't move. She tried to nod, and only the tiniest movement of her head resulted from the effort.

"Because I was afraid, Emilie. Because I have never felt even the slightest fraction of love for any woman, to match the love I bear for you. You are not a pawn to me. You are not a political object. A *vessel*, by God! You're all there is."

His left hand rested on his knee, closing and flexing. Emilie shut her eyes, because she couldn't bear the sight before her. She couldn't bear the sight of him, the Duke of Ashland, at her feet in his formal white shirt and satin waistcoat, his gleaming breeches. Immaculate, except for the pattern of red brown droplets sprayed delicately across his left shoulder.

"*You* are not a vessel, Emilie. *I* am. Everything I do, everything I have, everything I am, belongs to you. I don't . . . Emilie, I can't even describe it. I can't tell you the whole of it. I was frozen, asleep, and you brought me back to life. You healed me, you made me whole again. I felt myself a beast, alone and snarling in my cave, and you walked inside without fear and tamed me."

"What a bold mix of metaphors, my dear fellow," said the Duke of Olympia. "I feel I should be scribbling notes. There's a melodrama I've been thinking of writing, a sort of operatic saga, tragedy and betrayal and consumption of the lungs . . ."

Ashland reached out and took Emilie's cold hand. "I was

afraid that if I told you these things, you would run away. That it was too much, that *I* was too much: too big and too scarred, too demanding and too full of need for you. Because I do need you, Emilie. Every inch of you. I need your mind, your love, your companionship, your wisdom, the comfort of your body. Animal lust, my God! That isn't the half of it. I need your body, *your* body, Emilie, because it unites me with *you*. I'm no sooner quit of you, than I'm dreaming of all the ways I want to have you again . . ."

From across the room came the clink of the decanter. "Sherry, anyone?"

". . . and not simply because of this animal lust, this mad craving between us, but because it draws me into you. When I take you to bed, I feel as if I'm part of you, flesh of your flesh, in holy communion with the woman I adore. I am human again at last."

Olympia clapped his hands. "Excellent. Soundly argued. True loins equals true minds. Surely that's sufficient, my dear niece?"

Emilie opened her eyes, and Ashland's gaze fastened her at once. She saw him as if through a haze of emotion, though perhaps it was only the haze on her spectacles.

"On my knees, Emilie, I ask for your hand. I ask you to be my wife, to be mother to my children." He brought her fingers to his lips and held them there, closing his eyes briefly at the instant of contact. "In return, I offer you my heart, my home, and my fortune. And, yes, the protection of my name and my body."

Olympia groaned. A sherry glass crashed into the desk. "For the love of God and all His creatures, Emilie, tell him *yes*. Put us out of our misery."

Still Emilie couldn't speak. Her tongue, her throat were too full to move. Ashland's hand was strong around hers, his breath warm and even on her skin.

He bowed his head over her hand. "No more intrigue, Emilie. From now on, you command me. Not a single act without your knowledge and consent. And I swear on my life, Emilie, that your child—*our* child—will never have to bear what you have borne."

"Yes," she said.

Ashland looked up.

"Thank God," said Olympia. "Dowry and settlements to be arranged, of course, and naturally I shall want to give away the happy bride myself . . ."

But his words were lost in her ears. She was being hoisted up by a pair of iron arms and spun about in mad circles, kisses raining down upon her chin and neck and cheeks. "I love you," he said. "I love you, Emilie. Dash it all, didn't I ever say it before? I love you."

"Mind the floor lamp, there," said Olympia.

Emilie cupped her hands around Ashland's head and kissed him. "I love you. I loved you hopelessly from the first, far too much to draw you into all this . . ."

"But I gave you no choice."

"No." She kissed him again. "And having risked your life for me, you have as your reward only more of the same. A lifetime, if you're especially unlucky."

"Ah yes." Olympia heaved a relieved sigh and walked to a nearby bookcase. "The risk of assassination and whatnot. I've been thinking about that. Clearly, some sort of retreat is necessary. If not for Emilie's safety, then for my own health. Newlyweds have a somewhat deleterious effect on my digestion."

Ashland let her slide downward in his arms, until her feet rested—physically, at least—on the priceless Axminster below. "Retreat? What do you propose?"

Olympia reached out his hand and touched the globe on the shelf, spinning it idly. "As I understand it, the two of you are under a certain impetus to marry, as quickly as possible."

"That is not your concern, Uncle. It is a private matter between the two of us."

Ashland's voice rang out with conviction. "As soon as possible, in fact. Tomorrow, if we can arrange it. My animal lusts, you understand, cannot be reined in."

"Ahem. Yes. Good, then." Olympia twirled his globe. "As it happens, my personal steam yacht lies at anchor in Southampton, with a full complement of water, coal, and crew."

"Your steam yacht!" Emilie gasped.

Olympia's large white hand steadied the Earth. He turned to them, leaned back against the bookcase, and smiled. "Have you given any thought to an extended honeymoon?"

EPILOGUE

The Cook Islands
August 1890

Emilie opened her eyes when the shade shifted, exposing her to the white tropical sun.

For a moment, she didn't move. Her limbs were drowsy with warmth, her heartbeat slow and blissful. Her husband's arm curled just beneath her breasts, and as she lay there, she could feel her body rise and fall to the cadence of his breathing. She curled her toes into the powdery sand.

Her husband.

She savored the word in her head for the thousandth time. "Ashland," she whispered.

A grunt came from the sleeping form under her head.

She tried again, more loudly. "Ashland."

"Hmm?" His chest moved slightly; his arm tightened around her. "What is it?"

"The shade. It's gone. We'll burn in a moment."

Her husband smelled deliciously of salt and sand; Emilie wanted to lick it from his skin. He nuzzled her temple sleepily and said, "Bother the shade."

Emilie laughed and made a lumbering turn in his arms. She was wearing only her chemise, and the thin linen tangled about her legs. "Easy for you to say. You haven't got a baby inside you, kicking away at all that sunlight."

"Mmm." Ashland kissed her neck and found the bottom of her chemise with his long arms. He wasn't wearing anything at all. He was simply and splendidly naked, all gleaming tanned skin and endless muscles: the privilege of having anchored the yacht off an uninhabited island and sent the children off with the Doctor on a voyage of exploration to the other side of it. He'd spent the morning in a slow and painstaking exercise of his husbandly rights, from various inventive positions (the traditional ones having become a trifle awkward of late), and now, having refreshed himself with picnic and nap, seemed to find his bride overdressed. "How vexing, madam. And how long has this condition been troubling you?"

Emilie laughed again and pushed at his elbows, but it was no use. Ashland untangled the chemise with expert fingers and drew it upward over her belly, and she let her arms fall back into the sand. "Several months, in fact. And it grows worse every day. By the beginning of October, I shall probably explode."

"What a beast of a husband you have, putting you in such a state."

"A dreadful beast. And I suspect he feels no remorse at all."

Ashland lifted the chemise over her head and kissed her. "None at all?"

"None. Instead he looks at me with an air of the most insufferable self-satisfaction."

"The cat who caught the canary?" He bent to swirl the tip of her breast with his tongue. His shoulders, broad and hard with muscle, shimmered with the sun's own light.

"Exactly. Though I can't quite understand it, just between the two of us. These days, I begin to resemble the giant dodo more than the canary."

"I suppose your beast of a husband takes the opposite view. No doubt he, in his demented state, believes you grow more beautiful every day." His immense hand cradled her belly; he kissed the very top.

"Then I weep for him, for he has evidently lost the sight in his single remaining eye."

"Or perhaps he sees more clearly than ever."

Emilie giggled aloud. "You, sir, have turned out to be an appalling flirt."

"Ridiculous. I was an appalling flirt from the beginning. I

am grieved to say that by the age of twenty, I was notorious throughout London." He kissed his way back up her bosom.

"No doubt. I suppose you once had all those debutantes at your feet, with your Guardsman's uniform and your young Apollo looks."

"Only practicing for you, Your Highness."

Emilie wrapped her hands around his neck. He held himself effortlessly above her, his honed sinews betraying not a quiver. She ran one finger along the pits and scars of his jaw. "Beautiful man. I love you madly."

Ashland turned his head to kiss her finger. "Beautiful lady. I love . . ."

Three faint belches of the ship's horn carried over his words.

"What the devil?" Ashland rose to his knees.

Emilie tried to rise, failed, rolled to one side, and tried again. Her heart made a tiny skip against the wall of her chest. "Not the children, surely!"

"They've an armed guard with them, and the Doctor. I'm sure they're all right."

But Emilie knew his voice, and she could hear the faint note of alarm beneath his steady words. Four months ago in Sydney, they had taken aboard Dr. Yates, a physician with the highest reputation, to keep a watchful eye on Emilie as her pregnancy advanced and to assist with the delivery in October; he was also a devoted naturalist, and he acted in the double faculty of tutor for Freddie and Mary. He was brilliant and trustworthy, almost a member of the family. Surely he wouldn't take any undue risks?

Ashland was already thrusting himself into his shirt and trousers. "I'll go around the point with the glass. Should be able to see the signal flashes from there."

Emilie struggled with her chemise. By the time her head emerged from the neckline, Ashland was striding off at a jog to the rocky end of the lagoon where they'd set up their idyll this morning, deliberately out of sight of the Duke of Olympia's luxurious steam yacht and its curious crew.

She reached Ashland just as he was lowering the glass from his eye.

"Well? What is it?"

"It's your bloody uncle, of course. We're to head home at once."

"Head *home*?" Emilie said, as she might say, *Head into the guano-infested rocks at the entrance to the Underworld*.

"Head home." Ashland closed the glass and shoved it into the waistband of his trousers. He turned to her, bent, and caught her up in his arms, belly and all. "But I'll be damned if the old chap can't bloody well wait a few more hours."

And the Duke of Ashland carried his burgeoning young bride straight back to the powdery white sand of the beach, to her endless and rather noisy delight.

HISTORICAL NOTE

While Emilie, her family, and the principality of Holstein-Schweinwald-Huhnhof itself are entirely fictional, the dangers she would have faced as a European royal in 1890 were quite real.

If the eighteenth century was the age of great revolutions, the nineteenth century saw the rise of small ones. This was not for lack of big ideas. By the time of the short-lived establishment of the Paris Commune in 1871, any number of "isms" flourished in the cafes, streets, and universities of the Western world, addressing the great problems of social and political inequality with ambitious solutions. Moreover, they had acquired distinctly international goals, and conceived often violent means to achieve them.

The anarchism movement took many forms, but at its core rejected the state as unnecessary and evil, and authority itself as tyranny over the individual. For those who believed that violence was the only effective means of achieving the overthrow of state and hierarchy, the so-called *propagande par le fait* ("propaganda of the deed") held irresistible allure. In the decades before the outbreak of the First World War in 1914, assassination took the lives of tsars, kings, empresses, presidents, and prime ministers across Europe and the United

States: President McKinley, Tsar Alexander II of Russia, and the beautiful Empress Elisabeth of Austria were among the victims.

But among the organizations responsible for these assassinations—to say nothing of countless bombings, kidnappings, riots, and uprisings—the Revolutionary Brigade of the Free Blood does not, and never did, exist.

Turn the page for a preview of
Juliana Gray's next book

HOW TO MASTER
YOUR MARQUIS

Old Bailey, London
August 1890

The courtroom was packed and smelled of sweat.

James Lambert, the Marquess of Hatherfield—heir to that colossal monument of British prestige, the Duke of Southam—was accustomed to the stench of jammed-in human perspiration and did not mind in the slightest. He feared, however, for the young woman who sat before him.

Hatherfield couldn't watch her face directly, of course, but he could sense the tension humming away in her body, like the telephone wire his stepmother had had installed into her private study last year, in order to better command her army of Belgravian sycophants. He knew that her back was as straight as a razor's edge; he knew that her eyes would appear more green than blue in the sulfurous light waxing from the gas sconces of the courtroom, and that those same eyes were undoubtedly trained upon the presiding judge with a fierceness that might have done her conquering Germanic ancestors proud.

He knew his Stefanie as he knew his own hands, and he knew she would rather be boiled in oil than sniff a human armpit. His darling Stefanie, who thought herself so adventurous, who had proved herself equal to any number of challenges, had nonetheless been raised a princess, with a princess's delicate nose.

The judge was droning on, precedents this and brutal nature of the crime that, and Latin tags strewn about with reckless enthusiasm. He was a man of narrow forehead and prodigious jowl; the rolls about his neck wobbled visibly as he spoke. A large black fly had discovered the interesting composition of the curling white wig atop his pear-shaped head and was presently buzzing about the apex in lazily ecstatic loops. Hatherfield watched its progress in fascination. It landed atop the fourth roll of wiry white hair with a contented *bzzz-bzzz*, just as Her Majesty's judicial representative informed the mass of perspiring humanity assembled before him that they were required to maintain an open mind as to the prisoner's guilt *ad captandum et ad timorem sine qua non sic transit gloria mundi* et cetera et cetera et cetera.

Or perhaps he was now addressing the jury. Hatherfield couldn't be certain; the man's face was cast downward, into his notes; or rather into the jowls overhanging his notes. Like that chap at Cambridge, that history don, the one who would insist on taking tea at his desk and dropping bits of crumpet unavoidably into the jowly folds, to be excavated later as he stroked his whiskers during lectures. On a good day, the dais might be strewn with the crumbly little buggers, and a positive trail left behind him on the way back to his chambers. What had they nicknamed him? Hatherfield screwed up his forehead and stared at the magnificent soot-smeared ceiling above.

Hansel, that was it.

A flash of movement caught his eye. Something was going on with Stefanie's fingers: She was scribbling furiously on the paper before her, biting her tender lower lip as she went. She looked up, locked eyes with him, and flashed the paper up and down again, the work of an instant. He saw the words, nonetheless. They were written in large capital letters, underlined twice for emphasis:

PAY ATTENTION!!

Ah, Stefanie. He tapped his fingers against the rail before him and composed his reply in Morse code:

I am paying attention. To you. You look exceptionally handsome in that waistcoat. I should very much like to kiss you.

He watched as her eyes dropped down to his fingers. He tapped the message again.

She changed color. Well, he couldn't see her well enough to verify, but he knew anyway. The flush would be mounting up above her stiff white collar, spreading along the curving wedge of her regal cheekbones. The tip of her nose would be turning quite pink right about . . . now. Yes, there it was: a little red glow. Just like when he . . .

With her elegant and agile fingers, Stefanie tore the paper in half, and in half again; she assembled the quarters together and tore them rather impressively once more. She hid the pieces under a leather portfolio and locked her hands together. The knuckles were bone white; Hatherfield could see that from here.

Familiar words struck his ear, jolting him out of his pleasant interlude: his stepmother's name. ". . . the Duchess of Southam, who was found murdered in her bed in the most gruesome manner, the details of which will become clear . . ."

The Duchess of Southam. Trust her to toss her bucket of icy water over his every moment of happiness, even from the grave, merely by the sound of her name in a room full of witnesses. He had tried by every means to deny her that power over him, and still she laid her cold hands on his body.

Hatherfield found he couldn't quite bear to look at Stefanie now. He trained his gaze instead on the judge. The fly had disappeared, frightened away perhaps by the thunderous vibration of those tempting white curls, as the speaker worked himself up to an indignant climax—a theatrical chap, this judge, for all his comical jowls—and asked the prisoner how he pleaded.

Hatherfield's hands gripped the rail before him. He straightened his long back, looked the judge squarely in the eye, and replied in a loud clear voice.

"Not guilty, my lord."

Devon, England
Nine months earlier

Princess Stefanie Victoria Augusta, a young woman not ordinarily subject to attacks of nerves, found to her horror that her fingers were twitching so violently she could scarcely fold her necktie.

True, it was a drab necktie. She had longed for one in spangled purple silk, or that delicious tangerine she had spotted through a carriage window on a dapper young chap in London, before she and her sisters had been hustled away by their uncle to this ramshackle Jacobin pile perched on a sea-cliff in remotest Devon. (For the record, she adored the place.) But the array of neckties laid out before her on the first morning of her training had offered three choices: black, black, and black.

"Haven't you any *interesting* neckties?" she had asked, letting one dangle from the extreme tips of her fingers, as if it were an infant's soiled napkin.

"My dear niece," said the Duke of Olympia, as he might say *my dear incontinent puppy.* "You are not supposed to be interesting. You are supposed to be the dullest, most commonplace, most unremarkable law clerk in London. You are *hiding*, if you'll recall."

"Yes, but must one hide oneself in such unspeakable drab neckties? Can't they at least be made of silk damask?" Stefanie let the necktie wither from her fingers to the tray below.

"Law clerks do not wear silk damask neckties," said her sister Emilie. She was standing before the mirror with His Grace's anxious valet, attempting a knot with great concentration.

"How do you *know* they don't?" asked Stefanie, but Olympia laid a hand on her arm.

"Stefanie, my dear," he said affectionately, for she was his favorite niece, though it was a close secret between them, "perhaps you don't recall what's at stake here. You are not playing parlor games with your courtiers in charming Hogwash-whateveritis . . ."

"Holstein-Schweinwald-Huhnhof," said Stefanie, straightening proudly. "The most charming principality in Germany, over which your own sister once reigned, if you'll recall."

Olympia waved his hand. "Yes, yes. Charming, to say nothing of fragrant. But as I said, this is not a friendly game of hide-and-seek. The three of you are being hunted by a team of damned anarchist assassins, the same ones who killed your own father and kidnapped your sister . . ."

"*Attempted* to kidnap," said Princess Luisa, smoothing her

skirts, except that her hands found a pair of wool-checked trousers instead and stopped in mid-stroke.

"Regardless. No one is to suspect that you're being scattered about England, dressed as young men, employed in the most invisible capacities . . ."

"While you and Miss Dingleby have all the fun of tracking down our father's murderers and slicing their tender white throats from end to end." Stefanie heaved a deep and bloodthirsty sigh.

Miss Dingleby had appeared at her other elbow. "My dear," she'd said quietly, "your sentiments do you credit. But speaking as your governess, and therefore obliged to focus you on the task at hand, I urge you to consider your own throat instead, and the necktie that must, I'm afraid, go around it."

Four weeks later, the neckties had not improved, though Stefanie had become a dab hand at a stylish knot. (*Too stylish,* Miss Dingleby would sigh, and make her tie it again along more conservative lines.)

If only she could make her silly fingers work.

The door opened with an impatient creak, allowing through Miss Dingleby, who was crackling with impatience. "Stefanie, what on earth is keeping you? Olympia has been downstairs with Sir John this past half hour, and we're running out of sherry."

"Nonsense. There are dozens of bottles in the dungeon."

"It is not a dungeon. It's merely a cellar." Miss Dingleby paused and narrowed her eyes at Stefanie's reflection in the mirror. "You're not nervous, are you, my dear? I might expect it of Emilie and Luisa, straightforward as they are and unaccustomed to subterfuge, but *you*?"

"Of course I'm not nervous." Stefanie stared sternly at her hands and ordered them to their duty. "Only reluctant. I don't see why *I* should be the law clerk. I'm by far the shadiest character among the three of us. You should have made me the tutor instead. Emilie will bore her pupil to tears, I'm sure, whereas *I* would . . ."

Miss Dingleby made an exasperated noise and moved behind her. "Take your hands away," she said, and tied Stefanie's black neckcloth with blinding jerks of her own competent hands, to a constriction so exquisitely snug that Stefanie gasped for breath. "The decision was Olympia's, and I'm quite sure he knew what he was doing. Your Latin is excellent, your mind quick and retentive when you allow it to concentrate . . ."

"Yes, but the law is so very *dull*, Miss Dingleby . . ."

". . . and what's more," Miss Dingleby said, standing back to admire her handiwork, "we shall all be a *great deal* reassured by the knowledge that you're lodged with the most reputable, learned, formidable, and upstanding member of the entire English bar."

Stefanie allowed herself to be taken by the hand and led out the door to the great and rather architecturally suspect staircase that swept its crumbling way to the hall below. "That," she said mournfully, "is exactly what I'm afraid of."

Olympia and his guest were waiting in the formal drawing room, which had once been the scene of a dramatic capture and beheading of a Royalist younger son during the Civil War (Stefanie had verified this legend herself with a midnight peek under the threadbare rugs, and though the light was dim, she was quite sure she could make out an impressively large stain on the floorboards, not five feet away from the fireplace), but which now contained only the pedestrian English ritual of a duke taking an indulgent late-morning glass of sherry with a knight.

Or so Stefanie had supposed, but when she marched past the footman (a princess always greeted potential adversaries with aplomb, after all) and into the ancient room, she found herself gazing instead at the most beautiful man in the world.

Stefanie staggered to a halt.

He stood with his sherry glass in one hand, and the other perched atop the giant lion-footed armchair that had been specially made a century ago for the sixth duke, who had grown corpulent with age. Without being extraordinarily tall, nor extraordinarily broad-framed, the man seemed to dwarf this substantial piece of historic furniture, to cast it in his shadow. His *radiant* shadow, for he had the face of Gabriel: divinely formed, cheekbones presiding over a neat square jaw, blue eyes crinkled in friendly welcome beneath a high and guiltless forehead. He was wearing a uniform of some kind, plain and unadorned, and the single narrow shaft of November sunshine from her uncle's windows had naturally found him, as light clings to day, bathing his bare golden curls like a nimbus.

Stefanie squeaked, "Sir John?"

The room exploded with laughter.

"Ha, ha, my lad. How you joke." The Duke of Olympia stepped forward from the roaring fire, wiping his eyes. "In fact, my friend has the good fortune of traveling with company today. Allow me to present to you the real and genuine Sir John Worthingham, QC, who has so kindly offered to take you into his chambers."

A white-haired figure emerged dimly from the sofa next to the fire and spoke with the booming authority of a Roman senator. "Not nearly so handsome a figure as my nephew, of course, but it saves trouble with the ladies."

With supreme effort, Stefanie detached her attention from the golden apparition before her and fixed it upon the source of that senatorial voice.

Her heart, which had been soaring dizzily about the thick oaken beams holding up the ducal ceiling, sank slowly back to her chest, fluttered, and expired.

If Stefanie had been a painter of renown, and commissioned to construct an allegorical mural of British law, with a judge occupying the ultimate position in a decorous white wig and black silk robes, bearing the scales of justice in one hand and a carved wooden gavel in the other, she would have chosen exactly this man to model for her and instructed him to wear exactly that expression that greeted her now.

His eyes were small and dark and permanently narrowed, like a pair of suspicious currants. His forehead was broad and steep above a hedgerow brow. His pitted skin spoke of the slings and arrows of a life spent braced between the dregs of humanity and the righteous British public, and his mouth, even when proffering an introductory smile, turned downward at the ends toward some magnetic core of dole within him. Atop his wiry frame was arranged a stiff gray tweed jacket and matching plus fours, with each leg pressed to a crease so acute that Stefanie might have sliced an apple with it.

If Sir John Worthington *had* ever encountered trouble with the ladies, Stefanie judged, it was not without a significant intake of champagne beforehand. On both sides.

Still, Stefanie was a princess of Holstein-Schweinwald-Huhnhof, and what was more, she had never yet met the living being she had not been able to charm.

"Good morning, Sir John," she began cheerfully, and tripped over the edge of the rug.

Time was supposed to slow down during accidents of this sort, or so Stefanie had heard, but all she knew was a flying blur and a full-body jolt and a sense of horrified bemusement at the sensation of threadbare carpet beneath her chin. A feminine gasp reached her ears, and she was nearly certain it wasn't her own.

A pair of large and unadorned hands appeared before her, suspended between her face and the forest of chair and sofa legs. "I say. Are you quite all right?" asked a sonorous voice, which in its velvet baritone perfection could only belong to the Archangel.

Was it manly to accept his hand in rising? It was a marvelous hand, less refined than she might have expected, square and strong-boned, with a row of uniform callouses along the palm. The fingers flexed gently in welcome, an image of controlled power.

Stefanie swallowed heavily.

"Quite all right," she said, rather more breathily than she had planned. She gathered herself and jumped to her feet, ignoring the Archangel's splendid hands. "New shoes, you know."

A little giggle floated from the sofa.

Among the sounds that Stefanie could not abide, the female giggle ranked high: well above the drone of a persistent black fly, for example, and only just beneath the musical efforts of a debutante on a badly tuned piano.

She shot the sofa an accusing glance.

A young lady sat there, utterly dainty, perfectly composed, with a smug little smile turning up one corner of her mouth. She was beautiful in exactly the way that Stefanie was not: delicate features, soft dark eyes, curling black hair, rose-petal skin without the hint of a freckle. Though she reclined with languorous grace upon the sofa, one tiny pink silk slipper peeking from beneath her pink silk dress, she was clearly of petite proportions, designed to make the long-shanked Stefanies of the world appear as racetrack colts.

Except that Stefanie herself was no longer a young lady, was she?

"Charlotte, my dear," said Sir John, "it is hardly a matter for amusement."

"Nothing is a matter of amusement for *you*, Cousin John," said his dear Charlotte, with a sharp laugh.

Stefanie expected Sir John's face to empurple at this saucy (if accurate) assessment, but instead he heaved a sigh. "Mr. Thomas, I have the honor to introduce to you my ward, Lady Charlotte Harlowe, who lives with me in Cadogan Square, and who will, I'm sure, have as much advice for you as she does for me."

Lady Charlotte held out her spotless little hand. "Mr. Thomas. How charming."

Stefanie strode forward and touched the ceremonial tips of her fingers. "Enchanted, Lady Charlotte."

"Indeed," said Sir John. "And I believe you've already made acquaintance with my nephew, the Marquess of Hatherfield."

"Your *nephew?*"

"Yes. Hatherfield practically lives in our drawing room, don't you, my boy?" Sir John looked grimly over her shoulder.

Stefanie turned. "Lord Hatherfield?"

She spoke with solemn composure, but her head was spinning. The Archangel was a *marquis?* Good God! What other gifts could possibly have been lavished on his head by an adoring Creator? Did he spin gold from his fingertips?

A marquis. And Sir John's nephew. Practically living in his drawing room, the old fellow had said.

God help her.

The Archangel Hatherfield grinned widely and shook her hand. The callouses tickled pleasantly against her palm. "It's a great pleasure to meet you, Mr. Thomas. I admire your pluck enormously, entering into my uncle's chambers like this. I daresay you charm snakes in your spare time?"

"Oh, I gave that up long ago," said Stefanie. "I kept tripping over the basket and losing the snake."

Hatherfield blinked at her once, twice. Then he threw back his head and howled with laughter. "Oh, Thomas," he said, wiping his eyes, "you're a dashed good sport. I like you already. You've got to take good care of this one, Uncle. Don't let him near the cyanide tablets like the last poor clerk."

"Really, Hatherfield," said Sir John, in a grumbly voice.

"Well, well. This is charming," said Lady Charlotte, looking anything but charmed. "I look forward to hearing Mr. Thomas's witticisms all the way back to London. How lucky we are."

The Duke of Olympia, who had been standing silently at the mantel throughout the exchange, spoke up at last. "Indeed, Lady Charlotte. I do believe that you will profit enormously from Mr. Thomas's company, both in the journey to London and, indeed"—he examined the remains of his sherry, polished it off, set the empty glass on the mantel, and smiled his beneficent ducal smile—"in your own home."

Lady Charlotte's already pale skin lost another layer of transparent rose. "In our home?" she asked, incredulous, turning to Sir John. "Our *home?*" she repeated, as she might say *in my morning bath?*

Sir John, impervious Sir John, iron instrument of British justice, passed a nervous hand over the bristling gray thicket of his brow. "Did I not mention it before, my dear?"

"You did not." She pronounced each word discretely: *You. Did. Not.*

"Well, well," said Hatherfield. "Jolly splendid news. I shall look very much forward to seeing you, Mr. Thomas, when my uncle can spare you. You *will* spare him from time to time, won't you, Sir John?"

"I will try," said Sir John, rather more faintly than Stefanie might have expected.

She was not, however, paying all that much attention to Sir John and his ward. Hatherfield had fixed her with his glorious blue-eyed gaze in that last sentence, and she was swimming somewhere in the middle of him, stroking with abandon, sending up a joyful spray of . . .

"Nonsense," said Lady Charlotte. "Clerks are meant to

work, aren't they, Sir John? It costs a great deal to educate a young man in the practice of the law, and it must be paid *somehow*."

"Why, dear Lady Charlotte," said Hatherfield, without so much as a flicker of a glance in her direction, still gazing smilingly into Stefanie's transfixed face, "you speak as if you've ever performed a moment's useful work in your life."

A strangled noise came from the throat of the Duke of Olympia. He covered it quickly, with a brusque: "In any case, my friends, I see by the clock that you will miss your train if you delay another moment. I believe young Mr. Thomas's trunk has already been loaded on the chaise. I suggest we bid one another the customary tearful farewell and part our affectionate ways."

Hustle and bustle ensued, as it always did when Olympia issued a ducal decree. Stefanie's hand was shaken, her overcoat found, her steps urged out the front hall and into the chill November noontide, where the Duke of Olympia's elegant country chaise sat waiting with pawing steeds. To the left, the landscape dropped away into jagged slate cliffs, awash with foam, roaring with the distant crash of the angry sea.

"Cheerful prospect, what?" said Hatherfield.

"Barbaric," said Lady Charlotte. She reached the open door of the chaise and stood expectantly.

Stefanie, feeling unexpectedly lighthearted and therefore (as her sisters well knew) rather mischievous, grasped Lady Charlotte's fingers to assist her into the chaise.

A little gasp escaped her ladyship, an entirely different sort of gasp from the one that had greeted Stefanie's arrival on the threadbare rug of Olympia's Devon drawing room. She jerked her hand away as if stung.

"Is something the matter, Lady Charlotte?" asked Lord Hatherfield solemnly.

She raised one delicately etched eyebrow in his direction. "Only that I require your assistance into the vehicle, Hatherfield."

Hatherfield handed her in with a smile, but what Stefanie noticed most was not that golden smile, nor the unexpectedly gut-churning sight of his strong fingers locked with those of Lady Charlotte, but the expression on her ladyship's face. It had changed instantly at the point of contact, from sharp hauteur into something softer, something dulcet and melting and almost longing, something rather akin to . . .

Adoration.

The Marquess of Hatherfield swung himself into the carriage and tapped the roof with his cane. In deference to both Lady Charlotte and her august guardian, he took the backward-facing seat, next to young Mr. Thomas.

Mr. Thomas. Mr. Stephen Thomas. He glanced down at the plain wool legs next to his. Rather skinny legs, at that; particularly in comparison to his own, which were thick and hard, the quadriceps hewed into massive curves by nearly a decade spent powering racing shells through the rivers and lakes of England in an attempt to outpace the skulking shadows in his memory.

Yes, Mr. Thomas's legs had a curiously slender cast, beside his.

Which was only to be expected, of course, and not curious at all. For Hatherfield had gathered at a glance what the supposedly keen-eyed Sir John and the reputedly sharp-witted Lady Charlotte had, by all appearances, not begun to suspect.

It was quite obvious, really.

Mr. Thomas's legs were slender because *he* was a *she*.

A brash, clever, amusing, lovely, and elegant *she*. Ah, how she'd sprung right back up to her feet after her humiliating fall! How she'd joked about it afterward. A *she* for the ages.

The Marquess of Hatherfield straightened his gloves, settled back into his cushioned seat, and smiled out the window.

ETERNAL
ROMANCE

FIND YOUR HEART'S DESIRE...

VISIT OUR WEBSITE: www.eternalromancebooks.co.uk

FIND US ON FACEBOOK: facebook.com/eternalromance

FOLLOW US ON TWITTER: @eternal_books